# PRAISE FOR

## ENRAPTURED

"Filled with sizzling romance, heartbreaking drama, and a cast of multifaceted characters, this powerful and unusual retelling of the Orpheus and Eurydice story is Naughton's best book yet."
—*Publisher's Weekly*, starred review

## TEMPTED

"Endlessly twisting plots within plots, a cast of complex and eminently likeable characters, and a romance as hot as it is complicated." —*Publisher's Weekly*, starred review

"Ms. Naughton has taken the Greek Argonaut myth, turned it on its head, and OWNED it!" —*Bitten By Paranormal Romance*

## ENTWINED

"An action-packed creative wonder guaranteed to snag your attention from page one." —*Fresh Fiction*

"Do NOT miss this series!"
—*NY Times* bestselling author Larissa Ione

## MARKED

"Naughton has tremendous skill with steamy passion, dynamic characterization and thrilling action." —*Publisher's Weekly*

"Elisabeth Naughton's MARKED gives an incredibly fresh spin on Greek Mythology that is full of humor, action, passion and a storyline that keeps you from putting down the book."
—*Fresh Fiction*

## WAIT FOR ME

"Full of twists and turns, lies and deception, and the ultimate revenge, Wait For Me is a great romantic suspense read." —*Night Owl Reviews*, Top Pick

"This book blew me out of the water. Wonderfully written with characters whose emotional turmoil seemed to jump off the page and grab you." —*Cocktails and Books*

## STOLEN SEDUCTION

"This third book in the Stolen series is full of intrigue, secrets and undeniable love with characters you can't get enough of...an awesome read!" —*Fresh Fiction*

"An adventurous story of twists and turns, this story will keep you guessing until the very end. And the chemistry between Hailey and Shane is sizzling hot. Naughton combines passion and danger in one fast-paced story." —*News and Sentinel*

## STOLEN HEAT

"This book has got it all: an adventure that keeps you turning the pages, an irresistible hero, and a smoking romance." —*All About Romance*

"Stolen Heat is an awesome combination of deadly suspense, edgy action and a wonderful romance with characters that you'll laugh, cry and yell with." —*Night Owl Romance*

## STOLEN FURY

"A rock solid debut...Naughton's intelligent adventure plot is intensified by the blazing heat that builds from Lisa and Rafe's first erotic encounter." —*Publisher's Weekly*

"Naughton deftly distills deadly intrigue, high adrenaline action, and scorchingly hot passion into a perfectly constructed novel of romantic suspense." —*Chicago Tribune*

# A SECOND CHANCE

A knot twisted inside Ryan. He wouldn't survive it if Kate walked out on him now. Losing her the first time had broken him. A second time would kill him.

He knelt in front of her, knowing if he touched her, he wasn't going to be able to stop. But he needed that connection, needed to show her how much she meant to him. With shaking fingers, he clasped her hand in her lap. "You can't leave now."

Her eyes were full of anguish and remorse. He ached to wrap his arms around her and pull her close, to take away the pain for both of them.

"You can't possibly tell me any of this is what you want," she said quietly.

"I don't want this mess, no. But in some insane way, it brought you back to us. I wouldn't change it now for anything. What I want is to see you smile again, to figure out a way to make this easier for all of us. Walking away isn't going to do that. It'll just make things worse."

Her eyes slid shut. "I know."

Hearing the crack in her voice did him in. He could see himself pushing her back on the bed, tugging her clothes off, pressing inside her and driving the worry away. Wanted that so bad he could barely breathe.

Gently, she pulled her hand from his and ran it over her hair. "I'm just tired and not thinking clearly. I need some rest."

He didn't want to break the connection, but she'd already done it, was putting up those barriers again and blocking him out. Why couldn't he read her? Why couldn't he figure out what she was thinking? He'd always been able to do that with her. He didn't want to admit she was different, but she was. So much about her was different from what he remembered.

# Titles by Elisabeth Naughton

## Eternal Guardians Series
*(Paranormal Romance)*

ENSLAVED
ENRAPTURED
TEMPTED
ENTWINED
MARKED

## Firebrand Series
*(Paranormal Romance)*

SLAVE TO PASSION
BOUND TO SEDUCTION

## Stolen Series
*(Romantic Suspense)*

STOLEN SEDUCTION
STOLEN HEAT
STOLEN FURY

## Single Tituldn'tles

WAIT FOR ME
*(Romantic Suspense)*

## Anthologies

BODYGUARDS IN BED
*(with Lucy Monroe and Jamie Denton)*

# WAIT FOR ME

# ELISABETH NAUGHTON

*For all readers,*
*young and old,*
*who believe in second chances.*

# CHAPTER ONE

There was torture, and then there was rip-your-fingernails-out-by-the-roots-with-pliers pure agony. Right now, Kate Alexander was in the midst of the latter. Or at least it felt like she was.

She ground her teeth and tried to think of something besides the sweat slicking her skin, the ceiling entirely too close to her face, the fact she could barely breathe in this claustrophobic box. Nothing worked. The only thought revolving in her mind was the fact if she didn't get out of here soon, she was going to go batshit crazy on the tech behind the glass to her left.

"A little longer, Kate."

Great. Fabulous. Just what she wanted to hear. She knew not to move—that would only prolong her misery—but this little test had already taken way longer than it should. What the hell was he doing in there, throwing a party?

Patience had never been her strong suit. Her doctors had told her that lack of patience was probably the reason she hadn't stayed dead in the first place—that she'd given up waiting for the light to get stronger and had decided just to turn around and come back because she'd grown impatient. Kate wasn't convinced of that fact—she didn't remember any light. She didn't remember much of anything. But thanks to the trusty staff at Baylor University Medical Center in Dallas, Texas, her "death" had lasted only a mere ninety seconds. Ninety seconds that had changed her life forever.

She had no memory of the car accident that had left her snazzy Mercedes in a lump of twisted metal. No memory of the driver of the other vehicle who'd walked away while she'd lain on a cold slab fighting for her life. No memory of her life before the accident, period. But she'd learned one very important lesson that day: some things in life were worth fighting for.

Her mind drifted to Jake, their anniversary and the special dinner she had planned. Seven years... It didn't feel like seven years. In many ways, it felt like she barely knew him. The past eighteen months had been a blur of tests and more tests, settling into life in Houston, reacquainting herself with her husband and their friends all over again. A side effect of the accident he'd told her, one they'd get through together. Except…he traveled so much for work, it seemed like she was doing all that reacquainting by herself.

She wanted to sigh but knew not to. Okay, so he was dedicated to his job. He loved his work. She had to admire his passion. So what if their marriage was far from perfect? No one had a perfect marriage. But she'd been given a second chance. She planned to make the most of it.

She quietly rejoiced when the machine buzzed again and the table began retracting from the tunnel. Done. Finally. Twenty minutes of hell. And she hadn't needed to flip the tech off after all. A smile curled her lips at the thought.

The tech emerged from the screening room and unstrapped Kate's head and shoulders from the restraints. "Not so bad. How are you feeling?"

Kate sat up and rubbed the long scar on the side of her scalp. "Like a sardine."

He chuckled. "I hear that a lot. You'll need to hang around for a bit while we review the images and make sure we got everything we need."

She nodded, knowing the routine. She'd been through it before, and this wouldn't be the last.

She dressed then headed out into the waiting area where TVs flickered with a surreal image. Several people gathered around the three screens, staring at what looked like a war scene. Flames and billowing smoke, sirens blaring, lights flashing. Prickly fingers of fear ran over Kate's skin as she watched the horror unfold.

The camera zoomed in on plane wreckage. A ticker across the bottom of the screen flashed "Breaking News."

*"The crash happened at roughly ten-forty five, Pacific Time. Flight 524 from San Francisco to Houston crashed just after takeoff. Witnesses say the plane burst into a fireball only yards from the runway. NTSB officials are on scene, and an investigation is already under way. Early reports estimate there are no survivors."*

The air caught in Kate's lungs. She scrambled for her purse, one strap sliding down her arm as she frantically searched among receipts and fruit snacks for the note Jake had left her. His flight information and where he'd been staying for the conference in San Francisco.

"Kate? Is everything okay?"

She didn't look up to see who was talking to her. Couldn't focus. The purse slipped off her shoulder, landed at her feet with a clank. She dropped to her knees, frantically pawing through the contents, looking for his note. It wasn't the same flight. It couldn't be. He was probably landing right this minute. He'd laugh when she told him she'd dumped her entire purse on the floor at the clinic.

"Kate? What is it? What do you need?"

Vaguely, she realized Gina, the nurse, was helping her. Tears blurred her eyes. She shook her head. "A note. Jake's note. I have to find it. I have to—"

"We'll find it. Relax. Just breathe. I'm sure everything's okay."

She drew a deep breath, let it out. Gina was right. She was overreacting. Jake was fine. Blinking back tears, she scanned the floor and finally spotted Jake's slanted handwriting on a slip of paper just to the right of her hand. Her fingers shook as she drew it close so she could read the words.

*My flight info:*
*Outgoing: Houston to San Francisco, Flight # 1498*
*Return: San Francisco to Houston, Flight # 524*

The paper slipped out of her fingers. The room spun. Blackness circled in.

The CT scan, the anniversary dinner she'd shopped for earlier, the last eighteen months of her life swirled behind her eyes and mingled with Gina's voice, muffled now, calling to her from what seemed like a great distance. Only one thing made sense. Only one thought remained.

Her life had just shifted direction all over again. And this time, death had won.


"You really need to eat something." Mindy, Kate's next-door neighbor, set the steaming mug of tea on the kitchen table in front of Kate and sat in the chair to her right.

Without looking, Kate knew Mindy's freckled features were drawn and somber. The woman had adored Jake. Everyone had. None of their friends had known about his mood swings. Or the fact he purposely stayed away from home. Or that he and Kate fought about his work. But they didn't need to know those things now. No one did.

"Thanks." With shaky fingers, Kate wrapped her hands around the mug, holding on to the warmth. "I think I might just be ill if I smell one more cup of coffee."

There'd been a steady stream of friends through the house all afternoon and into the early evening. This was the first quiet moment Kate had found. And now...now she wondered why she'd wanted it.

"The tea should help you relax," Mindy said, pushing her red hair over her shoulder. "It's been a long day. How about a little soup?"

Kate shook her head. Food was the last thing on her mind. Her stomach would revolt if she tried to eat. Waving a hand, she blinked back tears that wanted to fall. She wasn't going to give in again. Not now. She'd save the waterfall for when she was alone. In that big bedroom she was too used to sleeping in all by herself.

"I'm not hungry." Silence enveloped the room. She knew Mindy disapproved, but she had a thousand other things on her mind besides food. "God, Mindy. I have so much to do."

Mindy's hand clamped over hers on the table. "There's plenty of time for all that."

"No. If I don't get it all taken care of, I'll go nuts." She leaned back in her chair. "I can't stay here."

"You have to give it time. You can't make rash decisions right now."

"No. This house was his idea. Living here..." Her eyes slid shut. "He made every major decision in our lives."

"He was your husband. And you've been through so much this last year and a half with the accident. Of course he made all the decisions. It's logical given your medical history."

Her medical history. The memory loss. It had been Jake's excuse for everything. Why he ran their finances, why he arranged it so she was never alone, why he'd chosen which publisher she freelanced for.

She should have insisted he include her in decisions. She should have played a bigger role in planning for a day like this. She didn't even know where to look for his life insurance policy.

Her stomach rolled, and she swallowed back the bile. Leaning forward to rest her elbows on the table and her head in her hands, she knew she needed to get as far from this house as possible. She'd felt the pull to leave months ago, but she'd fought it because of Jake. Because her life was here. Now...now she didn't know what to think anymore.

"Jake was the one who loved Houston. Not me." Her head throbbed. She wasn't taking pain medication tonight. Not when her mind was already in a fog.

"It's your home, Kate. You can't just leave. Jake's family's here."

A pathetic laugh erupted from Kate's lips. "He and his father haven't spoken in more than a year. The man barely even acknowledges he has a grandson. That's not the type of family I want for Reed." No family was better than that in her mind.

"Just promise me you won't make any spur-of-the-moment decisions. Please?"

Concerned brown eyes gazed into Kate's face. Mindy wouldn't get it. Not really. She wouldn't understand that this feeling of not belonging had been festering for a long time. That it had been haunting her ever since the accident. And tonight wasn't the night to get into it with her.

Kate squeezed Mindy's hand. "Sure. I'm not really thinking clearly tonight." Rising, she took the untouched mug of tea to the sink. "I need to turn in. Thanks for everything today. I don't know how I would have gotten through it all without you."

Mindy rose from her seat and rested both hands on Kate's shoulders. "Will you be okay tonight? Reed's already asleep upstairs, but I could take him over to my house if you need some time alone."

Kate looked to the kitchen stairs that led up to the second floor where her four-year-old son was sound asleep, then shook her head. She hadn't told him the news yet. She didn't want him hearing it from the neighbors. "No, but thanks. I need to be with him if he wakes. We'll be fine."

"I'm always here for you, Kate. Remember that. If you need anything, I'm just across the street."

"Thanks." Kate forced a smile she didn't feel.

With a quick hug, Mindy made her way to the front of the house. When the heavy mahogany door clicked shut, Kate turned and surveyed the empty house. She was alone. Totally alone. No car would be pulling into the drive in the middle of the night. Jake wouldn't come bounding through the door, apologizing for missing yet another dinner. She wouldn't see his face or feel his arms around her again. It didn't matter if he'd been a lousy husband. He'd been *her* husband. And now he was gone. From now on, it would just be her and Reed.

Shaky lips blew out a long sigh. She tamped down the grief that wanted to pour over her again. Even though it was close to midnight, she knew there was no way she'd be able to drift into a slumber, peaceful or otherwise.

Making her way into Jake's office, she rubbed the chill from her arms, then sank into the chair behind his desk, letting the butter-soft leather cushion her aching body. With trembling fingers, her hand feathered the dark wood in front of her.

Her gaze washed over the room. A tall bookshelf graced one long wall. Medical books packed the shelves from floor to ceiling. A computer blinked on the short arm of the L-shaped desk. A picture of Reed smiling in the summer sun faced her.

Jake's room, Jake's things. She'd rarely come in here because it was his private space. An odd sense of unease settled over her as she sat in his chair.

She flipped on the Tiffany lamp sitting next to the phone and fanned through the stack of mail on the corner of his desk. The mundane task took her mind off details she had yet to address, calmed her frayed nerves.

Bills, a renewal for a medical journal, a letter claiming they'd won ten-million dollars in a sweepstakes. She tossed junk mail into the garbage can at her knee, sifted Jake's professional mail into one stack, their personal mail into another.

She reached for the letter opener in the pencil holder and found it missing. Pulling open a drawer, she pawed through the contents, then another when she couldn't find it.

In the back of the third drawer, she found it, along with another unopened letter. Kate shook her head, a melancholy sensation deepening her sadness. Reed had probably put these here. He was always getting into stuff he shouldn't. Jake always got so upset when Reed moved his things.

But no one would have to worry about that anymore. With renewed sadness she ripped open the letter and glanced at the bill in her hand. Her brow creased when she saw her name. She reached for the envelope she'd just torn. Jake's medical office was listed as the address on the outside, but it was clearly a bill for her time in the hospital after her car accident. A revolving balance showed an amount of ten thousand dollars still owed.

Jake had told her their insurance had covered everything. Looking closer, she realized it wasn't a hospital bill at all, but an invoice from a nursing home.

Nursing home? That wasn't right. She'd been in the hospital for a little more than a week. Four days in a coma in ICU, another three until they moved her to a regular room, then five on the med/surge floor recovering from her injuries.

She looked at the bill again.

San Francisco.

No, that wasn't right either. The accident had happened outside Dallas. She'd been driving home from a geology conference in Ft. Worth. Her journal had been covering the event. She'd never even been to San Francisco.

The dates of service were wrong as well. They spanned more than two years.

Her hands shook as she set the invoice on the desk. A chill settled over her.

Medical records. Jake was meticulous about his files.

She swiveled toward the file cabinet and flipped through the files, looking for one with her name.

Nothing.

She yanked open the second drawer. Taxes, appraisal information on the house, medical journals he belonged to. The man even had a file with all his grades from college. He was OCD to the max.

But where were her files?

Impatience settled over her, a dismal feeling she didn't want to acknowledge. She yanked open the third drawer, breathing out a sigh of relief when she saw medical folders for Jake, Reed, and herself.

Yes, it would be here. Someone had screwed up, billed the wrong person.

She drew her folder open on the desk, flipped through the stack of forms. A claim for stitches in her toe when she'd stepped on a piece of glass last month. A dental claim when she had to have a tooth repaired last spring. Medical updates from Dr. Reynolds, the neurosurgeon she'd been seeing since the accident. Forms and evaluations spanned the last year and a half of her life, then stopped.

No records on her pregnancy, none on Reed's birth. Nothing

from her stay at Baylor University Medical Center where she'd been treated after the accident.

They had to be in different folders. Something separate, marked "delivery" and "accident". She closed the drawer, reached for the bottom one. It wouldn't budge.

She pulled again, only to realize it was locked.

She fumbled through the drawers of his desk, searching for a key. An odd sense of urgency pushed her forward. She tried the few keys she found but none fit the lock. Swallowing the growing lump in her throat, she pawed through his shelves.

Still no key.

The blood rushed to her head, intensifying that dull ache around her scar.

She scrambled up to the bedroom they'd once shared and yanked open his dresser drawers, fumbling through socks and underwear and old T-shirts.

It had to be somewhere. He wouldn't have locked the drawer and thrown away the key. Her fingers skimmed cotton and finally settled on cold metal.

Pressure settled on her chest as she pulled the key ring from the back of the drawer. Two keys glittered in the low light, one bigger than the other. On wobbly legs, she made her way back down to the office, kneeling on the floor in front of the file cabinet.

*Don't open it. Forget about the key. Forget about the drawer. Forget about that stupid bill. Nothing good can come from this. You've already been through enough today.*

She swallowed the lump in her throat. Before she could change her mind, she turned the key in the lock. The drawer gave with a pop.

Inside, a long metal box rested on the bottom of the drawer. She set it carefully on the desk, then sat in his chair and rubbed damp palms along her slacks. The second key slid into the lockbox with ease.

Drawing in a deep breath, she opened the lid. Medical forms, evaluations, bills filled the box. She extracted each paper, scanned the dates and contents. All referenced the nursing home in San Francisco. All mentioned dates two to five years in the past.

According to the papers, she'd been in a coma for almost three years, not four days. Reed had been born by C-section when she'd been in that coma.

Her eyes slid shut. It couldn't be. She'd had a long labor—over twenty-four hours. Jake had held her hand through the pain. She'd been wheeled into surgery when the labor had stopped progressing. Jake had been with her as her son was cut from her. He'd told her all about it. He'd relayed the story of Reed's birth so many times, she could see it in her mind.

Tears pooled in her eyes. She looked at the papers again as her brain warred with what she'd been told and the facts in front of her.

There were no pictures. No pictures of her pregnancy. None anywhere in the house. Jake had told her it was because she'd hated being pregnant, that she didn't want to remember what she'd looked like.

But there were none of her smiling in a hospital gown, either. None of her nursing her baby. She'd believed him when he'd said he'd forgotten the camera the day Reed was born.

She ran to the family room, yanked picture albums off the shelves, flipped through each page. Jake holding a newborn Reed. Jake giving him a bath. Jake feeding him his first solids. *Oh, God.* Jake smiling with him on his first birthday. In every picture, it was Jake. Not a single one of her and Reed until after his second birthday.

Panic washed over her. She'd always assumed she'd been the one taking the photos. She'd never even questioned it. Rubbing a hand over the pain in her chest, she tried to rationalize the moment. Couldn't.

He was a doctor. He was her husband. She'd believed him. It had never even occurred to her not to. Why? Why would he lie?

*No, no, no. This can't be real.*

On legs that threatened to give out, she made her way back into his office. Her eyes focused on an evaluation from a neurosurgeon she didn't recognize.

*Damage to the lateral cortex of the anterior temporal lobe as a result of severe trauma.*

*Prognosis: memory loss, possibly permanent and irreversible.*

Permanent memory loss. Coma. Three years.

Choking back tears, she continued flipping through the forms. Her stomach pitched when she saw Jake's signature on several of the papers. He'd been an attending physician.

*Her* attending physician.

*No, no, no.* Her husband never would have been allowed to oversee her recovery. Never. Not in a million years. She wasn't a doctor, but she knew the rules.

Sweat beaded on her neck, trickled down her back. There had to be an explanation. Something. *Anything!*

She lifted each paper out of the box in an urgent need to find the truth. Questions continued to swirl in her mind, memories she wasn't sure were real or contrived. When she drew out the last paper, the floor moved under her feet.

Her legs buckled, and she dropped into the chair. In the bottom of the box rested a photo. Her breath clogged in her throat. With shaking fingers, she extracted the picture, just as a stabbing pain cut right through her heart.

It was a photo of a young girl, roughly five years of age. She was sitting on a boat. Water sparkled behind her. Trees glinted off in the distance. A young girl with a disturbingly familiar face, a curly mop of brown hair, and the greenest eyes Kate had ever seen.

Kate's eyes. The same shape, size, color…the same exact eyes Kate stared at everyday in the mirror.

*Oh, God. Oh, God.*

The air clogged in her lungs. And a place deep inside told her this girl couldn't possibly be anything other than her daughter.

# CHAPTER TWO

Ryan Harrison tucked a towel around his waist as he walked through his hotel suite. He picked up the remote on the bed and flipped on the TV, then ran another towel through his dripping hair as he searched for CNN.

The shower still ran in the bathroom, but it didn't drown out the heavily accented lyrics to "Come What May" from *Moulin Rouge*. She always sang when she was satisfied. He, on the other hand, didn't feel like singing. What he really wanted was coffee. He thought about calling room service, but the commotion on the television caught his attention before he could find the phone.

Lights flashed on the screen, people scrambled, sirens shrieked. A reporter relayed the news from yesterday as Ryan sat on the end of the bed and watched the coverage of the plane crash in San Francisco.

His heart beat hard. His palms grew sweaty where they gripped the towel. It was like watching Annie's plane crash all over again. His stomach clenched at the memory, a sharp stabbing pain that cut right to the center of him.

His cell phone rang, startling him back to the present. Pushing to his feet, he ran a shaky hand over his face and pulled the screaming phone out of the slacks he'd tossed across the back of a chair only hours ago.

"Harrison."

"You rat bastard." Mitch Mathews's deep voice boomed through the line, concern more than evident in his brother-in-law's words. "Scared about ten years off my life. I've been calling you for hours. You see the news?"

Ryan couldn't seem to take his eyes off the screen. "Yeah, just saw it."

"Where are you?"

He glanced around the room. "New York."

"Thank God. I thought you were flying out of San Francisco yesterday."

"I was supposed to. Hannah rescheduled a meeting in LA. I flew there yesterday, then here after." He caught the airline and flight number when the reporter said it again and swallowed the lump in his throat. "Jesus, that was my flight."

"Son of a bitch," Mitch muttered. "You gonna be okay?"

"What?" Ryan was having trouble thinking. "Yeah, I'm fine."

"When are you coming back?"

"Tonight, I think." Ryan rubbed a hand over his forehead. "Julia's gonna be pretty upset by this. Go by and see her, would ya? Your folks are at the house with her."

"Yeah, sure thing. You might not be able to get a flight back into San Francisco."

"I know. I'll try Oakland or San Jose or Sacramento and drive. I want to get home."

"Okay. Call me before you leave."

"Will do. See ya."

The water had stopped, and Monique's voice was now louder as she sang with her sexy French accent.

Ryan closed his eyes and pressed the phone to his forehead. He didn't want to be with her right now. A thousand thoughts and memories and feelings were flooding through him, and none of them were things he wanted to share with her.

She was an attractive woman and he enjoyed her company when it was convenient, but he had no desire to get to know her hopes and dreams. And he certainly didn't want to share his with her. Or cry about his past. If there were two things he never discussed with anyone, they were his wife and daughter.

He turned back to the TV and clicked it off just as she stepped into the room. She wore a much-too-small towel wrapped around her curvaceous body, her wet, fire-red hair dripping down her back. A wicked smile spread across her lips.

"*Mon cher.*" She crossed the floor, her brick red-painted toes looking oddly like blood splatters on the plush, white carpet. "*Je me suis ennuyé de vous.*"

He knew enough French to know she was trying to lure him back into bed. He pulled away from her suffocating embrace. "I gotta go."

She batted her long, exotic eyelashes and stuck out her swollen bottom lip in a sexy little pout she'd perfected over the years. "*Nonsens.* You said they aren't even expecting you until after lunch. *N'était pas par le passé assez.* I want you again."

Her English was good, but she always slathered on the accent when she was trying to seduce him. He headed for the bathroom. "Yeah, well, as tempting as that is, I have to get to the office."

She followed, and when she rounded the corner, her eyes narrowed to see him already in his slacks.

"*Bien,*" she sighed in defeat. "I'll just have to wait for you to get back tonight." A bright red nail trailed down his bare chest and hovered at the top button of his slacks. Her eyes tipped up seductively to meet his.

He knew that look. And he knew she was going to be royally pissed in just a minute. "I'm not staying tonight. I have to fly home."

Her arms crossed over her breasts—breasts just a little too perfect, ones she'd never admit having work done to. "*Merde.* You said you'd be in town a few days!"

"And I planned on it, but something came up. It's family stuff. I have to get back."

She threw up her hands and marched back into the bedroom. "*Fils de chienne!*"

He also knew enough French to know when she was swearing at him. He followed as he buttoned his shirt. "Look, I'll make it up to you the next time you're in California."

"I don't plan to be in California anytime soon. I'm here now, *dammit!*"

"I know, and I'm sorry. It's just bad timing." He reached for her hand, knowing he was being a dick, trying to soften at least a little of the blow. "Cut me some slack, okay?"

"*Hybride*, you don't deserve it." But she smiled when she said it. "Just this once. And I'll expect you to make it up to me three-fold, mon cher."

He kissed her cheek. She liked men. He wasn't special. He also knew she'd find someone else to hang out with after he left, and it didn't bother him in the least.

"Thanks." He dropped to the end of the bed and reached for his shoes, itching to finish up his work and get home as soon as he could. "You're a gem, Monique."


Ryan pulled the car into the drive of his Sausalito house around seven a.m. the next morning, jet-lagged and exhausted. Getting home had proved to be more of a nightmare than he'd expected.

Flights into SFO had been rerouted or canceled. Luckily, he'd managed to catch a red-eye into Sacramento, then picked up a rental car. As he grabbed his bags from the trunk, he steeled himself for what he'd find inside. He hadn't had a chance to talk to Julia since the accident and he had no clue how she was reacting to it all.

Her bubbly laughter greeted him as he pushed the kitchen door open.

"Just roll the damn dice, would ya?" Mitch bellowed.

Julia giggled. "You'll never beat me at this. I'm a pro."

"There's no such thing as a pro at Yahtzee. It's pure luck."

"No, it's not. Yahtzee!" she shrieked as the dice settled. Mitch swore under his breath. "It's skill, see, Uncle Mitch?"

"You're not teaching my kid to swear, are ya?" Ryan forced a smile as he stepped through the door and glanced around the room. Julia looked up and grinned.

Mitch flashed the same deep dimple in his cheek he'd shared with his sister. "I save all the really bad words for when you aren't around."

"Hey, Dad!" Julia slipped off the chair and caught Ryan in a fierce hug. "What are you doing here? I thought you weren't coming back for a few more days."

"I finished early and thought I'd just come home." He dropped his bag on a chair and eased down so they were at eye level. Then he ran his finger down her button nose, the one that was just like Annie's. Every time he looked at her, he saw her mother. His heart took one giant roll. "I missed you."

She frowned, and those knowing eyes of hers swept over him. "You came back because you were worried about me, didn't you?"

"Yeah, so sue me. Are you okay?"

"I'm fine, Dad, really. You shouldn't worry so much. It's not good for your health. Gives you ulcers and can reduce your life span, not to mention pack on the pounds. And you're not getting any younger you know. You have to start thinking about your weight. Besides, I'm practically a grown-up. I can handle stuff."

"The grown-up part remains to be seen." He tried to hide the smile that wanted to creep up his face. "Where'd you learn about the effects of stress anyway?"

"At school. You know, that private institution you spend a fortune to send me to? I learn a lot at school."

"Nice to know my money's being put to good use." He headed

into the kitchen, grabbed a bottle of water from the fridge.

"I'm on the brink of womanhood," she said after him. "Lots of girls my age are already getting their periods."

He choked on his water. "Please. It's not even eight in the morning, I'm jet-lagged, and you're only nine."

"So?" She looked right at Mitch, who seemed to be enjoying the banter. "It's right around the corner. You're going to have to deal with it, Dad. And while I'm thinking of it, I need a bra. We should probably go shopping for one sometime soon. Maybe today." She reached for the dice, then flashed a devilish grin his way. "I was thinking of getting one of those red lacy ones like the girls wear in your Maxim magazines."

"God, help me," he managed, heat creeping right up his face.

Mitch laughed and walked into the kitchen. He poured himself another cup of coffee then patted Ryan on the back. "Damn it all to hell if she's not just like her mother."

"Don't I know it," Ryan said as he eyed his daughter. She not only looked like Annie, she sounded just like her too. Same smart-ass attitude and dry sense of humor. His chest tightened as he remembered Annie's quirky grin, the deep dimple in her cheek when she smiled. The way she could make him laugh no matter the situation.

"Are you okay, Daddy?" Julia's smile faded. She only ever called him Daddy when she was worried about him. The rest of the time it was Dad or more lately, just "hey, you".

"Yeah," he said quietly. "I am now."

"Good. Me too. I'm gonna go up and get dressed." She slipped off the chair again and crossed to him. When he eased down, she pulled him in for a tight hug and kissed his cheek. "I'm glad you're home. I love you, Daddy."

"I love you, babe." On a long breath, he watched her head out of the room and up the back stairs. He didn't need to worry about her so much, but he did. Truth was, she was way more together most of the time than he was. She'd had to grow up much too fast over the past five years. No nine-year-old should have to worry about her father's state of mind day in and day out, but Julia did.

He raked a hand through his already disheveled hair. "Son of a bitch, she's growing up way too fast."

Mitch grinned. "Yeah, I know. You're gonna be in a world of hurt in a couple of years."

"I know." Ryan rubbed a hand over his chest, trying to ease the knot growing there. "Maxim? Where the hell did that come from?" He shook his head. "It scares the crap out of me. Thank God you're here to shelter some of the blow."

"Don't look at me, buddy. I'm not a parent. I reserve the right to turn a blind eye to issues dealing with puberty and sex. I deflect all that crap back to you."

Ryan grimaced again. "Don't mention the words puberty and sex in the same sentence with my baby girl."

Mitch rummaged through the kitchen cupboards, searching for God only knew what. "Where are Kathy and Roger?" Ryan asked, watching him.

"We sent them off to get breakfast. Mom's been a little...stressed...since the crash yesterday. Too hard for her to deal with. I don't know that she's ever gonna get on a plane again. She may just be stuck here for good."

"God help us," Ryan muttered. He loved his in-laws, and he appreciated that they flew down from Seattle whenever he needed help with Julia, but a man had limits.

Mitch found a box of Froot Loops in the pantry. "Hot damn!" He leaned back against the counter and fished out a handful of cereal. "I haven't had this stuff since I was a kid."

Ryan glanced at the box. "That's probably from when you were a kid. I don't remember buying that."

"All those preservatives? It can't go bad." He propped himself up on the counter.

Sinking into a chair at the kitchen table while Mitch munched on stale cereal, Ryan massaged his aching forehead. A tension headache was settling right behind his eyes—the result of no sleep, too much traveling and stress on top of it.

"You look like shit, you know," Mitch muttered.

"Tell me something I don't already know." He hadn't shaved, he was still in the same clothes he'd worn yesterday, and he felt like he'd been on an emotional roller coaster the last few hours.

"Monique must have worked you over pretty good."

"About took my head off when I told her I was leaving so soon."

"I like her. You get tired of her, you pass her on to me."

Ryan chuckled. "She wouldn't go for you. She's not into the outdoorsy type."

Mitch glanced down at the worn jeans and dirty hiking boots he was wearing. "Are you saying I'm not classy?"

Ryan looked at his brother-in-law. Mitch needed a haircut, his light, brown curly hair was brushing his collar, and the goatee he was experimenting with looked downright pathetic. "I'm saying you don't have enough class in your left pinky for her."

"And you do?"

"No, I don't. But she hasn't figured that out yet." He pressed his fingers against his temples. "She's just using me for sex. One of these days, she'll figure out I'm a son of a bitch and she'll drop me on my ass."

Mitch laughed. "Can't argue with you there."

Rising, Ryan stifled a yawn. "You gonna stick around?"

"Yeah, for awhile. At least until Mom and Dad get back."

"Good. I'm gonna crash." He patted Mitch on the shoulder as he walked by. "Thanks, buddy."

"Sure thing."

Ryan stalked up the kitchen stairs, paused halfway, and glanced back. Just when they were all starting to get on with their lives, Annie's absence was slamming back into them, this recent crash reminding them what they'd lost. Whether Mitch or Julia wanted to admit it, it had hit them all hard, bringing back memories from five years ago.

He rubbed his aching head and continued up the stairs. Memories swirled through his mind as he flopped down onto the bed in his room. That last day—dropping her off at the airport that morning, kissing her good-bye, rubbing a hand over her flat belly and smiling at the secret she'd told him the night before, leaning in and taking one last whiff of her sweet lilac scent.

He'd give anything for one more hour with her.

His eyes slid shut. Tears he didn't realize were still there stung his eyes. He had trouble conjuring up her face these days. She was ingrained in his heart and soul forever, but that image was slowly fading from his memory, the edges turning fuzzy. Even her voice, that husky siren voice of hers that had always tugged at something deep in his soul, was hard to bring up now.

He swiped a hand over the burning pain in his chest. Part of him wished like hell it would just go away. The other part was holding on like it was his last lifeline. He'd already lost her once. He couldn't bear the thought of losing what little of her he had left.

# CHAPTER THREE

"Knock, knock."

Kate glanced up from her desk and smiled at the face in her doorway. The first smile she'd felt in days...maybe weeks. As she leaned back in her chair, late afternoon sunlight spilled through the windows of her fourteenth-floor office at McKellen Publishing, bathing her in warmth. "Hey, Tom."

Tom Adams, her managing editor, dropped into the chair across from her. "Looks like you're getting settled in."

She looked over her cramped office. Stacks of journals sat against one wall. A half-empty box was pushed up against the bookshelf. She'd managed to set out a few pictures of Reed, a chunk of conglomerate, an obsidian rock she'd picked up hiking a few months back. Papers littered her desk, and framed art leaned against the wall, waiting to be hung. "Trying to. Not making much progress, I'm afraid."

"How's the article coming?" He reached for the glass paperweight shaped like a frog that sat on the corner of her desk. Reed had given it to her for Mother's Day last spring, during his frog stage. Resting an ankle on his opposite knee, Tom passed the paperweight from hand to hand.

She ran her fingers over her hair, hoping to wipe away some of the tension coursing through her. It wasn't the job leaving her stressed but being here in San Francisco. So close to the answers she was searching for, so far away from them at the same time. *"Geochemical Discrimination of Five Lava Dams on the Colorado River?* It's coming along."

"Sounds interesting. Can't wait to read it." His hazel eyes sparkled. In the afternoon sunlight, she could just make out a patch of gray hair, right at his temples.

She couldn't help but laugh. Only a couple of science nerds could enjoy something like that. But she sensed he wasn't here because he questioned her work. He knew she was competent, that she knew the job inside out. Geology came to her like second nature. He was here because he was worried.

Her lips pursed. "Stop looking at me like I'm going to fall apart. I'm fine, Tom."

"Are you?" His brow lifted. "I wouldn't be much of a friend if I didn't worry."

"I know. And I appreciate it. But I'm fine. We're getting by. The place you loaned us in Moss Beach is perfect."

"I'm glad you like it. How's Reed?"

"Okay." She thought about her four-year-old son. "He loves being near the ocean. But…it's hard for him right now. He misses Jake." She did too, although she hated to admit it. No matter what he'd kept from her, no matter how strained their relationship, she still had trouble believing he could have intentionally done anything to hurt her. There had to be a logical explanation for the secrets he'd kept hidden for so long.

Which was why she'd called Tom and finally taken him up on his offer of a job here in San Francisco. Why she'd uprooted Reed clear across the country. She had to find the answers. She had to know what really happened.

"I know there's not a lot I can do," he said. "And I know you won't lean on me even if I offer."

A grin curled her lips. He knew her so well.

"Regardless," he went on, "I'm offering, Kate. I want to help."

"I appreciate it. Really. Just giving me a job was the best thing you could have ever done."

"That freelance work you were doing for the Dallas office wasn't anywhere near your potential."

Her smile faded. Jake hadn't wanted her to work. He'd wanted to her to stay home, to, as he put it, "get better". She'd started writing freelance articles for a geology magazine based out of Dallas because she'd needed to do something to keep busy. But they both knew if Jake hadn't died, she wouldn't be here now.

She forced a grin she didn't feel. "If I need anything, you'll be the first to know."

"Liar." He reached into his pocket, drew out a slip of paper. "And because I know how stubborn you are, I'm going to give this to you before you ask. That's the name of a lawyer here in town I've used before. I know you're running into a dead end with that nursing home. Someone knows something. A lawyer might be able to apply some legal pressure, open some doors for you. No one likes a pushy lawyer."

"Thanks. I'll give him a call later in the week."

He rose and set the paperweight back on her desk. "Do that. And zip me a copy of that article when it's done."

"Hey," she called, realizing she hadn't even asked about his wife yet. "How's Kari?"

A silly grin crept up his face. "Fat and happy."

"When's she due?"

"Four more weeks."

His beaming face brought a warmth to her chest. After Kari's bout with ovarian cancer, they'd never expected to have a baby. Thanks to new drug treatments, she was nearing the end of her pregnancy.

"Give her my best. Tell her I'd love to have lunch with her sometime if she's feeling up to it."

"I will. Cut out early, Kate. Go home to that kid of yours."

When he disappeared into the office chaos, Kate swiveled to look out at the view of San Francisco. Water glinted in the distance between towering skyscrapers. Cars honked below on the street. On a deep breath, she closed her eyes.

She'd been here a whole week now and hadn't remembered a single thing. Nothing was familiar to her. Not the city or the scenery or the atmosphere. She'd hoped beyond hope that something, anything would trigger her memory. Disappointment was something she was learning to deal with.

The nursing home had been a waste of time. She'd driven out to San Mateo, to the site of the home, but nothing there had tugged at her memory, either. The original facility had burned in a fire almost a year ago and the director of the rebuilt facility had all but slammed the door in her face, refusing to answer her questions. Every lead ended in a wall. Someone somewhere knew something. She just had to figure out where to start.

She fingered the lawyer's name and number Tom had given her as she gazed out at the city again. Swiveling back to her laptop, she pulled up the Internet and paused on the news page.

Along the right sidebar, under *Entertainment News*, a picture of a man—a really hot man with blond hair—had been posted. The most gorgeous woman Kate had ever seen was literally wrapped around him. His arm was tight around her waist, one of hers was hidden inside his open suit jacket, and the other was draped across his chest. And she was whispering something in his ear. Something that was making him smile like he'd just heard the naughtiest of secrets.

Jake had never smiled like that with her. They'd certainly never been so intimate in public. The pair made an attractive couple, yet…Kate's gaze kept straying back to the man's face. She was sure she'd never met him before, but there was something familiar in those piercing blue eyes. Something…

Excitement pulsed in her veins when she realized where her mind was going. She scanned the photo again. They were walking across some kind of lobby—a hotel, she'd bet. Heading toward a night of passion. *Lucky girl.* A burst of jealousy coursed through her as she read the caption below the photo: *Marriage Rumors Swirl Around Top Model and Pharmaceutical Giant.*

Kate's gaze snapped back to the woman, and in an instant, all that excitement deflated in her chest. No wonder something felt familiar about the pair. The woman was a model. An underwear model. Kate had seen her before in numerous magazines.

She frowned. Leaned back in her chair. Called herself stupid for getting so worked up. Over a paparazzi photo, no less. How on earth would she possibly know a pharmaceutical tycoon? The idea was ridiculous.

Putting the matter out of her head, she pulled up a search page and scrolled through the list of lawyers in the San Francisco area. The one name that stood out to her wasn't the name Tom had just given her.

She stared at it. Debated her options. She'd gone with her gut coming to San Francisco. While she appreciated Tom's help and his suggestion of a lawyer was a good one, she had to go with her gut again. Something in the back of her head said trusting her instincts was important here. More important than it had ever been before.

Ryan stood at the wall of windows in his office on the forty-eighth floor, hands on his hips, gaze sweeping over the city. The setting sun glinted off the bay. Alcatraz hovered in the distance, the buildings nothing but cold, empty shells of their former selves. Not all that different from him, really.

Shit. He swept a hand over his forehead. He was a fucking good time to be around these days, wasn't he? If he didn't find a way to bounce out of this rut he'd been in for the last week, Mitch would find a way to kick his ass out of it. And Ryan didn't need to give

Mitch another reason to kick his ass. Mitch had been gunning for him ever since that day back in college when he'd found out Ryan was dating his baby sister.

The knock at the door brought him around, breaking the memories loose before they could take root and suck him under. Hannah Hughes stuck her head through the crack. "You got a minute?"

"For you, I've always got a minute."

Hannah crossed the room like a female cat, all long-legged grace, the fitted red blazer and knee-length skirt highlighting her runner's physique. She nodded toward his desk. "Is that the new Reliquin promo?"

He turned the drug layout so they could both see it. "Marketing department just sent it up. It doesn't hit me."

Hannah crossed her arms over her chest, studied the page. "It doesn't scream happiness. This new breast cancer drug's supposed to make life better for women. You need an attractive woman, kids running around, maybe a few toys littering the floor. Something that says life goes on after cancer."

"Don't even think about it." He knew where she was headed. Hannah had her hand in every part of this company already. She didn't need to stick a finger in something else. "You have enough to do. Pretty soon, I won't be able to afford you."

"You can barely afford me now." She dropped into a chair across from his desk, pulled a file from her bag.

Knowing she was about to go over the day's nitty-gritty, Ryan reached for his glasses and eased into his leather chair. His daily meeting with Hannah was the one thing he looked forward to everyday. They had an easy working relationship, an unspoken admiration. She was never afraid to tell him just what she thought, and he respected her for it. Needed it. Promoting her to VP of Public Relations for AmCorp Pharmaceuticals was the best thing he'd ever done.

"The FDA's grumbling about our stage three clinical trial results for Omnitrol," she said, jumping right to her point. "They want a longer study."

Ryan took the report she handed him, studied the papers. The FDA's stringent requirements were a constant frustration. Forget about the fact there were people out there dying from cancers new drugs could possibly cure or prevent. But he knew the game, had played it for years. And his biotech company adhered to each one of the FDA's rules and evaluations. Sometimes it meant scrapping a drug they'd spent millions on in research and development. Other times it meant shelving one until further studies could be conducted. He had a sinking suspicion Omnitrol was headed in that direction.

"Okay. Get Angela on it. Have her contact Jim Pierson over at Biomed and find out what we need to do."

"Already have her on it." She shifted papers in her hands, handed him the next topic. "I'm flying out to Denver next week to check on Research & Development for Mediquin. They've started animal testing, and I need to get a handle on how things are going."

"Jack's there. He can formulate a report and fax it to us."

She tipped her head. "Ryan, Jack's swamped with the merger. The Grayson Pharmaceutical deal's causing him all kinds of angst. He asked me to come out and give him a hand with the R&D problem, run interference on the last few details of the merger."

He breathed out a sigh of frustration and raked a hand through his hair. This merger was causing more trouble than it was worth. Grayson Pharmaceuticals was a company he'd been eyeing for a long time. They had a long track record of good sales and important medicines, and he'd been lucky when their cash flow problems had made them vulnerable. But their R&D department was raising red flags with this new drug.

"Fine, but I need you back here ASAP." He jotted a note and looked up. "Anything else?"

She bit her lip.

"Hannah?"

"You made it into the *National Star* again."

His mood took a nosedive at the mention of his "favorite" tabloid magazine.

Hannah pulled the paper from her bag and tossed it on his desk. On the front was a picture of him and Monique walking through the lobby of his New York hotel on his recent visit.

"Fabulous," he muttered, easing back in his chair as he read the marriage rumor headline.

"It gets better. Inside, there's a nice little quote from Monique about getting creeped out in hospitals. A terminal patient at one of her runway shows tried to get an autograph, asked her to make an appearance in his cancer ward. She snubbed him. Told him he needed to go grow some hair. Press is all over it, especially with her connection to you. Not sitting well for us, Ryan."

He clenched his jaw. His relationship with Monique was anything but exclusive, and marriage was the last thing on his mind. He had no control over what she did or said. And they never talked business when they were together. Rarely talked at all, as a matter of fact.

"How do you want me to handle it?" Hannah asked.

"Don't. Ignore it."

"The press is going to play this up, and we don't need backlash right now with everything that's happening with Grayson. I really think we need to make a statement."

Like he cared. The press could print anything about him they wanted. "The Grayson deal's sealed. And I don't really give a shit what people think of me personally."

"Well, I do. It's my job to care. That's why you pay me the big bucks."

"I pay you the big bucks because you earn them."

"I'm trying to earn them now."

"Your opinion on the subject is noted."

"But you're going to do as you damn well please. And that means nothing."

He pushed out of his chair. "You want a drink?"

She frowned. "Just water."

He crossed to the wet bar, pulled two chilled bottles from the fridge, then handed her one. "What else?"

"What do you mean?" she asked, closing the file on her lap.

"I can see it on your face. What else?" She might be good with the press, but she couldn't hide anything from him. They'd known each other too long.

She let out a deep breath and leaned back in her chair, fingering the water bottle. "The Grayson deal has me curious."

"About what?"

"About your goals." When he raised a brow, she added, "Long-term goals. What's the plan?"

"I'm not following you."

"Well." She shifted in her seat. "Aside from wanting to excel in the pharmaceutical world, which you've already done, and wanting to expand your umbrella company, which you're doing by acquiring subsidiaries, I'm just curious where things are going."

He had a feeling he wasn't going to like where this was going. Moving back to his desk, he sank into his chair and waited for her to get to the point.

"Look, don't take this the wrong way, Ryan, but you're not exactly the norm for a CEO." She arched one perfect eyebrow. "You're a multimillionaire and are very successful at most everything you put your mind to, but you don't live like a man who rakes in the dough. You live in a nice house, but you could easily afford something bigger and way fancier. You drive the same car you drove five years ago, you don't have expensive spending habits, you don't own a yacht or sports cars or even take luxury vacations. Aside from the one week every year that you take to go somewhere with Julia, you never take time off. You belong to the country club, but you rarely go there, you barely use the car and driver you have on staff for the company, and you don't throw lavish parties or socialize with San Francisco's elite."

He swiveled his chair to look out over the bay as she talked. Darkness was setting in, and the lights of the city reflected off the water. Darkness that suddenly mirrored his sinking mood.

"My point is," she went on, "you don't seem to enjoy any of the benefits you have from the work you do, so I'm curious why you're pushing so hard to expand AmCorp."

"I have my own reasons." And he'd be damned if he was going to explain them to her or anyone else.

"But what's the point if it's not making a difference in your life?"

His gaze cut to her. "You're one to talk. You're as dedicated to this company as I am."

"Sure I am, but I also have a life outside the office. You don't."

His jaw clenched again. Any enjoyment he'd had in the meeting earlier had trickled away. He didn't need her blunt realism smacking him in the face. "My private life is none of your business."

Tension floated in the air as she stared at him. Their relationship was professional yet friendly, and they shared not only a love of this company but a mutual admiration. However, she'd just crossed a line—a big one—and they both knew it.

Long seconds passed in silence. Finally, she set her water on the table, then stood and retrieved her papers. "You're right," she said as she reached for her briefcase. "I'm sorry. I was out of line. I'm flying to Denver Monday morning, so I'll be around this weekend if something comes up."

Shit. Now he felt like an ass. But dammit, his personal life was just that—personal.

The knock on the door had them both looking over as Mitch peeked into the room. "You planning on sleeping here tonight or what? Hey, Hannah."

"Hey, Mitch." A weak smile tugged at her mouth as she finished gathering her things.

One glance at the clock told Ryan it was already after seven. He tossed his reading glasses onto the papers littered across his desk and scrubbed both hands over his face. "I didn't realize it was so late. We were just finishing up." He dropped his hands. "What are you doing here?"

"I thought I'd come rescue you." Mitch tipped up his blue Mariner's baseball cap. Unruly curls peeked out from beneath the hat. He dropped into a leather chair opposite Ryan's massive mahogany desk and propped his dirty sneakers on its sleek surface, then smiled Hannah's way.

Ryan's brows drew together. "You're gonna get crap all over my work."

"Your work is crap." Mitch grinned. "Wanna get a beer?"

A cold beer in a noisy bar where he couldn't think sounded like heaven right about now.

"Sure, just let me get my stuff together." He glanced toward Hannah, hoping to ease some of the tension still lingering in the air. "Hannah, you want to join us?"

"Tempting, but no. I have a date."

"With who?" Mitch asked.

"Kevin Moreland."

Ryan shot her an amused look. Kevin Moreland was doing a promo spot for one of their drugs. "Now who's handling the models?"

"*I* am not the CEO of this company. No one notices what I do."

Ryan slipped on his jacket, relieved her playful tone had returned.

"Besides," she added, "Mitch has never gotten around to asking me out, so I have to settle for the young, hot models to fill my time."

Mitch's brows snapped together. "Hannah, sweetheart, I would ask you out, but you scare me. A woman in a suit intimidates me."

She leaned close and ran a coral-tipped fingernail down the stubble on his cheek. "Power is a very sexy thing. You just never know what it's going to do next." She headed for the door. "I'll call you next week, Ryan."

"Hannah," Ryan called. She looked back. "What type of car should I buy?"

A wide smile spread across her face. "How about a Jag?"

He thought about it a minute, then nodded. "Tell Charlotte to get me some brochures tomorrow."

"I will." The door snapped shut behind her.

"A Jag?" Mitch asked. "Dude, if you're buying Jags, I'll take one."

"You'd take it into the mountains and coat it with mud. No way."

Mitch chuckled as he pushed to his feet. "Chicks dig dirty guys."

"In your dreams, mountain man." Ryan reached for his jacket. "Where's Julia? I thought she was with you this afternoon."

"Mom and Dad took her to get ice cream. I wanted beer. I was outvoted." He shoved his hands into the front pockets of his jeans while Ryan moved around the room, gathering his things. "They're leaving tomorrow morning and wanted to take her out for a little fun before they head back to Seattle."

Ryan was all too aware they were leaving. He loved seeing his in-laws, but this week had been too emotional with the recent crash. He was looking forward to getting his house back to normal. "I thought you were going to Chicago, some geologist's conference?"

"I was. Opted out. Not really feeling like traveling right now. I have a ton of work sitting on my desk. We've identified a new site off the coast of British Columbia. It's pulling in all kinds of controversy." He rolled his eyes. "This one chick, this editor for the *Geologic Times*, wrote this article totally bashing our oil company and any sort of exploration off Queen Charlotte Sound. Made some smart-ass comments about our drilling possibly causing massive earthquakes and tsunamis in the area. It's such bull, and she had basically no scientific evidence. So now I'm stuck running interference, trying to convince the investors it isn't a big issue. Like we're not monitoring the fault lines seismically and testing radioactive gas emissions day and night as it is anyway."

Mitch could drone on and on about geology and not care if anyone was listening. In that respect, he was just like Annie. In fact, this was one of those controversies Annie would have loved to argue with him about. She'd always goaded him about his career choice as an engineering geologist working for an oil-and-gas conglomerate. While she'd claimed her work as a seismologist was important to the world of science, she'd teased him that his was only important to the world of profit.

"I bet she doesn't even have a degree in geology," Mitch went on. "She's just some nut-job editor who's read one too many papers and now thinks she's an expert. I ran a search on her. No credentials listed at all. I bet she's some environmental hippie chick. Probably a tree hugger."

"Who?" Ryan was barely listening. He grabbed his cell phone and dropped it in his briefcase.

"That editor who wrote the article." Mitch followed him out into the lobby. "I think her name was Kate Alexander, something like that."

They rode the elevator to the parking garage while Mitch mumbled on and on about some article Ryan could care less about and the idiot who'd written it. Ryan pinched his forehead as they climbed into Mitch's mud-coated Land Rover.

"She's here in San Francisco. I think I'll go over to her office tomorrow and give her a piece of my mind." Mitch pulled out into traffic.

"You do that," Ryan said.

"Oh, hey, forgot to tell you. You got a call this evening, some lawyer here in town. Um, Simone Conners. Sounded pretty sexy."

Ryan recognized the name. "She's an old friend of Annie's." He knew Simone lived in the area, had seen her at several charity functions, but preferred to ignore her. He generally ignored anyone who had known his wife. Making polite chitchat about the good old days wasn't his idea of fun. "What'd she want?"

"Don't know, wouldn't say. If she was a friend of Annie's, she was probably calling about the crash the other day, though."

"Yeah, probably." Ryan looked out the window at the city lights.

"You gonna call her?"

"What?" He glanced over. "I doubt it. She was more Annie's friend than mine. I didn't know her that well."

"Sounded pretty hot on the phone."

"You can tell that just from hearing her voice, huh?"

"Oh, yeah."

"She was married the last time I talked to her, at Annie's funeral."

"So maybe she's not married anymore."

"She was Annie's friend, moron. I'm not interested."

"Why? Was she fat? Ugly? What's the story?"

"God, you're a piece of work. No, she was attractive, at least she was the last time I saw her. Petite, brunette, big eyes. You'd like her."

A grin tugged at Mitch's mouth. "Maybe I should pop over to her office tomorrow, scope her out."

"I thought you were gonna scope out the tree hugger at the publishing house."

"I can do both." Mitch's eyes flashed in the dashboard lights. "Now there's a thought."

"You're a sick and twisted man."

"You have no idea."

Ryan raked a hand through his hair. "I think I'm gonna need at least two beers tonight. Preferably big ones."

# CHAPTER FOUR

Kate stared at the computer screen. Photos of the Stromboli Volcano in Italy stared back at her, an article half done that needed a lot of work. She heaved out a sigh and pressed the heel of her hand against her forehead. There was no possible way she was going to be able to focus on editing today. The article would just have to wait until tomorrow.

Jill stepped into her office a few minutes later with a steamy mocha. "Sure to cure writer's block every time."

"Thanks." Kate smiled and reached for the cup. "You're a peach."

"I'm just buttering you up."

Kate sipped her drink and glanced over the cup with raised brows. "Why do I get the feeling I'm not going to like what you have to say next?"

Jill wrinkled her nose, the nose ring the twenty-something assistant wore making a clinking sound Kate didn't want to ponder too much. "Because I'm really bad at this kind of stuff. Here." She held out a note. "This guy stopped by today while you were out. Really familiar looking for some reason, but I can't remember where I've seen him. Anyway, he wanted to speak with you about something, but since you weren't here, he left you a message. His phone number's at the bottom."

Kate scanned the note, then looked back at Jill. "You've got to be kidding me."

Jill cringed. "Sorry."

Her day was heading straight for the toilet. Kate reached for the phone. The jerk had listed about ten facts from her article he deemed inaccurate and inconclusive.

She dialed and tapped her foot against the floor while she waited. With everything else going on in her life, she didn't need this crap right now. A woman answered. "Mitch..." Kate checked his name at the bottom of the paper, "Mathews, please." She waited another minute. "No, that's fine, I'll leave a message."

Cradling the phone between her ear and shoulder, she fished out a bottle of aspirin from her desk. After dry swallowing two pills, she glanced up at Jill, who was hovering in the doorway. A male voice clicked on the line, and Kate grasped the phone with her hand, wrinkled her brow. Something about the voice was vaguely familiar.

She looked back at the name. Mitch Mathews. Ran it around in her head. Didn't recognize it. But there was something so familiar in that voice...

Whatever. She'd never met the jerk before. After this wouldn't talk to him again. She waited for the incessant beep.

"Mr. Mathews," she began in a smug voice. "This is Kate Alexander at McKellen Publishing. I wanted to take the time to personally thank you for the kind note you left with my secretary today. We really appreciated the pointed and colorful language. Seeing as you had the time to not only track me down but also leave such a lengthy thesis on Queen Charlotte Sound, I must assume you are the *expert* in this field. From now on I'll be sure to defer all questions and comments about this and future articles straight to you. One note, however. Jackass is spelled with two s's, not one. I would have thought they'd teach you that in donkey school. Good day, Mr. Mathews."

Kate gathered the papers in front of her and pushed to her feet. "I have an appointment this afternoon, Jill. You can forward my calls to my cell."

"Ah, sure thing. Kate? Are you okay?"

"I'm fine. Why do you ask?"

"You just seem" —she glanced at the phone and back— "a little on edge."

Kate took a calming breath. "I'm fine. I'll be back later."

Glancing at her watch, Kate realized she was already behind schedule. She climbed into her Explorer and headed across town. Normally, reader comments didn't even faze her, but there'd been something in the tone of Mitch Mathews's note that had really grated on her last nerve.

She found a parking place two blocks from her destination and figured that was a sign her day had to be getting better. It couldn't get much worse. Her *life* couldn't get much worse. As she stood in the building lobby and waited for the elevator, a chill spread over her shoulders and a ripple of anxiety rushed down her spine. She was just nervous. That was normal. If this didn't pan out, she wasn't sure where to go next.

The elevator pinged, the doors opened. She drew in another calming breath as she stepped into the law firm lobby, which was quiet but for the click of fingers on a nearby keyboard. The secretary looked up as she approached. Kate tried to smile, but her insides felt like they were on a continuous loop-de-loop roller coaster. There had to be a reason she'd fixated on this lawyer's name amidst the hundreds listed on the Internet. "I'm here to see Simone Conners."

"Ms. Conners is fairly busy today," the secretary said. "Do you have an appointment?"

"Yes. Kate Alexander."

The young blonde picked up the phone, mumbled into it then glanced back at Kate. "Ms. Conners is expecting you. Go on in."

"Thank you."

Kate worked to settle her swirling nerves as she pushed open the double oak doors and stepped into the room. Wide windows ahead looked out over a view of San Francisco. To the right, bookcases lined with legal tomes filled the shelves, and to the left, a grouping of leather couches sat in front of a long conference table covered with books and papers.

But it was Simone Conners who drew Kate's attention. The petite woman rose from her desk in front of the windows with the whitest face Kate had ever seen. A face that wasn't the least bit familiar, dammit. "Oh, my God."

Kate looked behind her just as the door snapped closed. She didn't see anyone else. Turning back, she stared at the lawyer with chocolate brown hair cut in a stylish bob and bronze-colored eyes that looked like they'd just seen a ghost.

"Oh, my God," Simone whispered again. "Annie."

A chill spread over Kate's skin. "Um, no. I'm Kate Alexander. We have a one o'clock appointment. If this is a bad time, I could—"

"You..." The lawyer closed her eyes, shook her head, then opened them again. "I—I'm sorry. You look like a woman I used to know."

Excitement mixed with a good dose of fear flooded Kate's veins. No. It couldn't be this easy. Could it? She swallowed the lump in her throat. "You...you recognize me?"

"I'm sorry. It's not possible." Simone looked down. When she glanced back up, she'd fixed a polite smile to her face. "What can I do for you?"

"Why isn't it possible?" Too many questions swirled through Kate's mind. Too many fingers of hope. She tried to keep the desperation out of her voice, but wasn't sure she succeeded.

Simone sat again, the white, sleeveless blouse showcasing her toned arms, the slim navy slacks expensive and stylish. "The woman I was thinking of died almost five years ago. They say everyone has a twin. I guess I just met hers. Now that I look closer though, you're not identical. You just gave me a startle, that's all. I was thinking of her recently, which is why I jumped to conclusions that can't be real." She gestured to the chair opposite her desk. "Now, what can I do for you?"

Kate eased into the seat. Nerves bounced all around inside her. "What…what was her name?"

"My friend?" Simone rested her elbow on the armrest of her chair. "Why do you want to know?"

"Just curious."

Simone considered for a moment, then said, "Annie Harrison."

Kate rolled the name over in her mind. She'd never heard it before. That hope began to fade. "How did she die?"

Simone tipped her head. "I'm sure you didn't come all the way down here to discuss my friend, Ms. Alexander."

Kate ran a hand over her hair, stopping to rub her scar. "Please, just humor me for a moment. How did she die?"

"In a plane crash, just outside San Francisco. Very similar to the one that happened here not long ago."

A plane crash. No, that wasn't the same. Kate's eyes slid shut. Possibilities, scenarios ran through her mind. None made sense, none seemed feasible, but she had to ask. If she didn't, it would eat away at her. "What's different about her and me? I mean, you said we weren't identical. What's different?"

Simone's eyes narrowed. "Why are you so interested in my friend, Ms. Alexander?"

Kate focused on the petite lawyer. Tried to remember the woman. Couldn't. But there was that feeling…an odd sense of déjà vu. The same one she'd felt when she'd seen Simone Conner's name online. "I didn't know about your friend when I came in here. And I'm sorry for asking, but…"

"But what?"

Blowing out a shaky breath, Kate straightened. "I came here on the advice of a colleague. I'm having trouble tracking down some information, and he thought a lawyer might be able to apply some legal pressure that could help me find the answers I'm seeking. I found your name online. And...I don't know...something just told me you were the one I should see."

When Simone only continued to stare at her speculatively, Kate shifted. "My husband died in that plane crash here a few weeks ago."

"Oh." Simone's face softened. "Oh, I'm so sorry. No wonder you—"

"No, that's not it. But thank you." Kate took a deep breath. "After his death, I found some information that brought me here to San Francisco. I was in an accident several years ago and ended up in a coma." She frowned, shook her head. "Or so I thought. When I was going through my husband's papers, I found evidence I'd been in a nursing home here in San Francisco for over two years. Ms. Conners, I don't ever remember being here. I don't remember anything before waking up from that coma eighteen months ago. Nothing about my background, where I grew up, my family. My husband told me I was injured in a car accident, that I'd been in a coma for four days. Now...now I'm not sure what to believe."

Simone leaned forward, her brow wrinkling. "Where have you been living?"

"In Houston. My husband was a doctor. A neurosurgeon." She dug papers out of her bag. "He signed forms as my attending physician while I was here in San Francisco, though. He'd never have been allowed to do that if he was my husband."

"No, he wouldn't." With narrowed eyes, Simone took the forms, scanned the papers.

"The nursing home burned down a year ago. Coincidental, if you ask me. A new one was built in its place, but they claim all the records were destroyed in the fire. I can't get anyone there to answer my questions. I was hoping maybe you could help me talk to them. I was a patient. I have rights."

Simone read the forms in her hands, flipped from page to page. "Permanent memory loss," she mumbled, scanning the evaluation. "And you don't remember a single thing from the accident?"

"No. Nothing."

"What about after the accident?"

"I woke up in Houston. My husband was with me. I didn't remember him, either. It was like starting over."

Simone continued to read the papers in front of her. "This is pretty unique. It says the portion of your brain that was damaged deals with long-term memories, specifically personal ones, and personality. Do you have a career, Ms. Alexander?"

"Yes. I'm an editor for a geological publication. My doctor in Houston seems to think the part of my brain that was damaged was where personal memories are stored, which is why I'm able to remember things I've learned along the way—like the rate of converge of the Juan de Fuca plate—but nothing specific about where I learned it."

When Simone glanced up in confusion, a weak smile tugged at Kate's mouth. "Sorry. I forget others aren't interested in geology like I am. The running joke around the publishing house is that I'm the queen science nerd."

"Oh, my. Wow." Simone blew out a long breath and tossed the papers on her desk. With a hand that appeared to be shaking, she swiped at her forehead. "Did you find anything else with these forms?"

"Just this." Kate fished the picture out of her bag and handed it to her. "I don't have a clue who that is in the photo, but the eyes...those eyes are so familiar. They're just like mine."

Simone's mouth fell open. "Oh, my God."

"What?"

"That's Annie's daughter."


Mitch spent the better part of his afternoon at the lab, testing the rock samples his team had sent down from British Columbia. After several hours, he sat back and rubbed his tired eyes. There was still a lot of research to do, but he felt confident they'd made a good start. He'd have to take a trip up to BC soon, probably in a few weeks, but he trusted his team, and their initial tests so far were concurrent with his.

It was after four when he finally made his way back to his office. He smiled at Christy, his secretary, as he strolled in and tossed a bag of Mrs. Fields chocolate-chip cookies on her desk. "Take off, would ya?"

"You're sure in a good mood." She loved Mrs. Fields anything, and he knew it.

"Samples are looking good. Call Charlie and find out when they want me to come up. I'm thinking maybe two weeks from now.

Find out what sort of progress they're making and what their schedule's looking like. Then head home. You've been at it all day."

"You don't have to twist my arm." She followed him into his office and set down the report she'd just finished typing. "Here's the geochemistry profile on the site."

"Great." He flipped through it. "Did I get any messages?"

"You have a few on your voicemail. Mac also stopped by and wants a rundown on the biomarkers. I told him you'd call him tonight or tomorrow."

"Thanks, Christy. What the hell would I do without you?" With a sheepish grin, he leaned back in his chair and propped his feet up on the desk.

"Fall flat on your ass." She winked and walked out of the room.

Mitch picked up the phone and dialed in his access code. He didn't close his door, he never did, so when he fished out the baseball he kept in the top drawer of his desk and started tossing it in the air, the rhythmic swoosh and tap didn't even elicit a response from Christy at her desk.

His eyes slid shut as he listened to his voice mail and continued tossing the ball. It was mostly info about the site, a few messages from the lab about what they'd found earlier that morning.

The phone beeped and moved to the next message. When the husky female voice chimed through the line, he sat straight up in his chair.

The baseball he'd just tossed came down with a crack and hit him in the head. "Dammit," he muttered, rubbing his skull. But the pain quickly dissipated as his mind zeroed in on the voice. He knew that voice.

It was Annie's voice.

And it was ticked, which was why he was sure it was hers. He'd heard the clip in that voice thousands of time, the lithe way she said his name, the way her condescending tone drawled out the word *jackass*. The blood drained from his face as he scrambled for his phone so he could listen again.

No, it couldn't be real. He was imagining things. Conjuring. What the hell had his mother called it when he was a kid? Spacing out in the middle of the flippin' day.

His pulse picked up speed as he hit replay. The message was new. It was Annie's voice, and holy hell, it was from today. He listened again, this time trying to focus on the words, not so much the voice. She'd said her name was Kate Alexander.

Kate Alexander.

The nut-job from the publishing house? That didn't make sense. He knew that voice almost as well as he knew his own.

Scenarios, possibilities, questions swirled in his mind. No way. It couldn't be…

And yet… His heart thumped hard. Her body had never been found. She'd been sitting over the wing. The engine had exploded. No one around her had ever been recovered. They'd all hoped beyond hope that she hadn't actually been on the plane, that she'd changed her mind at the last minute after Ryan had dropped her at the airport. But that hope had died when Ryan had identified her belongings after the crash.

But what if she'd never gotten on that plane? Was it possible she could still be alive? The idea was crazy. Ludicrous. Virtually impossible. And still…the only thing he could think about now.

He had to know for sure. He dialed her number but it went straight to voice mail. Slamming the phone down, he grabbed his coat and ran for the door.

Christy stood when he tore past her toward the elevator. "Mitch, what—?"

He barely heard her. He was already in the stairwell. His watch said four-thirty by the time he made it out of the building. There was no way he'd get all the way across town before five. He wove right and left through traffic, yelled at an old woman crossing the street much too slowly, and finally found a parking place in front of McKellen Publishing just before five.

Screw the meter. He didn't even bother to see if he'd parked in a handicapped spot. He could only think about one thing. That goddamn familiar, irritating as hell, sweet voice.

He raced through the building, swore at the elevator when it didn't seem to move, then headed for the stairs. By the time he got to the fourteenth floor he was panting, but it didn't slow him down. He headed straight for Kate Alexander's office.

The secretary with the tattoos and nose ring he'd run into earlier stood when she saw him, her brows drawing together in an obvious sign of worry. "Mr. Mathews, you can't go in there!"

He swept past her, shoved the door open with his shoulder. The room was empty.

"Where is she?" He glanced around the cramped office that was the size of his bathroom.

"Ms. Alexander's not here. She's out for the afternoon. I can make you an appointment if you'd like."

He barely heard her. He scanned the room, for what though, he didn't know. Stacks of journals were shoved up against the wall. A bookshelf sat to his right, loaded with geology books and minerals. Her desk was a sea of papers, and the small window that looked out over the city cast late-afternoon light over the boxes and boxes of journals and books waiting to be unpacked.

Dammit, there had to be something, anything that would tell him…

"You can't be in here, Mr. Mathews," the secretary said louder as he rounded the desk. "I'm going to call security."

He flipped through the files on her desk, moved stacks of paper looking for…shit, he didn't know what. Just anything. His gaze moved to the photograph beside her computer. And everything inside him froze.

Holy shit.

With shaking fingers, he reached for the frame, then sank into her chair, barely believing what he was seeing.

It looked like Annie. Not the exact image he remembered, but close enough. It didn't matter that her nose was slightly different, her cheeks a little higher or that she had a scar near her temple. The face staring back at him had the same eyes, same chin, the same dimple that was in his own damn face. And she was cheek to cheek with a young blond boy.

A young boy who was the spitting image of Ryan.

Every ounce of blood drained from his face.

"Mr. Mathews," the secretary asked. "Um, are you okay?"

"Where is she?" he managed.

"I don't know. If you come back tomorrow—"

"I need to know now!"

The secretary jumped. "We don't give out personal information. If you come back tomorrow, I'm sure she'll see you."

"Dammit! This isn't about the goddamn article she wrote! This is personal. Where the fuck is she?"

"I don't know. Look—"

He clenched his jaw, realizing he wasn't getting anywhere with the gatekeeper. Grabbing the photo, he headed for the door. She ran after him, yelling something about stealing personal property, but he didn't care. All he cared about was getting to Ryan.

Now.

* * *

Her legs felt like they might just buckle.

Kate checked the address she'd pulled from the Internet. Simone had told her not to jump to conclusions, to let her do some research, but as soon as Simone had recognized Julia Harrison in that photo, Kate couldn't stop thinking about the coincidences.

There was a reason Jake had locked that photo in that box. A reason she felt a surge of déjà vu when she looked at it. A reason she'd found Simone Conners.

She'd gone back to her office. Ran a search on Ryan Harrison, the man Simone had told her Annie Harrison had been married to. Felt sick over what she'd found. Of course, she'd seen his face plastered on the covers of *Fortune* and *Money*, and more recently, the tabloid magazines, but she hadn't known much about him other than the fact he was incredibly attractive. Now she did. There were numerous reports on the Internet that he was a ruthless pharmaceutical CEO who had a reputation for aggressive corporate takeovers and for walking over anyone in his way on the road to success. The press dubbed him money-hungry and uncompromising. And he had a habit of sneering at the cameras whenever they got close. But he didn't seem to mind being photographed with a different woman on his arm every weekend.

There was no way she would have been with someone like that. Money? Power? Fame? None of that mattered to her. Someone so obsessed with those things would never have been attractive to her. There was no way she would have been…

She swallowed the lump in her throat, unable to say the words, let alone think them. She'd *had* a husband. Jake. A wave of nausea rolled through her as she fingered the ring still on her left hand. It didn't matter that Reed looked a little like this man. Everyone had a twin, right? Hadn't Simone said that to her only hours ago?

Oh, man, this was a bad idea. She closed her eyes and took deep, calming breaths. What the hell was she doing here? She never should have come to San Francisco. She never should have gone to see Simone Conners. She never should have looked in that damn drawer.

She opened her eyes, scanned the affluent street. Enormous maple trees lined each side of the road in the Sausalito hills. Lawns sloped from one attractive home to the next, each property stately and more impressive than the last. This was a mistake. This wasn't real. She needed to go before she made a complete fool out of herself.

She was just about to head back when the jingle of a bell sounded close. She looked up as a trio of young girls on bikes came whipping by.

The last girl slammed on her brakes as soon as she saw Kate. Her friends went sailing past, laughing, but she planted her feet and gripped the handlebars of her bike, then did that same damn I've-seen-a-ghost stare that Simone had done when Kate stepped into her office.

Kate swallowed hard. Every inch of her skin tingled like a thousand needles being stabbed into a pincushion. The face—the girl—she was the one from the picture.

She couldn't leave now. She had to see. She had to *know*.

Fear rippled through her. She didn't know what to say. Didn't know what to do. But something pushed her forward. "Hi."

"You," the girl said, still staring wide-eyed at Kate. "You...you look like—"

"My name's Kate. Are you Julia?"

"Yes." Her eyes narrowed. "How do you know my name?"

"A friend told me." The awkward silence and the way the girl continued to stare at her like she had a third head was more than Kate could bear. She glanced up the road. "I came to talk to your dad. Is he home?"

The girl jumped off her bike as if she'd just been slapped. "He's not home. He can't see you."

Kate's palms grew damp. "Wait—"

"Julia!" A male voice echoed from across the street. "Time to come in!"

The girl's bike crashed to the ground. She sprinted across the pavement and up the path toward a stately, three-story house. A man was just stepping down off the porch. A man dressed in slacks and a dress shirt with the sleeves rolled up to his forearms. A man with blond hair and a devastatingly handsome face that didn't even compare to the one Kate had seen in magazines or on the Internet.

A man, she realized as she drew in a sharp breath, who up close didn't just look a *little* like her son. He looked *just* like him.

# CHAPTER FIVE

Ryan's adrenaline surged as Julia tore straight at him, her face a mix of fear and anger and heartache.

"What is it?" he asked as he dropped to one knee in front of her, gripping her shoulders and scanning her body to make sure she wasn't hurt.

"I...go inside, Daddy. Go inside!"

"Julia, calm down. What's wrong? Tell me what happened." His gaze jumped past her, to her bike lying in the road. To the person standing in the middle of the street staring at them. To the woman who looked like...

The air whooshed out of his lungs. His knees turned to gelatin. "Oh, my God."

"No, Dad!" Julia pushed against his shoulders, tried to force him back into the house as he slowly rose to his feet. "No, Dad. It's not her. It's not her, Daddy. It just looks like her. Please, Daddy, please. Look at me."

His gaze dropped to Julia's tear-streaked face. Panic filled her eyes, but it barely registered. With shaking arms, he lifted her out of his way then looked toward the brunette standing still as stone in the road. Watching him like he was watching her.

His head spun. His pulse raced. It couldn't be.

He was vaguely aware of a car screeching to a halt next to the curb, of Mitch climbing out of his Land Rover, of Julia's hysterical voice as she tried to pull him back into the house, but he couldn't feel her hands. Couldn't seem to stop his feet from moving forward. He felt like he was in a fog. A dream. Like he was hallucinating in broad daylight.

Somehow he made it down the block, stopped in front of her. Stared at her in shock. At his side he heard Mitch mutter, "Mother of God."

No one spoke. For a long minute there was nothing but silence. And fear and hope and utter disbelief. And then his heart lurched in his chest.

"Oh, my God." He closed the distance between them, cupped her face in his hands, ran his fingers over the smooth skin of her jaw. This couldn't be real. It had to be a dream. Memories bombarded him from every side, condensed beneath his breastbone and squeezed as he soaked her in. As he felt her pulse beat beneath his fingers. As the heat of her body surrounded him to leave him foggy and light headed.

She was real. She was warm and soft and *alive* beneath his fingers. She was…Annie.

She stared into eyes. Recognition flared in the depths of those green gems. And that connection they'd had from the very start, from the first second they'd met so long ago, burned hot and bright, warming him in places he hadn't even realized had gone cold.

All this time. All these years…

"Annie," he whispered.

Her eyes darkened. The recognition fled. Was quickly replaced with confusion and…fear.

Before he could stop her, she jerked out of his arms, took a big step back. Held her arms out in a very clear don't-touch-me move. "No." She swallowed, looked from face to face with her brow drawn low, took another step away. "No, my name is Kate. Kate Alexander."

Pain slashed through him. He tried to reach for her again, but Julia tugged hard on his arm, stopping him. "Dad, I told you it's not her. It just looks like her. Dad, Daddy, listen to me. It's not her."

Not her? It had to be her. It had to be…

"Annie—"

She dodged his grip. And his heart felt like it shattered against the pavement at his feet. "I…I was hoping to ask you a few questions. I can see this isn't a good time. I'll just leave—"

"No!" Ryan and Mitch both said at the same time.

She jumped. Froze. Looked from face to face in bewilderment.

Holy God, it had to be her. It sounded like her. Ryan could never forget that voice. He didn't know what the hell was going on but he didn't want to scare her off. To keep from reaching for her, he scrubbed his hands over his face. Closed his eyes, shook his head, opened them again. She was still there. She wasn't a figment of his imagination.

Why wasn't she throwing herself into his arms? Why was she

standing there looking at him as if he were a stranger?

"No," Mitch said again, holding out his hands. "No, now's fine."

Her attention shifted his way. "Who are you?"

She didn't know Mitch? She had to know her brother. She was Annie.

"Mitch Mathews. Ah, his brother-in-law." Mitch nodded at Ryan. "Her...Annie's...brother."

Her brow wrinkled, then her green eyes grew wide. "Mitch Mathews. The geologist?"

A sly smile spread across Mitch's mouth. "Yeah, same one."

"Oh. Well." A nervous look crossed her face. A face that Ryan now saw was different from what he remembered. Different but still familiar. "This is a little awkward. I, ah, I had no idea." She ran a hand over her hair.

Ryan's stomach tightened. It was the same unconscious gesture Annie always made when nervous.

"Me, either," Mitch said. They studied one another for a minute. "I got your message."

A rose tint stained her cheeks. "Well, you, ah, seemed a little fired up about the article. I guess I just responded...badly, I might say now, in light of the situation."

Mitch grinned. Why the hell was he grinning?

"What are you two talking about?" Ryan asked, looking from one to the other. He felt like he was being hammered by prize-fighters from all sides, and they were acting like they knew each other. If Mitch had known Annie was so close and hadn't told him—

"This is the editor, Ryan, the one I told you about. The one who wrote that article."

Ryan looked back at her—at *his* Annie. At the woman who couldn't be anything *but* his Annie. Why was she acting as if she didn't know him? Why wasn't she grabbing Julia, hugging her tight? Hugging *him* tight? Holding on to him like he needed to hold on to her?

As questions tumbled through his mind and he scanned her features again, he realized what looked different. Her nose was thinner, her cheekbones a little higher, and there was a scar near her temple he didn't remember.

*Editor. The one who wrote that article. Kate Alexander.*

His chest pinched tight. Was it possible this woman wasn't

Annie?

His mind skipped to the conversation he'd had with Mitch in his office, and confusion replaced shock. "The nut-job?"

"Excuse me?" She shot a glare his way.

Mitch laughed. "No, no. It's nothing. Just a joke. Ah, this is a little awkward. You…you look a lot like my sister. We're all a little flustered, I think."

What the hell was Mitch saying? She was his sister. Wasn't she?

"Why don't we go inside," Mitch suggested. "You can tell us what this is about. Come on." He motioned for the house. She eyed Ryan with suspicion, then stepped well out of his reach and up next to Mitch.

Ryan turned, stared after her as they headed for the house. Tried to clear his head. Was it possible someone else could look so much like his wife? Sound like her? If she wasn't Annie, what was she doing here? Was this some kind of sick joke?

The sway of her step caught his attention. And his heart took a hard, sharp roll. She was built just like Annie, same strong legs and perfectly toned ass. She even walked like her.

Fate could not be so cruel. *God* could not be this cruel. There had to be an explanation. Pain lanced through his chest, speared what was left. He'd listen to whatever she had to say for Mitch's sake. Then she was gone. He couldn't take this in-your-face reminder of everything he'd lost.

He followed them into the living room where the leather couches Julia had helped him pick out formed an L-shape. She stood in the center of the room, staring out at the skyline of San Francisco for several seconds, then turned and glanced around the room. He didn't know what she was looking at—or for—but as her gaze swept over the photos of Julia, of Mitch, of Annie, Ryan's patience reached a tipping point.

Julia tugged on his arm, whispered, "Daddy" in a pleading voice, but he ignored her.

"Why are you here, Ms…what was your name again?"

She visibly jolted, then turned to face him, and from the way her green eyes widened, he knew the shock was gone from his face and had been replaced with the ice he felt inside. The ice he'd built up over the years just so he could survive.

He watched her pull up some invisible shield, watched her eyes harden as if she were looking at a complete stranger. As if the connection they'd shared in the street had never happened. "Your wife died in a plane crash, about five years ago, is that right?"

When he didn't answer, she added, "And she died here in San Francisco. Is that correct?"

"You already seem to know the answers to these questions. Why are you here?" he asked again.

"A year and a half ago, I was in an accident that landed me in a coma." She lifted her hand, rubbed at a spot on the side of her head. "When I woke up in a Dallas hospital, I couldn't remember the accident or anything about my life before it. The doctors said the trauma did something to my long-term memory. Retrograde amnesia, they called it. I'd been told I was in a car accident. But now, I'm not so sure."

"Why not?" Mitch asked, watching her closely too.

She glanced his way. "My husband died in that plane crash here a few weeks ago. After, when I was going through some of his papers, I found evidence that suggests I was in a nursing home here in San Francisco during that coma, not in Texas like I'd been led to believe. And that the coma had lasted close to three years, not four days. I'm not sure why my husband lied, or what it all means, but I came here to San Francisco looking for answers. I went to see a lawyer today for advice. The woman recognized me, said I looked a lot like Anne Harrison." She glanced back at Ryan. "Your wife."

Ryan's head spun, and his pulse beat so hard it was a roar in his ears. The story was ludicrous. Insane. No way it was real.

"Who was the lawyer?" Mitch asked.

"Simone Conners."

Mitch's eyes found Ryan's. He knew what Mitch was thinking. But it couldn't be her. Yeah, she looked a lot like her, but now that the shock was gone he could tell she wasn't the same. Annie's nose had been different, her cheeks not as sharp. Maturity could change a person's face and shape, but it didn't reshape bone structure. Besides which, Annie was gone. She'd died in that crash. They'd buried her. It didn't matter that they'd never had a body. No one had survived that crash.

"Simone thinks you might be Annie," Ryan said. "That's why you're here."

"No. Not exactly. In fact, she doesn't know I'm here. She told me not to come, but I…" She bit her lip, then reached into her purse. Her eyes cut to Julia, standing at Ryan's side, and a protective urge bubbled through him, one that made him want to tug his daughter tight to his side. With trembling fingers, she held a photo out to him. "I found this in a lockbox in my house."

Hesitantly, Ryan reached for the picture. Looked down. And felt his entire world tip right out from under him.

Julia's eyes widened as she glanced at the photo in his hand. "That's me."

Ryan's head darted up. When she turned to look at Julia and tucked her hair behind her ear, he caught sight of a faded strawberry birthmark just below her left ear where her jaw met her neck. An upside down heart. One he'd kissed and licked and nibbled so many times he knew it as if it were his own.

Hope burst into flame in his chest. It was her. She was alive. She was…

He moved to reach for her. She stepped back to avoid his touch, and when her gaze fell on his, the look in her eyes registered. No recognition. No love. Nothing but emptiness and distrust.

Her reaction in the street slammed back into him. And that hope was quickly doused with ice.

*Accident. Retrograde amnesia… Alive.*

Sickness pushed up his esophagus. The room closed in around him as it had at her funeral, when the reality that he'd lost her forever had hit him like a ton of bricks.

But he hadn't lost her. She was here. She was real. No matter what had happened to change her appearance, one thing remained. She was alive. She'd never gotten on that plane. She'd been here in San Francisco the whole time and he'd never looked for her. He'd never even thought to look for her.

Air choked in his lungs. The photo fluttered to the floor at his feet. He had to get away from her. Away from all of them before he lost it for good.

He walked out of the room. Didn't know where the hell he was going. At his back, he heard Mitch mutter, "Ah, just give us a minute, okay?"

He made it as far as the kitchen. Needed to go farther, wasn't sure his legs would carry him. Bracing his hands against the cold granite, he dropped his head, just focused on breathing. In and out. In and out. Hoped like hell it would alleviate the pain spearing his chest.

*Don't lose it. Keep it together for Julia.*

His eyes slid shut, and he forced back the tears. Of all the scenarios he'd imagined over the years, this wasn't one of them. In all of them, in the ones where she'd been alive, at least, she'd been as thrilled to see him as he was to see her. But this woman, this Kate Alexander didn't know him. She wasn't running into his arms. She wasn't professing her love for him. She was just standing there, staring at him like he was…nobody.

And she'd said she had a husband. That pain cinched down tight until he could barely breathe. She'd gotten remarried. Her life had moved on while his had stood rooted in time, the memory of her the only thing that kept him going day after day.

"Ryan."

Mitch. Dammit, he should have known Mitch would follow him.

He didn't turn, couldn't face Mitch's eyes. "She doesn't recognize us."

"No, she doesn't. It doesn't mean it's her."

"It's her. You saw the way she ran her hand over her hair. And she's got the same damn birthmark near her ear." His voice cracked. "That's Annie."

"We don't know that."

"I know it." Ryan finally turned Mitch's way. "I know it. I knew it as soon as I saw her."

"It's possible. But the chances are so remote. Look, I'll agree she looks like her. Christ." Mitch scrubbed at his jaw. "And her story, well, it could fit. But we don't know for sure. She could be some crazy loon looking for money. Ryan, I don't have to remind you you're practically a celebrity. That draws the sickos right out of the woodwork. We don't know if it's her. There are tests we can take. DNA sampling—from me, from Julia."

"It won't matter. You and I both know it's her, whether you want to admit it or not."

"I need to know for sure."

Ryan's eyes slid shut. Mitch was so rooted in science, in the black and white of everything. But this situation was nothing but gray. "She doesn't recognize us," he said again.

"Ryan, don't do this to yourself. Not yet. Let's see what we find out. This could all just be a huge coincidence."

Ryan turned to stare over the kitchen. Minutes ago, he'd been about to make Julia dinner. He'd planned to show her pictures of the new Jag Hannah had talked him into ordering. After, he was going to sit down with her and watch a movie. He was even going to let her choose one of her favorite Indiana Jones flicks that they'd already seen ten thousand times. Now...now he couldn't figure out what the hell to do next.

"I gotta get out of here. You...you take care of it. Tell her whatever you want. I'll go along with whatever you decide."

"Ryan—"

"I need a few minutes, Mitch," he snapped. He couldn't stand looking into her blank eyes again, knowing she wasn't remembering him or what they'd shared. He couldn't deal with the pain. Pain he thought he'd gotten through long ago. Pain that was now sucking him under all over again.

He opened the back door and left before Mitch could stop him.


Kate studied the photos on the mantel while Ryan Harrison and Mitch Mathews spoke quietly in the other room. The face in the pictures looked like her, albeit a slightly different her. A river of unease rushed through her veins as she looked from photo to photo. The Harrisons on what looked to be a hiking trip. Annie Harrison in a hospital bed, holding a newborn. A wedding photo of Ryan and Annie on the day they were married, both dressed to the nines and grinning from ear to ear.

Her chest tightened, and her skin grew hot. If it was her in the photos, she didn't remember any of the events. But the odd roll of her stomach told her that didn't mean it wasn't her either.

She looked quickly away from the photos, not wanting to go there yet, and scanned the room. Nothing about this house was familiar either. Not the furnishings or the pictures on the walls, though she did like the job Ryan Harrison's decorator had done. Leather couches, plush pillows, chunky wood tables and trendy lamps she might have picked out herself if given the chance.

Her stomach rolled again at that thought, and she turned to find Julia Harrison staring at her with suspicious eyes. The girl had refused to utter a single word the whole time Ryan and Mitch were in the other room. Kate's nerves kicked in. Staring down Ryan Harrison was one thing. Staring down his daughter when she very clearly wanted Kate gone was another.

She didn't need this. She had enough problems in her life right now—moving to a new city, getting Reed adjusted to life without his father, trying to figure out what the hell had happened to her. And now, add to all that a man who could possibly be her real husband and a daughter who looked at her like she was the anti-Christ?

It couldn't possibly get any worse, could it?

Mitch came back into the room, shot her a weak smile. Relief rushed through Kate like sweet wine when she saw him. As Julia slipped out of the room without a word, guilt rushed through Kate's veins. It couldn't be easy for the girl to see someone who looked so much like her mother. Kate hadn't considered the girl's feelings in all this when she'd decided to come by here today. She'd been so intent on finding answers, she hadn't thought of anyone but herself.

Mitch watched her leave, then turned to face Kate. Heartache showed clearly in his features. And that guilt expanded ten-fold as she stared at him. This was so much harder for all of them than she'd anticipated.

Mitch blew out a breath. "We, ah, we think maybe there are enough similarities to warrant some tests. DNA tests to either prove or disprove the whole thing."

She nodded, swallowing the lump in her throat. Was it relief or regret? At this point, she wasn't sure. "Yeah, that's what I was hoping. I can have my lawyer set it up. It should be easy, just a blood sample from you, her brother, and possibly her daughter." As she glanced around, her unease grew by leaps and bounds. Ryan Harrison obviously wasn't coming back out to talk to her. "I should go."

"Okay." Mitch raked a hand through his hair. "I, ah, I'll walk you out."

He led her out of the house and back down the street to her car. She wasn't sure why, but she felt comfortable with him, even if he'd been the one to leave her that nasty gram at her office. Funny...a few hours ago he'd been her biggest enemy. Now he seemed to be her only ally.

Which was ludicrous because she knew nothing about this man.

He was quiet as they walked, his hands shoved deep in the front pockets of his jeans, his eyes on the ground in front of him, and as they headed toward her car his words from earlier echoed in her mind. *Annie's brother...* Jake had told her she was an only child. That her parents had died years ago. She'd believed him. She'd believed so many things that now could very well be wrong. What else had he lied about?

She pushed that thought aside. Told herself she'd deal with it later. Right now, she had to stay focused on the moment or she'd break down.

When they stopped near her Explorer, she turned toward Mitch and looked into his eyes. Green eyes, she noticed now, that were eerily familiar. Like his niece's—Julia's—eyes. Like her eyes. "Can I ask you a personal question?"

"Sure."

She probably should let it go, but she was curious. "You seem like a really nice guy. So nice considering all this and what you must be feeling that I'm having trouble figuring out which guy you really are. The pompous jerk who left me that note this morning, or the supportive brother-in-law you seem to be this afternoon?"

He chuckled and looked down at his feet.

"What?"

"Nothing. That's just something my sister would have asked me."

"Oh." The implication of those words hung in the air between them. He thought she was his sister. She could see it in those emerald eyes. Did she want that? Panic spread through her chest. She didn't know what she wanted. Was seriously starting to doubt whether coming here had been a smart idea or not. God, why hadn't she just waited like Simone had told her to do?

She ran a hand over her hair. They stood in silence for several seconds, then her curiosity finally got the best of her. "So which is it?"

"Both, I guess."

"I see." But she didn't. Not really. She didn't see anything. Doubted she ever would. And that fact left her feeling more lost than anything.

She drew in a deep breath that did nothing to ease the ache in her chest and glanced back toward the house. "I don't think he likes me very much."

"He's been through a lot. You have to understand, when Annie died, it changed him. They had something special, something most people don't find in a whole lifetime of looking."

"I find that hard to believe. I've read a lot about him, and nothing I've ever seen leads me to believe he's a caring individual."

"Don't believe everything you read." Something in his voice warned her to be careful about her choice of words. But that voice softened when he added, "Seeing you today, well, it's something I think he's dreamt about for years. I just don't think he ever expected Annie not to remember him. It's like losing her all over again."

"I'm not Annie," she said quietly.

"No. Not yet. At least, not that we know for sure."

There it was. Spoken aloud she didn't know what to think. What to feel. What to do for that matter. "He thinks I am."

"He knew her really well. They were together for ten years."

Guilt tightened the already snug feeling in her torso. "I didn't come here to hurt anyone. I hope you know that. I just need answers. You don't know what it's like to go through life not knowing who you are. A person without a past, well," she shook her head, "it's an anomaly."

"And scary, I bet."

"Yes, very," she whispered as he stared into her eyes. And though she fought it, she couldn't deny the jolt of déjà vu that coursed through her when she looked at him. "I'm just looking for answers, one way or the other."

"I get it."

She didn't answer, was too afraid of what would come out if she tried. Her pulse beat hard. If he was really her brother, she'd remember right? But there was nothing. No memory flashes, no images in her brain, nothing but this feeling of...familiarity.

When she realized she was staring, she quickly looked away. "I have to go. I'll, ah, call your office when I have the details mapped out for the test."

"Okay."

"Okay." Her feet didn't seem to want to move. But she forced them to. For her sanity as much as his. "Okay," she said again with a shaky voice as she climbed into her car.

# CHAPTER SIX

Midmorning sunlight glinted off the bay, the tall spires of the Golden Gate Bridge rising against a dense, green backdrop of trees and hills. Salt and the ripe stench of fish wafted on the air as Kate sat on a park bench, digging her fingers into the seat. Around her, seagulls swooped, their cries echoing through her mind, jangling her already overstressed nerves.

What she needed was a good kick in the pants to get off her duff and get back to work finding out what had happened to her. What she was doing was waiting for Ryan Harrison.

After three days of biting her fingernails to the quick, languishing over news from Simone about the blood test results, she'd finally given in and called him. She didn't know why she felt compelled to talk with him, and couldn't explain why his reaction to her affected her so much. All she knew for sure was that guilt had consumed her every minute of every day since their meeting. And if she didn't do something to fix it, it was going to eat away at her and prevent her from finding the answers she desperately needed.

She knew what it was like to lose someone you loved. And because of that, she tried to put herself in Ryan's position, to imagine what she'd do if Jake suddenly returned from the grave.

Her fingers dug deeper into the seat as anger coursed through her. The first thing she'd do is handcuff him to a chair until she got the answers she was looking for. Then she'd sandblast him for putting her through this nightmare.

On a deep breath, she forcibly released her grip and ran her hands over her hair. Jake wasn't going to rise from the dead. And she was stuck without a past.

She spotted Ryan walking along the waterfront path before he spotted her. That odd sense of déjà vu she'd felt in the street outside his house rushed through her as she watched him. His hands were tucked in the front pockets of his slacks, and he wore dark sunglasses over his eyes, but she didn't miss the scowl on his face. Or the rigid shoulders and stiff back that screamed of his unease at the current situation.

He stopped a few feet away. Clenched his jaw. When she stood to meet him, her stomach pitched, a reaction she wasn't prepared for.

"Thanks for coming," she managed.

"I'm not entirely sure why I did." There was an icy tone to his voice she didn't like. Did he use it in his business dealings to intimidate and influence? If so, it was effective.

"I appreciate it, all the same." She shifted her weight, not sure what she wanted to say now that he was standing in front of her. An awkward silence spread between them like a vast ocean.

"I doubt you know anything yet, so why this little meeting?" he asked.

For some reason, she wanted to reach out and bridge the gap between them. To comfort him. Which was an unexpected reaction. "No, I don't. Simone said it would take probably a week for the test results. Which, by the way, I wanted to thank you for agreeing to."

He didn't respond, just rocked back on his heels and watched her. A whiff of his scent drifted on the air, and a shiver of awareness swept over her when she drew it in, that musky spice oddly familiar.

Not familiarity, she told herself. Awareness. He was an attractive and powerful man, and underneath it all, she was still a woman. Even before any of this had happened, she'd thought he was handsome. The tabloids and magazines, though, didn't do him justice. His nose was straight, his jaw square and clean shaven, his features chiseled and so very masculine. And his mouth…

Her gaze traveled to his lips. Full. Smooth. Tempting. She wondered what it would feel like to brush her thumb across that bottom lip, to trace the faint scar down the right side of his chin. The man had a sensual mouth that at one time she'd probably kissed and tasted and claimed as her own.

*Whoa.*

Where the heck had that come from? She forced her gaze away from that tantalizing mouth and back up to his eyes—or his sunglasses, to be more precise.

And because she couldn't see those eyes, she was having an increasingly difficult time reading him. It only added to her unease.

"Okay, look," she said, straightening her back, putting the

hormonal thoughts out of her mind. "I just wanted to apologize for all of this. I know you're not very happy with me. And I want you to know that I'm really sorry. I just want to know the truth. You have no idea what this is like for me."

"For you?" His blond brow raised behind dark glasses. "I don't know what this is like for you? Try being in my place for ten seconds."

A sigh escaped her lips. "I have. I know this isn't easy for you, for any of you. I didn't intentionally wake up one morning and say, 'Hey, I think I'll find Ryan Harrison and screw up his life.' I'm not like that."

"Oh really? Because that's just what you did." He started to walk away, stopped, and turned back to her. "Do you have any idea how many freaks are out there trying to mess up my life? My personal life is my business, no one else's. Dammit! If the press gets one whiff of you, they're going to gather like flies on shit. Did you even stop to think about the consequences, even for a minute? My daughter is going to get sucked into this. The press will have a field day with her, and I've spent the last five years making sure she's been shielded from them. It would be one thing if you came looking for us because you cared, but just to show up on our doorstep because you're curious? It's crap!"

There was more anger in him than she'd realized. She tried to keep her voice even and calm. "It's not like that."

"It is like that. We mean nothing to you. I can read it on your face. I saw it the day you stood in front of my house. You look at us and see nothing. And we look at you and see everything. And it doesn't matter one damn bit." He scrubbed a hand through his hair, irritation radiating from his strong, muscular body.

Kate dropped to the bench, all the fight suddenly gone. "It does matter. If it didn't, I wouldn't be here. It's not just about knowing. It's more than that. If I turn out to be Annie Harrison, then that means Julia is my daughter. And I can't turn away from that. I never would have left my daughter on purpose. And I wouldn't want her growing up thinking I did. If I didn't do something to set this right, I'd never be able to live with myself."

She swallowed hard at the implications of what she'd just said. If she turned out to be Annie Harrison, and Julia really was her daughter, then there was a strong chance Reed was Ryan's son. Not Jake's as she'd been led to believe. Reed looked so much like Ryan—even she could see that—was she fooling herself thinking she wasn't Annie Harrison?

She forced back the fear. No matter what, she had to know. One way or the other, she had to know the truth.

She glanced up, wished desperately that he'd take off those damn glasses. "I don't want to screw things up for Julia. I don't, please believe that. And I wouldn't want to put her in harm's way. But…but if she's my daughter then I have to know."

For a minute, she was sure he was going to turn and walk away, but then he eased onto the bench next to her, slid off his sunglasses, and rested his head in his hands. A man defeated. One who was hurting, just like her. "Don't you think I've thought of that? Christ, that's all I've thought about for the past three days. Julia's my whole world. And she's pissed about this. She doesn't understand it. She's a very grown-up nine-year-old, but she doesn't understand any of this. I don't, either, for that matter."

"That makes three of us."

He looked out over the water. "I've been racking my brain trying to figure out how this could even be possible. What happened to you between the time I dropped you off at the airport and that plane took off without you on it? They said you were on that flight. I identified your purse and laptop from the wreckage afterwards. Whatever happened to you had to have occurred in the time-span of less than an hour. For the life of me, I can't figure it out."

"If I knew the answer to that question, this wouldn't be so hard to take."

He shook his head, looked down. "No. Nothing could make this easier."

His words settled between them, his heartache over the situation hanging in the air. When he finally looked over at her she saw honesty and truth in those brilliant blue eyes. And a jolt ran through her, one she wasn't prepared for.

"If I had known you weren't on that plane, I swear to God I would have been looking for you."

The determination in his voice shook her right to her core. Those fierce, unwavering eyes seemed to be looking all the way into her soul, and no matter what she did, she couldn't break away from his gaze. It drew her, tugged at something that felt like it was awakening inside her. "I believe you," she whispered.

He closed his eyes, then looked back over the water, breaking the spell pulling her under. "So, what do we do now?"

"I...I don't know. Wait, I guess."

"We already know the answer. I know it. You know it too, or else you wouldn't be sitting here with me right now."

A lump clogged in her throat, the realization hitting her that he was right. She shook her head. "I need to know for sure. Julia's not going to want to have anything to do with me until we can prove it one way or the other."

"She's probably not going to want to have anything to do with you regardless of the outcome. She's been through hell and back."

A dull ache settled in her chest. She didn't want that. She only wanted to make things better. For all of them. "I don't want to hurt her, or you."

"No matter what you do, it's going to hurt us." He stood and slipped his sunglasses back on. The glint of gold caught her attention as he moved, and for the first time, she noticed the ring on his left hand.

"We'll deal with it when we know for sure." His voice was no longer soft but hard and cold. "Until then, don't try to go see her. She needs time to get used to this whole thing. Your hanging around would just confuse her more."

Kate nodded, unable to make sense of the changes that came over him. She'd never experienced anything like it. One moment his voice was tugging on her heartstrings, and the next it was slicing through her, straight to the bone, sending chills up and down her spine. "Okay. I can understand that. Are you going to be okay?"

"Me? Yeah, I'm pretty much used to hell. I'll get by."

She watched as he walked away. But she didn't feel any better than she had before. If anything, she felt worse. Talking with him had only proved he'd loved his wife a great deal more than she'd anticipated.

*Page not found.*

Kate glared at the computer screen, the blinking cursor only accentuating the tension headache behind her eyes. Waves crashed outside on the beach. A gray drizzle slapped at the second-floor window outside her home office.

She should be keying in edits on an article that was supposed to be finished two days ago. Instead, she was running another search on Ryan Harrison.

So far, she'd found pictures of him cozied up to a black-haired vixen at some charity function. Another hit showed him with a blonde on his arm at a baseball game. And the *National Star* had a whole file of pictures of him with that voluptuous, redheaded model.

The man obviously got around.

"Mama?"

"Hmm?"

Why did she care? Just because he *may* have been her husband? That was stupid. She'd been married to Jake, after all. It wasn't like she had a reason to be jealous.

But what did surprise her was that from all her research, his life had apparently changed after his wife had died. Before, he'd been vice president of a small pharmaceutical company. After, he'd branched out on his own, expanded, and made a killing in the field. Was it just a stronger work ethic since becoming single? Or had he used his wife's life insurance money to expand his company?

Either way, he'd benefited immensely from Annie Harrison's death.

Kate typed in AmCorp Pharmaceuticals and came up with their home page. She scanned the technical information. Mostly cancer drugs. Specialized cancer drugs that often were pushed through the FDA because of need and a promise of significant benefit.

"Mama," Reed said from her feet where he lay on his belly on the floor next to her, playing with his Power Rangers, "I asked you something."

She tore her eyes from the computer. "What, baby?"

"Where do you go when you die?"

Her fingers paused on the keyboard. Reed hadn't once asked about death in the weeks since Jake's passing. "To heaven."

He rammed a red motorcycle into a black one, his gaze intent on the destruction he was causing. "You don't come back?"

Oh, man. Of all the topics to bring up, he had to go for this one. Easing off her chair, she settled onto the rug next to him. "Who said you come back?"

"Michael at preschool says when starfish die, they come back to life."

A smile tugged at her mouth. "Starfish can reproduce by something called regeneration. When an arm is cut off, a whole new starfish can grow out of it. It doesn't mean they die, though, and then come back to life. Once a starfish dies, it's gone for good."

His sapphire eyes lifted to meet hers. Eyes, she realized, that were just like the eyes she'd seen on that computer screen. "To starfish heaven?"

A laugh escaped her lips. "Yeah, baby. To starfish heaven."

He went back to his toys. "But you died and came back."

Kate drew in a breath. How did he know that? Had Jake told him? "That was different. Reed, look at me." His gaze lifted. So innocent and adorable. Her only link to her past life. The only thing she really had left. "Mommy's heart stopped because of an…accident. The doctors started it again. It's different from someone dying. When you die, you don't come back."

"Not ever?" Tears swam in his eyes.

An ache filled Kate's chest. She knew he was thinking of Jake. A four-year-old shouldn't be asking questions about death and dying. He shouldn't have to go through losing a parent. But here he was, growing up much too fast, having to deal with things no preschooler should have to face.

She rubbed a hand across her chest. Surprisingly, the pain wasn't for Jake like she expected. This time, it was for a family she didn't know. For a man and his daughter who'd lost someone they loved deeper than she'd expected. All her research didn't change that fact. She'd seen the heartache on their faces. Was Julia asking these questions? Wondering why her mother was back from the dead and what it all meant in the long run?

Shouldn't Kate be the one answering them for her, trying to set some of this right?

"Mama?"

Reed's voice drew her attention. Smiling, she ran a hand over his blond hair. If the tests came back positive, she'd have to tell Ryan about him. Dread coursed through her at the thought. What would he say when he found out he'd missed out on four years of his son's life? That Reed thought of another man as his father? It would only make things worse.

She didn't have answers to the questions swirling in her mind. And at the moment, she didn't want to think of them. She just wanted to focus on her sweet son's face and remember why she was here, why she was digging for information that she may never find.

"Yes, baby?"

"I love you."

Her face softened, and she drew him into her arms and onto her lap. "I love you, sweetheart. More than you will ever know."

# CHAPTER SEVEN

"See that?" Mitch pointed across the ravine to a fan-shaped deposit of sediments marking a dried riverbed. "It's an alluvial fan."

"What causes that?" Julia asked with sincere interest.

Ryan fought the urge to roll his eyes. He'd taken the day off, unable to concentrate on much of anything besides the turmoil inside him, and headed up to the mountains at Mitch's insistence. How the hell he'd let Mitch talk him into this, he didn't know.

"Generally, a stream drags the sediments with it, depositing them at the bottom," Mitch explained. "Sometimes a landslide can do it."

"Give it a rest, Mathews." Ryan used the back of his forearm to wipe the sweat from his brow.

"The kid likes it," Mitch said, grinning at Julia.

"Does she?"

Julia smiled his way. "The kid does."

"I don't know what the hell's in the Mathews's gene pool, but whatever it is got passed down to her." Ryan slapped a mosquito that landed on his arm. "Son of a bitch, I'm getting eaten alive out here."

Mitch elbowed Julia. "He's such a city slicker."

They both laughed.

"Enough playing in the dirt today," Ryan announced. "I'm filthy and tired. Let's head back."

"Dad, you're such a party pooper." Julia caught up with him and grabbed his hand. He slung an arm over her shoulder as they headed down the path. Behind them, Mitch continued to shout out geologic markers they passed.

"See what you started?" Ryan mumbled.

Julia giggled. "Imagine what he's like on a date."

"That's why he doesn't date much."

"What the hell are you two talking about up there?" Mitch hollered.

"Nothing," Ryan shot back.

"Just the native dating rituals." Julia giggled again.

"Or lack thereof," Ryan added under his breath.

"You two are a bunch of comedians," Mitch said. "Just so happens I've got a hot date tonight." He winked at Julia as they climbed into his dusty Land Rover. "It's more than I can say for your dear old pop here."

Ryan eyed him across the console. "Who the hell would go out with you?"

"Okay, it's not so much a date as a meeting. But if she's as hot as you say, it could turn into a date."

The rig bounced down the gravel road. Ryan had a sickening feeling as to where this was headed. "Please tell me you aren't seeing Simone Conners."

Mitch glanced in the rearview mirror. "Why not? You yourself said she was my type."

Ryan rested his elbow on the window ledge and massaged his aching forehead. "I lied. She's got a kid. You don't date women with kids, remember?"

"I like kids. Look at Julia."

"Julia's an anomaly. Normal kids don't give a rip about geology. Besides, I thought you were seeing some archaeologist. Redhead, looked like a model?"

Mitch shrugged. "I was. She took off on a dig. Didn't work out."

"Does it ever with you?"

"Hey, now. Don't get all pissy with me just because you're in a bad mood. Maybe Simone Conners is 'the one'."

Ryan let out a smug huff. "There is no 'one' with you, Mitch."

"There could be. Did it ever occur to you that maybe I'm tired of chasing skirts?"

"Yeah, right. And the moon is made of cheese."

"Hey, I have a soft side. There's nothing wrong with wanting to cuddle now and then. It's not always about sex."

"If you even *think* about uttering the words love and marriage right now, I'll puke."

Mitch frowned. "Look, if it makes you feel any better, I'm sure, hot or not, she won't go out with me. Not now, at least."

Something in his tone and the way he checked the rearview mirror again made Ryan glance back at Julia. Her eyes were already closed, her head resting against the window.

"She's representing Kate," Mitch finished quietly.

Ryan's head snapped around. "What do you mean, representing?"

"As in, Simone is Kate's lawyer."

"For what reason?"

"I'm not sure." They pulled onto the highway. "Right now, it sounds like she's the one handling the DNA testing. Once that's done, there could be...other...legal issues."

"Goddammit. We don't even know anything yet, and she's already hired herself a fucking lawyer?"

"Don't get all worked up. Yet. You and I both think she's Annie. If she is, there'll be some legal things to decide."

"You mean custody issues." Ryan swore under his breath and looked out the window.

"She's not gonna make a move for Julia when she doesn't even know her."

"Yet," Ryan murmured. Dammit, if she was Annie, he wanted her to get to know Julia. He'd never try to block that. But he wouldn't put up with her forcing her way in, either. "She's not gonna waltz in here and fuck up my life. How long have you known this little bit of info?"

Mitch grimaced, keeping his eyes on the road. "A few days. Look, I'm with you on this one. I don't think she should get custody, but Ryan, if she's Julia's mother, she has a right to get to know her."

"Do you think I'd get in the way of that?"

"No, *I* don't. But *she* doesn't know that. If her story's straight, then she doesn't know a thing about us. She doesn't know what we will or won't do. As much as I hate it too, she was smart to get a lawyer."

Ryan glared out the window. "I don't want you meeting with Simone Conners."

"That's my call, not yours."

Ryan felt that short leash on his emotions unraveling. "She was my wife."

"And she was my sister. I have as much right to find out what's going on as you do."

"Don't pull the *I knew her longer than you did* card on me, Mitch. It's not the same, and you know it."

"I do know it," Mitch snapped. "But I loved her too, you son of a bitch, and I'm hurting right along with you. And if meeting with Simone Conners can give me any hint as to what's happening and when we'll know more, then I'll do it."

Ryan clenched his jaw, looked out at the hills rushing by his window. He wasn't pissed at Mitch. He was pissed at the whole situation. And his inability to deal with it all when everyone else seemed to be coping just fine. "Dammit, this isn't the way it's supposed to be."

"I know." Mitch softened his tone. "Nothing's happening yet. I just wanted you to be prepared for it, if it does."

Ryan nodded, though what he wanted to do more was put his fist through the window. None of this was what he'd expected. Every time he thought about the whole fucked-up situation, something new hit him. And now all he could focus on was a possible custody battle down the road.

He wasn't losing Julia too. She was all he had left. He'd fight to the end to keep her with him, whether Kate Alexander was his wife or not.

Simone pulled up in front of Chaser's, the sports bar where she'd agreed to meet Mitch Mathews. Nerves bounced around in her stomach as she checked her lipstick in the rearview mirror. It wasn't unethical for her to meet with the man. After all, she'd known his sister. They had a mutual acquaintance. And until they knew for sure that Kate really was Annie, Simone wasn't crossing any attorney-client lines.

Her nerves told her otherwise. They all thought she was Annie. Meeting with him was only going to cause trouble down the line. But for some reason, when he'd called and asked, she'd found herself saying yes. Maybe because she'd heard the desperation in his words and knew what it was like to lose someone you loved. Maybe because she was hopeful this family could find a happiness she'd never get. Maybe because for years, she'd been wondering about Annie's single, geologist brother, and when he'd called, his sexy voice had overridden mere common sense.

Yeah, it was the last. Simone frowned as she climbed out of her BMW and locked the door. She'd gone too long without a man in her life if one sexy voice and a little mystery had lured her here.

One drink. She'd have one drink, make small talk, then be on her way. Tomorrow, they'd hopefully have the test results. If things went as Simone expected, she'd be representing Kate in legal proceedings, which would make any contact with Mitch Mathews and his brother-in-law, Ryan Harrison, unethical outside of work.

She moved into the dimly lit establishment, scanned the area. A long wooden bar ran the length of the back walls. Huge, flat-screen TVs seemed to occupy every inch of wall space. Baseball games flickered on screens, but luckily the sound was muted so she heard only the normal rustle of any bar—glasses clinking on tables, patrons chatting, the sizzle and pop from the kitchen.

She looked across the tables and booths for Mitch. Spotted him instantly. In the back corner, a man with curly, sandy brown hair and an athlete's body pushed out of a booth. A man with a face that could only be related to Annie Harrison.

Those nerves jumped a notch, but she straightened her shoulders and pushed them down as she wove between tables toward him. When she reached him, he held out a hand. "Simone Conners?"

"Mitch Mathews?" Damn, but his hand was warm, the palm rough from physical work, so unlike Steve's smooth attorney hands had been.

"The one and only," he said with a lopsided grin. "Have a seat."

"Thank you." She slid into the circular booth, set her purse between them. Before she could ask why he'd called her and requested this meeting, a server approached.

"What'll you have?" Mitch asked her. A dent creased his face as his lip curled in a half smile.

Dimples. The man had dimples in addition to the sexiest voice she'd ever heard. Oh, hell, she was in trouble.

"Um…" She glanced at her menu as words jumbled in her brain. *Vodka, straight up, with a twist. Make it a double.* "The house chardonnay is fine."

Mitch tapped his near-empty beer. "I'll have another."

The waiter left, and silence settled over them. Simone watched a pretty blonde get up and move toward the bathroom. Wondered if Mitch noticed. But when she glanced his direction, he was staring only at her.

Her stomach tightened. She cleared her throat. "So…"

"So," he said, still looking at her, those green eyes of his throwing her completely for a loop. "Ryan tells me you were a friend of Annie's. Before."

Small talk. She could do small talk. "Yes, I was."

"How well did you know her?"

"Really well, actually, probably better than a lot of her local friends. We met through a mutual friend when Annie was in DC for a conference one time, hit it off. My daughter, Shannon, is the same age as Julia."

"How long have you lived in San Francisco?"

"Only about two years. I moved here from Baltimore after my husband passed away."

"I'm sorry."

She didn't want to talk about Steve. Not tonight. "Thank you."

The waiter arrived just in time, set her wine in front of her. She took a big drink.

"Why did you call Ryan recently?"

She thought about how to answer as she fingered her wineglass. It was always hard for her when someone wanted to talk about Steve, but it hurt more when people who'd known them both acted like he'd never existed.

"Honestly?" she said, "I've thought about calling him several times. Annie brought Julia out to see us one time and the girls hit it off. I'm sure they'd love to get together for a playdate. But you know how life is. Things come up. You get distracted. And then that crash happened here recently, and I knew how hard it had to be for him. I just wanted him to know I was thinking of him."

When Mitch only nodded, she felt the urge to explain, though why, she wasn't sure. "I've only run into Ryan a handful of times since I've been here, and I got the impression he wasn't too thrilled to see me those few times."

"It's not personal," Mitch said, setting his glass on the table. "Ryan doesn't keep in contact with any of his old friends, especially any of Annie's old friends. He wasn't planning on calling you back, and he's pretty pissed at me for meeting with you tonight. Things have been…rough for him."

She could only imagine. But her concern was Kate right now, not Ryan Harrison. She took another sip of wine. "So, Mr. Mathews, why did you want to see me?"

He leaned forward, stared into his beer, seemed to contemplate his words. "Annie was my sister, and I loved her. If there's a chance this woman, Kate Alexander, is her…well, I just wanted to get your take on it all. You knew Annie before, and you've spent more time with Kate than we have."

She saw the heartache in his eyes, felt the pain. This had to be killing him inside. "You two were close, weren't you?"

"Very. Oh, she wanted to pummel me on a regular basis when

we were growing up, just like any good sister, but yeah, we were tight. I miss her."

Simone didn't have any siblings, but she knew all about loss. "And you and Ryan? You're close too, I take it?"

"The closest. We've been friends for years, ever since college. Almost had to kick his ass when I found out he was sleeping with my baby sister."

Simone laughed, feeling oddly at ease with this man she'd just met. "I bet that made for interesting times."

"It did. Ryan and I played baseball together in college. We were seniors the year Annie started school. One spring day we've got a home game, and I'm out at shortstop, and I glance in the stands between innings and see Annie there. She's smiling and waving, and I'm like, 'Cool, she came to a game.' Then I realize, she's not smiling and waving at me. She's making moon eyes at Ryan over on second base. Took me all of like ten seconds to realize what was going on."

Simone smiled. "Then what happened?"

Mitch frowned, leaned back against the booth. "There wasn't much I could do during the game except get worked up. I stayed away from Ryan in the dugout so I didn't lose it. Then ended up getting ejected when I threw one measly little bat at the umpire."

"You didn't."

He cringed. "I did. But in all fairness, the man needed glasses. No way those pitches were strikes."

She lifted her wine, sipped, felt herself relax for the first time in days. "What happened after, with Ryan?"

"Well, I had plenty of time to get good and pissed. I showered, changed, left, then went back to confront him after the game. Stupid move. I should have done it off campus. When I got back, I saw him and Annie outside the ballpark together. He was kissing her and...I lost it. He needed stitches. And I'm pretty sure the black eye lasted a good week."

"Nice."

"Then Coach came out and suspended us both for fighting."

"Oh, even better," Simone said, still smiling. "What did Annie say?"

"Annie didn't speak to me for a month." He looked into his beer, and the humor faded from his voice when he said, "Thing is, Ryan had a reputation in school for being a player. We both did. When I found out he was seeing her, I was sure he was just using her. I was wrong. In fact, he never looked at another girl after that. He still doesn't."

"I've seen Ryan at functions. He's not lacking for female companionship."

"No, he's not. But the truth is they come on to him because he's got money and power now. And I'm pretty sure the only reason he dates is because it takes his mind off the fact he's alone. In five years there's never been anyone who's meant anything to him. I know for a fact he'd gladly give it all up just to have Annie back. That's why this is killing him. The not knowing, especially."

"I don't know what to tell you, Mr. Mathews—"

"Mitch."

The spark in his eyes sent her stomach free floating. "Mitch," she said slowly, wondering why the hell he was having this effect on her. She was never interested in a client. Or the relative of a client. Clearing her throat, she looked back at her glass and traced the condensation on the stem. "We'll know more when the tests come back."

"I know we will. What I'm curious about is your gut reaction."

Her gut reaction wasn't always right. She hadn't trusted her gut since Steve had passed away. She'd been so sure he would beat the cancer, but he hadn't. "It's not my job to speculate. It's my job to deal in facts. And the facts are simple. There's a very strong chance that Kate is Annie."

He seemed to ingest that. "Ryan will fight a custody suit. He's got power behind him."

And here was the meat of the meeting. Simone's back tightened. "Well, you can reassure Mr. Harrison that if it comes to that, Kate has power behind her too."

A slow smile spread across his face. And that damn dimple winked at her. "I like you, Counselor."

He liked baseball. He was sexy as hell. And she'd gone way too long without. She shouldn't care what Mitch Mathews thought of her, but she did. Dammit, she really did.

He leaned forward, resting his forearms on the table, his hand so close to hers, if he moved just a fraction of an inch, they'd be touching. But she didn't need to touch him to feel the heat rolling off him in waves. The same heat was rolling off her. "I'd like to take you out to dinner. In a real restaurant."

For a split second, she was tempted to say yes. Then reality settled in. "I don't think that's a wise idea."

"Why not?"

"Because I'm you sis—" She stopped herself just in time, but she saw the way his brows lifted in optimism.

"Kate's attorney," she corrected, hating that a part of her now hoped Kate turned out not to be Annie. It would make this…what was happening between them…a whole lot easier. "It would be unethical to have a personal relationship with you."

"Is that what we're doing here, Counselor? Starting a personal relationship?"

Big red warning flags went off in her mind. The way he was watching her, the sinister smile, those sexy eyes. If she wasn't careful, she'd get herself disbarred.

"I think it's time for me to go, Mr. Mathews."

He didn't try to stop her as she reached for her purse. And she was thankful the lust was gone from his voice when he asked, "So you think we'll find out tomorrow?"

"I'm hopeful, yes. But it might be as late as next week." As she pushed out of the booth, he was right there, reaching for her arm, helping her up. Tingles rushed over her skin where they touched, and she looked up into mesmerizing green eyes. Eyes any woman could get lost in without much effort.

"So maybe tomorrow I'll be calling you for that dinner."

Heat slid through her veins, warming her from the inside out. She fought it though, working for that professionalism she'd perfected over the years. She held out her hand. "Perhaps. Thank you for the drink, Mr. Mathews."

"Mitch," he said with that damn sexy, lopsided grin, caressing her hand in both of his, giving her just a taste of what it would feel like to be caressed elsewhere by those big, masculine fingers.

"Mitch," she heard herself repeat.

She swallowed hard as she let go and exited the restaurant, telling herself the whole time no matter what happened tomorrow, Mitch Mathews was a man who wouldn't take no for an answer. The question was, what would her answer be next time?

Kate sat at her desk Tuesday afternoon, trying to edit a piece about geoscientists working in conjunction with the Peace Corp. Easing back in her chair, she glanced out the window toward the bay. The article wasn't enough to hold her interest.

Not today.

With a huff, she tossed the article on her desk, unable to read anymore. It was more sociological and political fluff than out-and-out science.

Not that she'd be able to read it even if it was the most compelling article on the planet. She scrubbed her hands over her face and tried to calm her frazzled nerves. She was sitting on pins and needles waiting for word from Simone, wondering what Ryan Harrison was doing and thinking.

Her pounding head signaled a need for caffeine.

She rose, headed to the lounge where she poured herself a thick mug of black goo, then took a big drink. It tasted awful, but if it would help her headache, she didn't care.

She slipped into her office without looking up and closed the door softly behind her. When she turned, she was surprised to see Simone standing behind her desk, looking out across the bay.

"Nice view," Simone said.

"Hi. I didn't expect to see you today."

"I know. We need to chat."

Oh, man. Something in her gut signaled this wasn't good. On a deep breath that did nothing for her now frantic nerves, Kate wove around her desk and sat.

Simone sat across from her. "Okay, first of all, I need to share something with you. I had drinks last night with Mitch Mathews."

Kate's brow lifted. "Really?"

"Yes, really." Simone straightened. "It wasn't personal. I mean, okay, it could be personal. He called, I think, to talk about you, but there was a spark there. Nothing happened but...I'm only telling you this because I'm your attorney, and I want you to know you come first. I told him flat out that I wasn't going to see him again unless the test results came back negative. And I won't."

Kate didn't know what to make of that news. "Wow. You believe in being blunt."

"It's the only way to get the point across. I like Mitch, but he's not the first man I've met that I like. I just didn't want you to hear this from him later or for it to come up out of context."

"I like Mitch too," Kate said. "What I know of him so far. He seems like a nice man. If you'd told me you had drinks with Ryan, well, I think I'd have a problem with that. He hates my guts."

"He doesn't hate you, Kate. He's confused. There's a big difference."

"Doesn't seem like a big difference to me." She studied Simone.

"You're allowed to have your own personal life, Counselor."

Simone's brow wrinkled, and Kate sensed she wanted to say something but didn't.

"So is that why you came by today?" Kate asked.

"No." Simone extracted a folder from her briefcase and drew in a long breath. "I got the DNA report back. I wanted to talk to you about it first. I called Ryan earlier. He's meeting me at my office this afternoon."

Kate swallowed the lump in her throat. *Here we go.* "Okay, let's have it."

Simone passed her the file, waited and watched as Kate scanned the page. "It's a preliminary report, Kate. But it's a pretty good match. They'll want to take samples from Mr. and Mrs. Mathews to match parentage. I'm told they live in Seattle. I don't believe they've been informed of your possible identity yet."

Kate set the file on her desk. Rising, she walked on shaky legs to the window and crossed her arms over her chest where she blew out a calming breath. Then another that did little to slow her racing pulse.

It was true. She was Annie Harrison. Ryan was her husband. Julia was her daughter. The reality of the moment cut right through her, grabbed on to her heart and squeezed tight. She'd lost five years of a life she didn't even know. And now she was left with…what? A family she couldn't remember and a future that didn't look any brighter than it had five minutes ago. If anything, that future looked a thousand times more confusing.

Swallowing the lump in her throat, she forced herself to speak. "I had a feeling it was going to work out this way."

"I think everyone did. If it's any consolation, I think they already know. I got that sense from Mitch last night. Maybe that'll make it easier."

"I expected it, but it doesn't make it easier." Wiping the tears from her face, she turned. So many thoughts, scenarios, questions swam in her mind, but she couldn't focus on those yet. Pain lanced through her chest at what would inevitably come, but she tried to breathe through it. Knew she just had to get it out there. "Okay, Counselor. Time to earn your retainer. I have a son."

Simone looked up sharply.

Kate's lungs felt three sizes too small, but she forced herself to go on. "He's four and a half. When I woke up from that coma, he was almost three years old. I didn't bring it up before because I had to be sure before I pulled him into this."

Kate closed her eyes to block the tears. "When I asked you for legal advice, should I turn out to be Annie Harrison, it was with Reed in mind. I think it's probably a safe bet he's Ryan's son. He looks a lot like him. I'll want to have him tested as well, just to be sure."

"Of course."

"And I want to tell Ryan about him. I'd appreciate it if you'd not say anything today."

"Of course not." Simone jotted a few notes on her legal pad.

Kate massaged the scar on her head, thoughts of Ryan circling in her mind. Of Julia's reaction to her. Of what they would both say and do when they found out about Reed. "He's going to want to get to know Reed, in the same way I'm going to want to get to know Julia. It could get sticky with visitation issues, etc. He already doesn't like me. I don't see this making things any better."

"We'll work it out. Don't worry about that. Ryan is a fair and honest man. Regardless of what the press says, regardless of how he's feeling right now, he'll cooperate."

"I'm not so sure." Kate ran her hands through her hair as tears filled her eyes. Why did this hurt so bad? She should be happy. Ecstatic that she had her answer. She finally knew who she was. Why wasn't that enough?

Simone skirted the desk between them and wrapped her arms around Kate. "Just breathe. We'll get you through this. I promise."

Kate closed her eyes. Focused on the push and pull of air in her lungs. Centered herself on that one small thing she could do now. Everything else…everything else would work itself out. She had to give it time. Her head knew that even if her heart didn't totally understand.

She pulled back and wiped her eyes. "Thank you. I…I appreciate everything you're doing for me. I appreciate your help and friendship. I didn't realize how much I missed having a friend around until now."

Simone smiled. "I liked Annie a great deal. We were good friends. But I like you a lot, too. I'd be your friend whether I'd known her or not."

"I appreciate that too," Kate whispered. She dried her face and looked at Simone again, this time knowing she could get through the emotional fallout from this so long as she stayed focused on her goal. "There's one more thing I'd like to discuss."

"Okay, shoot."

"I've been doing some research, trying to find answers. It was only speculation before, but now that we know for sure... I don't know if it will make a difference in the long run, but I need to know what happened to me. Jake knew something. He had to. There has to be a reason he lied. Was I living a double life? Did someone intentionally try to hurt me only something went wrong? Did I run away from my family? I can't go through life not knowing the truth."

Simone leaned back against Kate's desk. "Go on."

Kate paced in front of the window. "Well, from what I can deduce from the crash records, my body was never recovered, obviously," she added sarcastically. "But there was a body in my seat."

"Correct." Simone went back to her briefcase, flipped through her file on the crash. She'd obviously done some research herself. "The manifest shows you checked in on the flight, which means the stewardess did a head count and your seat was accounted for after the bulkhead doors closed. You'd made it through security with your boarding pass and ID. And your personal belongings were recovered after the crash—your suitcase, but also your purse, specifically, found wedged under a seat. Ryan identified it."

"Do you think he still has it?"

"I don't know. I could ask. What's on your mind?"

"I don't know. Maybe I'm just hoping seeing it might bring back a memory. I've had no luck at that nursing home. They won't even let me through the door anymore. But I really feel like that's a starting place."

"They haven't returned my calls, and I don't have enough here to get a court order to go through their files."

"I know." Kate pinched her throbbing forehead. "If I could just get in their record room myself."

Simone reached back for her file and opened it on her lap. "Where is it? San Mateo?" She skimmed the information she'd jotted down. "You know, I think I've got a friend whose mother is in this home." She bit her lip as if pondering their choices. "I might be able to get inside, go in to see her."

Kate's brow lifted. "You wouldn't be suggesting something illegal now, would you, Counselor?"

Simone frowned. "Why do you call me that?"

"What?"

"Counselor."

Kate shrugged. "I don't know. You are one, aren't you? Does it bother you?"

"Yeah, I am one. And no, it doesn't bother me. It's just weird that you and Mitch use the same word."

"Not so weird. Not anymore."

Simone stood and tried to smile. "No. I guess not anymore. Tell you what. I'll make a call, talk to my friend and find out if her mother's really there. If she is, I'll let you know, and we'll decide what to do from there."

"Okay."

Simone gathered her things. "I'm going to meet with Ryan. You take some time and figure out what you're going to tell him. If you want me to be there, we can set it up in the office. However you want to handle it."

"Thanks, but I think I need to do that on my own."

"Okay." Simone shot her a quick smile. "I'll call you after I speak with him today."

# CHAPTER EIGHT

Simone's gaze snapped to the door when it pushed open. Ryan and Mitch stepped into her office, presenting a unified front.

Brothers.

Regardless of their individual characteristics, they were brothers at heart, and it showed. Ryan with his sharp, clean, good looks, and Mitch with his rugged, outdoorsy ones. They were roughly the same height and build, but so different in every other way.

She rose, stepped to Ryan, hugged him quickly. "I'm sorry for all of this."

"Thanks." He pulled back. "I'm sorry about Steve too. I...I should have called you."

"It's okay. I understand. These things are hard. They bring up emotions we don't always want to deal with."

He nodded. Her gaze cut to Mitch. He'd gotten a haircut and shaved off the goatee. He looked good, but she missed the wispy curls near his collar.

Dragging her gaze away from him, she rubbed her hands together. "Okay." She moved back behind her desk, switching to lawyer mode. "Have a seat, and we'll get started."

"She's not coming?" Mitch asked.

"No. I've already spoken with Kate. We felt it best to do this separately. She wanted time to absorb the results before she spoke with either of you."

Mitch and Ryan exchanged glances. She noticed their apprehension and took out the test results. No sense prolonging their misery. She handed a copy to each of them. "These are the preliminary DNA reports. It's not entirely conclusive, but I think you'll see it's close enough. We'll need to get samples from your parents, Mitch, but I think we can say with ninety-eight percent accuracy, Kate Alexander is Annie Harrison."

Ryan leaned back and closed his eyes. Heartache raced along his features, but she could tell from his quiet reaction he'd already expected this news. As Kate had said, however, knowing didn't make any of this easier.

Mitch took his time studying the report. When he glanced up, Simone saw the pain in his eyes, too. This was hard on both of them.

She rose and moved around the desk, leaning back against the mahogany surface where she picked up another folder and handed papers to each of them. "Here are copies of her medical records. She wanted you to see them. The accident she was in damaged her face. She went through several reconstructive surgeries to both her nose and cheek areas, which is why she doesn't look exactly like she did before."

She waited while they each flipped through the files. "I know it's one thing for her to say she can't remember anything. It's another for you to see it in black and white. She was being treated by a neurosurgeon in Houston. I've tried to track him down but am running into a wall. It seems like each of our leads are ending that way."

Dismissing the thought, she added, "As far as her brain trauma, her records indicate there was some sort of damage to the lateral cortex of her anterior temporal lobe, the part of the brain that deals with long-term memory, specifically that area which focuses on personal memories. So things she learned say, in school, haven't been affected because they're stored in a separate part of the brain—or so the theory goes. Where she learned those facts, though, is a different story because that would be a personal memory, like where she went to college. It explains why she does so well in her current field, remembering technical information about seismology and geology, even though she doesn't know what sort of degree she holds. As I've learned through research on this case, most of what the medical community knows about the brain is pretty inconclusive, especially those parts of the brain that deal with memory."

"So she really doesn't remember anything?" Ryan asked in a weak voice.

"No," Simone answered. "And there's one other major thing you should be aware of." When they both looked up, she said, "That portion of the brain is also responsible for personality." She wanted to make this part perfectly clear so they both understood. "She's not the same person she used to be. If you spend time with her, like I have, you'll notice similarities—gestures, looks, that sort of thing. But there are some very glaring differences as well that you need to be prepared for. Kate's personality now was developed *after* the accident. She reacts differently to situations. Whereas Annie was emotional and quick to respond, Kate is more reserved. She thinks things through before jumping to conclusions or voicing observations. That's a minor point, but it becomes important when you get to know her. I don't want either of you thinking you can just pick up where you left off five years ago and everything will fall in line."

"Is she ever going to get her memory back?" Ryan asked.

"From my discussion with Dr. Allan, a local neurosurgeon who's looked at her charts, it's not likely. Most amnesiacs remember something, anything, especially from their childhood, but Kate's case is very unique. She hasn't remembered a single thing. She'd hoped being in San Francisco would trigger her memory, but so far, nothing."

She softened her tone. "I'm sorry, Ryan. I know that's not the answer you were hoping for."

He nodded, stared down at the report. Several seconds of silence passed before he said, "Who would do this to her? Who would do this to us?"

His head snapped up, but instead of pain, this time Simone saw anger. A hell of a lot of anger Ryan had every right to be feeling. He pushed out of his chair. "Who the hell was that sonofabitch who took her away from us?"

"His name was Jacob Alexander," Simone answered. "He was a doctor in the Houston area. He was also a passenger aboard the plane that crashed here recently, which is how Kate came to find me and then you. Apparently he was here in San Francisco for a medical conference, though Kate doesn't know the name of it. I don't have a lot of information on Alexander yet, but Kate's asked me to do some digging."

"What kind of digging?" Mitch asked.

Simone looked his way and saw the anger in his eyes as well. They'd all lost so much time. Time they couldn't possibly get back. But hopefully knowing the why would help alleviate some of that hurt. "Kate needs to know what happened to her. She's as confused by all this as you both are, except in her case, she's trying to figure out which parts of her life are lies and which parts are truth. We're starting with the nursing home where she was in that coma, although we're running into obstacles. Ryan, you identified her belongings after the crash, correct?"

"Yeah." He crossed his arms over his chest. "There wasn't much there, just her purse and charred laptop."

"Do you still have them?"

"I might, somewhere. I boxed up a lot of her stuff right after that. What the hell will that tell you?"

"Probably nothing, but she'd like to see them just the same. Mitch, can you get a hold of the university and find out what projects she was working on before her disappearance?"

"You think all this might be related to her work?" Mitch asked.

"I don't know. What we do know is that Ryan left her at the airport, and she woke up from a coma almost three years later. If this had been a random act of violence, a kidnapping, something like that, she'd be dead now. Someone took the time to make it look like she was on that flight, then to take care of her after God only knows what kind of accident. It could very well have been related to a project she was working on."

"And if it wasn't?" Ryan asked.

"If it wasn't, we'll cross that off our list and move on to the next possibility. In the meantime, I'm going to keep hounding that doctor in Houston who's listed on Kate's medical records and try to find some answers there. Kate also mentioned her father in law—Walter Alexander—who seems to have disappeared just after his son died. I want to track him down as well."

Simone caught the fire in Ryan's eyes. Fire that said it was a good thing Jacob Alexander was already dead. Simone understood his rage and frustration, but of more importance to her was Kate, and making sure Kate had what she needed to get through the next few days in one piece.

"So what now?" Ryan asked.

"Well, that's really up to you and Kate," Simone answered. "She isn't asking for anything at this point. She needs some time to absorb it all, but I'm sure she'll be contacting you shortly. She's not asking for any sort of legal visitation with Julia, if that's what you're concerned about. She's expressed a strong desire to get to know Julia, which I'm sure you're aware of, but I think you two need to try to work that out on your own before bringing in legal representation. I think the next step is notifying your parents, Mitch, asking them for blood samples, just to verify the whole thing."

Mitch nodded. Simone glanced between the two, wishing she could do something, anything to make this easier on them. Knew, unfortunately, that she couldn't.

She pushed away from the desk and stepped forward, indicating the meeting was pretty much over. "You're welcome to take those reports. I don't suspect they'll help much now, but maybe they will in the future."

Ryan thanked her, turned and looked at Mitch, who was still seated. "I'll see you outside."

When they were alone, Mitch looked up at her. "What's this investigation about?"

"If it were you, wouldn't you want to know what happened?"

He shook his head, glanced down at the report still in his hands. "I get Ryan's anger and his need to know and all. I'm as angry as he is about the fact she was taken from us. But this...it just seems like a wild-goose chase."

"It could be. We're taking it one step at a time. In the meantime, it makes Kate feel like she's doing something, like she has some control over her life. I think she needs that right now."

"How'd she take it?" he asked quietly.

"Not well. She knew before I said it, though, just like Ryan did. They have a lot to work through."

He glanced back at the closed door. "I don't know how to make this easier for him."

"Just be there for him. It's about to get sticky, Mitch."

His gaze locked on hers. Then his eyes widened. "Oh, hell. The boy."

"You know?"

"I didn't, until just now." His eyes slid shut. "I saw a photo on her desk. Shit." He told her about the visit to Kate's office only days before. "I didn't put two and two together until right now. Things have been so...crazy. God Almighty." He rubbed his forehead. "I thought things were bad before."

"You can't say anything to Ryan. She's going to tell him. She needs a little time to figure out how. We have to let them work through this on their own."

"I'm torn on this one, Counselor. She's my sister, and I love her, whether she remembers me or not. But he's, by every right, my brother, and I love him too. And he needs me."

That revelation touched her in a way she didn't expect. She crouched in front of him, her fingertips gently brushing his cheek. "You're doing the right thing already. I'm sorry you're stuck in the middle of all this. Can I do anything?"

He looked up, and that sexy grin spread across his face. The one that brought out that deep dimple that did insane things to her pulse. "You could have dinner with me."

Oh, but she wanted to. "I can't, Mitch. Not so long as I'm representing Kate."

His eyes locked on hers. She saw the same disappointment she felt reflected there. "I want you to tell her to find another attorney, for my own sake, but I can't. She needs you. She needs someone on her side."

"She's got all of us on her side."

"Yeah, but Ryan…" He looked to the door. "I have a feeling this is gonna get bad before it gets better."

Unfortunately, Simone had a sinking suspicion he was right.

Ryan checked the address he'd finagled from Annie's secretary and glanced at the small, two-story cottage along the beach with gray shaker siding and seagull wind chimes hanging from the front porch. Nothing like his house in Sausalito. Not even close to the place they'd shared together in San Francisco. But still, property in Moss Beach wasn't cheap. He wondered how she had the funds for a place out here.

As he took in the small beach houses on the treeless street, he rubbed the dull ache in his chest with the palm of his hand. He wanted to see her, needed to see her. There were things he needed to say now that they knew for sure. He couldn't sit around and wait for her to make the first move.

On legs more unsteady than he wanted to admit, he made his way up her walk, knocked on the door. When no one answered, he paused to listen. Voices echoed from the back of the house. Trying to figure out where they were coming from, he headed around the side.

The yards were unfenced. Grass gave way to sand, which bled into the Pacific. As he reached the back of Annie's cottage, a young boy crouched in the grass playing with a pile of sticks stood up and stared at him with big, blue eyes.

Eyes that were just like Ryan's eyes. Same shape, same color. The blond-haired boy even had the same shaped face.

"Um, hi," Ryan managed when he could find his voice.

"You're a stranger." The boy turned and took off running. "Mama! A stranger!"

Mama? Ryan stepped out of the trees along the side of the house to get another look at the kid. He ran up to a woman seated on the sand. She turned and shielded her eyes from the sun to look back across the yard, then jumped to her feet.

The pair spoke for a moment. Then the boy shrugged and ran toward the house. He paused when he approached Ryan again, this time smiling, flashing that same dimple Ryan had seen so many times before on Mitch's face, on Julia's face, on Annie's face. "Mama said I could watch cartoons."

He disappeared into the house. The screen door slapped shut behind him.

Ryan's pulse raced as he stood in the yard, sunglasses in hand, trying to figure out what the hell he'd just seen. No way that was real. He mentally ticked off time in his mind as his gaze shifted across the sand to Annie. Words choked in his throat. Snapshots of their life together flashed behind his eyes, memories of a pregnancy that had only just begun before she'd left on that trip.

"I didn't expect to see you today," she said as she approached slowly.

"Yeah, ah, I can see that." He looked back toward the house, still too stunned to do anything but stare. "The boy…"

"He's my son." When Ryan looked her way again, she added, "I'm pretty sure he's your son, too."

"My…" he swallowed hard "…*son*?"

She crossed her arms over her middle, looking gorgeous and nervous and a thousand other things he couldn't describe because he was too wigged out to think clearly. "He was almost three years old when I woke up. He was born by cesarean when I was in that coma. He's four, and he doesn't know anything about this yet. I haven't told him about it, about you." She hesitated. "He thinks his father died in that plane crash."

Ryan couldn't seem to take his eyes off the house. "I have a son."

A son. A four-year-old boy who looked just like him. With his blue eyes and his blond hair and Annie's silly dimple. His heart felt like it kick-started right there in his chest. A son he hadn't once let himself dream about over the years because it was too painful to think of one more thing that he'd lost.

But he hadn't lost him. He was here. He was as alive as Annie. He was…

A son who, after seeing him, he knew couldn't possibly belong to anyone else. A son he was only just now finding out about. Over a week after she'd come into his life.

The surprise and elation he'd originally felt morphed to confusion. He turned to face her. "You didn't say anything. All this time, and you didn't say anything?"

"I didn't know for sure until yesterday. I still don't. I didn't have him tested."

"You're pretty sure now."

"I've a strong hunch. It's not the same."

"A strong hunch. It doesn't take a strong hunch to see he looks just like me." He raked a hand through his hair. "Dammit, all this time and you didn't tell me? Were you ever going to tell me?"

"Yes, of course. I wasn't planning on keeping it from you."

"Well, isn't that what you're doing? You obviously didn't tell me when you found out who you are."

"Ryan, it's only been a day."

Her impassive tone only infuriated him more. "Only a day? A day is like a lifetime to me. I assumed you lost the baby!" He drew in a deep breath, tried to calm his raging temper. It didn't work. "Son of a bitch, he's my son? Do you have any idea how much I wanted that baby? My God, I didn't just lose you. I lost him, too. And now you're telling me it's only been one goddamn day?"

He paced away, then back again, not trusting himself. Why couldn't he control his emotions when he was around her? Why was everything getting worse instead of better? He had a son. *A son.* He should be happy. Thrilled. Instead, all he felt was pain, confusion, and a mountain of misery.

"Don't do this," she said. "I'm telling you now."

"You didn't tell me. I found out on my own, accidentally!"

"I was going to tell you."

"When? When it was convenient for you? Did you even think what I'd need? How I'd feel? No, because you can't remember anything about me. Convenient, isn't it? To have such a candid excuse for not caring about anyone else's feelings."

"Kate?"

They both glanced toward the screen. A middle-aged man with thinning hair stood on the other side of the door. "Is everything okay out here?"

"Who the hell are you?" Ryan asked.

"I'm a friend of Kate's. Who are you?"

"I'm her goddamn husband. Can't you feel the love?"

Annie closed her eyes.

The man pushed the screen open, squared his shoulders.

Annie jogged up the steps and pushed him back into the house. "Tom, now's a really bad time."

"I came by to make sure you were okay. You skipped out on a meeting today."

She herded him inside. "I'm fine. I'll explain it later. Right now, I need to take care of this."

From the yard, Ryan heard the man say, "Do you want me to stay? That guy looks pissed. Are you sure you're okay?"

Annie's voice—shit, Kate's voice...his Annie would never do this to him—echoed from inside, but Ryan blocked it out. Closing his eyes, he rested his hands on his hips, breathed deep, and tried to find control. In his business dealings, he was all about control, but with her...with her, he'd never had control. She'd wrapped him around her finger from the first moment they'd met, and he'd been under her spell ever since. She'd brought out the deepest emotions in him, from the most intense passion to the most excruciating pain. And that pain was lingering from one freshly inflicted wound to the next, dragging out his anger in ways he didn't want but needed to contain.

He had to stop letting his emotions lead him. She didn't remember him. She didn't care about him. He had to think about Julia and...his son. He had to start thinking of this as a business transaction.

He slipped on his sunglasses, crossed the grass, and dropped into the sand, perching his forearms on his knees as he stared out at the roaring waves and waited.

Long minutes later, he heard the screen door open and sensed more than heard her move up behind him.

"Is he gone?" he asked.

"Yes."

"Who was he?"

"My boss. This is, technically, his house. We're renting it from him."

That explained how she was able to afford a place way out here.

"What's my son's name?" He knew his tone was harsh, but he didn't care.

"Reed—" she blew out a breath "—Jacob Alexander."

"You gave our son his name." His jaw clenched.

"Ryan, I didn't name him. I was in a coma when he was born."

He closed his eyes and forced himself to remain silent as he tried like hell to lock his emotions deep inside. It just didn't fucking work. "I want visitation. If you won't agree to it, I'll take it to the courts. My lawyers will get it."

"I'll agree. I don't want to keep him from you."

"Good. You tell him. Tonight. If you don't, I'll do it. I'm not going to pretend like he's not mine. We both know he is. I've waited too damn long already."

"I'll do it. Ryan—"

"And I want his name changed. I want him to have my name. *Our* name, dammit." He glared at her over his shoulder. Knew it wasn't her fault. Knew none of this was directly her doing, but, God, he hurt. And she was the cause. "Keep the fucking middle name if you have to but his last name will be Harrison."

He stood and brushed the sand off his slacks. "We'll meet Saturday, ten in the morning, at Golden Gate Park, on the steps outside the Conservatory. Don't be late, Ms. Alexander."

Her hand closed around his arm, stopping him. "Hey. This isn't easy for me. None of this is. I'm trying to do the right thing here."

"The right thing? Which one is the right thing? Not telling me about my son or getting married when you were still married to me?"

She let go but didn't step back. "That's not fair. I didn't know I was your wife when I was with Jake. He led me to believe we were married. It wasn't like we went through a ceremony."

"How convenient for you."

He saw the hurt in her eyes, but he also saw the anger. That familiar independent spark that he had once both loved and hated. "You use that word, convenient, a lot. I seem to be a convenient target for you. If you've got something to say, Harrison, go ahead and say it."

"Fine, I will. I don't like you."

She let out a sour laugh but didn't smile. "Then we're even because right now I think you're an ass."

He clenched his jaw to the point of pain, stared hard at her. At the woman who was still his wife. *His* wife, dammit. No one else's. It didn't matter that she didn't remember him. It didn't even matter that she hadn't consciously married that rat bastard Alexander. All that mattered was that she'd let the asshole trick her into thinking she had. After everything they'd shared, she should have known in her heart the prick was lying to her. She should have known she belonged with someone else.

He left her standing in the sand. Knew she was right. He was an ass. A grade-A ass. But all he could think about was the fact she was wearing another man's ring. That and the fact he had a son. A son she'd named after the son of a bitch.

# CHAPTER NINE

A heart attack had to feel better than this. The wretched ache in Kate's chest was worse than any physical pain she'd endured during or after her time in the hospital. And that was saying a lot considering she'd already died once.

Unable to bear it anymore, she slipped out of her office and made her way over to see Mitch. He seemed to be closer to Ryan than anyone else. Maybe he could tell her what she should do.

He was on the phone when she peeked her head around the doorjamb, standing near the window, tossing a baseball in the air. When he turned her way, she forced a smile she didn't feel and waved.

Mitch motioned her in and gestured he'd be just a minute.

She checked out his office while he finished his conversation. Shelves were in various states of disarray. Field research lay scattered across his desk. A framed Mariners poster hung on one wall, and a bat leaned against a corner. A wry smile spread across her face when she realized this guy was a baseball freak.

Moving by his desk, she noticed the framed photo next to his computer. It was of her, Ryan and Mitch. She was standing in the middle, wearing a cap and gown, grinning from ear to ear. Mitch had his arm around her neck, sporting the same goofy smile, and Ryan was on her other side, his arm around her waist, a smirk across his handsome face.

She picked up the photo, ran her finger along the faces. Was it really her? It was like looking at someone else's life. She didn't remember the day. Couldn't, for the life of her, figure out why they were all smiling.

"College graduation," Mitch said softly.

"I see that." She hadn't even heard him end his conversation. "I guess it never occurred to me you'd have pictures. From before, I mean."

"We have lots of pictures. I can get you some if you want. You can look through them, see if it helps."

"I think I'd like that." She set the frame down and drew in a deep breath. "I was hoping we could talk. If this is a bad time, I can come back."

"No, this is a good time." He glanced out the door. Kate didn't miss the way his secretary was staring at them with suspicion. "Are you up for a walk?"

"Yeah."

Mitch led her down to the lobby, slipped on his sunglasses. They headed toward the waterfront.

"I'm assuming you heard about what happened yesterday?"

Mitch slid his hands into his pockets. "Yeah, I did. Are you okay? You don't look very good."

Her brow quirked. "No, huh? Well, I don't feel very good. Nothing like having everything hit all at once. Ryan was a little ticked when he left."

"Ryan has a temper," he said as they walked into the park. "He doesn't handle it well sometimes."

"Well, that's a surprise," she tossed back sarcastically. "He wouldn't even let me talk."

"You've got to understand, this is really hard for him. He changed after you disappeared, shut down in a lot of ways."

"Just what is your relationship?"

"He's my best friend. He was before you two were even an item. But," he added, "that doesn't mean I won't kick his ass when he's being a jerk. Especially when it involves you."

The determination in his voice made her smile. "Why is it so much easier for me to talk to you than it is to talk to him?"

"Because I'm your brother."

Warmth closed around her heart. She'd never thought she had a brother.

"And I don't want anything from you," he went on. "Except to get to know you again, to be your friend. Ryan wants his wife back."

She dropped onto a bench, a deep sigh escaping her lips. "I'm not his wife. I may have her body and her face and her voice, but I'm not her. Not inside."

"Yeah, you are." He sat beside her. "You just can't see it because you don't remember it. But you're still her. Things you say, things you do, the way you carry yourself. You're still ready to bite my head off when I disagree with you about geology." She looked down at her hands and smiled. "And you have the same gentle spirit she did."

"But I'm different."

"Yeah, you're that too. But it doesn't mean you aren't who you are now because of who you were then. People change all the time. If this whole situation didn't change a person, they wouldn't be human. Ryan's different. I'm different. It makes sense that you, of all people, would be different."

"He's so cold. I can't believe he was ever the sort of man you all describe. You and Simone, you make him sound so warm and friendly, but everything I've seen of him in the last week makes him look exactly like the cold-hearted, arrogant, ruthless tyrant the media makes him out to be. I can't read him. I don't know that I'll ever be able to."

Mitch smiled. "That's Ryan. He keeps his emotions closely guarded. But he wasn't always like that."

"What changed him?"

"Losing you changed him." He shook his head when she looked away. "Ryan closed in on himself after we lost you. He exists for two reasons these days—to work and to take care of Julia. Nothing else in his life matters—not the money or the fame or the power. He only works as hard as he does because it's a distraction from having to feel anything. It's the game that keeps him going. If he lost it all tomorrow, he wouldn't care as long as he had Julia. He'd just start all over. You have to understand that although he wants you to get to know Julia, the thought of losing her at all is terrifying to him."

"I'm not trying to take her from him."

"I know that," he said softly.

"I feel like my life is split into two parts, the person I was before, and the person I am now. I don't know how to blend them."

"You're trying too hard. It'll happen when it happens. I know it's hard. I know you think about her and you see Annie, and you think about yourself and you see Kate—two different people, two different lives—but deep down, they're the same. You just need some time to figure it out."

"And in the meantime, I'm just making a mess out of everything."

He brushed a hand over her shoulder. "You guys will get through this. Give Ryan a day or so. Once he spends time with Reed, all of that anger about not knowing about him will slip away.

Trust me, I know the guy. He's hard as steel around the edges, but inside, he's one big, gooey mess."

"So I shouldn't go see him today?"

"No way. He's brooding today. You won't get through to him."

"I don't know what difference a day will make. I just seem to set him off every time he sees me."

"You think you didn't set him off before?" He grinned. "You think you two never crossed sparks? You did all the time. It's what made your relationship so fun to watch. He always thought you were too independent. It used to bug the hell out of him. Deep down, he feared you didn't need him the way he needed you. I guess in some way, this is just the same old argument magnified about a thousand times."

He reached for her hand, and she noticed their fingers were the same length. The same shape. His were thicker, more masculine, but their hands were similar. Worn. Weathered. Solid.

"He's a good guy, Kate." One side of his lips curled in a smirk as he studied her fingers, and the dimple she'd seen so many times in the mirror creased his cheek. "God, it's weird to call you that. But I'll get used to it. You just have to give him time too. This hurts him because he wants more from you than you can give him right now."

She almost laughed. "He's got beautiful women draped over him all the time. What could he possibly want from me?"

"You really don't know?" There was amusement in his voice. "He wants you back."

An ache settled in her chest. "I don't know if I'll ever be able to give him what he wants."

"You have to jump off that bridge when you get to it. In the meantime, think about Julia and Reed and how you're going to handle them. That's the most important thing at this point."

"I know."

He hesitated, then said, "You also have to understand that knowing you were married, that you were with someone else, it's eating away at him."

Frustration welled inside. "Well, that's just great. He can go off with a different woman every weekend, but I happened to be in a committed relationship and I'm the one feeling guilty."

"Ryan may date, but he hasn't opened his heart to anyone since you left. I think the realization that you did is what's making this so hard. He loves you as much as he did before you disappeared, and you don't. That hurts him."

She closed her eyes. "I don't want to hurt him."

"Were you in love with the other guy?" he asked gently.

She pushed off the bench, unable to sit anymore. "I thought I was. Although now I'm wondering why. There were inconsistencies, but I thought it was the stress of my illness. Of his job. How could I have been so wrong about someone? It makes me question my judgment."

Mitch crossed to her. "There's a reason all of this happened. You have to believe that."

"I don't really know what I believe anymore."

"I'll tell you one thing." He slipped on his sunglasses. "I believe in a higher power pushing all of us together. I never used to, but I do now. You can't not believe when you look at the situation."

"How can you think that? How can you believe God would let us go through this hell?"

"Because you have to think of the alternative. If it hadn't happened the way it did, you'd have been on that plane. You'd really be gone now. There'd be no second chances. There'd be no Reed."

She hadn't thought of it that way. The realization sent a chill down her spine.

"I have to get back," he said. As they turned and headed back out of the park, he shot her a look. "You know, we need to call my...our," he corrected, "parents."

She grimaced. "I was afraid you'd say that."

"I was thinking maybe Sunday, after you and Ryan have a chance to see the kids. I'd really like you to be there when I call them. We could do it at my house, if that makes you more comfortable."

She nodded, though what she wanted to do most was run away.

"They're going to want to fly right down and see you."

"I thought of that too."

"Are you okay with that?"

"Do I have a choice?"

"Not on your life. They're good people, Kate. I'll be there with you."

"Okay." She blew out another breath, wanting to lighten the mood. "So, I hear you've got the hots for my lawyer."

"Why? Did she say something about me?"

Kate couldn't help it. She laughed. He looked and sounded like a middle schooler. "You like her."

"Yeah, I do. But this might not be the best time to start something."

"Because of me?"

"Because of…a lot of things."

"Mitch, don't let me hold you back."

"I'm not. It's not just you. My life is complicated. I travel a lot. Sometimes I'm gone for months at a time. I don't make good boyfriend material."

"I don't believe you. Something tells me you'd make great boyfriend material for the right woman. And I'd feel a lot better if at least someone in this mess was happy."

With a grin, he swung his arm over her shoulder. The small gesture warmed her. "One step at a time, sweetheart. We'll get you there. Just have faith."


A little faith would do them all some good.

When Mitch strolled into Ryan's house later that evening, he found himself in the middle of a war zone.

"I'm not going!" Julia screamed from upstairs and slammed her door.

"Yes, you are, young lady. You don't have a choice!" Ryan quieted his voice as he yanked open the refrigerator. "If I don't have a fucking choice in this, you don't have a fucking choice in it."

"You can't make me go! I won't go!" Julia screamed down the kitchen stairs, then slammed the door again.

"I hope this isn't about my date with her tonight," Mitch said as he walked into the kitchen. "Because it's really going to mess up my plans if she's bitching like this."

"Heaven forbid we should cramp your plans." Ryan scowled, moved to the stove and slammed a pan on the burner. "She's pissed off about tomorrow. She doesn't want to go see Annie…or Kate…or whatever the hell she's calling herself these days."

"Oh." Mitch sank into a chair at the bar and popped a grape in his mouth from the bowl on the counter. "And it's Kate. You call her Annie, it's going to piss her off too."

"At this point, I don't give a fuck if she's pissed or not."

Mitch blew out a breath and glanced around. Definitely not a good night in the Harrison household.

Julia stalked into the kitchen, glared at her father, then moved to

Mitch. "I'm not going tomorrow," she said, fisting her hands on her hips. "You can just tell him that, because he's not listening to me."

Mitch caught Ryan's tight jaw out of the corner of his eye. "I think he can hear you loud and clear, sweetheart."

"I don't want to see her. I don't want to have anything to do with her. She's not my mother!"

"Julia, dammit," Ryan said. "We've been through this a thousand times. I'm not thrilled about the situation, either, but she's your mother, and she wants to see you. And you'll just have to get used to it."

She crossed her arms over her chest. Her little eyes filled with tears. "I don't want to go. I hate her! I don't want to have anything to do with her!"

Ryan stepped forward, but Mitch saw the fire in his eyes and sent him a warning look. Nothing Ryan had to say was going to get through to her.

"You know what, Julia?" Mitch asked. "I love you. I even like you, a lot, which is pretty important to me because love is a requisite in families, liking each other isn't. But you're acting like a spoiled brat right now." Her mouth fell open in surprise. "You're talking about my sister there, and I'm not gonna let you badmouth her in front of me. You can be upset and frustrated with this whole situation, just like we are, but you're going to have to get used to it. She *is* your mother, and she *does* deserve a chance to get to know you. And you can glare at me and your dad all you want, but it's not going to change that fact."

Tears fell down her cheeks. She turned and ran out of the room.

Ryan braced his hands on the counter and dropped his head.

"Let me go to her," Mitch said, already pushing off his stool. "I'm the one who yelled at her. I'm the one she's mad at right now."

"She's mad at the whole goddamn world."

Mitch patted his shoulder. "So are you, buddy. Bad combination."

Mitch didn't bother to knock when he reached Julia's room, just pushed the door open. She was sitting on her bed, arms crossed over her chest, glare of the century on her face.

The full-size bed dipped as he sat next to her. "How long are you planning on being pissed at me?"

"As long as I feel like it."

He checked his watch. "Well, we've got plans tonight. I had to work my ass off to get this playdate for you. I'm trying to put the moves on this hot little lawyer and if you don't show up to entertain her daughter, it shoots my chances to hell."

"Is that all I am to you, just some kid you can use to get a girl?"

A grin tugged at his mouth. Now there was the feisty nine-year-old he knew and loved. "Basically. You got a problem with that?"

"You're incorrigible."

He couldn't help but laugh. "Where'd you hear that?"

"At school. And you are. And you're obnoxious too." She released her arms and sighed. "And I'm not mad at you. I just don't want to see her tomorrow, that's all."

He slid his arm around her shoulder and pulled her close. "I know, sweetheart. I know this is hard. It's hard on all of us, especially your dad. You've got to cut him some slack on this one."

She swallowed the tears and leaned into him. "I like things just the way they are, with you and me and Daddy. I don't want her around messing things up."

"She won't."

"She will."

"Give it a chance, okay? Just give it a chance, Julia."

"I don't want to."

"Then do it for me. She's my sister, and I love her. And you're my niece, and I love you. Do it for me if you can't do it for any other reason."

On a long sigh, she pulled back and wiped her face. "Okay. But you owe me." Her eyes narrowed. "And you owe me for tonight too. If this girl ends up being a total bore, you're gonna owe me big time."

"Thanks." He nudged her off the bed. "Now get your shoes. We're late."

Mitch glanced over at Julia and studied her profile illuminated by the dashboard lights. She needed a firm hand right now, someone to tell her the way it was going to be. Ryan was having problems of his own. He wasn't exactly handling any part of this well.

Who could blame him, though?

"Now don't go embarrassing me," he said, refocusing on the road.

"Would I do that?" Julia batted her lashes.

"Yeah, you would, especially when you're pissed at me. No telling amusing stories about me or bringing up personal stuff."

"Like how you drink milk straight from the carton? Or how you wear your jeans until they're basically walking before you wash them?"

He cringed. "Yeah, like that. And no bringing up past girlfriends with her, either. I'll have to take you down if you do."

She smiled. "You like her."

"Yes, I do." A frown tugged at his lips. "Why does everyone keep saying that?"

She reached over and tickled his side. "Aw, she's your penguin."

"My what?" He wiggled his way out of her grasp. "Cut that out."

"Your penguin. You know, penguins. They mate for life. Penguins are one of the only animals on the planet that do that, like humans. It's sweet. You've got yourself a little penguin, Uncle Mitch."

"I didn't say I was mating with her for life. Where the hell do you pick up this crap?"

"At school. School's full of crap."

"God, you've got a smart mouth. And no swearing in front of her, either."

"Why not? You do it."

"Yeah, I also get drunk and burp. Doesn't mean I want you doing it." He pulled to a stop in front of Simone's big old Victorian house. "Try to play the nice, polite niece part for me, at least for tonight. I know it's a stretch."

She eased out of the car and eyed the house. "Three new album downloads for my ipod."

Mitch squinted at her across the hood of his Land Rover.

"What?" Julia asked, looking shocked and surprised by his reaction. "I figure this is worth at least three. I'll make you a list. You can download them for me tomorrow when I'm off doing you yet *another* favor."

"Blackmail doesn't work with me."

"Oh, it will," she said with a grin and headed up the front steps.

Simone answered the door in bare feet, snug jeans, and a fitted T-shirt that accentuated her perky breasts. Damn, she was hot. He wasn't in the market for a penguin, but he wanted at least one date with the curvy lawyer.

"Hi," he said. "Sorry we're late. The shrimp is Julia."

Julia frowned up at him, then held out her hand. "Hi."

Simone shook her hand, her brows lifting as if she were impressed with Julia's manners. Score one for the shrimp. "It's nice to see you again, Julia. You probably don't remember me, but you and your mom came to visit us a few times when we lived in Baltimore."

Julia studied her face. "Um…no. I don't remember. I must have been little."

"You were. Why don't you come on back to the kitchen." Simone led them through the house. "Shannon's helping me get dinner going."

A long hallway cut the house in half, opening to the kitchen in the back and a large great room with windows that looked across a big yard.

Shannon stood at the counter, tossing a salad. Long hair the color of Simone's fell down to her shoulder blades. She eyed Julia warily as they came into the room.

"Julia, Mitch," Simone said. "This is my daughter, Shannon."

"Hey," Shannon mumbled.

Julia sent Mitch a wary gaze. Behind her back she held up four fingers.

No way he was buying her four albums. He elbowed her in the ribs and stepped around her into the kitchen. "Hi, Shannon. Your mom's told me a lot about you."

Shannon glanced at her mother across the room but didn't respond. Mitch caught it, watching their eyes and body language. Definite tension there.

"Shannon," Simone cut in. "Why don't you take Julia upstairs and show her your room."

Shannon shrugged as if she didn't care. "Okay. Come on."

Julia shot Mitch a less-than-amused glare as he nudged her out of the room. The two girls disappeared down the hall.

He looked back at Simone. "Well, that went well."

Simone blew out a sigh. "We're hitting the preteen years. Everything I do is wrong these days." She scrunched her nose as she looked down the hall. "Sorry, she's in a mood tonight. I probably should have cancelled. I have no idea how you talked me into this in the first place."

"What? It's just a playdate."

The yeah-right look she shot him sent heat careening through his veins. He cleared his throat and shoved his hands in the front pockets of his jeans so he wouldn't be tempted to reach for her. "I'm actually glad you didn't cancel. Ryan was having a rough night with Julia. I think it was good for both of them that she got out of the house."

She crossed into the living room, sank onto a plush couch, and tucked one leg under her. The room fit her, tall ceilings, big furnishings, comfy chairs. "What's going on?"

He dropped onto a chair opposite her. "Julia's upset about tomorrow."

Simone nodded. "And how's Ryan?"

"Upset about tomorrow."

Simone smiled. Man, she had a great smile. Full lips, straight white teeth. He really wanted to taste that mouth. Feel her give in and open for him. "Things will get better, Mitch. You just have to have faith."

He'd said that same thing to Kate. Now he just needed to believe it himself.

He leaned forward. "How much better do they have to get before you'll go out with me?"

"Now you're pushing your luck."

"Damn." He eased back into the cushions. "Shot down again. It's starting to become a routine."

She laughed. He could get used to that laugh. He found himself smiling too. Really smiling, for the first time in weeks. "Do you know you're the first lawyer I've ever met who *doesn't* want to screw me over?"

"Trust me, Mitch, I'm sure there are others."

"Shot down and put in my place. I'm batting a thousand tonight. Tell you what, Counselor, you can ease my pain by feeding me. You got any food in this house?"

Simone pushed up from the couch and grinned. "That I can do."

# CHAPTER TEN

Kate changed her clothes three times. She started off in gray slacks, slipped into a skirt, then slid on jeans. Jeans. Yeah, that was the way to go.

Calm and casual.

Glancing at her reflection in the mirror, she frowned. She was fooling herself. She didn't look calm. And there was no way anyone would believe she felt casual.

She messed with her hair for the hundredth time. She'd had it up, then down, then up again, finally deciding to let the wild curls fall where they may. It looked like one giant rat's nest.

It didn't matter what she looked like. This wasn't a date. After checking her reflection in the mirror one last time, she took a deep breath. Now or never.

By the time she loaded Reed into the car and headed toward the city, she was thoroughly exhausted. And it wasn't even nine-thirty yet.

This was a bad idea.

Sunlight glinted through the trees in the park as she and Reed walked toward the Conservatory of Flowers. They were the first ones there, so they sat on the bottom steps of the massive building while she tried not to stress out about a situation that was totally out of her control.

Her whole life felt like it was out of control these days.

Ryan and Julia strolled up about fifteen minutes later. Kate's stomach took one odd roll when she saw Ryan. Her palms grew damp. Wearing loose-fitting jeans and a short-sleeved shirt, and hiding his eyes behind dark sunglasses, he looked calm—and casual.

And dammit, sexy as hell.

Kate's gaze cut to Julia. The girl sent her a wicked glare, her disdain for the entire situation evident on her face.

Kate straightened her back. It was going to be awkward no matter what. She might as well get it over with.

Letting out a sigh, she picked Reed up and set him on her hip. "Baby," she said quietly. "This is Ryan." She swallowed the lump in her throat. "This is your...your father." She'd tried to explain things to him last night, but the poor kid was so confused, she had no idea what he'd say or do.

Reed looked at Ryan, his little brow wrinkled. Chubby fingers reached out and pulled the sunglasses off Ryan's face. "You have the same eyes as me." He turned toward Kate. "Blue eyes, Mama. Not like yours."

"Yeah, I know, baby."

He wiggled to the ground and looked up at Julia. "You don't have blue eyes."

Julia crossed her arms. "No shi—"

Ryan nudged her in the ribs.

"...kidding, Sherlock," she corrected with a scowl.

Reed didn't seem to notice her sarcasm. "Come on. Let's climb the stairs."

Julia shot Ryan a pathetic look.

"Go," he told her firmly.

She rolled her eyes and followed Reed.

Ryan slipped his glasses back on. For a moment, Kate had seen his eyes, and they'd looked tired and sad and a bit overwhelmed. But she'd also seen pure joy flash in those deep blue pools when he'd looked at her son. And in that one moment, she'd seen a part of him she didn't know existed.

"So," he said. "I was thinking maybe we could split up for a few hours, you take Julia, I'll take Reed, we'll meet back here around noon?"

"Okay." She looked up the steps at the two kids. What a picture they made, Reed running up and down, Julia tagging along behind. Julia didn't realize it, but she was already playing the protective big sister, making sure Reed didn't trip on the steps or fall flat on his face.

"Ah." Ryan shifted his feet, bringing her attention back to him. "Julia's been a little" —he scratched his head as if searching for the right word— "shocked, by this whole thing. You let me know if she gets out of line. She can be a handful sometimes."

"I can handle it, Ryan."

He nodded. "Okay, I'll see you back here around noon."

A weight settled on her chest. How did he do that? Act like none of this mattered? If he was feeling even a fraction of the agony she was, it had to be ripping him apart.

He stepped away from her and up the steps. When he crouched near Reed, he slipped off his glasses. A wide grin spread across Reed's little face, and he giggled, then slid his hand into Ryan's and headed back down the steps with him.

"Bye, Mama!" He waved as they headed down the path together.

Her chest tightened, and an ache cut through her soul as she watched the pair walk away. She'd seen Reed hold Jake's hand time and time again, but it had never affected her the way this picture did. Father and son, one almost a carbon copy of the other, both heading off into the sun together.

She rubbed the pain with the palm of her hand and blew out a shaky breath. This had to get easier. It just had to.

Julia stepped up beside her and crossed her arms.

Kate turned her way. "How do you feel about ice cream?"

"It's barely ten in the morning. It'll rot my teeth."

"So, you'll get water. Come on."

They settled into a booth at Ben & Jerry's. Kate ordered coffee. Julia decided on a root beer float after studying the menu for what seemed an infinitely long time. So much for rotting teeth. Kate eased back in her seat and studied Julia across the table.

Julia flipped her curly hair over her shoulder, leaned down, and took a sip of her soda through the straw. When she glanced up, her eyes were distant. "I don't need a mother."

Kate nodded. And so much for being polite.

"I'm only here because my dad and my uncle asked me to come. If you'd have asked, I'd have said no."

Well, this was going well. Kate pursed her lips. "I see."

"No, I don't think you do. I don't care what those stupid test results say. You're not my mother. My mother died five years ago."

"I realize this is hard for you, Julia. It's hard for all of us. But I assure you, I am your mother."

"That's just biology." Julia folded her arms across her chest. "Lots of women have kids. That doesn't make them mothers. Mothers stick around. They care about their kids. They don't…" She swallowed. Tears glinted in her eyes. "They don't disappear and then come back not remembering anything."

Kate's heart broke for the girl. "If I could change it, Julia, I would. I would in an instant."

Julia looked away. "Doesn't matter. It still doesn't change the fact that I don't need you or want you around. And neither does my dad."

The words felt like a slap in the face. Kate recognized the girl was striking out, but it still stung.

"He loved my mother, a lot," Julia went on. "And seeing you has been hard on him, but he's not in love with you. He knows that now. He's only being nice to you because of those tests, because of your...boy." She pushed her soda away in disgust.

"Julia." Kate tried to keep her voice calm and soothing. She was the adult. She had to remember that. Although, at the moment, she really wanted to run screaming out of the restaurant and indulge herself in a good long cry. "I'm not trying to get in the way of you and your father. I wouldn't do that. I just want to spend some time with you, get to know you a little. Your dad wants to do the same with Reed."

Julia bit her lip. "They said you already got remarried."

Kate's chest tightened. "They did? Your dad told you that?"

"Not exactly." Julia looked down at the worn table. "I heard him talking to Uncle Mitch about it. Did you?" When she shot a nervous glance up, Kate saw the questions swirling in her green eyes.

This wasn't the way she wanted the conversation to go. But she couldn't change the subject. Not when it was so important. Figuring honesty was the best route to take, Kate nodded. "I thought so. I don't really know how to explain the situation because I don't quite understand it myself. But I thought I was married. If I had known about you and your dad, though, things would have been different."

"He died, right? That's why you came looking for us."

"Yes, he died. That's how I found out about you."

"What was his name?" Julia glanced back down again. Kate could see this was hard on her but that she was curious, so she let the topic continue, for now.

"Jake. He was a doctor."

"Do you miss him?"

Kate let out a breath. "I don't know what I feel right now, Julia. Things are pretty messed up at the moment."

"But you weren't really married to him, right? 'Cause legally, you're still married to my dad."

Oh, man. There was a thought. And a reality. "No, I guess I wasn't. Your dad and I haven't even talked about that yet, though."

Julia twirled the soda glass between her hands. "You will. And you can fix it. People get divorced all the time. My dad will go for it."

Another slap. Kate didn't quite know why it hurt so much.

"He's over you, you know," Julia went on. "He dates lots of women, has since just after you left. I think he stays with them when he goes on trips. One time, I called his hotel, and a girl answered."

Heat crept up Kate's face.

"I'm more grown up than I look," Julia said. "I know a lot about what adults do."

Kate ran a hand over her forehead. This definitely wasn't what she'd wanted to talk about today. She needed to get the conversation back on neutral ground.

"Julia, let's try to focus on you and me. We're here because we need to get to know each other. Your dad and I will work things out on our own. I don't know what will happen, but I'm going to be around, for you and for Reed. I promise you that. I'm not leaving."

"You said that once before." She glanced away. "Whatever. Can we go back now? I want to see my dad."

This was going to be a lot harder than Kate had originally thought. All those nifty ideas about being one big happy—albeit dysfunctional—family dissipated into thin air.

Kate paid the bill, and they drove back to the park in silence. Julia refused to talk to her in the car. She'd closed down already, exhausted her conversation base, put up those walls her dad was so good at building.

Walking back toward the Conservatory, they spotted Reed and Ryan sitting on the bottom steps, sharing an ice-cream cone. Julia went running up to them, dropped into her father's arms, and sank onto the steps at his feet. The transformation in her mood was incredible. One minute, she'd been grumpy and depressed. Then as soon as she'd seen her father, she'd shifted to happy and elated.

Kate stopped and took in the scene from a distance. They seemed to fit—all three of them. Ryan and Reed had obviously gotten along just fine. Reed was smiling and laughing and trying to climb on Ryan's back. That didn't surprise her, though. Her son was a happy boy. He liked people, and he'd been enthralled by Ryan from the start.

And Julia even seemed to be warming up to Reed. She shot him a quick smile when she thought no one was watching.

Kate was the only one who didn't fit. She was the one causing all the confusion and hurt. She was the one who didn't know how to make this whole damn thing work.

Her eyes slid shut, and she turned before the tears could fall. This day had been so much harder for her than she'd ever imagined. Not just her conversation with Julia but all of it. Seeing the kids, watching them with Ryan, sensing how at ease he was with them and realizing how uncomfortable she felt about everything.

She headed back down the path to catch her breath, to check her emotions and regain composure. Breaking down in front of them wasn't an option. Just a few minutes, that's all she needed.

Ryan watched Annie disappear back down the path. He glanced down at Julia, then over at Reed. They looked happy. But Annie definitely didn't.

*Shit.*

"Julia, keep an eye on Reed."

"Ah, Dad, do I have to?" Julia whined.

He shot her a warning look. "Yes, you have to. You guys stay here and don't wander. I'll be right back."

Following the path, he spotted Annie on a bench about fifty yards away, nestled between the trees. Her head was resting in her hands, and while he couldn't make out her expression, he didn't need to see her face to know what she was feeling. He'd seen her beaming with joy, so angry she could spit fire, and in the throes of bitter tears. And every time, he'd known what to say or do to make things better. This time, he didn't.

He eased down onto the bench next to her. The scent of lilacs wafted in the air around him. He sucked in a breath and closed his eyes. After five years, she still wore the same perfume. Why hadn't he noticed that before?

"Was she that bad?"

She shook her head but didn't look up. "No. Just honest."

He glanced through the trees toward the Conservatory where the kids were chasing each other up and down the steps. "That means bad."

"No, Ryan, she was fine. Don't get upset with her."

When she lifted her head, he couldn't help but see the tears in her eyes. And his heart clenched at the sight. "I'm sorry. I don't know what to do to make this better."

She wiped at the tears with trembling hands. "It's okay. It's me. I'm the one making things so difficult."

"No, you're not."

"Yeah, I am. This is just..." She closed her eyes and covered her face with her hands. "It's just more real than I thought it was going to be."

Instinct overcame reason. He reached out to her before he thought better of it, slid an arm around her shoulder, pulled her close to his side. Her body stiffened in defense, then relaxed when he didn't let go. His body heated as she sank into him. Warm. Solid. So very real. And when her face turned into his chest, his heart squeezed even tighter.

How could he have forgotten what she felt like? Memories flashed in his mind, ones he'd pushed down over the years to keep from feeling that mind-numbing pain. Her lying in his arms in their bed, her skin sliding over his, her lips pressing against his neck, her mouth whispering what she planned to do to him.

With her body close to his like this, every minute of their life together flashed in front of his eyes. She felt so good, so right. He didn't want to let go.

"Don't cry," he whispered. "Dammit, don't cry. I never could take it. You're supposed to be the tough one."

She gulped in steadying breaths. Her breasts pressed against his side. As her hand moved across his chest, his skin tingled beneath the thin fabric of his shirt. The casual touch sent a jolt of electricity through his entire body, spurring all kinds of thoughts, a host of memories. He wanted her hands on his skin, her lips pressed against his, her body below, above, against his any way she wanted. As many times as she wanted.

She eased back enough to look up at him. And when she did, those deep green eyes tugged at something in his soul no one before or since had ever been able to touch. So soulful and expressive, those eyes had haunted his dreams since the day she'd disappeared.

Her hand lifted, and she paused, then reached out and slid the sunglasses off his face. Her gaze settled on his, and recognition sparked in her glittering eyes. Recognition, followed by stark fear.

She pulled away and sat up, dropped his sunglasses on his chest then rubbed her hands over her face as if wiping away what she'd seen.

Ryan's skin chilled. He watched her reel in her emotions and wanted to ask why she was fleeing from a connection they both so obviously felt. But he couldn't find the words. In that instant, he'd seen a glimpse of the woman she used to be, but she'd pushed it down so fast, he didn't know how to respond.

He dropped his hands, slipped on his sunglasses again. Then he stood and tried like hell to keep his voice even when he said, "I guess we're going to head home."

Annie nodded, slipping on her own glasses.

He rested his hands on his hips, trying so hard for normal when this situation was anything but. "I need some time to talk to Julia. But I want to see Reed again, soon. I was thinking maybe we could meet somewhere, after work, mid-week. Maybe swap for a few hours again."

"Okay. I can do that."

Her voice was steadier, more sure. No longer filled with emotions he wanted to tear out of her.

He forced back the hurt. "I want them to get to know each other too. Maybe we can set up some kind of alternating weekend thing down the line, where you have both, then I have both. They need time together as well."

She nodded again. "Yeah, that sounds okay."

"Okay." He looked over at her again. Part of him wanted to just grab her. Part of him wanted to run. "I'll call you."

"Ryan." She stood.

He watched her face for any sort of indication she felt even a fraction of what he did. He couldn't see it. He couldn't see any of it.

"Thank you," she said quietly.

"Yeah, sure."


Laughter echoed from Mitch's backyard when Kate and Reed walked up to his front door. The crack of a bat sent Reed's eyes wide. As Kate rang the bell and waited, she heard feet moving across the floor and was surprised when Simone opened the door.

"Hey, come on in." Simone moved aside and made room.

"I didn't know you'd be here," Kate said.

"Well, I was talking to Mitch this morning because Shannon and Julia are trying to arrange another playdate, and he said you were coming by. I have some news for you. I hope you don't mind. He invited us for a barbecue, said Reed would be here." She glanced down and grinned. "Hiya, Reed."

Reed smiled, looked past her legs to see into the house.

"No, I don't mind," Kate said. "In fact, a little fun sounds fabulous right now."

"Stressful day?"

"Stressful life." As if her meeting with Ryan yesterday hadn't been enough, today she had to call her parents.

Right. Like that was going to make things better.

At the sound of the bat cracking again, Reed let out a whoop and tore off through the house toward the back door.

"Come on." Simone led her through the small house. "Shannon's playing baseball with Mitch. They've struck up a little connection there."

They stopped in the patio doorway. Kate watched Mitch pitch the ball to Shannon. She hit it, sending it sailing over his head. Reed ran around his feet, scrambling for the ball.

"They make quite a picture, don't they?" Kate asked. She hadn't even introduced her son to Mitch yet, and the two were automatically drawn to each other.

"Yeah, they do," Simone said.

Kate looked toward her lawyer, who seemed to be staring only at Mitch. "You've got a pretty sappy look on your face there, Counselor."

"What? No I don't." Simone frowned, turned back into the house and sat at the kitchen table. "And before you ask, there's nothing going on between me and Mitch. I'm only interacting with him because of Shannon and Julia."

One corner of Kate's lips curled. Her lawyer had a major case of denial.

"So," Simone said, pulling a file from her briefcase on the table, "while they're all occupied outside, I thought we'd go over a few things."

"Okay."

"No one seems to know where your Houston doctor is. The man's simply vanished into thin air." She slid a paper across to Kate. "This is his last known address. He put in a request for leave from the hospital and said he was taking a 'mental health' vacation. That was three weeks ago. I have a PI trying to track him down, but so far nothing."

Kate's brow wrinkled.

"I also can't find anyone by the name of Walter Alexander who fits the description you gave me," Simone added. "It's like he never existed."

"That's not right."

"It's a common name, but the man you've told me about doesn't live in Houston, never did, for that matter. Did you ever hear Jake refer to him by a different name?"

Kate rubbed her throbbing head. "I don't know. They didn't exactly get along. Jake avoided him whenever he could."

"Did he ever say why?"

"No. His relationship with his father was off limits. We never talked about it."

"Well, see if anything comes back to you. At this point, I want to find Dr. Reynolds first. His disappearance right now is really fishy."

No kidding. "What about the nursing home?"

Simone let out a breath. "I do have a connection there. Visiting hours run until eight p.m. How do you feel about a little moonlighting tomorrow night?"

"Just tell me when. I need in there."

"I didn't think you'd argue. Monday nights seem to be the slowest. Only two security guards on duty and a nursing shift-change around seven thirty. Janitors come on around six. I think that's our best bet."

"Okay. Did you say anything to—?"

They both glanced up when the front door opened. Julia and Ryan walked through the archway and into the kitchen. Kate's stomach tightened.

Julia scowled when her eyes landed on Kate. "Great," she muttered under her breath.

Ryan squeezed her shoulder. "Be nice," he mumbled.

Julia headed out to the backyard, letting the patio door slam behind her. It was all Kate could do not to close her eyes and draw in a calming breath.

"Hi, Simone." Ryan's forced smile screamed of frustration. "I didn't know you'd be here."

"Mitch invited me. I hope that's not a problem."

"No, it's great to see you." He glanced out the window. "As long as you don't mind fireworks."

Simone smiled. "I have a nine-year-old myself. I know the

ropes."

Ryan glanced over at Kate, raised his brows in acknowledgement of her presence, and moved into the kitchen.

Simone cast a quick glance between Kate and Ryan, obviously sensing the tension. She stood and gathered her papers. "Well. I guess that's it. We can talk more later." She headed for the refrigerator. "I told Mitch I'd get him a beer."

The screen door slapped behind her as she left. In the silence that followed, Ryan popped the top off a beer, leaned back against the counter, and took a long pull from the bottle. "I didn't mean to run her off."

Nervous tension ran through Kate. Just being in the same room with him reminded her of the insane emotions she'd felt yesterday when she'd looked into his eyes on that stupid park bench. She really didn't need to be feeling anything for him, especially not those crazy tugs she couldn't define or understand. And definitely not that low pulse of arousal she had to tamp down whenever he got close.

"We were basically done. I didn't know you'd be here today."

"Mitch asked me to come."

"I see." Mitch, the peacemaker.

"I can go if you want me to."

"You don't need to go on my account."

His wary gaze rolled over her. It only unnerved her more. She ran a hand over her hair and straightened her back.

He moved to the refrigerator, took out another beer, popped the top, then walked to the table and handed it to her. She looked up in surprise. As her fingers closed around the cool bottle, he sat in the chair Simone had vacated.

She lifted the beer to her lips, took a sip. The amber liquid tasted like heaven. Silence stretched across the table, only heightening her nerves.

"You don't look so good," he finally said.

Kate stifled a pitiful laugh. "So nice of you to notice." She leaned back and closed her eyes. "Rough life."

"You wanna talk about it?"

She opened one eye. "With you?" Was he serious? They couldn't even be in the same room without getting into an argument.

"Might help me understand where you're coming from." His gaze dropped to her left hand and the ring she still wore.

Frustration bubbled through her. He had no right to make her feel guilty over her life with Jake. If they didn't get it out in the open, it was just going to keep on festering. "That really bothers you, doesn't it?"

The muscles in his jaw flexed. "You're damn right it does."

"I don't wear it to irritate you. I don't even realize I'm wearing it most of the time."

"And the rest of the time?"

"The rest of the time, I'm trying to figure out how this could have happened. I have a very hard time believing Jake did any of this on purpose."

Ryan took a long drink. Tension caused fine lines to deepen around his eyes. "Maybe you didn't know him so well."

"Maybe I didn't. It's a little unnerving to think I could have been so wrong about someone."

"Did he hurt you?"

His tone was cold, but there was a tender look in his eyes that eased the frustration inside her. "No. I know you may not want to hear it, but he was very decent. We argued some. Things weren't always great, but he never physically hurt me. And he doted on Reed. I never once questioned his devotion."

"Trusting." The sarcasm tightened her spine. "The woman I knew would never have blindly gone along with just anything. It didn't strike you as odd at all? You just accepted everything he told you?"

"He was a doctor. He said he was my husband. Everyone around me supported that. I never questioned it because I never had a reason to." Her anger kicked up. "You don't know what it's like to wake up with no memory, with no idea of who you are. Until you do, don't pass judgment on me."

Silence stretched over the room. Her words hung in the air between them. Every time they talked, things just seemed to get worse. Kate drank her beer and counted the seconds that ticked by on Ryan's watch. The low din was like a cannon going off in the room.

"Were you in love with him?"

His quiet voice brought Kate's eyes up. He didn't meet her gaze, instead kept looking out the window. But she didn't miss the way his whole body tensed as if in preparation for the answer.

She didn't want to lie. But she wasn't overly elated about the truth, either. For the first time, she felt torn.

"Yes," she said more hesitantly than she intended. "I thought so. Now…"

His intense sapphire eyes turned to her.

She lifted a shoulder and let it drop. "Now I don't really know. I don't know much of anything."

"Shit." Ryan's jaw tightened. He pushed from the chair and went back into the kitchen to get another beer.

Kate took a deep breath and tamped down the frustration and guilt burning in her chest that she shouldn't even be feeling. "Do you think there will ever be a day when we can have a conversation without you swearing at me for one reason or another?"

"No." His tone was cold and impassive, his eyes fixed out the window toward their kids.

She stood. "Well, we must have had one hell of a marriage if this is any indication. What on God's green earth ever convinced me to marry you in the first place?"

"I hate to bust your bubble, babe, but we're *still* married."

"You don't have to remind me." She was well aware of that fact now more than ever, and the reality of it was the only thing that made her rein in her emotions. "Look, Ryan, I know this is hard for you. I understand what you're going through, even if I can't relate. I've tried to put myself in your shoes a hundred times, and I can't. But it doesn't mean I don't care."

She wished he'd look at her, but he just kept staring out that damn window. "I'm not going to lie to you. There's something about you that…intrigues me. Although what it is, I have no clue. You're obnoxious, obtuse, rude and cold. And every time I'm around you, I'm reminded of those facts. You're living up to your heartless reputation, Mr. Harrison."

The look he sent her could have turned flesh to stone. She knew from his reaction what she'd said had hit its mark, so she softened her tone when she added, "And even with all that, I'm still at a loss, because even though I may not have memories, I can still feel things. Yesterday at the park, it was like an odd sense of déjà vu. I recognized something about being close to you. And I felt something I haven't felt before. But I don't know what it means. I don't know if it's just recognition of something we once shared, or if it's something pushing me toward you. And frankly, at this moment, I can't even think about it. I don't even want to."

She ran a hand over her hair. "I'm overwhelmed. I have to think about Reed and what's best for him. And how to get Julia not to hate my guts. And what the hell I'm supposed to tell my parents when they show up." She massaged her throbbing scar. "It's more than I can handle. And I can't even begin to focus on you until I get some of those things worked out first. I don't want to hurt you any more than I already have, but I can't lie to you and tell you that I didn't have feelings for Jake or pretend like the last year and a half with him didn't happen, because it did. Neither of us can change that. All we can do is try to make things easier for the kids from here on out."

He was so quiet and still, she half expected him to explode at any second.

"I can accept that," he finally said. "The kids are a priority for me too."

He set his beer on the counter and stalked toward her. "But you accept this. I'm not that patient. I've been through five years of hell while you've been off having a life. I'm not going to just sit back and let you figure everything else out first and put me on the back burner until you're ready to deal with me."

He moved closer, and she stepped back until her feet hit the wall. His face was only inches from hers, his breath warming her skin, causing a trickle of awareness to course through her. She smelled the soap from his shower, felt the heat radiating from his body. And had a sudden, wicked, senseless urge to wrap her hand around his neck and pull his mouth down to hers.

Which was off the charts *insane*.

"You're just gonna have to deal with me now," he said in a husky voice. "Right along with everything else."

Those sapphire gems were full of rolling emotions. Emotions and heat and need and challenge. A challenge something deep inside told her she'd faced before.

Instead of grabbing his face and taking a taste of that mouth as her body suddenly wanted her to do, she poked his chest with one hard index finger. "And you're just going to have to grow up, Harrison. This isn't all about you. I'm doing the best I can. I'm trying to be sensitive to your needs and Julia's feelings. Nothing's easy. For any of us."

Frustration and anger and loss and fear welled up and overtook her. She curled her fingers into the front of his shirt, moved in until she was close enough to take that taste, but now didn't want it so much. She was too damned pissed. He wasn't the only one who could be a jerk when they were hurting.

"And remember this," she added. "I'm here because I want to be here. I didn't have to come looking for you. And there's nothing making me stay except me. So suck it up and deal with it, just like I'm dealing with you."

She released his shirt with a push, barely enough to move him. But Ryan took a step back anyway. And when he stared at her, his eyes glittered with a mix of shock and anger and, she could swear, a touch of admiration. Admiration that sent a thrill straight to her belly.

Strange yet familiar sexual sparks flared between them. Sparks that told her they'd had this argument before. Not this exact one, but this face-off. This sexually charged confrontation. She didn't need memories to know the chemistry between them was combustible. She could feel it. Could feel it had always been combustible. But unlike arguments of the past, this one wouldn't end in sweaty, sexy, passionate sex. She wouldn't let it.

After everything she'd already been through, she wasn't setting herself up to get burned again. Especially not by a man like Ryan Harrison.

She stepped past him and headed out into the backyard.

# CHAPTER ELEVEN

"Don't worry." Mitch squeezed Kate's knee as she leaned against the side of his desk in his home office. "They're not going to freak out."

She raised her brow and crossed her arms.

A sly smirk tugged at his mouth. "Okay, they'll freak a little. But not that much."

"I still don't know why I have to be here," Kate said.

"Moral support." He picked up the phone and dialed. "I've had to deal with them by myself for five years. It's time you started pulling your weight again."

He swiveled away and began speaking into the phone.

Kate glanced at Ryan, who was leaning against the doorjamb. She wanted to be outside with Simone and the kids, not shut up in here with Ryan and Mitch. "Is he always this pushy?"

"Pretty much," Ryan said, crossing his arms over his chest.

"Did I used to like it?"

One side of his lips quirked up in a winsome smile. The first inkling of smile she'd seen on his face. "Not a bit. You pushed right back. Just like you did with me in the kitchen."

She turned away from the way Ryan held her gaze, looked back to Mitch and tried to tamp down the thrill Ryan's words sent through her body. Mitch was doing his best to explain the situation to his mother. A frown tugged at Kate's mouth. "It doesn't sound like it's going well."

"Mom," Mitch said into the receiver, "I'm putting you on speaker."

Kate's eyes grew wide, and she nudged him with her knee and shook her head, but it didn't stop him.

"Okay, Mom," Mitch said, "we're all here."

The line was quiet. Then Kathy Mathews's voice chirped through. "Is Ryan there?"

"I'm here, Kathy," Ryan said, stepping into the room.

"Ryan, is he telling the truth, or is this one of his jokes? Because if he's kidding on this one, he's definitely out of the will. You got that, Mitch?"

Ryan glanced at Kate. "No, Kathy. He's not kidding. She's real."

There was silence again. "Is...is she there?"

Kate glared at Mitch. Oh, he was in so much trouble for this. "I'm here, too. He's not lying."

The line seemed to go dead. Then they heard sobbing. Followed by Roger's voice. Mitch picked up the handset, turned off the speakerphone, and patted Kate's knee. He went through the story with his father a second time.

When Mitch hung up, he let out a deep breath. "They're coming down tomorrow. I managed to convince them to give you a day instead of jumping on the first plane out of Sea-Tac."

"Fabulous," Kate muttered. "That was really sweet of you, by the way, throwing me under the bus like that. Remind me to return the favor."

"You'll feel better once you have some food. You always were a grump when your blood sugars dropped." He pushed out of his chair and headed toward the kitchen.

Kate knew Ryan was still behind her. How, she wasn't sure. She just sensed him. "How do you think they're going to react to all of this when they get here?"

"They'll be fine," Ryan said. "They're good people. I'd be sure Reed's with you tomorrow when you see them, though. That'll give you a buffer."

"Good idea." She looked his way. "Will you be there?"

"I think I'll sit this one out. Mitch will be with you."

She nodded. But why did that bother her?

"I guess this is the last big shocker for awhile," she said quietly.

Ryan looked down at his feet. "Yeah, I guess so. I told my parents this morning. They're coming down later in the week, but you don't have to worry. They'll want to see you, but they're mostly coming down to see me and Julia, and to meet Reed."

"Okay." The whole conversation was just awkward. Meeting her parents, meeting her in-laws, it was bizarre. "Just let me know when they get here. I'll bring Reed over." She tried to read his thoughts. Couldn't. Doubted she ever would. "Did they not like me?"

"What?"

"Your parents, did they not like me? It doesn't sound like they're overjoyed at the thought of seeing me again. Not like

Mitch's parents." She frowned. "My parents." It was still a hard idea to get used to. She actually had parents.

"Yeah, they liked you." His voice turned soft, the tenderness in it tugging on her. "They loved you." He shook his head. "They know this is awkward for me, for us. They don't want to make you any more uncomfortable than you already are."

No matter what anyone did or didn't do, it was still uncomfortable. She didn't know what to say in response. She desperately wanted to do something to make this better, though.

"Come on," he said, breaking the silence before she could. "Let's go get some food and see what the kids are doing."

Thankful for the distraction, she followed him out into the kitchen, vaguely aware he was trying to keep the sarcasm and anger out of his voice. Since their moment in the kitchen, he'd been trying a lot harder to treat her with some sense of compassion, or at least with a little less hostility.

When they walked into the room, Mitch and Simone were working in the kitchen together, getting hamburger fixings ready to go, while Julia and Shannon set out chips and condiments. The girls had already struck up a fierce friendship. Reed just ran around getting in the way, like he was a regular fixture in the group. They looked normal. Like two families hanging out for a backyard barbecue.

It was only when you looked closer you saw it was just one giant mess.

The flickering lights of the TV in the corner of the room caught Kate's attention. No one seemed to be noticing it, so she moved to turn it off, but her hand paused on the power button when the reporter mention Ryan's name. Then her face flashed on the screen. And she sucked in a gasp.

Ryan stepped up next to her. The reporter was standing outside Ryan's downtown office building.

"*Channel Two News has recently learned that pharmaceutical giant Ryan Harrison, whose wife died aboard U.S. Airlines flight 1466 which crashed shortly after takeoff from San Francisco five years ago, received shocking news earlier this week. His wife may still be alive.*

"*Sources confirm this woman, Kate Alexander, agreed to undergo DNA testing to verify suspicions she is Harrison's estranged wife. A source close to Ms. Alexander also confirms she suffers from a rare form of amnesia, which has blocked out virtually all of her long-term memory, making this discovery even more amazing.*

*"Harrison, shown here in video from the Governor's Ball last winter, and his lawyers are not commenting at this time, but sources do tell us it is highly likely Ms. Alexander is in fact Anne Harrison. Ryan Harrison, CEO of AmCorp Pharmaceuticals, has very rarely spoken publicly about his deceased wife. His company has been involved in several questionable take-over mergers lately…"*

"Fucking press." Ryan flipped off the TV and headed for Mitch's office.

Kate sank down onto the couch and covered her face. With trembling fingers she tried to rub away the headache already pounding away at her brain. As if things weren't bad enough, now the story was all over the news.

Simone ushered the kids outside and sat next to her. Mitch followed Ryan into the office.

"Talk to me, Counselor," Kate said.

"Well, I want to hear what Ryan's PR people have to say, but I'm thinking you're both going to have to make a public statement. It's the only way we're going to get the press off your backs. Odds are good they're at your house right now, and at Ryan's. I think you lucked out today by being here. As of yet, they haven't found you, but they will."

"Fabulous."

She pushed off the couch and walked into Mitch's office. Ryan was pacing with the phone pressed to his ear. Mitch stood in the corner of the room listening, his hands on his hips.

A chill spread over Kate. Ryan had definitely been frustrated and angry with her before, but this was different. His voice was icy, his face hard and rigid, and whomever he was talking to—and she assumed it was one of his lawyers—was taking the brunt of his fury.

"I don't give a damn what they want," he said into the phone. "My personal life is my own fucking business. I've never commented on it before. I'm sure as hell not going to start now."

Kate listened to his end of the conversation, not feeling any better judging by the number of times Ryan swore. When he was done, he tossed the cordless phone on the desk, dropped into Mitch's leather chair, leaned his head back, and closed his eyes. "What do you want to do?"

The question was meant for her. Kate looked to Simone, then back at Ryan's hard face. "If we ignore it?"

"They'll hound us until we break."

Kate caught Simone's nod of agreement. "So we face them head on."

He met her gaze with steely eyes. "I don't want my personal life strewn across the front page of the *National Star*."

"Ryan," Simone interjected for the first time, "I don't think you have a choice in the matter right now. Either we give them something to print, or they're going to do their damnedest to make up something much worse. I realize your need for privacy, but it's the lesser of two evils we're concerned with now."

Ryan turned his icy gaze on Simone. "I hate the fucking press."

She smiled at the confrontation. "I'm sure they feel the same way about you."

Simone slipped an arm around Kate's waist. "I think we need to go over our game plan. We make it clear the children are off limits. You make a joint statement, act like you're on civil speaking terms" —she shot a speculative glance at Ryan— "then answer a few brief questions. The whole thing will be over in a few minutes."

Ryan let out a huff.

"And you, Mr. Multimillionaire," Simone said. "You'll be polite and courteous. The press will tear Kate to shreds if you're an ass to them. I know it's worked for you in the past, but this time you have other people to think about. This time, the press isn't interested in your business. They're interested in your family. It's a whole new ball game."

Not even a torrential downpour could keep the press away. Kate glanced out the window of the penthouse suite in the Hawthorn Hotel at the sheets of rain slamming the city. Dark and gray, much like her mood, no end in sight to the depressing day.

Turning away from the rain, she tried to refocus on what was about to happen, but every time she looked at Ryan, she was startled by the image he created. Surrounded by a group of men and one woman, he looked every bit the power player he was. He wore an expensive navy suit with a crisp white shirt and blue-checked tie, and somehow, dressed like that, in this environment, she could easily see why people were so intimidated by him.

She wished Simone was with her but she'd already gone downstairs to herd the press. While Ryan continued to ignore her and talk to his team instead, Kate's anxiety amped. She'd seen how angry he was yesterday when the story had broken, but he had to know this wasn't a normal event for her. Would a little humanity right now be too much to ask for from the man?

A member of Ryan's team peeked his head in the door. "It's time, Mr. Harrison."

Kate's stomach fluttered. *Here we go.* She dropped her arms, straightened her jacket, all the while wondering how the hell her life had gotten so complicated. Before she could take a step toward the door, the lone woman in Ryan's group approached her.

"Ms. Alexander, I'm Hannah Hughes, Vice President of Public Relations for AmCorp. Ryan's brought me up to speed. I realize this is probably a lot to deal with right now and if there's anything AmCorp can do to make you more comfortable, please let us know."

Kate was about to respond when Hannah stepped past her and out into the hallway with the rest of Ryan's team. Okay, so much for chitchat. That felt scripted.

Kate turned when Ryan walked up beside her.

"Ready?" he asked.

She nodded and swallowed the growing lump in her throat.

He stayed next to her as they walked down the hallway, the expression on his face blank and emotionless. For the first time since she'd met him, Kate wished desperately he'd say something, anything to her. Even yelling at her was better than this.

They rode the elevator in silence. No one—not a single member of his team—spoke. When the elevator pinged and the door opened, though, they were instantly swarmed by the press, by cameras flashing and reporters hollering questions. Ryan reached for her elbow and guided her into the conference room. TV cameras were shoved in their faces, blinding lights and microphones. For the first time, Kate caught a glimpse of Ryan's public image, of how frustrating it must be to be in the spotlight. She didn't like it. And she didn't want it.

At the far end of the room sat a long table and a podium with a bank of microphones. Ryan's team of lawyers filtered to the mikes where Simone was already waiting. Kate and Ryan stepped up behind them.

Simone leaned over. "You okay?"

Kate nodded, though what she really wanted to do was throw up.

Hannah Hughes spoke first, bringing a hush over the fifty or so reporters gathered in the room. "Good morning," she said in a firm and confident voice. "I'm Hannah Hughes, Vice President of Public Relations for AmCorp. I'd like to lay some ground rules before we get started. Mr. Harrison and Ms. Alexander have asked me to read a statement, during which we request you refrain from asking questions. Afterwards, Mr. Harrison and Ms. Alexander will open the floor up for a brief question-and-answer session."

She slipped on her glasses and glanced down at the prepared statement. "Five years ago, Mr. Harrison's wife of seven years, seismologist Anne Harrison, boarded flight 1466 bound for Denver, Colorado." What followed was a vague description of the events that brought them together.

Hannah didn't seem to miss a beat as she read through the statement. She kept right on going, her gaze steady across the sea of reporters, never looking at any one person for very long, never showing a hint of emotion. The reporters listened intently, jotting notes and focusing on her words. Hannah glanced up when she finished, then stepped back and let Kate and Ryan approach the mike. Nervous tension ran through Kate, but she did her best to smile when the cameras turned on her.

"Good morning," Ryan said. "If we'd have known there was going to be a three-ring circus here today, we'd have booked a clown for the festivities." He flashed a mesmerizing smile—one Kate had never seen before—and several people in the audience laughed.

"Unfortunately," he went on, his face hardening, "this situation is anything but a laughing matter. I don't think I need to tell you that we're just as shocked by recent developments as you are. Upon completion of this press conference, neither Ms. Alexander nor myself will be answering questions regarding our personal lives. I'd appreciate your cooperation in this, and request that you give us the space we need to deal with this situation on our own."

As soon as he paused, a wave of arms shot into the air, followed by voices trying to be heard. Ryan pointed to one reporter and waited. "Can you tell us who recognized Ms. Alexander?" the man asked.

"Yes. Simone Conners, a lawyer here in the city."

"Ms. Alexander," another reporter asked, "can you explain how your memory has been affected since your accident?"

"I can try," Kate said with a smile. "I'm not able to remember anything before waking up from that coma. My memory basically started eighteen months ago."

Hands went up all over the room, and Kate pointed to a young female with red hair. "Ms. Alexander, how did you end up in Houston?"

"If I had the answer to that question we wouldn't be standing here right now, would we?" She smiled and called on another reporter.

"Ms. Alexander," a bald man with thick glasses asked, "did you recognize Mr. Harrison when you saw him?"

"No. I've seen plenty of pictures of Mr. Harrison, his reputation is legendary, but I never recognized him."

"Ms. Alexander," another reporter asked with a smile. "What do you think of Mr. Harrison's renowned and somewhat ruthless reputation?"

For reasons she'd never understand, the press seemed to be focusing in on her. Kate tried to keep a calm outward appearance, but inside her stomach flopped all over the place like a fish out of water. Working for a smile, she said, "Mr. Harrison appears to be a shrewd business man, but I assure you he's human just like everyone else."

Her response garnered a wave of laughter from the crowd and raised brows from Ryan.

Kate pointed to another man. "Mr. Harrison," this one asked, "how does it feel to see your wife again after five years and not have her recognize you?"

Ryan ignored the question, pointing instead to a young blonde in the front row. Kate shifted her feet, recognizing the tension pulsing from Ryan.

"Ms. Alexander," the female reporter asked. "What are your intentions at this point?"

"At this point, I simply want to get to know my family again. I'm going to expect the press gives us time to accomplish that goal."

Kate pointed to a reporter in the third row. "Mr. Harrison, what was your reaction when you saw your wife for the first time?"

"Shock." He pointed to another reporter, obviously not wanting to elaborate or give them anything to go on.

"Ms. Alexander," the man asked, "how did Mr. Harrison react when he found out you'd been remarried?"

How did the press know that? They hadn't given any specifics about Jake or her marriage in that prepared speech. Kate saw Ryan's jaw clench out of the corner of her eye. It was the only time through the whole press conference she'd seen him flinch.

"Ask another question," Ryan cut in before she could answer.

"Ms. Alexander," another reporter asked. "Have you filed for divorce from Mr. Harrison?"

Again, Kate watched Ryan's jaw tighten, and she quickly answered before his temper kicked in. "At this point, we've hardly had time to digest the information, let alone make any decisions about the future." She pointed to another reporter.

"Ms. Alexander, we understand you have a son. Have you had paternity tests run to verify if Mr. Harrison is his father?"

"We will not be discussing our children," Ryan said before Kate could answer. "Any reporter who attempts to question our children will have to deal with me personally."

Kate sensed his waning patience. "We'll take one more question." She pointed to a bald man in the fourth row.

"Mr. Harrison," he began. "Considering California is a community property state, what legal action have you taken to protect yourself financially from Ms. Alexander and her lawyer from filing for divorce and seizing half your assets? It's basically a foregone conclusion at this point. Isn't it a nice little coincidence she waited until your net worth was at its peak to suddenly show up on the scene?" There was a hint of sarcasm in the man's voice that said he couldn't wait to see Ryan Harrison knocked down a notch.

"I'll kindly remind you that you're speaking about my wife," Ryan snapped before Kate could step in and diffuse the question. "I don't give a rat's ass what conclusions you draw from the situation. Your freedom of speech doesn't give you the right to pry into my personal life. This press conference is over." He stepped away from the mike, grasped Kate's hand, and pulled her behind him out of the conference room.

His assistant was already holding the elevator when they swept into the hall. Ryan let go of Kate's hand as soon as the doors closed behind them. A muscle in his jaw twitched like it had a life of its own.

Kate swallowed, not quite sure what to say or do. When the elevator doors opened, Ryan yanked off his tie and unbuttoned the collar of his shirt. He tossed his jacket across the back of the couch and stalked into the adjoining bedroom. Kate let out a deep breath and closed her eyes as the door slammed shut.

That had gone about as well as a root canal. She couldn't wait to see the papers tomorrow morning.

The door opened behind her, and a wave of suits filled the room. Hannah Hughes strolled in, slipped off her glasses, and pinched the bridge of her nose. "Well," she said on a sigh, "that went well. So much for all the prep work we did with Ryan."

Talking with Ryan's VP of whatever wasn't high on Kate's list right now. She headed for the bedroom.

"I'd rethink that if I were you, Ms. Alexander," Hannah said as she sat on a barstool and one of the other suits handed her a drink. "You'll want to give him a while to calm down."

"The hell I do." Kate thrust the door open with her hip. It slapped closed behind her.

Ryan stood across the room with one hand braced high on the window frame, looking out across the bay at the waves of rain dousing the city.

"You really have a way with reporters, Ryan. I can see why the press loves you as much as they do."

"Go away. I'm not in the mood."

A half laugh, half yell bubbled through her. "I don't really care what you're in the mood for. You weren't the only one in that room downstairs and if anyone should be upset it's me. They didn't sandblast your character or your intentions in this situation, just mine. They made me out to be some slut gold digger who turned up on your doorstep because she wants your money."

When he didn't respond, she stepped farther into the room, a little concerned he actually believed that bullshit they were throwing around down there. "Turn around when I'm talking to you. I've a right to see your face when we're arguing."

He spun around, and the enraged eyes and bulging vein in his temple told her his temper had reached its limit. "You've got no rights when it comes to me. You relinquished your rights when you walked out on me five years ago!"

"What the hell kind of statement is that? You're blaming me now for this whole mess?"

"You were always too goddamned independent. I asked you not to go on that stupid trip, but you wouldn't listen to me. You had to do just as you damn well pleased, like always, and now look at the fucking mess we're in."

Kate's eyes narrowed. "You son of a bitch. How dare you bring up something like that, something I don't even remember. As you so easily reminded me yesterday, I'm your wife, not some measly peon you can order around and treat like garbage."

She turned to leave, but he crossed the floor, grasped her arm, and whirled her around before she could get away. "My wife? That's a laugh. Yesterday you didn't want to have anything to do with being my wife, and now, when it's convenient and you can use it, you throw it in my face?"

"Take your hands off me."

"Or what?" He backed her against the wall, his height a looming advantage, more than evident to her at the moment. "If you're my wife, don't I have the right to touch you? Or are you the only one with rights around here? There's a whole slew of reporters downstairs. Why don't you just run down and tell them what an ass I am. They're looking for something else to print about me."

The heat from his hands all but burned the skin of her arm beneath her jacket. A dark fire brewed in his eyes, a hint of danger. Her pulse quickened, her senses peaked when she caught a whiff of his musky cologne.

She wasn't attracted to arrogant, domineering men. She wasn't. Not at all.

So why was her heart thumping wildly in her chest?

"Let go of me," she said with as much calm as she could muster.

His jaw tightened. His eyes locked on hers. Long seconds passed as he stared at her. And in the silence, that connection she'd felt to him in the park flared hot all over again, dousing her anger and filling her with regret.

"Damn it." He let go. Turned away.

She grabbed his arm. "Ryan."

His whole expression softened when he looked back at her. And something in that look shot straight to her heart—a feeling she wasn't prepared for or even expecting.

"Oh, hell." His hands tangled in her hair as he pulled her mouth toward his. Those tempting lips crushed over hers. His tongue, rough and hot, dipped into her mouth when she opened. She reached for him before she even realized what she was doing, grasped his arms at the elbows. Dark flashes of arousal coursed through her, erupted in her center, spread through every limb and nerve ending.

He pressed her back against the wall, changed the angle of the kiss, took her deeper. The contrast in textures blew her mind—hard and firm against her hips, soft and sensual at her mouth. Need pumped through her, shooting spears of heat through her entire body.

She didn't think to push away, only wanted more. More of his touch. More of his mouth. More of his wicked body pressing into hers. She trembled when his hands combed through her hair, streaked down her shoulders and arms to grasp her waist. Her skin tingled with each touch, every caress.

Those delicious lips trailed the line of her jaw, pulling a moan from her chest. She threaded her hands into his hair, the silky blond strands wrapping around her fingers. Dropping her head back, she offered him her throat. Shivered when his lips moved down her neck.

*More, more, more.* The words pounded in her brain, tightened her breasts, spread heat straight to her sex. An ache pulsed between her legs, one that needed to be filled. One that needed him to fill it. He fumbled with her jacket, thrust it over her shoulders, trapping her arms at her sides. The buttons on her blouse gave one by one; the front clasp on her bra popping open with little effort.

He eased back just far enough to look down, and a moan slipped from his lips. A moan laced with hunger. Kate's skin tingled as he stared at her, and her nipples puckered when his hands moved over her breasts, teasing, molding, taking.

She wanted him. Needed this. When his mouth found hers again, she opened on reflex, drew him deep, tangled her tongue with his, and groaned when she felt the hard length of his erection press against her lower belly.

"I can't believe how good you feel," he murmured against her lips, his fingers rolling her nipples, sending shock waves of pleasure between her legs. "I'd forgotten what you taste like."

She struggled against him, finally freed her arms and yanked the shirt from the waistband of his slacks. She needed to touch, wanted that sizzle of skin against skin.

"More," she said against his lips, kissing him again and again. Common sense fled. Fire raced along her skin when he lifted her leg around his hip, when his hands hiked up her skirt, when his fingers brushed her mound.

Not enough. She had to have skin, needed heat.

He was wearing too many clothes. Dammit, she couldn't get at him fast enough. She fumbled with his belt, then the button on his slacks while his mouth ravaged hers again. He stroked his fingers across her panties. His hips pressed into hers, his cock hard and pulsing against her. A promise of everything she wanted and needed and hadn't realized she'd craved.

An irritating pounding sounded somewhere close.

She lifted her leg higher, rubbed against him. Moaned when tingles spread through her lower body.

"Kate?" Simone's muffled voice echoed through the room. "Mitch is here with your parents. Is everything okay?"

*No, dammit. Definitely not okay. Go away.*

"Ignore her," Ryan mumbled, kissing her jaw, her ear, her throat as he slid his fingers beneath the edge of her panties, so close to her heat.

"Kate?" Simone knocked again.

*Dammit.*

Kate's head rolled back and hit the wall. Ryan's hand stilled and his lips hovered against her neck. Long seconds passed in silence, then he dropped his face against her shoulder and let go of her leg, bracing his hands on the wall behind her.

She didn't want to let go. She didn't want to face reality. She trailed her fingers through his silky hair, trying to hang on to the moment.

"Kate?" Simone knocked once more.

"Answer her," Ryan murmured.

Kate swallowed, struggling to breathe. "Yeah, I…I'll be right out."

"Okay," Simone said.

"Jesus," Ryan said. "I feel like I'm twenty-two again and your parents just walked in on us."

"Did that happen?"

"More than once."

"Oh, great. Now I'm going to have that in my mind when I meet them."

His lips were but a breath from her skin, and as she felt his chest vibrate, she realized he was chuckling. It was a good feeling. A warm feeling. An I-didn't-expect-this-but-I-only-want-more-of-it feeling.

But he pushed himself away before she could have more. And in his absence, her skin chilled with the reality of what they'd just done.

"Ryan."

He stopped halfway to the bathroom, held his hands out to show her he wasn't nearly as under control as he needed to be either. "I don't think your parents need to see me like this."

If his features hadn't been cool and guarded once more, she might have laughed. Instead, her eyes slid shut as he closed the bathroom door. The room was suddenly too big, her skin too cold, and he'd just pulled up those damn walls again.

Had she really almost slept with Ryan Harrison after the way he'd just treated her? She cringed. No, sleeping with him implied something a bit more tender, a tad more intimate. What she'd almost done was let him screw her against the wall while his employees waited for him in the other room.

*Way to go, Kate. So much for that resolve not to get sucked into combustible chemistry.*

Considering her purse was out in the living room, she did the best she could with her appearance. She finger-combed her hair and wiped away her streaked makeup, then re-buttoned her shirt. Smoothing out her skirt, she checked her reflection one last time.

Her hair was one big tangled mess. Her lipstick was gone, and she had a sinking suspicion Simone would take one look at her and know exactly what had been going on in the bedroom while she and the other lawyers waited on the opposite side of the door.

Was she a complete moron?

Oh, yeah. It appeared so.

She ran her hands across her face, wished it would wipe away her stupidity. Unfortunately for her, it did nothing but remind her how sensitive her skin still was from Ryan's mouth. She was fully aware of his reputation as a womanizer and a heartless bastard. And hadn't he just proved it to her?

She smoothed out her hair one last time and lifted her chin. The key word in all of that was *almost*. Now that she was in control again, she could keep it from becoming an absolute foregone conclusion. Fate had stepped in and spared her this time. Next time, she'd be a little more cautious and a hell of a lot stronger against his advances.

Dammit. She chastised herself. There wouldn't *be* a next time. She wasn't going to become one of Ryan Harrison's little bimbos, even if she was his wife.

# CHAPTER TWELVE

Kate was wrong when she assumed it was Simone's wary gaze she'd have to avert. When she stepped into the living room of the suite, Mitch was leaning against a bar stool alone. His head came up when he saw her, his eyes as fiery as she'd ever seen them.

"What the hell's going on?"

Lovely. This so wasn't what she needed right now. Thankfully, the suits were gone and her parents were nowhere to be seen.

Kate held up her hands to stop him from going into the bedroom. "Mitch, let it go. I've already had to deal with one irate man today, I can't take another."

"He's being an ass, isn't he? We heard the press conference in the car on the way over, but it doesn't give him the right to treat you like this."

"I can handle Ryan. I'm not some wimpy girl. Where are your...my...*our* parents?"

"Simone took them in the other room so they didn't have to listen to World War III."

Kate's eyes slid shut. Great. Just great. Their first impression of her would be her screaming at her husband.

"You did great today," he said softly. "That's part of the reason Ryan's so pissed. You had those reporters eating out of the palm of your hand."

She stifled a pathetic laugh. "Really? That's not the impression Ryan gave me."

The door opened behind her, and she sensed Ryan step into the room.

Mitch shot him a glare. "Are you done throwing your little temper tantrum?"

"Kiss my ass."

Mitch took a step toward him. "I'd rather kick it. You're being a complete jackass, and you know it."

"You wanna take a swing at me?" Ryan huffed, throwing his arms out invitingly. "Go ahead. You aren't the first Mathews's to want to do that today."

Kate pushed her way between the two. "Knock it off right now. You're both idiots if you think this adolescent sparring's going to help the situation at all. What is it about men that makes them think throwing a punch is going to make them feel better?"

Ryan's gaze shot to her, and his face paled. "You're bleeding."

"What?" Kate touched her lip. "Damn. It's just a bloody nose." She tilted her head back and took the tissues Mitch offered, pressing them against her face.

The door across the room opened. Ryan grasped her hand and pulled her back toward the bedroom. "Come on, let's get you cleaned up before you have to see them. Mitch, run interference…please?"

Mitch frowned but nodded and headed in the opposite direction.

Ryan propped Kate up on the long marble vanity in the suite's master bathroom. He handed her fresh tissues while she pinched the bridge of her nose to stop the flow of blood.

"Don't look so concerned," she tried to joke. "It's no big deal. I get them all the time."

"You do?" He took the bloody tissues, grimaced, and handed her a fresh one.

"Yeah, usually when I'm stressed. I think this whole day classifies as stressful."

Ryan rested his hands on the counter, one on each side of her thighs. "I'm sorry. I was out of line yelling at you before. I'm not mad at you. I'm just frustrated with this whole thing. And now to have the press swarming… It infuriates me. I shouldn't have taken it out on you."

Kate looked at him over the mound of tissues pressed to her face. "Did you mean it when you said this was all my fault?"

"No. If you haven't figured it out yet, I have a temper."

"Did you always?"

He pulled the tissues away and checked her nose. "No. I know you won't believe this, but I was pretty even-keeled when we were married. I'm definitely not the same person I used to be."

Her fingertips grazed his hand when he reached up with a washcloth to wipe the blood from her lip. "Neither am I, Ryan."

His hand stilled, and his eyes locked on hers, eyes that seemed to be seeing a part of her no one else could touch. She felt herself being sucked back under, felt her heart thump rapidly, felt her skin tingle with that crazy need to be touched only by him.

This close, she could easily see why women were drawn to him. On the outside, he was hard and rough, seemingly untouchable. But underneath there was something soft and gentle struggling to break free. More than one woman had probably tried to crack through the icy exterior to free the passionate man underneath. Was it possible?

When he touched her, when she remembered how his mouth had claimed hers and his hands had stroked her body in almost frantic motions, she was almost sure it was possible. But when his eyes changed and he looked at her with that steely gaze he was so famous for, she wasn't so convinced anymore. If there was softness in Ryan Harrison, it was hidden deep within. And she wasn't sure anyone—especially her—would ever be able to reach it.

She broke the connection she knew he felt too, looked away.

He swiped the washcloth over her skin one last time. "I think you're all better now."

She started to move away from him, but he caught her chin and tipped her face up to his, stopping her. "I'm sorry about what I said but not about what happened after. I've been dying to touch you for the past two weeks. This wasn't the best time or place, and that I regret, but not the rest of it."

Determination lurked in his eyes. And behind that, a glint of gentleness, the softness she knew was there.

"Next time," he said, "we won't be interrupted."

"Would that be a foregone conclusion?"

A smirk tugged at his mouth. A really sexy, mesmerizing smirk. God, he was handsome. Too handsome. She was toast if he ever turned the full force of that smile on her. "Absolutely."

She eased off the counter. She had to find control. She wasn't going to let him manipulate her. "I'm not one of your brainless bimbos, Ryan. Contrary to what happened here earlier, that's not my style."

He pulled her close before she could turn away. The fluidity of the movement took her by surprise, and she found her body molded tightly to his, knee to chest, every line and muscle and plane of his body flush against hers. She pressed her hands against his biceps, but it was his lips grazing her temple that stilled her and kept her from pushing back. "I'm not interested in brainless bimbos."

The moment was so tender, and so unlike him, she wasn't sure how to respond. She hesitated, tried to resist the pull. Lost when her heart contracted.

He didn't try to kiss her, didn't make any advances, just held her tight and rubbed his hand down her back like he needed this. Needed the contact, the connection. Needed her.

And, oh, man. That gentle caress did more than his mouth had done earlier in the bedroom.

Her eyes slid shut even as she fought back the desire rebuilding inside. Her skin tingled under his breath. Heat pooled in her belly. Want and need pulsed through her veins until she wasn't sure which was which.

"You want to tell me about this little expedition you're going on with Simone tonight?" he said into her hair.

"Who told you?"

"Mitch."

She pursed her lips as she eased out of his arms, thankful he'd changed the subject and she'd gotten away before she'd done something stupid. Like pushed him to the ground and jumped his bones. "Figures."

"Why didn't you tell me?"

"Ryan, we haven't exactly been on the best speaking terms."

"Well, we are now. Is this really important to you?"

"Don't you want to know what happened?"

"Yeah, of course I do. But not if it's just going to add more complications we don't need."

She sighed. "I have to know. I lost five years of a life I didn't know I had. Someone somewhere knows something."

"Okay," he said after several seconds. "I'll go with you."

"I don't need you holding my hand."

Irritation flashed in his eyes. "This changed my life too. I'm going with you."

He wasn't going to take over. She wouldn't let him. But if he wanted to tag along, she wouldn't stop him at this point. And he was right. He deserved answers as much as she did. She nodded. "Okay."

Relief rippled over his features. Relief that surprised her. Had he thought she wouldn't agree? From one minute to the next, she didn't know how he was going to react. "Now that we have that out of the way, why don't we go meet your parents?"

She glanced to the door. Winced when she realized what awaited her. The press was one thing. Her parents? She pressed a hand against her stomach as it rolled and tossed on a sea of worry. "Right now, I think I'd really rather slit my wrists."

He reached for her hand, brought her wrist to his mouth and kissed her gently, right over her vein. "And scar these perfect wrists? Never."

That wicked kiss brought every nerve ending to life in her body, all over again. And that connection she'd felt before with him flared hot and bright.

"C'mon."

When he tugged on her hand, she faltered. "I...I thought you didn't want to be involved in this?"

"When did I say that?"

"Yesterday, at Mitch's house."

"I think a lot's happened between yesterday and today, wouldn't you agree?"

Emotions flickered in his eyes. Emotions she wasn't sure she was ready for. He confused her. He frustrated her. He infuriated her. And then, in an instant, he dazzled her.

He was a complex puzzle that seemed to have no possible solution, and just when she thought she had him all figured out, he'd go and turn himself into something she totally didn't expect. She didn't know if she'd ever be able to keep up with him.

It scared her. It aggravated her.

And dammit, it electrified her.

With no other choice, she followed him out into the living room and stood face-to-face with her parents.


"This is the dumbest idea ever." Mitch rested his hands on the steering wheel of his Land Rover and surveyed the dimly lit parking lot.

Ryan looked up from the backseat. Early evening had settled over San Mateo. Street lights flickered and popped on. With any luck, Annie was already on the other side of the building by now.

Mitch was right. It was a dumb idea. They should have stayed with Annie's parents and had dinner with the kids. As awkward as it was for Annie, it was safer than what they were doing now.

"All you have to do is drive the get-away car," Simone said from the passenger seat. "Stop complaining." She popped her door. Ryan followed from the backseat. "We'll be back."

"Next time, I get to be the spy," Mitch called to their backs.

"How long do we have?" Ryan asked as they headed for the front doors of the nursing home. A security guard sat just inside. Video cameras monitored the parking lot.

"Visiting hours are over in thirty minutes. They'll boot me out by then. Do you have the ID card Alice swiped this morning?"

He patted his pocked. "Got it."

"I don't want to bail anyone out of jail tonight," she said under her breath.

He shot her a look. "You don't think I'm stupid enough to get caught, do you?"

"I sure the hell hope not, Harrison."

Simone plastered on her lawyer smile as they entered the lobby and approached the front desk. "We're here to see Gillian Rogers. I'm a friend of the family."

A large woman with gray hair was seated behind the reception desk. "Sign in. You've got about twenty-five minutes before visiting hours are up."

Simone signed the log, handed Ryan the pen, and waited.

The receptionist slanted a disapproving glance over them. "I'll need to see ID." She checked her computer and waited while Ryan and Simone fished out their wallets. "Mrs. Rogers is in D wing, room 438." She tapped a pencil against a photocopied map. "Here. Take that hallway, there." She pointed toward a set of double doors.

"Thank you," Simone said.

"Friendly," Ryan muttered as they pushed the doors open.

When they were alone in the hallway, she glanced at her watch. "Don't be late."

"Got it. Have fun."

"Yeah. Fun." Simone frowned. "Gillian has Alzheimer's. She doesn't remember me. This'll be a hoot."

Ryan winked, then ducked into a janitor's closet.

Institutional cleaners assailed his nostrils. He flipped on the pocket flashlight he'd brought with him and scanned the small room. Like Gillian's daughter Alice had told Simone, a janitor's uniform hung on a hook against the wall. He slipped it on, clipped the ID badge with his picture taped over the top to his shirt pocket, and wheeled the cart out into the hallway.

He made his way through the building at a slow pace, whistling as if he didn't have a care in the world. A nurse passed, stopped, and glanced back. "You're new. Where's Jimmy?"

He swiveled and flashed a smile. "Sick. I'm fillin' in."

"There's a spill in 218 that needs to be cleaned up."

"Yes, ma'am. I'll get right on it."

"I need you on it now. Come on." She waggled a finger at him.

Shit. He didn't have time for this right now. But it was either follow or raise suspicion, something they definitely didn't need.

He whipped the cart around. 218? Where the hell was that? Ryan glanced down at the building map he'd laid out below bottles on the top of the cart. Dammit. Opposite side of the building from the records room.

The nurse pushed open a door. "Mr. Anders?"

A muffled grunt was the only response.

Ryan left the cart in the hallway. His nose puckered when he stepped into the room. Mother of God, he had not signed on for this. The old man's bladder had all but exploded right on the floor.

"We'll get this cleaned right up for you, Mr. Anders," the nurse said. She nodded at Ryan to get moving.

Colorful language bubbled through his head, but he made his way back to the janitor's cart and grabbed supplies he hoped would work. Twenty minutes later, he was once again pushing the cart through the long hallways. His skin itched, and he felt the need for a shower to wash off the stench of that room. And he definitely didn't want to get old.

A woman was keying information into a computer when he made his way to the business offices. He lifted his ID badge. "I'm here to empty the waste baskets."

She barely glanced at him. "Fine. Don't be long. I need to lock up."

"Yes, ma'am."

He went around the room, performing the menial task. When he finished in the outer office, he moved to the record room.

The spring-loaded door snapped closed behind him. He quickened his pace to the window and popped it open.

Annie stood from her spot below the window where she'd been hiding. "What the hell took you so long?"

"Old man's bladder exploded on the other side of the building," he whispered.

"What?"

"I'll explain later. We don't have long." He helped her through the window. "There's a secretary out front itching to get home."

She went straight to the file cabinet, jerked the top drawer open and pawed through records. "There's no Alexander."

"Check Harrison."

She closed the top drawer and dropped to the next one.

Ryan emptied the trash. The metal blinds clinked as he ran a broom over them to disguise the sound of the file cabinet squeaking open and closed.

"Nothing," she whispered.

He looked back. "Mathews?"

"Here it is," she whispered. "So much for the records being destroyed in a fire." She pulled the file out, flipped it open, scanned each page.

Her sharp intake of breath brought his attention around. "What?"

"Jake's signature is all over in here." She kept flipping, her face so pale he was tempted to make her sit down. "There's a nurse's name on a lot of these. Janet Kelly."

"Got it." He moved to another cabinet and looked for personnel files. "They're not here."

"Another office?"

"Probably," he said, flipping through drawers.

"What's Midazolam?"

Ryan glanced up. "It's a benzodiazepine."

"What's that?"

"A drug used as a hypnotic sedative."

Her gaze shot to him. "Sedative? Like for a coma?"

"Maybe. If it's combined with a paralytic agent, yeah."

Kate swallowed and glanced back at her chart. "Like Anectine?"

*Oh, shit.* "Yeah."

"What about Tabofren?"

Ryan's hand stopped moving through files. "Say that again."

"Tabofren. It's all over in my chart."

"It's a cancer drug."

Annie looked up sharply. "I didn't have cancer, did I?"

He shook his head, but worry rippled through his chest.

A hand pounded on the door. "Hey, are you done in there? I have to lock up."

"Shit." Annie ducked behind the desk.

Ryan pulled the door open. His adrenaline pumped, but he forced a smile. "Sure thing. Just gotta get new bags." Whistling, he made his way back to the cart, found what he needed, and came back. With a frown, Annie waved him out from her space behind the desk.

He took his time, made sure the window was closed, then eased out of the room.

The secretary checked her watch. "Took you long enough." She flipped off the light and ushered him out of the main office, then locked the door.

"Night," he drawled.

She didn't answer, just headed down the long hallway, the clicking of her heels the only sound echoing in the empty space.

Ryan pushed the cart into the nearest janitor's closet and carefully made his way back to the business office. He knocked, glanced around, and waited. The door opened a crack, and he pushed his way through then locked it behind him.

Annie's green eyes sparkled in the darkness. "You sure know how to show a girl a good time."

"This wasn't my idea. Check that office. I'll take this one." They split up, each searching file cabinets and desk drawers. When Annie whispered from a nearby room, he closed the drawer he'd been searching and followed the sound of her voice.

"I found it," she said. "Janet Kelly was let go almost a year ago. 794 Harbor Drive."

"That's on the waterfront."

"I can't find anything on Jake."

Keys jangled in the outer office.

"Shit." Ryan pushed her toward the window. "Go." She yanked it open and slithered through. Ryan followed and did his best to pull the window closed behind them, then crouched down next to Annie in the bushes.

Light darted through the window, sweeping over the bushes. Ryan held his breath. When a giggle slipped from Annie's lips, he slapped a hand over her mouth.

No sound echoed from inside the room, but the flashlight beam stayed on. After what seemed like an infinite amount of time, the light flipped off. Feet shuffled, a door opened and closed. Then silence stretched out behind them.

"Are you trying to get us caught?" Ryan whispered.

Annie pulled his fingers away from her mouth. "Sorry. I couldn't help myself. I've never seen you move so fast."

"I can see the headlines in tomorrow's paper. *Pharmaceutical CEO arrested for breaking into Backwater Nursing Home.*"

Annie giggled again. "Afraid you'll tarnish your pretty-boy

image?"

"It's already been tarnished. And no. I'm afraid of going to jail and getting a cellmate named Bubba." When she laughed, his heart bumped. "And I don't want our kids left in Mitch's incapable hands. Julia already has a smart mouth."

"And she definitely doesn't get the swearing from you, right?" Her eyes danced, and the dimple in her cheek shot his pulse up.

"Absolutely not.

She grinned. God, he'd missed that smile. The way her whole face lit up, the way it made her green eyes sparkle. The way it sent heat careening to his belly. He ached to kiss her. Ached to touch her. Ached to finish what they'd started earlier.

As soon as they got back and sorted through everything they'd just found, he planned to do exactly that.

He grasped her hand. "Come on, let's get the hell out of here."


Light from the dashboard illuminated Simone's face in the front passenger seat of Mitch's SUV. She and Mitch were arguing about which turn would take them back to the freeway. They sounded like an old married couple.

Kate glanced at Ryan seated next to her in the back. He'd ditched the janitor's uniform in the bushes outside the nursing home before they'd left. At the moment, he was studying her chart intently. Deep worry lines creased his forehead.

That couldn't be good.

"You have the worst sense of direction," Simone grumbled. "No, turn right at the next light."

"We passed a McDonalds on the way in," Mitch said. "I distinctly remember. It's that way." He pointed ahead.

"No, it's not," Simone tossed back. "It's on the next street. Just turn." She reached for the wheel.

"Damn, woman. Let me drive." When she flashed him a look, he frowned, shook his head then made the turn where she'd pointed. The golden arches glowed bright down the street.

"See? Told you. Never argue with a woman about directions. Freeway entrance. There"

"Especially one who's a lawyer," Mitch grumbled. "I've got eyes, sweetheart, and I want points for remembering Mickey D's. Speaking of which, I'm hungry."

"I need to get to the office," Ryan said.

"Why?" Kate asked. The way he kept staring at her chart and his lack of amusement at the show in the front seat set her nerves on edge.

"I need to look something up. Drop me off downtown and I'll grab a cab home."

"Bye-bye double cheeseburger." Mitch sighed and drove past the fast-food restaurant. He pulled onto the freeway headed toward the city.

"Talk to me, Ryan," Kate said. "What's in there that's got your attention?"

He flipped papers in his lap. "It looks like you were in a natural coma for quite some time. After Reed was born, though, you were given coma-inducing drugs. Almost as if you'd come out of it on your own, only someone didn't want you to wake up."

Kate's stomach tightened. "What about the other drug?"

When he didn't answer, she said, "Ryan. Tell me."

His lips thinned. Then he finally said, "Tabofren was an AmCorp drug in stage one clinical trials five years ago."

Simone whipped around in her seat. Mitch glanced in the rearview mirror.

"*What?*" Kate's eyes widened.

"We pulled it because the FDA had some serious issues with side effects."

Kate felt the blood draining from her face. Felt the walls closing in around her.

Ryan's hand brushed hers on the seat. "Don't freak out yet. Let me do some research."

She nodded, though inside she didn't know what to think. What to do for that matter. With shaky fingers, she rubbed the scar along the side of her head. Swallowed back the fear.

It didn't work.

Mitch pulled up outside Ryan's building. "Simone and I'll go grab some take-out and meet you both back here."

"You don't have to," Ryan said, easing out of the car. He grasped Kate's hand and helped her out.

"Don't argue, Ryan." Simone reached through the window and squeezed Kate's fingers. "We'll be right back."

Why did she have such a bad feeling about this? Kate ran a hand over her hair as she walked into the building with Ryan. Tingling fingers of dread coursed over her, much as they had the day she'd knelt on the floor in Jake's office and unlocked the file cabinet that had changed her life.

"Hey, John." Ryan nodded at the security guard seated at the lobby desk.

"Mr. Harrison. You're here late tonight."

"Have a little work I need to do. My brother-in-law and a friend will be by later. Let them up when they come in."

"Sure thing, Mr. Harrison. Looked good on the TV today," he added with a lopsided grin.

"Thanks." Ryan placed a hand at the small of Kate's back and urged her toward the elevators. A hand that was warm and solid and sent tingles all along her lower back where he touched her.

She couldn't deny she felt a connection to him. She just didn't know what to do about it or how to deal with it when everything else was happening at the same time.

Ryan's office was a huge expanse of dark wood and metallic chrome. A wall of windows looked out over the skyline of San Francisco. Lights glinted in the city below, and the Golden Gate Bridge lit up in the distance. A wet bar was positioned across the room; two couches and a few low tables scattered in front of it. Ryan's massive desk sat on the other side of the room, a wall of bookshelves to the right.

Intimidation swept over Kate the moment she stepped into the room. Her scrawny office would fit in one small corner of this colossal space. The press conference flashed in her mind, and she remembered the steely look in his eyes when he'd dealt with the reporters. Ryan Harrison the business mogul was nothing like the tender man who'd held her so carefully after her nosebleed.

"Grab us something to drink, would you?"

Thankful for something to do, Kate wound to the wet bar. Ryan sat in the chair behind his desk and flipped on his computer. His fingers danced over the keys, his eyes intent on whatever he was looking for. His silence told her he wasn't willing to share his concerns just yet.

Kate bit back the urge to hover over him. She busied herself pouring them each a drink, then took the glasses to his desk.

"Is there a bathroom around here?" she asked.

He nodded toward a door. "Through there."

"Thanks."

She spent as much time in the lavish corporate bathroom with its marble counter and huge shower as she could, splashing water over her face, trying to get a handle on her emotions. When she finally worked up the nerves to step back into Ryan's office, she found him still sitting behind his desk. But this time, his head was cradled in his hands, his elbows propped on the surface in front of him. The computer screen blinked with images of Julia as the screensaver.

Tension seeped from his body, rushed across the space separating them and wrapped around Kate's chest, sending her nerves into the out-of-this-world range. Trembling, she eased around his desk to stand next to him. "Ryan?"

Without looking up, he grasped her by the waist and pulled her in front of him. His knees pressed against her inner thighs, sending shivers across her skin. Then he leaned forward and rested his forehead against her abdomen as he drew in deep, ragged breaths.

Something was wrong. Whatever he'd found was so bad he couldn't even look at her. She thought about walking away, just forgetting this whole mess. She could get on a plane and go back to Houston if she wanted, forget about Ryan Harrison and his daughter. That was probably the smartest idea all around.

But even as she thought it, she knew she wouldn't leave. She was connected to him now whether she wanted to be or not. Not just because of Julia and Reed, but because of something else. Something that drew her to him even when she wanted to run. Something she didn't understand but was desperate to see through.

She threaded shaking fingers through his hair, ran her hands down his neck to his shoulders, feeling the knot of stress bunched there. "Ryan, you're scaring me."

He didn't answer. Just pressed warm, firm, solid fingers tighter against her hip bones, as if holding on for dear life.

"Talk to me," she whispered.

His rugged features were laced with heartache when he looked up. And fear spread to panic when she saw the guilt seep into those mesmerizing blue eyes of his.

She drew in a sharp breath.

Without even asking, she knew somehow he was involved in whatever had happened to her.

# CHAPTER THIRTEEN

He stared at her so long with that guilt-ridden look, Kate wanted to shake the words out of him. "Ryan, what?"

"Tabofren showed promise in shrinking certain inoperable tumors. But the FDA put a stop to the clinical trials when major side effects started popping up, questioning its safety."

"You already said that in the car," she reminded him.

"I know. I just couldn't remember what those side effects were."

"Why do I have a feeling I don't want to hear about those side effects?"

He swallowed and glanced at her abdomen. "The drug targeted a signaling pathway that stimulates tumor growth in patients with advance-stage cancers. We were really excited about it after initial animal testing, and so was the FDA. They fast-tracked it into clinical trials."

"And?"

"Minor side effects included skin irritation, rashes, and dry mucous membranes. Nothing out of the ordinary. But the ones that caused the FDA to pull it were more serious. They were generally seen in patients with brain and spinal-cord tumors— severe headaches, changes in mood and personality, and...and memory loss."

*Oh, God.*

Ryan's fingers tightened around her waist, preventing her from easing away. "When patients in the clinical trials started reporting the symptoms, especially the black-out style memory lapses, they were backed off the drug. Most of them didn't suffer any long-lasting effects."

"Ryan, why would I have been given that? I don't understand. You said I didn't have cancer."

"You didn't. I don't...I don't quite know what's going on here, but..."

"But what?" She couldn't seem to keep the panic out of her

voice. When he didn't look up, she cupped her hand around his chin and lifted so he would look at her. "What, Ryan?"

He sat back and scrubbed his hands over his face. "Take a look at the screen and tell me if you recognize that man."

Kate ran her fingers over the keypad of his computer. The screensaver blinked off. Jake's face popped up. "Oh, my God."

"I'll take that as a yes," he said quietly.

"Why do you have Jake's picture?"

"That's Dr. Jacob McKellen. He developed Tabofren. He was heading the clinical studies."

*No.* Kate turned to the screen then backed away. No. Not possible. Words choked in her throat. This wasn't happening.

Ryan pushed out of the chair, grasped her by the shoulders. "Don't. Don't close in on me right now. Stay with me."

"No. You're wrong. There's a different explanation. There has to be."

"Babe—"

"Why? He did this to me on purpose?" How could the man she'd loved, had lived with for over a year, had trusted with her son...how could he intentionally have done something to hurt her?

"We don't know that. This doesn't make sense to me, either, but we'll figure it out." He pulled her into the warmth of his arms before she could back away.

She let him hold her, but she couldn't take her eyes off the screen. Off Jake's face looking back at her. Memories of their life together flashed in front of her eyes—Jake holding Reed at a backyard barbecue, dancing at a hospital fundraiser together, making love with him in their bed. A shudder ran through her, and she tried to wiggle away, but Ryan held her tight.

"You're okay," he said quietly. "I've got you." She struggled but didn't have the energy to fight him when he tightened his hold. Finally, she sank into him while emotions poured through her. How could she have been so wrong? How could she have not seen what Jake was underneath? Had she been blind? Or had she just not wanted to look close enough?

Ryan smoothed a hand over her hair, his lips whispered reassurances in her ear. But his earlier words echoed in her mind.

"You...you said his name was McKellen."

He didn't loosen his grasp. "Yeah. Jacob McKellen. His family's owned and operated McKellen Publishing for years."

Her shoulders slumped. Bile rose in her throat. "He...he said he never wanted me to work, but he didn't object to my freelancing. He knew at some point I'd end up working for McKellen Publishing."

"I thought of that. I don't want you going to work tomorrow."

"Ryan—"

"No, listen to me." He pushed back to look down at her, his fingers gripping her shoulders with intent and compassion. "This is bigger than we thought. Millions of dollars were dumped into Tabofren. People were pissed when it was pulled. Your chart shows it was administered long after the FDA yanked the plug. Someone was testing it, either because they had a buyer, or they were trying to get around the FDA. Either way, your snooping around won't sit well with whoever was behind this."

She didn't like what he was implying. "I thought Jake was behind this."

"I don't think he did this alone. I don't think he could have. People at the nursing home knew. Someone at the publishing house knew."

His words settled in the air between them. A clock ticked on the wall across the room. "Did you know him?" she asked quietly.

His eyes held hers, but she couldn't read his thoughts. "I met him a few times. I didn't know him well."

Her eyes fell closed. They'd met. They'd talked. Her being with Jake wasn't a coincidence.

He tightened his grip on her shoulders. "We'll get to the bottom of this, but I need you to be careful. Your face is going to be all over the papers. People will know you aren't dead."

One more thing to worry about. "I…I hadn't thought of that."

"I want you to see a doctor. Tomorrow."

She swiped at her cheeks. "I'm fine."

"Don't argue with me on this." The tone of his voice told her not to even try. "Tabofren was never tested long-term. We don't know what the long-range effects could be."

"I had a CT scan just before Jake died. It came back normal."

"It was done by the doctor in Houston who disappeared, right?"

"Yes." Her stomach rolled all over again. "You don't think he's involved too, do you?"

"I don't know. But we need to be cautious. We're not taking any chances here."

"Oh, God," she muttered again, sinking back into him. It was getting worse. Every new clue, every bit of information made her question just what she'd gotten herself into. What she'd gotten Reed into. What she'd dragged Ryan and Julia into.

He wrapped his arms around her and rested his cheek against her hair. Warmth, safety, strength cocooned her. "I'm not going to let anything happen to you."

Held tight against him, she wanted to forget everything they'd found, to cling to the lifeline that had become his body, to believe his words. His scent wafted in the air, brought a familiar sense of déjà vu. Closing her eyes, she turned her cheek against his chest and held him right back.

The rhythmic thumping of his heart reminded her she was alive. And in the silence, she could almost imagine what life with him had once been like. What he'd been like before...before losing Annie. Happy. Whole. A man who would move heaven and earth for the woman he loved.

But this wasn't then. Neither of them were the same people they'd once been. And even though she wanted to lean on him and let him be her rock, there was still so much she didn't know. About what had happened to her. About him. About how all of this—him included—was connected.

The truth would set her free. She couldn't let this break her. She wouldn't. She'd already come so far. The only thing she could do now was search for the answers she knew were out there.

And deal with the fallout when it happened.


"This cluster fuck just gets bigger and bigger." Mitch stood at the wet bar in Ryan's office and tugged a hand through his hair.

"Tell me about it." Ryan poured soda into a glass and glanced across the room at Annie and Simone, both of whom were sitting on the floor near the windows, quietly talking. Annie had put on a good face when Simone and Mitch had shown up, but he didn't miss the way her hand trembled whenever she reached for her glass of wine or picked at the Chinese food they'd brought back. "She won't come back to my place tonight, she's too damn stubborn, but I don't want her alone all the way out at that beach house."

"You really think someone would go after her?"

"Thanks to that press conference today, her face has been plastered all over the media. She's been snooping around that nursing home for weeks. Someone saw her and wouldn't let her in.

They know she's looking for answers." He glanced over at her again. "She's been through enough, and I didn't want to worry her, but I didn't tell her everything."

"Why doesn't that statement leave me feeling all tingly inside?"

Ryan turned so the girls couldn't hear him. "Jacob McKellen was pissed when Tabofren was pulled. He'd invested a good chunk of his own money into the R&D. He showed up here and about took my head off when he found out we decided to bag it. Told me he'd find a way to get it approved with or without my help. I brushed him off. Mitch" —he leaned forward— "two weeks later, Annie was gone."

"Oh, shit."

"It gets worse. I heard through the grapevine a few years ago that there were some clinical studies of a drug similar to Tabofren going on in Canada. They don't have a watchdog group like the FDA up there. It's easier to get government approval there, and when a company has the data, it's easy to slip it in under the radar here in the US if you know the system. If a company can prove the drug is safe and works, the FDA will open it up for consideration."

"You think he was testing it on his own?"

Sickness and a good dose of guilt swept through Ryan. "I don't know. But that's my hunch. I think he was using the nursing home as his test facility, then exporting the data to a Canadian company. We need to find the nurse who's listed in Annie's chart—"

"Kate's chart," Mitch cut in.

"Yeah," Ryan said quickly. "Maybe she knows who McKellen was working with on this."

"You two done whispering?" Simone set her wineglass on the bar and popped the cork out of the half-empty bottle of Merlot. One glance told Ryan Annie had stepped out of the room.

"We're just bragging about our sex lives." Mitch winked her way. "I got Ryan beat."

Simone refilled her glass, slanted him a look. "Two middle-aged men talking about their conquests. There's a shocker. Ryan, your company doesn't happen to sell any of those nifty erectile dysfunction drugs, do they?"

"No, sorry. I can set you up with someone who does, though, if you're in need."

Simone shot Mitch a wicked grin. "There's this guy who's been trying to get me to go out with him. But I'm a little worried about his staying ability."

"You're both hilarious," Mitch cut in. "And, sweetheart, anytime you want to go for a test drive, just let me know."

Simone laughed, the sound easing the knot in Ryan's chest, if even for a moment. "I'm pretty sure that'll never happen. But I am glad to see you two are on speaking terms again."

"Ryan can't stay mad at me," Mitch said. "I'm the only friend he's got."

"Yeah, like that's true." Ryan turned his attention toward Simone. "Any chance you can swing staying at Annie's tonight?"

"You mean Kate's?" Her gaze cut to Mitch.

"Yeah. I don't want her out there all by herself."

"I have Shannon. She's with a sitter at home. Kate and Reed could come to our house, I guess."

Annie reemerged from the bathroom, and they all fell silent.

"Quick," she said stepping up to them at the bar, working for a smile that didn't reach her eyes. "Change the subject. She's back in the room."

Mitch draped his arm around Annie's shoulder, the move so casual, so comfortable, Ryan ached to be able to do the same. "So far we've covered sex and drugs. Rock-n-roll's the next topic on the list. Pick a group."

A grin spread across her face. One that tightened Ryan's chest. He'd missed that and so much more these last five years.

"No?" Mitch raised a brow. "Okay, how about sleeping arrangements. Take your pick. You can have Simone, me, or Ryan."

Her gaze darted from face to face, finally settling on Ryan. His heart bumped under those watchful eyes, and heat pooled in his gut. He'd give anything to have her come home with him.

"You guys aren't serious, are you?"

"Afraid so." Mitch sighed. "Consensus is you shouldn't be alone."

"I'm a big girl. I can take care of myself."

"Kate," Simone said. "You've had a stressful day. Just humor us for tonight."

"I have Reed to think about."

"He and Julia are with Mom and Dad," Mitch told her. "They're probably swimming in the hotel pool or raiding the minibar. Trust me, he's fine."

She bit her lip. Tension flowed from her body, and when she reached up to rub her head, Ryan's fingers itched to slide into that mass of curly chestnut hair and rub it for her, to take away some of the stress he'd ultimately caused. If she'd let him, he'd do just about anything to ease that anxiety and worry running through her whole body.

"Okay," she finally said. "You win. I'm too tired to fight about this tonight." She glanced at Simone. "But I know you have Shannon to worry about." Then to Mitch, "And if this is as bad as we think, it's not smart for Simone to be alone, either. It was made common knowledge today that she's my lawyer. That she's the one who recognized me first."

"Kate—" Simone started.

"Humor me, Simone. I'll feel better knowing you're not alone, either. I don't want to be the cause of anyone getting hurt. And we're not all invading your house."

"I'm not—"

"Don't argue with the woman," Mitch said quickly. "She's always been smart."

Simone frowned and crossed her arms over her chest. But in her eyes, Ryan saw she wasn't going to argue. She was as freaked out by all of this as the rest of them. "This doesn't mean I've changed my mind about anything, Mathews."

"Yet," Mitch said with a grin.

Ryan wanted to laugh, but the situation was anything but funny. Then he realized what it all meant. When he looked toward Annie again, she was already eyeing him. His stomach flipped.

"I guess that leaves you and me," she said. "My place or yours?"

Ryan tossed his keys on the entry table and closed the front door behind Annie. She wandered into his living room without a word and stopped in front of the fireplace, where a series of framed photos of their life together still sat on the mantel. Their wedding photo, the day they'd brought Julia home from the hospital, a picture of the two of them on a hiking trip up one of those stupid mountains she'd always been dragging him to.

What did she think when she looked at those pictures? Did she feel anything? His palms grew sweaty. His stomach churned like it was set on the spin cycle of a washing machine.

Guilt slithered in as he watched her look from photo to photo, clamped on tight to his heart. Guilt for not looking for her when he should have. Guilt for what was happening now. Guilt over the fact someone had purposely hurt her five years ago and that it could possibly be because of him.

He raked a hand through his hair, knowing dwelling on that guilt wasn't going to change anything. The only thing that mattered now was keeping her safe. "Are you tired?"

She turned to face him. Moonlight spilled through the picture window, illuminating her features. Those deep green eyes, the high-set cheekbones, that mass of curly hair that fell to her shoulders and which he ached to slide his fingers through. "Exhausted."

Her tired voice was like velvet and sandpaper all wrapped up together. He wanted to hear her say his name in that same sleepy tone like she had so many times before. Wanted to pick her up and take her to his bed. Wanted to wrap her in his arms, slide inside her body, and block out the rest of the world.

But he knew he couldn't. She still wasn't sure of him. He'd been an ass to her when he'd first found out who she was, and now they both knew he was indirectly responsible for her accident. Her wariness was warranted, and he didn't want to push her. As much as he wanted—needed—to touch her, he wanted her to want him back. Even if it was only a fraction of his want for her.

"Come on," he said, gesturing for her to follow. "I'll show you the guest room."

He picked up her bag, the one they'd driven out to Moss Beach to get, and headed up the stairs. Her feet shuffled behind him, her sweet scent of lilacs drifted in the air. He hardened at just the thought of her lying in a bed down the hall from him tonight, so very close. So completely alive.

Cold shower. That's what he needed right now. Maybe two. Or ten.

He pushed the guest-room door open, and when she eased by him, those silky strands of hair brushed his shoulder. Heavy tingling sensations shot straight to his groin.

"This is nice," she said, turning a slow circle as she took in the pale blue walls, the white comforter on the queen-sized bed, the whitewashed furniture a decorator had picked out.

But nice wasn't the word he was thinking of. Dressed in jeans and a fitted T-shirt, she was gorgeous. Curvy at her hips, tight through her legs and ass, and when she turned, the swell of her breasts tempted not only his body but his control. He'd had his hands on those luscious breasts earlier today, wanted his lips there now.

"Ryan?"

He glanced up and noticed her curious expression. "Sorry. Punchy. It's been a long day."

"Yeah, I guess it has."

He set her bag on the bed, moved to open the adjacent door, and flipped on the light. Tried like hell to stop being so aware of every sound and movement she made. Couldn't. "Bathroom's through here."

"Did I live here before?"

The soft-spoken question drew him around. What would it be like not to remember who or what you were? To have to rely on others to fill in the gaps? For the first time since she'd come back into his life, he realized how hard this must be for her.

He checked the urge to reach out to her and instead shoved his hands into the front pockets of his jeans. "No. I bought this house about four years ago."

"Oh."

She ran her hand over the blue-checked blanket folded at the foot of the bed. He wished she'd touch him like that, couldn't help but remember the way heat had sizzled all along his skin when her hands had brushed over him earlier in the day.

"Where did we live before?"

"We had a place in the city. After you…left…I couldn't stand being there by myself."

That was partly true. The real truth was he hadn't been able to step foot in a single room in that house without remembering her being there, smiling at him, making love with him. Being in that house without her had almost killed him.

"Oh," she said again. On a deep breath, she dropped her hand and looked at her feet.

Talking about the past wasn't putting her at ease. And he didn't want her uncomfortable. He went into the bathroom and pulled towels out of the linen closet, then set them on the counter. When he made his way back out into the bedroom, she was already going through her bag.

Her face was drawn, her mascara smudged under her eyes. She looked like she could nod off to sleep at any moment. "I guess I'll just let you get some rest, then."

"Ryan?"

"Yeah?" He stopped at the open door, glanced back.

"I'm sorry."

"For what?"

"For this...for putting you out."

"You're not."

She shook her head. "Yes, I am. I'm sorry about all of this. I shouldn't have come to San Francisco. I didn't stop to think about how this would affect anyone but myself. I've sucked you into this nightmare. I've caused nothing but confusion and heartache for Julia and Reed. And now I've put Simone and Shannon in danger."

"You didn't do anything wrong," he said softly.

"Yeah, I did. I told myself I had to know the truth. Now..." She lifted her arms, dropped them in defeat, and sank down onto the edge of the bed. "Now, I'm not so sure I want to know anymore. Maybe it would just be better if I packed up and left."

A knot twisted inside him. Panic trickled through his chest. He wouldn't survive it if she walked out on him now. Losing her the first time had broken him. A second time would kill him.

He knelt in front of her, knowing if he touched her, he wasn't going to be able to stop. But he needed that connection, needed to show her how much she meant to him. With shaking fingers, he clasped her hand in her lap. "You can't leave now."

Her eyes were full of anguish and remorse. The sadness he saw there tightened his chest to painful levels. He ached to wrap his arms around her and pull her close, to take away the pain for both of them.

"You can't possibly tell me any of this is what you want," she said quietly.

"I don't want this mess, no. But in some insane way, it brought you back to us. I wouldn't change it now for anything. What I want is to see you smile again, to figure out a way to make this easier for all of us. Walking away from me and the kids isn't going to do that. It'll just make things worse."

Her eyes slid shut. "I know."

Hearing the crack in her voice did him in. He could see himself pushing her back on the bed, tugging her clothes off, pressing inside her and driving the worry away. Wanted that so bad he could barely breathe.

Gently, she pulled her hand from his and ran it over her hair. "I'm just tired and not thinking clearly. I need some rest."

He didn't want to break the connection, but she'd already done it, was putting up those barriers again and blocking him out. Why couldn't he read her? Why couldn't he figure out what she was thinking? He'd always been able to do that with her. He didn't want to admit she was different, but she was. So much about her was different from what he remembered.

Reluctantly, he pushed to his feet. "Okay. I guess I'll see you in the morning."

"Thanks."

She smiled when he didn't move. Not a seductive, made-for-him grin, but a forced, uncomfortable curl of her luscious lips that said it was way past time he left.

He pulled the bedroom door closed behind him, then gripped the handle for support. And alone in the empty hall, he closed his eyes and rested his head against the door. Everything he'd ever wanted was inside that room, and he didn't know how to get it. Every move he made was the wrong one. Each step he took seemed to push her further away instead of draw her closer. Was he fooling himself into thinking he could ever win her back?

He sure the hell hoped not. Because he knew for certain he'd never survive losing her again.

# CHAPTER FOURTEEN

Simone sat upright in bed when she heard the crash.

Glass breaking. From somewhere downstairs. Someone was in the house.

She threw back the covers, reached for the baseball bat she kept under her bed, then opened her bedroom door as quietly as she could. Nothing moved in the hall. The only light shone from a nightlight in the bathroom. She padded soundlessly across the hardwood floor, pushed Shannon's door open. Her daughter lay on her belly, arms over her head, dead to the world in deep sleep.

Her pulse pounded hard as she moved for the stairs. Two steps from the bottom, the wood creaked, and she froze. Her heart lurched into her throat. From the direction of the kitchen, she heard the sound of broken glass being scraped across the ground.

She swallowed hard, lifted the bat above her shoulder, and inched her way toward the kitchen. Steve had always talked about getting a gun. She'd told him he was stupid. But right now…now she wished she'd listened. She was five feet two, and even though she could swing a bat with the best of them, against a home invader, her measly DeMarini was nothing. She just hoped she got in one good shot that scared the bastard away before anything bad happened.

"Dammit."

She froze just outside the kitchen door at the sound of the voice. Shit, she needed to call 911. What the hell was she doing trying to handle this alone?

She took a step back just as the kitchen door pushed open. Without thinking, she lowered the bat and swung.

A muffled oof echoed to her ears, followed by the sound of a body hitting the floor. Hard. Adrenaline surging, she rushed into the kitchen, lifted the bat again, ready to strike out. Mitch held up a hand to block her.

"Dammit, don't hit me with that thing again!"

"Mitch?"

"Who the hell did you think it was?" He gripped his stomach as he lay on the floor, his upper body twisted in on an odd angle against the island cabinets. "The tooth fairy? Dammit, woman, I think you cracked a rib."

She let go of the bat. *Oh, shit. Mitch.* Wood clattered against the floor. Stepping over to him, she dropped to her knees and lifted his face to hers. "What are you doing in my kitchen?"

"I was hungry. Chinese food always leaves me hungry in the middle of the night."

The Chinese takeout. Ryan's office. Kate asking Mitch to stay with her and Shannon tonight because she was worried about them. She'd been so freaked out when she'd awoken, she'd forgotten everything else.

"Oh, my God. I'm sorry," she said, helping him sit up. "How bad is it?"

"Bad enough. But my ego's bruised more than my body. I just got my ass handed to me by a girl."

He was cracking jokes. He couldn't be hurt that bad. A little of her anxiety eased. "I heard glass shatter. I thought someone was breaking in."

In the dim light she watched a nervous expression creep over his face. "Yeah, that was me. I dropped a pitcher of lemonade trying to get to a beer in the back of your fridge."

"You—" She eased back onto her heels and laughed.

"Now you're laughing at me? Great. My manhood is shot."

"It's not you," she said between giggles. "It's this. All of it. This entire situation is completely insane."

"Tell me about it. And what the hell are you doing coming down here when you hear a suspicious noise anyway? We need to have a chat about you not being the too-stupid-to-live horror-movie chick."

She shot him a look. "While we're at it, we'll discuss your caveman tendencies."

He rubbed his ribs. "Damn, you hit hard."

"Here, let me look at it."

He pushed her hands away when she reached for the hem of his shirt. "What are you, a doctor now too? No way."

"I'm not gonna hurt you."

"You already did that." He shifted out of her reach.

"You're being a total baby. Just let me have a look."

He deflected her touch once more.

"Mitch."

"Simone," he tossed back, staring at her.

There was just enough light coming from the pantry that she could see the intensity in his eyes. "Why won't you let me touch you?"

"Because you said it wasn't a good idea. These are your rules, not mine, sweetheart."

"I don't—"

"Understand? Yeah. I get that. So let me spell it out for you." He dragged a hand through his hair. "If you touch me, I'm gonna touch you back, how about that?"

"Oh." Her skin grew hot. Her hands stilled on her knees. The temperature in the room seemed to jump ten degrees as they stared at each other. Sparks of awareness arced between them.

What was it about him that called to her? It was more than his good looks. More than his silly sense of humor. It was something else. Something she wasn't ready for.

Long seconds later, he broke the eye contact, then grunted as he pushed himself up from the floor. All long legs and sculpted muscle. "Yeah, you know, I'm just gonna clean up the mess I made."

She rose, reached out to him. "Mitch—"

He captured her wrist so fast, she didn't expect it. Heat gathered beneath his fingers, and when he turned to face her, she saw the hunger in his eyes. A hunger that radiated all through her body and lit up her skin like an electrical current had been turned on.

"Okay, here's the deal, Counselor. I'm crazy about you. In a way I've never been crazy about anyone else. Ever. I realize you're representing my sister. I realize I'm a conflict of interest to you. But if you touch me again, I'm gonna forget all about your irritating ethics and take you right here against the cabinets. No ED drugs needed. And trust me when I say, you will enjoy it. We both will."

The air choked in her throat. Desire coursed through her body. A desire she hadn't felt in years. The carefully constructed life she'd created since Steve's death hovered as if on a precipice.

"Mitch..."

A muscle twitched in his jaw. "Yeah?"

"Kiss me before I have a chance to say no."

His mouth was on hers before she even heard him move.

* * *

Water beaded on Kate's skin. Bubbles slid down to pool at her feet. She closed her eyes and drew in the fresh, clean, soapy scent, the same one that lingered close to Ryan's skin, the one she'd smelled when he'd pressed that muscular body of his against hers last night.

She turned her face under the hot spray in his guest bathroom. After a sleepless night, she was more exhausted than she'd been yesterday. Had he slept in that guest bed recently? She'd been sure she could smell him on her pillow, all but feel him on the sheets.

The muscles in her stomach bunched as she ran the bar of soap down her skin, over her abdomen, imagining his hands doing the same…his lips. A sharp ache pulsed between her thighs. Heat shot straight to her center.

He'd said he wanted her, that he'd been dying to touch her. But that was before they'd discovered her records at the nursing home, before he'd realized what this was all about. Since then, he'd been gentle and caring but somewhat withdrawn. Almost as if he were afraid to get too close.

Her fingers skimmed her breasts, and shards of desire ricocheted through her body. For some crazy reason, she didn't want him to back off. What she wanted was his hands on her like they'd been before, that sensuous mouth devouring hers, to feel him deep inside her body. That burning ache grew to fiery levels as she imagined him in the shower with her, imagined tracing the hard lines of his body with her fingers. With her tongue.

He was just down the hall. All she had to do was go to him, to ask for his touch. Shaking with need, she braced both hands on the tiled wall of the shower and drew in gulps of air. Technically, he was her husband after all, wasn't he? That wouldn't be asking too much.

Common sense seeped in, dampening the fire. Yes, he was her husband, but she didn't know him. Not in any way that mattered. All she knew was she was wildly attracted to a man she barely knew. That they had some incredible connection she couldn't comprehend. That she wanted him with a passion she hadn't experienced before.

Would wild sex solve any of her problems? Would it make her remember a life that seemed foreign to her? Would it help her understand what had happened? Would it make him see her as Kate?

That was the most important question.

She hadn't missed the fact he had yet to call her that, that he avoided saying her name altogether. She knew when he looked at her, he saw Annie. He didn't see the woman she was now. Would sex change that?

Probably not. But, oh, it would be good. And it would crush the pulsing ache she felt now and whenever he was close.

The sharp knock at the bathroom door brought her head up. She flipped off the water and ran unsteady hands over her hair, squeezing out the moisture to run down her body. "Um...just a minute."

"Coffee's done," Ryan said through the closed door. "Breakfast is almost ready."

He was just on the other side of the door, in her bedroom. She had but to flip the lock and he could be here with her, right now. Had he read her mind?

Shaking, she stepped out of the shower and grabbed a plush white towel from the rack, then wrapped it around her body. Her breasts tingled. Warmth pooled in her abdomen. On a deep breath, she forced herself to relax. "Okay. I'll, um, be right down."

"Do you need anything?"

*Yes. You. Now.*

She swallowed the words before they could slip out of her mouth. "Um, no. I'm fine."

"Okay. Don't take too long."

When his footfalls fell silent, she dropped to sit on the closed toilet lid. A smart woman would recognize she was in over her head and get the hell out of his house. But of course, she wasn't going to do that. She was going to stay here and suffer until she worked through these insane desires.

Or until she jumped his bones. Either way, she was screwed.

She put the thought out of her mind, slipped on jeans and a T-shirt. Then she brushed on mascara in the hope it would hide that tired look in her eyes, and slicked on some pale lipstick. Glancing at her reflection, she couldn't do anything but frown. Her curly hair was a mass of wetness, but she didn't want to take the time to dry it. She needed coffee and a good dose of reality more than a dry head.

She made her way into the kitchen and found Ryan standing at the stove with his back to her. That fire built again, heat careening through her veins as she watched him. He was barefoot, wearing loose-fitting, faded jeans and a light blue T-shirt stretched seductively across wide, toned shoulders. His blond hair was still damp at the edges from his shower, and her fingers itched to tangle in it like they had yesterday.

Oh, man. If she didn't get in control of this wild need, she was in for big trouble.

Clearing her throat, she stepped into the room. "Smells good. I didn't know you cooked."

Ryan turned at the sound of her voice, and heat arced between them. A heat she saw from the way his eyes darkened, he felt too.

He looked away quickly, but not before her breasts tingled all over again.

"Coffee's over there." He gestured with the spatula in his hand.

She poured a steamy cup of coffee, drew in a deep whiff of the enticing brew. Prayed it would settle this impossible hunger inside her. But something told her this hunger would only be sated one way.

She turned, leaned back against the counter, and eyed him over her mug. God, he was sexy. Not for the first time, she was awed by the fact she'd been able to snag a man like Ryan Harrison. Those shoulders, the tapered waist, that firm butt… She couldn't take her eyes off him. She'd felt that body pressed up against her yesterday. Had tasted that mouth with her own. If they hadn't been interrupted, she'd have known what every inch of him felt and looked like.

Fire flared in her veins. Shot straight to her sex.

She was losing it. She needed to remember what was important. Finding answers. Not wild, erotic, X-rated sex with the man in front of her.

She cleared her throat. Sipped her coffee again. "This is wonderful."

He flipped off the burner, turned, and crossed to her. She looked up with surprise and confusion as he plucked the mug out of her hand. Something dark lingered in his eyes. Something dangerous and, oh, yes…something *hot*.

He slid a hand around the nape of her neck, then pulled her to him and covered her mouth with his own.

Her legs nearly went out from under her. She dug her fingers into his shirt and held on for dear life, opening her mouth to his, drawing his tongue inside, sliding hers over and around his as she returned the kiss with everything she had in her.

*Yes, yes, oh, finally, yes.*

He tasted like mint and coffee, smelled like the soap she'd run all over her body, and felt like pure heaven. Her hands streaked up into his hair and fisted, her mouth turned wild and greedy against his. Her blood pumped hot as his hands slid down to her waist, drawing her even closer to his body. When his hips pressed into hers, she felt his erection, already hard and hot and so very eager for her.

"I couldn't sleep last night," he murmured against her lips, tipping her head with one hand to kiss her deeper, using the other to draw her shirt up so he could palm her breast. He squeezed just hard enough to make her gasp. But it didn't hurt. It felt good. So good. "All I could think about was you in that bed, naked. I was hard the entire night."

"You were?" she managed. The news thrilled her. Exhilarated her. Made her wet with anticipation. She kissed him harder.

"Yes," he groaned, kissing her again and again. He let go of her neck, used both hands to push her shirt up over her breasts, then pulled back and looked down at her puckered nipples. And when he groaned all over again, her sex contracted.

"You're so beautiful," he whispered. Warmth unfurled in her belly as he palmed one breast, as he lowered his head and laved his tongue across her nipple.

Pleasure arced to her pelvis. She dropped her head, threaded her fingers in his hair, leaned back against the cabinets and moaned long and low as he licked her again and again, as he flicked her nipple with his tongue, as he drew her deep into his mouth and finally suckled.

If he touched her between the legs, she knew she'd come. Every nerve ending in her body was alive and on fire. She pressed her hips against his, felt his cock swell even bigger behind his jeans.

"Ryan," she managed as he moved to her other breast. Her elbow knocked into a bowl. She heard something crash at her feet. Could only think about one thing. "I need you."

His head came up. His hair was messed from her fingers, and those achingly familiar eyes of his flashed with the same hunger devouring her.

He pulled her away from the counter, turned her for the back stairs, moved his hands to her hips, and pushed her backwards. "Come to bed with me."

"Yes. Yes," she groaned, slanting her mouth over his and wrapping her arms around his neck.

His body pressed into hers. His arms slid around her waist. He lifted her feet off the floor. He was close, but not close enough. She tangled her tongue with his as she tried to wrap her body around his.

The front door opened, and voices echoed down the hallway. Kate stilled in Ryan's arms. He froze near the bottom of the stairs. Julia's laughter echoed from the front of the house.

Ryan tightened his arms around her waist and dropped his head to her shoulder. A strangled groan resonated from his chest, one that vibrated through her whole body. Though she tried to stop it, a chuckle bubbled inside her.

"This isn't funny," he mumbled as he lowered her feet to the floor.

"I know. I'm sorry." Her back hit the stairwell wall.

"I think your parents have a hard-on radar. Anytime I get turned on, they show up."

Her chuckle turned to a full-blown laugh.

"That's not funny, either," he said into her shoulder.

"Imagine how much worse it would be if we were already upstairs."

"I can lock the door upstairs." He eased back and looked down at her. But he wasn't mad or upset or frustrated like the last time they'd been interrupted. Laughter glinted in his eyes. Laughter that made her chest constrict. "What was I thinking? I should have locked the front door."

She laughed again, brushed her fingers through the silky hair at his nape. Was this the same man who'd ranted and raged at her only a few days ago? The one who'd looked at her like she was destroying his world? She couldn't believe the changes in him. She'd done that, she realized. It was because of her the lines around his eyes looked softer now. Because of her, he looked…almost happy.

The realization sent warning signals running through her mind. But before she could overanalyze them, Reed burst into the kitchen. "Mama!"

She eased quickly out of Ryan's arms, dropped to her knees, and gathered her son in a bear hug.

Ryan moved behind the counter to hide, she knew, what was still a rather large erection. She'd done that too, she thought with a wicked flare of heat in her belly. She glanced over Reed's head and saw Ryan was watching them. And that heart that had only just started to warm to him took one long, hard tumble when she recognized the emotion flooding his mesmerizing blue eyes.

Love. For a son he hadn't known. For a wife that wasn't her.

Her stomach pitched. And fear brewed inside at the realization that the fire between them was only physical. She'd never be the woman he remembered. With how fast she was falling for him, she didn't think she could take it when he realized that for himself.

Julia emerged from the hall, her face full of smiles. When she saw Kate in the kitchen her expression dropped.

Tension seeped into the room, a tension Kate didn't know how to break. No matter what happened between her and Ryan, she had to be here for her daughter.

Kate slowly pushed to her feet and lifted Reed to sit on her hip. "Good morning, Julia."

"What is *she* doing here?" Julia asked, glaring at Ryan.

"She," Ryan said firmly, "is about to have breakfast. And so are you. Go wash up."

Julia's eyes narrowed, and she glanced from her dad to Kate. "I'm not hungry."

Kate knew what the girl was thinking, and she wasn't far off base. One look and it was obvious what had been going on. Kate's hair was likely disheveled, her lipstick smeared. Julia was a smart kid. She'd obviously seen her father with other women before. Unease and guilt and fear tumbled together in Kate's chest all over again to make drawing air downright painful.

"I don't really care if you're hungry or not, missy," Ryan snapped. "We're about to eat, so go wash up."

Kate looked to him, saw the anger in his eyes. And felt the need to defend Julia. But before she could, tears filled the girl's eyes, and she darted for the stairs.

"Ryan," Kate said in the quiet that remained. "Don't be mad at her."

"I won't put up with her treating you like—"

"Hi, dear." Kate's mother rounded the corner and shot her a beaming smile, oblivious to the tension in the kitchen. Kate's father followed closely on her heels. "We didn't expect to see you so early."

Oh, crap. Her parents. Panic swamped Kate, and she tried to smooth her unruly hair with the arm not holding Reed. "Well, uh…"

She looked to Ryan for help, but he only tipped his head and grinned, as if to say, *busted*.

Some help he was. Kate scowled his way, then looked back at her mother. Dammit, what was she going to say?

"We have some errands to run this morning," Ryan said to her parents, rescuing her when she'd thought he'd let her flail in the wind alone. "Any chance you two can watch the kids for us today?"

Roger settled onto a stool at the bar. He reached for a grape from the bowl. "Sure thing. Giants are playing this afternoon. Kids'd love it. You two want to go?"

"I don't think we're going to have time," Ryan said, "but thanks."

A door slammed upstairs before Kate could wonder too much about what he had planned. She watched as Ryan's eyes shot to the ceiling and frustration settled over his handsome features.

The guilt Kate had gotten so used to over the last few days ramped up a notch. "I should go talk to her."

"Let me." He reached out and squeezed her arm. Warmth circled from that spot and spread straight to her heart.

"Come on, Reed," Kathy said, reaching for Kate's son as Ryan disappeared up the back stairs. "Let's help your mom finish breakfast. My goodness, what happened to these eggs?"

One glance over confirmed Kate's worst fear. The bowl she'd hit with her elbow lay upside down amidst a giant, goopy mess of shattered raw eggs.

She closed her eyes. Wished like hell she could just disappear into the background. Knew she couldn't. Not only was her life a mess, but her daughter hated her, her parents had all but just walked in on her having sex with Ryan, and worst of all, she was pretty sure she was falling hard for the man.

A tumble, she feared, that would no doubt lead to nothing but heartbreak down the line, for all of them.

Ryan rubbed a hand over his chest as he made his way up the stairs. Hearing Annie say she needed him had sucked the air out of his lungs. But seeing her holding his son and the love that radiated between the two had nearly brought him to his knees.

He wanted his family back. He wanted the happiness they'd all missed out on. But mostly he just wanted her in his life permanently. Wanted to see her smile every morning, wanted to cuddle with her and Reed and Julia, wanted her looking up at him with those big green eyes heavy with desire and focused solely on him just as they'd been in the kitchen. And he wanted her telling him again and again that she needed him. That she wanted him. That she loved him in the same way he loved her. He didn't care that she couldn't remember what they'd once had. What was happening now between them…it was hotter than anything they'd ever had before.

He stopped outside Julia's room, gathered himself. When he knew he wasn't going to embarrass himself, he knocked gently on her door.

She didn't answer, but he knew she was in there. He turned the knob and pushed the door open with his shoulder.

She was sitting on the window seat, leaning back against the wall, staring out at the trees in the backyard. Her arms were crossed, her brow furrowed in anger, her eyes so full of pain and anguish, for a moment he didn't know what to say or do. She'd been his rock after Annie's death. She'd been the only thing keeping him going. He ached with the knowledge that while he felt like he'd been given a second chance, she was suffering.

He eased down next to her. "Do you want to talk about it, or do you just want to stay mad?"

"I want to stay mad."

"Well, I want to talk about it."

She stared out the window. "I don't like her."

"You haven't given her a chance yet."

"I don't have to give her a chance. I already know I don't like her."

Ryan massaged his forehead. "Julia, I don't know what to do to make this easier for you. You have to try. I know this isn't easy, but you have to at least try. The rest of us are giving it a shot."

Her eyes darted to his. Eyes that were hard emerald gems, just like her mother's, glittering with tears. "I don't want to give it a shot. I don't want to try to get to know her. I don't want to be around her. And I don't know why you do. She's not the same. Why can't you see that?"

"She is the same, deep down. You have to give her a chance to show you."

"She's fooling you, can't you see it? She's just going to mess everything up." Julia jumped to her feet. "She doesn't love you, she doesn't love us, and when she figures that out, she's going to leave again!"

"No, she won't," he said softly, hating that she had to deal with this.

"Yes, she will! And this time, it'll be her choice. It won't be an accident." Tears streamed down her little face. She wiped at her cheek. "I don't want to have that happen again. I don't want it to happen to us again!"

"Oh, baby." He pulled her close and wrapped his arms around her even though she struggled. "That's not going to happen, I promise."

But how could he be sure? Annie had all but told him last night she wanted to leave, to forget the whole mess. He couldn't make her stay, not if she didn't want to. But he wouldn't let her go without a fight, either. Not after this morning.

When she stopped struggling, he eased back, swiped tears from her cheeks. "I love you, Julia. I'm not going to let you get hurt again. I promise."

Her arms slid around his neck, and she rested her head against his shoulder. "Why do you have to date her? Why can't you just be friends?"

"Because I love her, baby," he said softly into her hair. "Because I have for a long time, since way before you were born. That doesn't stop just because someone says it should. It doesn't stop because time goes by. It's always there."

"But you don't love her. You love Mom."

He leaned back to look at her. She was so much like her mother. The same eyes, the same chin. The same silly dent in her cheek. That same stubborn nature. With gentle fingers he brushed back a lock of her hair. "She is Mom, baby."

She pulled him back, hiding her face in his chest.

"Please, Julia." Tears stung the backs of his eyes. "Please try, for me. I need you to at least make an effort. This friction is killing me."

She sniffled and wiped her eyes, clinging to him as if he were her last lifeline. She was silent for so long, he didn't know what to say or do. They had to get through this. They had to.

"Okay," she finally said. "I'll try, but not for her. Only for you."

It wasn't the answer he longed to hear, but it was a start. And it was more than he'd had yesterday.

When he moved back, he wiped her tear-streaked cheeks again. She was his everything, but even for her he couldn't stop loving the only woman he'd ever wanted.

"Thank you, Julia." He smoothed her hair back from her face.

"Are we okay here?"

"Yeah, I guess so."

She was lying. He could see it in her eyes. But he wanted to believe her words, needed to in order to stay sane. "Good."

He rose and grasped her hand. "Come on. I'm starving. We need to get downstairs before Grandpa eats everything. You know how he likes eggs and pancakes."

Julia followed him out the door, and as he headed toward the laughter coming from the kitchen, for the first time in months—years—Ryan felt that ice in his chest begin to thaw. For the first time in forever, he had hope.

Ominous gray clouds threatening rain hovered over the city. A thin fog settled on the ground, and a gentle breeze rustled leaves in the trees. If the weather was any indication of what lay ahead, Kate wasn't sure she wanted to keep searching.

They'd gotten a later start than she'd hoped for. After retrieving her old laptop and purse from the attic where he'd stored it after her accident, Ryan had left for an hour to deal with a situation at work. Seeing her old things did nothing for Kate's memory, but she hadn't expected much. Still, it was weird to look at something that had once been hers. And to feel nothing.

Shaking off the melancholy that brought, she arranged for some time off from the journal at Ryan's insistence. Tom's secretary hadn't sounded happy about passing on her request, but Kate wasn't up for arguing with Ryan over this one. At least not until she found out who at the publishing house had been involved with her disappearance.

She checked addresses as Ryan drove along the waterfront. The car bounced over a speed bump along Harbor Drive, and she shifted in the leather seat. Ryan's new Jag stuck out like a sore thumb down here, black and shiny, so unlike the rusted pickups and worn compacts parked in most driveways along this dilapidated stretch of road.

Glancing sideways at him in the fancy car, she was reminded of his success. There were moments she forgot he was practically a celebrity, forgot about his wealth and prestige. When they were alone together, he was just like any other guy. He didn't live like a man who made millions, didn't act like he could buy and sell you at the drop of a hat. But then there were moments she'd see a look in his eye or hear him on the phone with a business associate, and she'd remember how powerful he really was.

Which was the real Ryan Harrison? Cold and businesslike as he'd been when they'd first met, or warm and compassionate like he'd been with her the past few days?

She couldn't deny the sexual charge she felt whenever he was close, or the unexplainable tug she felt towards him in her soul, but doubt lingered doubt her judgment skills. Hadn't she learned that the hard way with Jake?

Her conversation with Ryan the night before ran through her mind. He'd known Jake. They'd worked together. Regardless of what he'd told her, she had a sinking suspicion he wasn't being totally honest.

"I think that's it." Ryan's voice cut through her reverie.

"It's a houseboat."

Ryan pulled the car to the curb and shifted into park. "Looks like nobody's home."

"Just our luck," she said with a frown.

He opened the car door. "Come on. Let's go take a look."

The dock rocked gently under her feet. Kate's fingers dug into her palm as she walked, and she bit back the desire to run back to dry land.

"What's wrong?" Ryan asked.

"I'm not wild about boats."

"Since when?" He stepped around a bucket left on the dock.

"Since forever."

"Never bothered you before. You used to spend hours on our boat."

She stopped at the front door of the houseboat. "You have a boat?"

"Had. I sold it a few years back."

Strange. She couldn't imagine ever wanting to be on a seasickness machine. Just one more thing to prove she wasn't the woman he remembered.

She lifted a hand and knocked. When no one answered, she knocked again.

Ryan turned and surveyed the area. "Stay here. I'll be right back."

"Where are you going?"

"Just checking something out."

Fabulous. She hated being kept in the dark. Hated even more

that she was standing on a boat, of all things. She looked over the side at the murky green water below and felt her stomach tumble. Why anyone would want to live on a boat was beyond her.

The front door popped open, and Ryan's face appeared behind the screen.

Her eyes widened. "What are you doing?"

"Come on." He drew her into the house. "Back door was unlocked."

"Ryan, this is breaking and entering," she said when the door closed behind her.

"You didn't have a problem with it last night."

"That was different. It was for a reason. This just feels like…like we're invading someone's privacy."

He chuckled and walked through the small living area. "Don't grow a conscience on me right now. Look around. See if anything stands out. I'll check the upper level."

He disappeared up the small flight of stairs. Frowning, Kate took in the orange-and-brown afghan tossed over the back of a worn leather Barcalounger with holes in the armrests. Gossip magazines lay scattered over a scarred, oak coffee table. An empty coffee mug sat on an end table.

She surveyed the adjoining kitchen. Papers littered the Formica kitchen table. A half-eaten bagel sat on a paper plate in the kitchen.

Moving around the counter, she ran her fingers against the coffeepot. Still warm. The light blinked red, indicating the machine was still on. Either Janet Kelly had left in a hurry, or she wasn't too worried about burning down her humble abode.

Kate flipped through the papers on the table. Bills, receipts, a fashion magazine. The woman had a penchant for shopping. Kate continued searching, hoping to find anything that might link Janet Kelly to the nightmare that had become her life.

Nothing stood out. She scanned the room again. On the opposite side of the kitchen lay a newspaper. Sighing, she moved to it and flipped it face up.

Then drew in a breath.

The front page boasted a photo of her and Ryan at the press conference yesterday. The photographer had captured a moment when she'd been answering a question, and Ryan had glanced her direction. He'd either been surprised by something she'd said, or moved. There was a gentle expression across his face. One at major odds with the way he'd looked at her earlier that day. But what caused Kate to stare wasn't merely the picture but the red circle that had been drawn in marker around her face.

The squeak of floorboards above drew her attention. Grabbing the paper, she made her way up the stairs.

The second floor consisted of one large bedroom divided into a sleeping area and an office. Along one wall sat a desk and computer. Papers littered the surface. A lamp hung down from above.

Ryan looked up from the stack of papers he was flipping when she came into the room. "Janet Kelly left in a hurry."

"Yeah, I got that impression." A sense of dread slithered beneath her skin. "Coffeepot's still warm downstairs."

"Find anything?"

"Just this." She tossed the paper on the desk in front of him.

He stared at it. She couldn't read his expression.

"What about you?" she asked, shaking off the foreboding sense of fear coursing through her.

"Not a lot." He lifted a torn sheet of notebook paper and handed it to her. "You recognize any names on there?"

"My name's on here."

"I know."

There were roughly fifteen names on the sheet, over half of which were crossed out in red. Hers was circled at the bottom.

"What is this?" she asked quietly.

"I don't know. But I think we need to start checking out the other names on that list, then find Janet Kelly and figure out what the hell's going on."

# CHAPTER FIFTEEN

She did *not* want to be here.

Being shoved into a tiny tube while strapped to a table wasn't Kate's idea of fun. She ground her teeth and took calming breaths. She'd much rather be out making phone calls with Ryan than having the CT scan he'd insisted on this afternoon.

The test was taking entirely too long. Didn't they realize she was claustrophobic?

The machine buzzed and whirred, and the table retracted from the tube.

*Thank God.*

Ryan was waiting for her in the reception area when she reemerged from the dressing room. His head was down, his fingers rubbing his temples. Tension surrounded him. She swallowed the lump in her throat as she walked across the room. He hadn't looked that worried before she'd gone in.

"Ryan?"

When he glanced up, those worry lines faded from his handsome face. A forced smile curved his mouth, one that didn't reach his eyes. "Done?"

"Yeah. Dr. Murphy said to come back in an hour."

He rose. "Let's get something to eat while we wait." With a hand at the small of her back, he urged her toward the elevator.

Kate settled into the dimly lit booth in the pub a block from the hospital. After their orders were taken, she said, "What did you find out?"

He draped an arm over the back of the booth and tapped a straw against the wooden table. "Nothing."

He was lying. She could feel it. "Come on, Ryan. Don't hold out on me."

"How do you feel about a vacation? We take the kids and go off somewhere for a while, use the time to let Reed and Julia get to know each other. Beach or mountains, your pick."

"Mitch told me you never take vacations, Mr. Harrison. You're starting to worry me. What's going on?"

As he glanced around the bar as if to see who was listening, her gaze followed. A bartender worked the long, mahogany bar. Two patrons sat on barstools at its sleek surface. A few tables throughout the space were occupied by tourists.

She looked back at him. "Ryan, what aren't you telling me?"

He finally fished out the torn slip of paper from his pocket they'd taken from Janet Kelly's house earlier that morning and passed it to her. "Each of the people crossed out are dead."

"*What?*"

He looked pained when he pointed at the names on the list. "Heart attack, car accident, drowning. One even died of a drug overdose just a few days ago. No indication of foul play in any of the incidents."

Four names were still uncrossed, including hers. "What about the others?"

"The top two I couldn't find, or there was no answer. The last one before yours, Kari Adams—it's a common enough name. I didn't have time to go through the phonebook for her."

Kate's brow creased. Why was that name so familiar?

Their food was served, and she set the paper on the table next to her beer, though the last thing she felt like doing was eating.

Ryan squeezed her hand. The casual connection sent a tingle of awareness over her skin. But when she looked up, she saw the worry in his eyes. "It doesn't mean anything," he said gently. "It could just be a coincidence."

"You don't believe that. I can see it on your face. You think those people may have been at the nursing home too, don't you?"

He sat back, trying to look shocked, not doing a very good job of it. "Where'd you get that idea?"

"I'm not a moron. I know pharmaceuticals are a billion-dollar industry. Do you think Jake was doing his own research? Testing it himself? Hoping to push it through for FDA approval?"

"It's a theory."

She glanced down at the paper again. "And you think these people were test subjects. That Janet Kelly knew about them, knew about what was happening."

"I don't know. Maybe. It doesn't explain why they're dead now, though."

"It does if someone's trying to cover up the evidence. What he was doing was illegal, right?"

He blew out a breath. "Yeah."

"And until I showed up here, no one really knew anything about this."

"I didn't say that."

Her gaze locked with his. "But you're thinking it."

"I think I'm hungry. And it's been a long day. And you need to eat so we can get back over to the hospital and find out about your test."

She eyed her plate. Why had she ever thought finding the answers would make a difference? Now all she wanted to do was turn back the clock, forget about what had already happened.

Ryan's hand closed over hers again. "Babe, don't," he said softly. "Let's just take this one step at a time, okay?"

With a nod she picked up a french fry and swallowed back the fear as she tried to eat.


Kate crossed her arms over her chest and stared out at the buildings from Dr. Murphy's office. Afternoon sunlight glinted off wood and stone. Ryan sat in a chair near the doctor's oak desk, waiting. She could all but feel the stress and worry seeping from him, recognized it in her too. Patience had never been her strongest attribute, and it seemed like the past few days, waiting was all she'd done.

Ryan stood when the doctor entered and shook his hand. Kate joined him at the desk.

"Well," Dr. Murphy said. "Let me start by saying we got all the images we needed." He pulled up her brain scan on the computer and swiveled the screen so they could see.

He tapped the screen. "This is the area we're most concerned with. It appears the injury happened to this section of the brain, where memory and personality are developed. My guess is a hematoma of some sort, judging by the craniotomy incision along your scalp, Kate."

"Not a tumor?" Ryan asked.

"No. No indication of one. There's definite damage to the skull, which indicates an accident or trauma of some kind."

That didn't make sense. Kate rubbed her scar. Why would she have been given a cancer drug if she'd never had cancer in the first place?

"The memory loss is a tough one," Dr. Murphy went on. "This

portion of the brain deals with memory, so if she suffered a major impact, it's possible that might be responsible for her amnesia now. However, most retrograde amnesiacs remember something, however trivial, from their childhood. Amnesia tends to be concentrated around the time of accident, sometimes erasing whole years of memories, but rarely an entire lifetime. Kate's case is pretty unique."

"What about the drug?" Ryan asked. He and Dr. Murphy had discussed her situation earlier, and Ryan had given him a copy of the chart they'd found at the nursing home.

"Well, as you know, I can't speak about that until we know more. Tabofren was never studied in a clinical setting in the U.S. I do remember reading something about a similar drug a while back in a medical journal—some study going on up in Canada—but I can't remember the specifics. In any case, it's possible if it was being administered while she was in a coma, it might have amplified her memory loss from the accident."

Dr. Murphy flipped through her chart. "It looks like you weren't given Tabofren for at least six months after the accident."

"I was pregnant."

"At least someone had the good sense not to give it to you during a pregnancy," the doctor said. "There's no telling what an experimental drug like that would have done to a fetus. Your child doesn't show any symptoms?"

"No."

"I'd like to have Reed tested, just to be safe," Ryan cut in, glancing at Kate. When she nodded, he looked back at the doctor. "What are the chances she'll get her memory back?"

"At this point? I wouldn't count on it. It's been almost two years, and she hasn't remembered anything yet. You've been back in San Francisco, what, a month, Kate?"

"Yes, about."

"And in that time, any memories?"

There were feelings. Mostly déjà vu feelings, but those weren't memories. She shook her head.

Dr. Murphy nodded. "Sometimes memories are triggered by familiar faces and locations. If that hasn't happened yet, I'm not overly optimistic it's going to."

That wasn't a surprise to Kate. She hadn't expected to remember anything. One look at Ryan, though, and she saw he'd been hoping for different news.

She willed herself not to let Ryan's disappointment affect her. "What about now? Am I in the clear, or should I be worried about any long-lasting effects?"

Dr. Murphy leaned back and brushed a hand over his bald head. "I wish I could give you a better answer. The reality is, we just don't know. Your scan looks fine now. I don't see anything that would cause concern. However, you received an experimental drug, and we don't know what that might do to you down the line, if anything. For now, I wouldn't worry too much, just be cautious of any changes you experience."

"But I'm not totally in the clear. That's what you're telling me?"

He leaned forward, his face softening. "You could be hit by a car and killed tomorrow, Kate. Worrying about what might happen isn't going to change anything. But you're high risk. I wouldn't ever forget about that fact or pretend it isn't an issue, because it is. My advice would be bi-yearly checkups at this point, unless something changes."

Ryan nodded, glanced at Kate. "That's doable."

Doable but not what she'd been hoping for. She would always worry. Every time she mixed up colors or numbers like she still so often did, she'd worry it was something more.

Dr. Murphy rose, and she and Ryan followed suit. Ryan thanked him.

"No problem. Set up an appointment for your son on your way out. We'll just make sure everything's fine with him as well."

"Thank you." Kate followed Ryan out the door.

When the elevator door slid closed behind them, he wrapped his arm around her shoulder and pulled her close. She could feel the relief in his body and the disappointment lurking beneath. "That's good news," he said into her hair.

Why didn't he sound more sure? She rested her head against his chest, fought the urge to sink into him and let him be her strength. She wasn't stupid enough to think there was any sort of happily ever after for them. Not when she knew what was going on between them was just physical, that it wasn't strong enough to last.

When his lips grazed her temple, her eyes slid shut. He was warm and comforting, everything she needed right now. And it scared her to death.

"Yeah," she whispered. So why didn't she believe it?

"Something's going right," he said quietly.

She nodded in agreement. She wasn't going to die of cancer. She might turn out okay even with all the drugs they'd pumped into her. But would she survive whoever was out there snuffing out research patients?

That was the question swirling in her mind now. That and what the hell she was going to do about the man next to her.

Kate let her head fall back against the headrest and closed her eyes. The rhythmic clicking told her they were still on the bridge, that in good traffic she had another twenty minutes to ponder the nightmare that was her life before they made it to the beach.

What she wanted was a long, hot bath, an enormous glass of wine, and solitude. What she had was Ryan Harrison. Seated next to her, he radiated tension and worry. And it only grated on her more.

Her cell phone rang, startling her out of her depressing musings. She reached into her bag and lifted it to her ear.

"Kate, is that you? It's Simone."

"Hey."

"Where are you?"

"In the car, on the way out to Moss Beach."

"Is Ryan with you?"

Kate's gaze flicked sideways at Ryan's tense shoulders as he turned the wheel of the Jag. "Yeah, he's here."

"I wasn't able to find him. His secretary said he was out today, but that he had his phone on him."

"He must have turned it off." During the appointment with Dr. Murphy. When they'd been talking about her future. A future that didn't look as optimistic as it had only a few hours ago.

"Regardless, I'm glad I found you," Simone said. "I have news. We found Reynolds."

"You did?"

"Yeah. Facedown in his swimming pool in Houston."

"Shit."

Ryan's gaze shot to her. She saw the questions in his eyes but glanced away. She couldn't deal with his worry. Not yet.

"Yeah," Simone went on. "Authorities are calling it an accidental drowning. He was bloated for two full days before the neighbors found him. Turns out he took an unexpected trip to Canada, just after Jake died. Neighbors didn't even know he was back yet."

"Oh, my God." Kate closed her eyes.

"They're not ruling out foul play, but at the moment, it doesn't look like they have any leads."

"How convenient."

"Kate." Simone paused again. "There's more."

She swallowed hard. Did she really want to know? No. She didn't. "Tell me."

"My PI has a lead on Walter Alexander. He thinks he's found him up in Vancouver, BC. I've got some business in Seattle later this week. I think I might catch a flight up and see if I can find him."

Panic coursed through Kate. "No. Don't do that."

"Relax, it's no biggie. The firm won't even miss me."

"Simone, you don't understand. Things are getting out of control. Don't go up there. Just walk away."

"Kate, I really don't think—"

Ryan plucked the phone out of her hand. Her fingers clenched into a fist. Her jaw tightened. Anger and frustration at the entire situation welled inside her. As he listened intently while Simone relayed the information to him a second time, Kate closed her eyes and dropped her head back against the seat. If he wanted to take over, she'd let him. She couldn't do anything about it. He had as much at stake here as she did. But his overbearing reaction was just one more reminder that he expected her to be the docile wife he remembered, and that wasn't her.

He ended the conversation just about the time he pulled into her drive in Moss Beach. His strong hand reached for hers, and she fought the urge to cling to him. "Are you okay?"

"Yeah, I'm fine."

"Talk to me," he said quietly.

That wouldn't solve anything. It would only make it worse. A tender conversation about her fears and anxieties would only land her where she really didn't need to be, and that was in his arms.

She needed to keep perspective, to figure out what the hell she was going to do next. To stop being distracted by a crazy attraction that would only lead to heartbreak.

"I'm fine," she said again. "I just need a few minutes."

With hands more steady than she expected, she eased out of the car. He followed her into the house and stood in the entry with his hands on his hips, watching her. She turned to face him, avoiding his gaze, avoiding the comfort she knew was right where she wanted it. "I need to go get a few things upstairs. Just…just make yourself at home. I'll be back."

She wasn't sure how she made it up the stairs, but she paused at the top, looked one way, then the other. Her bedroom was to the right, Reed's bedroom and her office to the left. If she went into her bedroom and Ryan followed, her willpower would break, and they'd end up in bed. If she went into her office, she'd have the buffer of walls between her and that soft, sweet spot she wanted to tumble across with him.

Sinking into the chair behind her desk, she dropped her hands in her lap and glanced around. Boxes still sat near the window. Pictures leaned against the wall, waiting to be hung. So many things she'd *meant* to get to, but had never found time for.

"What are you doing?"

Ryan's voice didn't surprise her. She'd known he'd follow, that he'd be worried. Why was she able to read him so well all of a sudden?

"Storm's coming in," she said quietly, staring out the window.

"Looks pretty calm to me."

"It's deceptive. You can tell when a big one's coming. The wind dies down. There's the slightest hint of darkness on the horizon. And when you step outside, you can almost smell it in the air."

He crouched in front of her, resting a hand on her thigh. Her skin sizzled through the thick denim of her jeans. Her body ached to be caressed by those firm hands.

It wouldn't help.

"Everything's going to be okay," he said gently. "Don't worry."

*Don't worry. Just like that. If only.*

She mustered up as much courage as she could and faced him. "I don't need you to make it okay for me, Ryan. I know you think you have to swoop in here and protect me from this whole thing, but I can handle it."

His back straightened, but he didn't move his hand. "That's not what I'm doing."

"Yes, it is. I know you're just trying to help, but you're smothering me. I came up here with the intention of getting my things to go back with you but realized what I need is time to sort through everything on my own."

His eyes narrowed. "I missed something between this morning and now. What's going on?"

She brushed his hand away and rose. Telling him to leave when his touch was searing her skin wouldn't work. She needed space between them. "You didn't miss anything from this morning. Maybe you just missed it in general."

He pushed to his feet. "You're going to have to explain, because I can't seem to read your mind."

She lifted her hands, dropped them. "What do you see when you look at me?"

"Is this a trick question?"

"No. It's an honest one. I know what you see. You see Annie."

"And that's bad because…"

"Because, Ryan, I'm not her."

A frown tugged at his mouth. "What are you talking about?"

He didn't get it. She wasn't sure he ever would. And even though it wasn't the most pressing issue at the moment, it would always be a problem between them. Dealing with it now, before either of them got more hurt in this crazy situation was the best idea.

"I'm talking about this." She waved her hands. "This, this thing going on between us isn't working. Every time you look at me, you see someone who doesn't exist anymore. You have this need to protect me, but it's not me you're worried about, it's someone I used to be. Someone I'm not anymore."

"Run that by me again, because I'm a little lost."

She let out a breath. "Ryan, in all the time we've been together, you haven't once called me Kate."

"Yes, I have."

"No, you haven't. I've been listening." Her heart clenched, but she refused to acknowledge the pain. A pain that was a thousand times sharper than she'd expected. "I can admit I'm wildly attracted to you, but that's just physical. It doesn't mean anything. You're attracted to someone who's not here anymore. I don't know how to be that person, and I'm not even sure I want to try. I like who I am now. And the person I am now doesn't need you hovering over her, trying to shelter her from this whole mess."

He shifted his weight. "What are you saying?"

"I'm saying…I don't think this is going anywhere. I appreciate your help, that you've given up time today to check things out with me, but going back to your house with you tonight isn't going to help matters. Reed and Julia are already confused. Being near you, acting on this combustible attraction isn't going to help make things better. We both know this isn't going anywhere, that neither of us is what the other needs or wants in the long run."

The muscles in his jaw tightened. "So this morning—"

"This morning was me being emotional and overreacting to the stress I've been under. It didn't mean anything."

Anger flashed in his eyes. Swallowing the lump in her throat, she stood her ground. If she were lucky, he'd get the hint soon and leave before she changed her mind.

Because she really wanted to change her mind. She wanted to throw herself into his arms and hide from everything going on around them. She wanted to forget he thought of someone else when they were together, because she wanted him more than she wanted to think logically.

"I think you should go, Ryan," she said quietly.

"Just like that?"

"Yes."

"This is crap. Tell me what's really going on."

"This is what's really going on." He wasn't getting it, so she put as much emotion into her voice as she could, hoping that would get her point across. "I don't need you. And I don't want you. And the sooner you get that, the better off we'll all be."

His eyes locked on hers. Steely, cold eyes. The same hard, emotionless eyes he'd turned on her at the beginning, before the press conference, before he'd kissed her, before she'd realized just what kind of caring man he was inside. "Fine. Whatever."

He brushed by her. She listened as his footsteps echoed down the stairs. Flinched when the front door opened and slammed shut.

Shaking, she sank to the ground and leaned back against the wall. Tears pooled in her eyes, and her chest ached with a fierceness she hadn't expected. This pain was so much worse than when she'd lost Jake, and it only made her realize just how much she did want Ryan. She'd fallen for him against her better judgment. And now, no matter where she went, no matter who she met, the reality of what she'd just let slip away would haunt her forever.

The first drops of rain pelted the window. The wind picked up, and waves pounded the shore like a mighty fist. She glanced out at the gray clouds even as tears slid down her cheeks.

# CHAPTER SIXTEEN

Ryan stood on Annie's front porch and drew in deep, calming breaths. He didn't need this shit. He'd been on an emotional roller coaster since the day she'd shown up on his doorstep, and it was only getting worse. And he definitely didn't need a woman telling him what he thought and felt. He knew, dammit.

He jogged down the front steps and walked through the rain to his car. If she wanted to be alone, he'd just leave her alone. He'd been through enough hell because of her.

*This morning was me being emotional and overreacting to the stress I've been under. It didn't mean anything.*

Her words ran through his mind as he pulled the car door open, and he remembered the look in her eyes when she'd said it. That haunted emotion brewing deep inside. His chest tightened. He'd been so focused on her words, he'd almost missed the most important sign.

Up until they'd seen Dr. Murphy, she'd been fine. She'd handled the news about the phone calls with a calmness he hadn't expected. She'd even accepted Dr. Murphy's explanation of her injury. It was only when Ryan had asked if she was going to get her memory back that she'd pulled up those damn invisible walls. Since then, she'd been withdrawn, reserved, hiding behind those barriers.

Dammit. She was pushing him away because she thought he was only interested in who she used to be. She couldn't possibly know he was starting to question that himself. That he'd already noticed the differences in her, that the attraction he felt to her was stronger than it had ever been before.

And she was sugarcoating it by implying she didn't need him to take care of her. Then he remembered the panic in her voice when Simone had mentioned going up to Canada.

She wasn't just scared. She was protecting him too. Not wanting him to get too involved. Doing exactly what she'd told him not to do.

*Son of a bitch.*

Water ran in rivulets down his face as he slammed the car door, as he jogged back up the front steps. He didn't knock, instead thrust the door open with his shoulder and took the stairs two by two until he got to the top. When he rounded the corner into her office, he found her slumped against the wall, her elbows crossed over her up-drawn knees, her face buried in her arms.

So much for not caring. She was lying through her teeth.

Her head darted up when she heard him. Tears streaked her cheeks. She swiped her hand across her nose. "What are you doing…?"

He grasped her by the shoulders, plucked her off the floor, and pressed her back against the wall. Then he closed his mouth over hers, hot, hungry, his kiss filled with all the anger and frustration and need swirling inside him.

Her hands bunched in his wet shirt, and she tried to wiggle free, but he held her tight, pressed his body into hers. He kissed her hard, demanding a response. She bucked beneath him, but he felt the moment she gave in. The moment she grabbed on and pulled him tighter instead of pushed him away. The moment she opened her mouth and drew his tongue into hers, drawing his heart right along with it.

A strangled moan resonated from her. Desire tightened in his stomach. Blood rushed straight to his groin. Grasping her T-shirt by the hem, he yanked it over her head and dropped it on the floor.

"Tell me I don't mean anything to you." He nipped her ear, sucked the lobe deep in his mouth, pressed his lips against that upside down, heart-shaped birthmark near her jaw. The one he'd licked and nibbled a thousand times before. The one that was familiar and new all at the same time.

She shivered. Her head fell back as she wrapped her arms around his shoulders, pulling him closer. She arched into him, offered more of her neck to his mouth, ground her hips against his erection. "You don't. It's…it's just sex."

*The hell it is.*

With hands he knew were way too rough, he grasped her bra and yanked. The front hook gave with a pop. He shoved the lacy garment aside, closed his hands over her naked breasts, bruising, kneading. He lowered his head to her right nipple, flicked the tip with his tongue, drew it deep in his mouth. She cried out when his teeth scraped the sensitive tip, hardening into a little bud, but she didn't push him away, and he wasn't done yet. He repeated the process on the other side, groaning himself when she thrust her hips into his in response.

"Say it again," he said as he kissed her collarbone, her throat, as he found her mouth again. "Tell me this isn't real."

She shook her head, grasped his soaked shirt, and pulled it over his head. "It's not."

"You lie."

He yanked the buttons open on her jeans, had his hands inside pushing them down before she even got the top button of his undone. In one swift move, her jeans and underwear lay in a pile on the floor.

Gasping, she reached for him. He captured her wrists, pinned them to the wall over her head with one hand. "Still nothing?"

She swallowed, shook her head. But he saw the desire in her eyes. Saw the hunger. Saw the need.

For him. Not for anyone else. Just him. Only him.

His mouth closed over hers. She opened for him, tangled her tongue with his. He brushed a hand down her belly, felt her quiver when his fingers slid into her curls. Groaned when he felt the hot, sweet wetness between her thighs.

"You're dripping. You need to come, don't you, baby?" She trembled at his words while he kissed her lips, while he circled his finger in her wetness until he found her clit. "Tell me how much you need me."

She groaned, pushed her hips forward. He slid his finger lower, inside, knew exactly where she liked to be stroked.

"Ryan..."

"Tell me," he said against her ear. "Tell me you feel what I do. I know you do. I know you can't fight it anymore than I can." He added a second finger, stroked her deep, found her clit with his thumb and circled until she cried out and came, her whole body trembling with her release.

"You're so fucking hot," he whispered in her ear. "So incredibly sexy. You make me so hard, baby. Tell me."

His name was a strangled cry from her lips. He captured it with his mouth, continued to drive her mad with his hand.

"Stop," she mumbled against him.

"No." He wasn't satisfied with her body. He wanted her soul too. Wouldn't settle for anything less. "Go up again. I want to watch. I love watching you come."

"I can't," she muttered, pushing against him. "It's too much."

He nibbled at her throat, at her breasts; all the while, he continued to stroke the fire inside her with his fingers. She twisted, her thighs clamped around his hand as he took her to the edge again. "Ryan, please."

"Tell me, baby. Tell me you don't feel anything when you're with me. Tell me I don't matter. We both know you can't, because this…you and me…this is all that matters."

"Dammit," she groaned. "I do care, you son of a bitch. Too much. I don't want you to matter this much. I don't want to feel. I don't want to hurt. I just want…you."

Her words shot straight to his heart. He released her arms, tangled his hands in her silky hair, and pulled her mouth to his. His lips softened, his kiss gentled, and when he tasted the salt from her tears, tenderness consumed him.

Her hands scrambled for the waistband of his jeans. Her probing fingers slid into his pants, then wrapped around his cock, causing his whole body to jerk.

He needed to be inside her. Couldn't wait. He dragged her to the floor. Wrestled with his pants and shoes. A groan tore through him when her mouth closed over his, and she pushed him back into the carpet, then straddled his hips, all her wet, moist heat so close he could barely breath.

She closed her mouth over his, kissed him deep. A shudder ran through him when she eased back, when she wrapped those long fingers around his cock then drew it toward her sex. And he lost all ability to think when she positioned him at the entrance to her body, lowered, and took him in.

His heart clenched so hard he gasped. He reached for her, pulling her mouth back to his, threading his fingers in her luscious hair. Everything else up to this point seemed unimportant. He drank her in with large gulps, reveled in the softness of her skin, the sweetness of her mouth. A low moan ground through him as she flexed her hips, as she lifted and lowered, as he tried to get as close as he possibly could.

He'd never thought he'd be with her like this again. Hadn't realized just how much he'd missed her, how much he'd needed her, how empty his life had been without her. She enveloped him. She surrounded him. She consumed every single part of him.

*Annie.*

Her name hovered on his lips, the desire to call out to her stronger than he expected. So many years. So many things he wanted to make up for. He wanted to give her what she needed. Needed to let her know he'd heard her words.

Her names melded into one. "Look at me, Katie."

Her eyes locked on his. And for a second, the connection he felt arc between them was so intense, so all-consuming, it devoured him. She touched his soul in a way no one before or since her ever had.

He knew she felt it too, could see by the look in her eyes she was as powerless as he against the emotions flowing between them. Tears glinted in her eyes, and he brushed back her hair to focus on her face.

"Only you," he whispered, pulling her brow against his. "Only this, only us."

Emotions pulsed through him when her lips slid over his. When she whispered his name. The muscles in his body tensed and he thrust harder, pulling her tight against him.

"Wait for me," she whispered, kissing him harder, riding faster.

How could he tell her he'd been waiting for her his whole life?

He held back. But when she arched, when she tightened around him and he knew she'd reached the peak, he let go, making sure she went over that edge with him.

Pulse pounding, Ryan wrapped his arms around her and just held on. She fell against his chest, drew unsteady breaths. His lips trembled at her temple. His heart beat frantically against hers. For the first time in forever he felt...whole again.

He closed his eyes. Breathed deep. Hung on to the feeling. But when she turned her face into his shoulder, and he felt the cool tears trickle across his skin, the reality of the moment hit him.

That wasn't what he'd meant to do. All his careful plans to woo her back had just crashed and burned, all because he hadn't been able to control his temper. And, judging from the sobs gripping her, that wasn't what she'd wanted, either.

"I'm sorry. God, I'm sorry. Don't cry." He rolled her over, brushed her hair away from her face. "Please don't cry."

She covered her face with both hands.

"I'm sorry," he said again, kissing her cheeks, the corners of her mouth, wanting to do anything to make it up to her. "I'm so sorry. I—"

She pressed her fingers over his lips. "Don't say it again. I'm not crying because I'm upset."

He stilled. "You're not?"

She shook her head, then slowly lowered her other hand and stared up at him. "No."

"Then why?"

She wiped a hand across her cheek. "Because you said my name. I didn't realize how much I needed to hear it."

He thought he'd fallen earlier, but he'd been wrong. Her sweetness overwhelmed him in a way it never had before. How could he love her more now than he had back then? Something about her today touched him in a way Annie never had. He didn't want to think about the absurdity of what that implied. He only wanted to be with her again, to feel her and know her all over.

"Oh, Katie. Come here."

He lifted her from the floor, carried her into her bedroom, sat on her bed, and cradled her in his lap. He nuzzled her neck, drew in her scent. Reveled in just being close to her.

"That's not the way I wanted it for you. Not the first time."

She rested her head against his neck, clasped her arms around his shoulders. "I'm not complaining."

She smiled, and he kissed her, softly, gently, wanting her to feel what was in his heart. She sighed and kissed him back. Her fingers laced through his damp hair to draw him closer.

When he eased back and looked down at her he realized one other thing he'd majorly screwed up on. His eyes slid closed. "Shit. Condoms."

"What about them?"

"They're in my pants pocket. After this morning I grabbed some, just in case."

"Hopeful, were you?"

He opened his eyes, saw the humor glint in hers. She didn't look upset, if anything she looked…amused. "I…I didn't mean to—"

Her soft fingers landed on his lips. "Don't apologize again. You may have started it, but I'm pretty sure I'm the one who finished it. I didn't give you a chance to say no let alone find a condom."

She hadn't, that was true. His lips curled and his blood warmed at the memory.

"I won't get pregnant, Ryan. I have it covered."

He wanted to tell her he'd be thrilled if she wound up pregnant from tonight. Just the thought of seeing her carrying his child, getting to experience everything he'd missed out on with Reed, warmed him from the inside out. But he knew she wasn't ready to hear that. Not yet.

"Plus," she added. "I've been through every test under the sun and I can say for certain, that's one part of my body that's completely healthy. And I trust you. I'm not worried."

He hated that they were having this conversation. That it was even an issue. "I was always careful. I want you to know that. If I had thought there was any chance, even a minuscule one, that you were still alive, I never would have been with anyone else."

Her eyes darkened. "I believe you."

He didn't want her to believe it. He wanted her to feel it. To know she was the only one he'd ever wanted. He brushed a curl back from her face. "I would never do anything to hurt you."

"I know that too," she whispered.

He leaned in and kissed her, felt his heart swell when she kissed him back.

"I can do better," he said against her lips, running his hand down the soft indent of her spine.

"Right now? Are you up for that already?"

"Babe, I've been up for it ever since you walked back into my life."

When she laughed, relief swamped him. He pulled her down onto the plush, red comforter, rolled her over, kissed her again, then eased back just long enough to look down into her eyes. "Did you really think you could get rid of me so easily?"

"Too obvious?"

His fingers tangled in her hair. "You almost had me convinced, until I remembered your eyes could never lie. They still can't." He kissed her eyelids, slid down to her mouth, traced his tongue along her lips until she opened and drew him in.

"I'll have to remember that," she mumbled when they were both breathless.

"Tell me what you want," he whispered as he ran his hand down her side, grazing his knuckles against the swell of her breast.

"I don't want to think. I just want you to touch me like you did before. I want to forget everything but you."

"Oh, babe. I think I can help you out there."

"Good. Because right now, all I need is you, Ryan."

And those were all the words he ever needed to hear.


Kate flexed her toes, stretching out her foot. She couldn't remember a time she'd felt so relaxed, so sated, so calm. Every muscle in her body was loose and invigorated.

She glanced down at Ryan, and a smile slid across her face. His head lay pillowed on her chest, his arm draped across her waist, his legs tangled with hers. Even in sleep he didn't seem to want to let go of her. Her fingers knotted in his hair, the silky blond tendrils tickling her skin. She'd never felt as desired, as wanted as she had the last few hours.

They'd made love twice more before he'd finally pulled her close and drifted off to sleep. Rain pelted the window outside, waves crashed against the shore in the dark, but in the confines of her little house, she was warm and content. And, for the moment, happy.

The kids were still with her parents, the phone was unplugged, and the nightmare that was her life shifted to the back of her mind. She'd deal with all that later. Right now, she just wanted to enjoy the moment, in case it didn't last.

"Don't," Ryan said without moving.

Her fingers paused in his hair. "You don't like that?"

"No, I love that. Keep doing it. Just stop thinking."

She smiled wider. "How do you know that's what I'm doing?"

"Babe, I can practically hear the gears grinding away in that thick skull of yours."

"They were not," she said playfully. "And it's not that thick."

A chuckle bubbled through him, one that vibrated in her own chest as he nuzzled her bare breast. "If you say this was a mistake I'm going to have to make love to you again until you stop thinking."

"I wasn't going to say that."

"No, but you're thinking it."

"Well, of course I was thinking it. I'm a smart woman."

With a smile, he skimmed his hand up her thigh and pressed his fingers into a pressure point in her hip. She giggled and tried to move away.

"Okay, you were warned." His lips trailed across her chest, up to her neck. Warm hands slid up her body to caress her breasts. Arousal coursed through her again.

"You're insatiable, you know that?" she whispered as his lips worked their way up to her ear.

"But in a good way."

She couldn't help but laugh. She hadn't known she could feel this relaxed with him. Didn't expect the warmth in her chest every time he kissed her.

He eased over onto his side, ran his hand up her shoulder, down her arm, his fingers intertwining with hers. He brought her hand back to his mouth and kissed her fingers one by one. Tiny threads of emotions coursed through her, the gesture so endearing, so tender.

She let her fingertips graze the scar on his chin. "How did you get this?"

"Mitch."

"How?"

"We got into a fight."

"About what?"

"You."

She traced the curved line, feeling the worn ridge. "Why?"

"I'm not sure how to say this, but back in college, I was sort of…" He paused as if embarrassed. "Well, I dated a lot."

She couldn't help but smile. A player. "Like Mitch."

He laughed. "Yeah. Probably why we got to be such good friends. Anyway, you and I had just started seeing each other, and you came to one of my games. Mitch and I played—"

"Baseball," she finished for him. "And Mitch saw us together and got so mad he got ejected from the game."

"How do you know?"

"Mitch told me the story. But not about the scar. He said he hit you when you came out of the clubhouse."

One side of Ryan's mouth curled. "He did. Man, he was pissed. And you…you were even more mad."

"I was?"

"Yeah. Said we were acting like children. Actually, it wasn't all that different from what you said to us after the press conference yesterday."

She ran her fingers over the scar again. "How many stitches?"

"Four. I knew Mitch was right. He had every reason to be pissed at me. I went to break up with you that night. But I took one look at you standing on the porch of your sorority house, and saw how worried you were about me, and…"

"And what?"

"And I fell for you. Hard."

Her heart thumped. She could imagine the scene. She just wished she could remember it. "You did?"

"Yeah. Plus, it didn't hurt that you took me back to my

apartment, doted on me, kissed all my wounds."

She laughed, then glanced down at her hand in his. Her fingertips grazed the platinum band edged in gold. "Why do you wear this?"

"Because I'm married."

"You were wearing it when we met. You didn't know you were still married then."

"I always wear it." His fingers slid along hers.

"You've worn it all this time?"

"Yeah. Does that surprise you?"

She shook her head, fighting back emotions she couldn't define. "Why? It's been five years."

"Because I got married, once, for better or worse. Forever. I found the woman I wanted to spend my life with. I have no intentions of getting married to anyone else."

"You'd rather be alone? What if you'd met someone?"

"I've met lots of women. None of them ever came close to you."

"Ryan." Emotions flowed through her. Tears stung the backs of her eyes. Under that tender gaze, her heart was dangerously close to the edge.

His fingers tightened in hers, and he glanced down at her left hand. "I noticed you took yours off."

She followed his gaze. "He wasn't my husband. I couldn't wear it once I knew the truth."

He lifted her hand, kissed her naked fingers. "I wish I knew what happened to your ring. I need to get you a new one."

She saw the determination in his eyes, and her stomach tensed in reaction. Loud warning bells went off in her head. She wasn't ready for that. Wasn't sure she ever would be. She tried to sit up. "Ryan—"

He leaned in and feathered his lips across hers with the most wicked of smiles. "Don't."

"Don't what?"

"Don't think. I don't want you to worry about tomorrow or the day after. I don't want you to overanalyze what I say. I just want you to feel."

His mouth nibbled its way down her neck. She sank back into the pillows and closed her eyes. As his hands caressed her body, glided over curves and angles, she drew in a breath. Desire coursed through her all over again as his tantalizing fingers slipped between her thighs. Heat pooled in her core with each gentle stroke.

She couldn't deny the tug she felt for him deep in her soul. It was more than physical, more than just blind attraction. It was so much deeper, so much more real than she'd ever expected or experienced.

And it scared her, more than she wanted to admit. The thought that it might be love, so soon after meeting him, made her palms sweaty, made her pulse beat faster. That couldn't possibly be what she was feeling already.

He eased between her legs and kissed her as he slid deep inside. And her heart turned over as she pulled him close, as she opened her mouth and body and mind and soul to him.

"Are you thinking?" he whispered in her ear.

"No. Definitely not." His slow, gentle strokes brought a sigh from her lips. She lifted her hips to meet him, ran her hands down his back, loving the texture of his skin, wanting to memorize every curve of muscle, each and every play of bone.

He smiled against her ear. "Good. I want your mind completely empty when I tell you that I love you."

Her whole body tightened. "Ryan—"

"I do," he said softly, drawing slowly out, pressing back in again until she gasped. "I can't pretend that I don't. What I love about you is deep inside. It's there whether you call yourself Annie or Kate. It's there whether you remember me or not."

"This is crazy," she whispered.

A smile twisted his mouth, and he kissed her again. Drew out and back. "No. Crazy would be denying what's real. I don't expect you to say it back, not yet, at least. I just want you to know it's there. That it's always right there."

She trailed her fingers through the hair at the nape of his neck, pulled him close. Kissed him again and again as they made love. The words hovered on her lips, but fear held her back. Fear of what would happen in the light of day. Fear of how he'd feel about her when he got to know her better. If she allowed herself to fall all the way in love with him, and he woke up one day realizing she was different from the woman he remembered, she wasn't sure her heart could survive the loss.

And she couldn't give him all of her until she knew for sure she was what he really wanted.

Tonight, though, she could pretend like tomorrow didn't exist. She might not be able to say the words, but she could show him what she felt instead.

Taking his face in her hands, she kissed him deeply, then rolled him to his back. "Let me love you, Ryan."

# CHAPTER SEVENTEEN

"I don't want you going up there alone." Mitch stood in Simone's bedroom, watching her toss clothes into a suitcase. "Did you hear me?" he asked when she didn't respond.

She patted his cheek as she brushed by and headed into her bathroom. "Careful, sweetheart, you're starting to sound a lot like your domineering brother-in-law."

Her insult barely registered. He followed, stood in the doorway while she moved around gathering her things. "I talked to Ryan earlier. He doesn't think you should go up there alone, either."

She dropped cosmetics into her travel bag, grabbed her favorite shampoo from the shower. "Please. Like I'm going to listen to two men? Mitch, I'm going to Seattle on business. Besides, no one will know I'm even there. In fact, I'll be safer there than I am here. Shannon's staying with my parents. Everything's fine. And I haven't even decided if it's worth it to go up to Vancouver yet. I'll wait and see what my PI finds."

Yet. He'd heard that little addendum loud and clear. She was too independent. Too stubborn. It was one of the reasons he'd never been attracted to successful women. She'd been dodging him ever since their night together, and he'd worked so late last night that he hadn't been able to come by and see her until this morning. He was supposed to hop a flight up to Queen Charlotte Sound today to get the project back on track, but now that he'd gotten a whiff of what she had planned, he couldn't leave until he knew she'd be safe.

"I'd go with you if I could but I can't. Damn, this is shitty timing."

"Don't worry about it," she said, grabbing hairspray from a basket on the counter.

She was avoiding his eyes. It didn't take a rocket scientist to figure out what was going on here.

"I know what you're doing, Simone. You don't have to go up to Vancouver because of what happened between us."

"I don't know what you're talking about." She slipped a hairbrush in her bag, zipped it closed.

Yes, she did. She knew exactly what he was getting at. He'd seen it eating away at her the second after they'd made love. Forget what was happening between them. She thought she'd let her client down. "Kate and Ryan are not going to be upset with you over this. You're allowed to have a life. You didn't do anything wrong."

She closed her eyes, drew in a breath. Emotions played over her face, but when she opened her eyes again, they were gone. She grabbed her bag and pushed past him into the bedroom. "I'll talk to Kate about it all when I get back."

He caught her by the arm. "Stop and look at me."

She turned dark eyes his way. Eyes that were haunted. Eyes that were guilt-ridden. Eyes that tightened his chest like a drum.

"Don't throw what's happening between us away because you're worried what someone else is going to think," he said.

"This was a bad idea. It never should have happened, and you know it. As for my going to Seattle, it's not your call. I'll be fine. Now, could you please let go of my arm so I can finish packing?"

He felt like she'd just stabbed him through the heart. As he released her, he tried to figure out what the hell was happening. When had he gotten so attached? He never worried about anyone besides family. When had Simone—a woman he barely knew—become as important, if not more, than the people he loved?

His chest stretched even tighter.

Heart thundering, he followed her back into her bedroom. She was zipping her garment bag, her chocolate hair falling across her cheeks. Rain drizzled outside the window, casting an eerie gray light through the room. In her snug skirt and fitted blouse, she couldn't look more angelic if she tried.

Oh, man. He was so screwed here.

He ran a hand over his face, tried to settle his racing pulse. When she turned to set her bag on the floor, he grasped her arms and drew her close. "I don't do long term. Casual. That's as serious as I get. But you, Counselor… With you I don't want casual."

"*What?*" Fear slid into her eyes. The same damn fear he felt but was pushing down. "Are you…?" Her eyes narrowed. "Did that bat hit you in the head? I thought it got you in the stomach."

He couldn't help it. He smiled. "No, *you* hit me over the head. The first time I saw you. The other night—thank God for the other night—I realized I've been head over heels for you from the start. Since then I've been thinking about the whole deal—marriage, family, kids, a minivan."

Simone jerked out of his arms and pressed a hand to her belly. "Oh, my God. A minivan? Are you sick? What the hell's come over you?"

"I don't know," he said quietly, watching her stunned reaction. Feeling it himself. He sure the hell hadn't expected to say that, but now that it was out there, he didn't want to take it back. "Shocked?"

"Um, yeah. We slept together. Once."

He dipped his hands into the pockets of his jeans. "As I recall, you enjoyed it. More than once. Many times more than once."

"I..." she sputtered, waved her hands. "Mitch, we barely even know each other."

"So let's get to know each other. Stay here. Stay safe. As soon as I get back, we'll focus on nothing but learning what irritates us most about each other."

She dropped onto the end of the bed. "This is a joke, isn't it? Please tell me it's a joke."

Not the reaction he'd hoped for. Hell, it wasn't even the conversation he'd planned on having. "No joke. You hooked me, Simone. Basically knocked me on my ass. I'm as shocked as anyone."

When she didn't say anything, just stared at him with wide eyes, he scratched the back of his head, feeling like an idiot. "Okay, I can probably do without the minivan. We can negotiate that later."

"You're certifiable, you know that?"

He felt himself cracking, and he was a man who never cracked. "Look, I've avoided relationships for a long time. For a variety of reasons. And after I watched Ryan go through hell over my sister's death, I told myself I'd been smart and that relationships weren't worth it. But now...after everything that's happened...I don't know. I just realized life is precious. That you gotta go after the things you want, because they might not be there when you finally pull your head out of your ass and realize they're important. I don't want to miss that opportunity with you, Simone. I'm not asking you to marry me. I'm just asking you not to end what's growing between us. And I don't want you to go to Canada because you feel guilty over it. I couldn't bear it if something happened to you."

He pulled her from the bed and gripped her hands. "Take a chance on me, Counselor. You might be surprised at what you find."

"I might end up in a padded cell."

A smile curled one side of his mouth. "Wouldn't be so bad if we were there together, would it?"

"Mitch—"

"Just think about it, okay? Think about you and me and what could just be the best thing in your life."

"I have a sinking suspicion that's all I'm going to be doing for the next few days." She frowned, but she didn't pull her hands from his. And he took that as a good sign. "You're like a tornado, you know that, Mathews? Devouring everything in its path and not caring about the consequences."

"I care about you. And Shannon, and keeping you both safe. Promise me you won't go to Canada."

She didn't answer, only curled into him, then slid her arms around his waist and held on. And as her heat enveloped him, his heart took one hard roll. Because right then he knew she wasn't going to do what he wanted. And that meant any plans he'd made for the next few days were going to take a drastic turn.

Hopefully not for the worst.


"What are you doing?"

Kate jumped from her spot on the floor in the living room and swiveled toward the stairs. Ryan stood on the bottom step, wearing nothing but faded denim low on his hips. His feet were bare, his eyes sleepy, and his blond hair had that tousled just-woke-up look.

She pressed a hand to her chest. "You scared me."

He walked into the room. "You were expecting someone else?"

Early morning sunlight glinted off his bare chest. Her skin tingled as she remembered tracing the lines of those muscles last night with her fingers, with her lips.

"Katie?"

Tearing her gaze away from his exquisite male body, she glanced up at his amused face. "What?"

"Are you okay?"

"I'm fine." She turned back toward the stack of journals she'd been flipping through and bit her lip as heat crept up her face. Sex was supposed to sate a person, not turn them into a randy teenager.

He slid to the floor behind her, one leg on each side of hers. Warmth radiated from his body. She shivered, itching to be touched, wanting those hands on her like they'd been last night. When his fingers slipped around her waist, she drew in a breath and smiled as his lips grazed the nape of her neck.

That's what she wanted. But oh, man. If he kept that up, she'd never get through these journals.

"There's my shirt," he said, trailing his hands under the cotton and up her ribcage to cup her bare breasts. "I was looking for it."

Desire pooled in her core. A low fire built when he pinched her nipple. She swallowed hard. "Sorry. I just grabbed the first thing I saw."

His chest vibrated at her back when he chuckled. "In the office? Across the hall? I think that's where it landed when you ripped it off me last night."

She bit back the smile, remembering the night before. She'd never been so aggressive, hadn't known she could be so passionate. Closing her eyes, she enjoyed the sensation as his teeth nibbled her neck and his hands continued to tease her breasts. "It's soft. And it smells good. You can have it back in a minute if you want."

"I do," he mumbled against her. His hand grazed her hip, slid down between her thighs. "I don't like waking up alone. I want you back in my bed."

His fingers danced across her mound. Made her shiver with anticipation. "I think it's my bed."

"Minor technicality. What are you doing down here, anyway?"

She looked back at the journal splayed in front of her, tried not to moan as his finger rested against her clit. Even through the thin fabric of her panties, he had to feel how turned on she was. "I couldn't get Dr. Murphy's conversation out of my head."

"Babe, don't—"

"No, not that. He said he remembered reading something on a study about Tabofren. Ryan, I read it too."

"You did?" He moved his hand from between her legs, reached for a journal in front of her.

She tried not to be disappointed she'd distracted him from touching her. After all, finding out what had happened to her was more important than another round of mind-blowing sex. Though at the moment—at any moment—mind-blowing sex sounded a hell of a lot more fun.

"Yeah. I remember because it sounded so cutting-edge. I know it's in here somewhere." She tossed the journal she'd been studying in a pile of others and grabbed a new one from the coffee table.

"What are you doing with all of these?"

"McKellen Publishing handles several scientific journals, including medical ones. Occasionally I'll paw through them if something on the cover catches my eye. I know I saw it somewhere." She glanced around the room. Journals littered the floor. She'd already been through all the ones she had at home.

She pushed to her feet. "I need to go into the publishing house today."

Ryan rose. "No way."

One look and she saw the worry in his eyes. Why did she have that strange feeling he was keeping something from her again?

"Ryan, I'll be fine. I can check the database at work. The article I'm thinking of will be listed there. I need to find it."

"I don't want you going there. Not until we know who's connected to this."

Fighting him on this wasn't going to help. He was stubborn and domineering and way too sexy standing there in her living room for her to want to argue with him.

Biting her lip, she rested the palms of her hands on his chest and tipped her eyes up. "You could come with me."

His hand slid up to cover hers. "Teasing me will not get you what you want."

She moved closer, rose up on her toes, ran her lips softly over his. "Why not?"

"Because I'm not that easy."

She laughed, trailed her lips across his jaw to his ear, pressed her body against his. His sharp intake of breath told her she was doing a good job at seducing him. His arms came around her, and the muscles in her stomach tightened when his lips caressed her neck. She felt his arousal against her hip.

"You can have your shirt back if you go with me," she said in his ear.

He walked her forward until she bumped into the couch. Swift fingers streaked up under the hem of his shirt, whisking it over her head. It landed on the newel post. He flipped her around and bent her over the arm of the sofa. "I think I get my shirt back either way, babe."

She gasped, then shuddered when his lips found her nape again, when his hand dipped between her legs. Then finally sighed when he stroked the fire already burning inside her and made her forget everything but him.

* * *

Kate slipped on her sunglasses as she stepped from Ryan's Jag. She waited on the sidewalk with a frown while he took his sweet time. He'd been dragging his feet all morning, almost as if he didn't want to help her after all.

He'd wasted time making her breakfast, had lured her into a long, hot shower where he'd washed her with his hands and tongue, then convinced her he had to stop at his house on the way in to change clothes and see the kids before they left again. It was now close to noon. Not that she was complaining about any of it, but she was itching to find that article. And his snail pace was grating on her nerves.

"You're worse than a woman."

He slipped the keys into his pocket. "Don't start with me. I have a bad feeling about this."

Okay, so he was worried. She could deal with that. Then why was that underlying feeling that there was more to this still eating at her? Shaking off the thought, she tucked her arm in his and pulled him toward her building. "Come on. We'll be in and out. No one will even know we're there."

The office was abuzz when they stepped out of the elevator and onto Kate's floor.

"Kate, you're here. Thank goodness." Jill scrambled from her desk, grabbing a handful of messages. "The phone has been ringing off the hook since Monday morning."

*Oh, great.*

Kate glanced at Ryan. "Jill, this is Ryan."

To his credit, Ryan said nothing about Jill's nose ring. Or the plethora of tattoos up and down the twenty-something girl's arms. "Hi."

Jill's gaze darted from Kate to Ryan and back again. Her eyes widened when she finally recognized him, and a silly grin spread across her face. "Oh. Hi."

"Go on in, Ryan. I'll just be a minute." Kate motioned toward her office

When he was gone, Jill asked, "Is that who I think it is?"

"Yes."

"Is he really your husband?"

"Looks that way. I'll take those messages." Kate pried the messages from Jill's fingers.

"Oh." Jill finally tore her gaze from Ryan, standing in her office.

"And Tom's looking for you."

"How does he know I'm here?"

"Rumor mill. Honey, you're practically a celebrity. And you go anywhere with Ryan Harrison, and people are going to talk."

"Fabulous," Kate muttered. She moved toward her office. "I'm not staying long. I just need to check on something. I'll take a stack of work with me, but if anyone asks, I'm not here. Got it?"

"Sure. Hey, Kate?"

Kate stopped with one hand on the door.

"Is he as good as he looks?"

Kate feigned disgust. "You're hopeless." Then added with a smile, "Better."

Ryan was studying the pictures on her shelf when she stepped into the room.

"Not as big as your office," she said, closing the door behind her.

"Where was this taken?" He lifted a picture of Reed playing in the sand.

"On the gulf. He loves the beach."

Emotions brewed in his eyes when they turned toward her. And, for the first time, she realized he'd lost time too. "I have more pictures at home. I can show you if you want."

A faint smile tugged at the corner of his mouth. But his eyes were distant, almost as if he were holding something back. "I'd like that." His voice changed before she could ask what was bothering him. "Where do we start?"

She moved to a shelf across the room and pulled out medical journals. "You can flip through these while I pull up the database on my computer."

He dropped into a chair opposite her desk and lifted a stack. She scrolled through screens on her computer. The quiet hum of the outer office was the only sound in the room.

"Kate?" The intercom buzzed. Jill's voice chimed through the quiet. "Heads up, Tom's on his way—"

Her office door pushed open before she could respond, and Tom Adams strode in without knocking.

"You dodging me?" he asked.

Kate stood. Ryan rose too, eyeing her managing editor with suspicion. He obviously recognized Tom from that day at her house when he'd come to talk to her and had learned about Reed. So much for avoiding anyone at the office. "Tom Adams," she said, making introductions, "Ryan Harrison."

"Jesus," Tom muttered. "It's true."

"I'm not staying today, Tom. I know the office is in an uproar, so I'll get out of your hair. I'm just looking for something."

"Looking for what?"

"An article about a cancer drug tested in Canada."

The color drained from his face.

"Son of a bitch." Ryan stepped around Tom and closed the door. Then he glanced at Kate. "I think we just found our link."

# CHAPTER EIGHTEEN

Tom Adams's Victorian row house sat on a quiet street in Pacific Heights. Ryan tapped a hand against his knee as he and Kate waited in the immaculate living room. Wide windows looked out over the city. Trees swayed gently in the afternoon breeze.

Kate caught Ryan's tense shoulders, his tight jaw. "Relax, would you? You're stressing me out."

He shot her an irritated look and went back to tapping.

Kari Adams came down the stairs with Tom at her side. Her face was drawn, the swell of her very pregnant belly protruding from her slim body. "Sorry we kept you waiting."

Ryan tensed at Kate's side, but she ignored him. "It's all right. I'm sorry we're bothering you. I know how tired you must be."

Kari smiled, running a hand over her belly. "I'm not able to sleep much these days."

"Practice for B-day," Tom said, his fingers skimming their baby.

"Look." Ryan shifted his feet. "I don't mean to be rude, but we really need some answers. The first of which is why you dragged us all the way over here when you could have answered our questions at Katie's office."

Kate slanted him a warning look, which he ignored. The man had no tact when he was on a mission.

"That's my fault." Kari sank onto the floral couch. Even with her pregnant belly, the couch seemed to gobble up her petite body. "Tom knew I'd want to be involved."

"I'm not following you." Kate sat in a plush, cream chair across from Kari. "How do you have anything to do with a medical study?"

"Do you recognize me at all?" Kari asked.

"No, should I?" Worry tickled the back of Kate's throat.

"I suppose not. We only spoke a few times when I was in the nursing home, but I could never forget your eyes."

Kate glanced up at Ryan. His jaw twitched. Kari Adams. Why hadn't the name clicked when she'd looked at the list from Janet

Kelly's house?

Tom stepped behind his wife, rested a hand on her shoulder. "Kari had ovarian cancer. We decided to try experimental treatments after we'd exhausted all other avenues."

"I didn't think I'd make it," Kari said, looking down. "But Dr. Alexander was so optimistic, he gave us hope. The treatments lasted over six months. I was in and out of the nursing home, being monitored by the staff there. That's when I met you."

Kate's eyes widened. "I was awake?"

"Some. You'd been in a car accident, were in a coma for several months. Your husband…" She glanced at Ryan. "Dr. Alexander, I mean, had you relocated to the nursing home so he could keep an eye on you since that's where most of his patients were. After your baby was born, you woke up, but you were in and out of consciousness for quite some time. One day you'd be up and moving around, the next completely out."

She'd been awake. She'd been moving. Which explained why her recovery hadn't been so extreme. Why her body had bounced back relatively quickly. People had seen her, talked to her. And she couldn't remember any of it.

"Go on," she said, swallowing the lump in her throat. "Jake said he was my husband?"

Kari nodded. "Yes. Another doctor was overseeing your care. I didn't know his name. Tall, dark hair, the lightest blue eyes I've ever seen. They seemed to know each other well. I think it must have been his nursing home—or he knew the person who owned and operated it."

"Reynolds." Kate glanced at Ryan again. He'd been right. Her Houston doctor had been involved. Had probably been killed because of that involvement.

"What was the name of the experimental drug treatment?" Ryan asked.

"Amatroxin," Tom said. "It completely cured Kari's cancer. A handful of other patients were taking it as well. Last year, Dr. Alexander compiled a list of research and he and another doctor published this article in our medical journal." He handed Ryan a journal from the table behind him.

"This references a study in Canada," Ryan said.

Tom swallowed. "Yes."

"You published false data?" Kate asked.

Tom drew in a deep breath. "Yeah."

"Why? Why didn't you tell me any of this, Tom?"

Tom shifted his weight nervously, gripped Kari's shoulder tighter. She reached up and grasped his hand in a sign of support. "Jake and I had an agreement. He let Kari into the research project, and I kept what I knew about the studies to myself. When the time came to publish the information, I'd help. We were desperate, and willing to try anything. After it cured Kari's cancer, I owed him. He needed to show proof the drug worked; I knew it did. The way I looked at it, it didn't really matter where the studies took place."

"Tom didn't know you were married before, Kate," Kari cut in, her eyes shifting from Kate to Ryan. "What he knew was you were in the nursing home under Jake's care, that you were his wife. Jake asked him to keep things quiet around you. He said that the trauma from the accident had been especially bad. Jake was very worried about your prognosis."

Kate rubbed the scar on her head. So much of this still didn't make sense. "And when I woke up, he arranged for me to do freelance work for the publishing house." She glanced up at Tom. "You never questioned my background? What I knew?"

Tension gathered in fine lines around Tom's eyes. "I didn't know he was a McKellen until after he'd moved you to Houston. When I saw your name listed on one of your freelance articles, I contacted him. He said he didn't like to use the McKellen name because of a falling out he'd had with his family. I believed him. He's the one who set you up with the Dallas branch. I wasn't in a position to question anything he told me. It made sense, and I was indebted to him. And then when I saw your work, I realized he was right. You're more knowledgeable about geology than anyone I know."

"You still didn't say anything after Jake died. Why not? I was here in San Francisco. You knew I was looking for answers. You knew I'd been to that nursing home, but you didn't say anything?" She stood, anger bubbling through her. Ryan reached for her arm to steady her.

"I don't think you understand what's going on here, Kate," Tom said. "Someone doesn't want you to find answers. After you called me and asked about a job here at the San Francisco branch, we started getting warnings."

"What do you mean, warnings?" Ryan asked.

"Anonymous phone calls, mostly," Kari answered. "They never referenced your name, Kate, but they said to keep what we knew about the nursing home to ourselves. That it would be in Tom's best interest not to be involved if word of the study leaked."

"Then why did you suggest I see a lawyer?"

Tom sighed. "I wanted to help. I saw how frustrated you were. I thought maybe if you could find the answers on your own, if I wasn't directly involved, it wouldn't hurt to give you a little push. I didn't know the lawyer you picked was going to recognize you."

So Kate was the link. If she hadn't come to San Francisco, if she'd never called Simone and scheduled that appointment, if Simone hadn't recognized her, it was likely none of this would be happening now. The lies would still be truth.

Ryan looked to Kari. "Did anyone else visit Katie at the nursing home, that you know of?"

Kari bit her lip. "There was another man, older, white hair, large build. And a young woman once that I remember. Other than that, I'm not sure. Kate was there for a long time, though."

An older man and a young woman. That could be anyone.

"I'm not much help, I'm afraid," Kari said softly. "My memories from that time are pretty vague."

The anger seeped out, was replaced by a weary disappointment. Everything Kate discovered just seemed to confuse her more. She was learning the how but not the why.

"No." Kate blinked back frustrated tears. "You've been a big help."

"Kate." Tom stepped around the couch.

Out of the corner of her eye, Kate caught Ryan's tense shoulders, the way his arms dropped to his side in a protective measure. She held out a hand to stop him and glanced at Tom. "What?"

"If I'd known what was really going on, I wouldn't have kept quiet. I thought Jake was on the up and up. After your press conference the other day, I knew I needed to find you. To tell you what I knew. I've been trying to get hold of you since."

So many lies. Every time she turned around, there seemed to be one more, smacking her in the face. She wasn't sure what to believe anymore. "I need to find the answers, Tom. I'm not going to stop until I do."

"I'm not so sure that's a good idea."

"Nothing's going to happen to her," Ryan interjected firmly from across the room. "If anyone tries to hurt her, they'll have to get through me first."

There was a warning laced through his words that had both Kate and Tom turning. A muscle in Ryan's jaw twitched. His eyes hinted of vengeance.

Tom nodded and glanced back at his wife. "I know how you feel. If there's anything we can do, let us know. We want to help."

Sweat trickled down Kate's back under Ryan's intense gaze. She could see he was serious, that he'd take on anyone who came after her.

And for reasons she couldn't explain, that knowledge scared her more than what the truth held.


"We've been driving around for an hour, sweetheart," Mitch complained from the passenger seat of Simone's rented SUV. He flipped the map in his lap, studied street signs, then glanced back down. "Your sense of direction's crap."

Simone shot him a less-than-amused look. She was still having trouble dealing with the fact he'd changed his work plans and pushed his way onto this trip with her. Not only was he now seated beside her as they searched for Walter Alexander's home in the suburbs of Vancouver, he'd waited patiently while she'd finished her business in Seattle. Hadn't even complained once. She knew he was supposed to be at the Queen Charlotte Sound site doing whatever work an engineering geologist does, but every time she'd brought it up, he'd brushed her off and told her he was right where he was supposed to be.

What kind of man did that?

*One who's crazy about you.*

Her pulse picked up speed, and her hands grew sweaty against the wheel.

A minivan? He was clearly certifiable. Problem was, the idea didn't sound as insane to her as it had before. Which meant he'd sucked her into his alternate reality and that *she* was certifiable now too.

"Tell you what?" she said, trying not to think about the future and what she was going to do about Mitch Mathews yet. If she did, it'd just make her scream. "If I find it in the next ten minutes, you let me do some shopping on Robson Street before we head home."

"Fine with me. I'll hang out in the hotel."

"We aren't staying in a hotel, sweetheart."

"Don't remind me. I'm already bitter about that fact. My plans to seduce the hell out of you keep getting shot down."

Seduce the hell out of her? Oh, shit. She was in serious trouble with this one.

"So you'll come shopping with me," she said, trying to change the subject.

"I'd rather die a slow and agonizing death at the hands of a sadistic dominatrix." A grin quirked his lips. "Now there's a thought."

She couldn't help it. She laughed. He was one great big walking hormone. And God help her, she loved it.

"Now, Mitch." She turned down a side street. "We'll get to your fantasies later. Right now, we're talking shopping—just an hour or so of male torture. Trust me, you'll love it. There are some adorable boutiques on Robson Street."

"Kill me now. Wait. Do they have a lingerie store?"

Her stomach fluttered. "Probably."

"Think you can find a little black, lacy number?"

She pulled to a stop in front of a rambling cedar-sided house on a quiet street. "They might not have your size, honey."

"Very funny."

"And since I found the house, that hour's mine."

He grasped her arm before she could climb from the car and pulled her close. "Take me to that lingerie store, and I'll make it worth your while."

The heat from his eyes all but seared her veins. But when he kissed her, she forgot everything. Why they were here, what they were looking for, why the hell falling into a relationship with him was such a bad idea.

When he eased back, his eyes were dancing with a mixture of heat and humor. "Forget black lace. I think I want you in red leather."

Red leather? Oh, man.

Her nerves were a jangled mess by the time they walked up the front steps and rang the doorbell. She flipped her hair back from her face, straightened her jacket. "Let me do the talking. We don't need to scare Walter Alexander off first thing."

"If you use that cool, professional tone on me while wearing red leather lingerie and holding a whip, I'll definitely listen."

Her elbow connected with his sternum and he sucked in a breath. But his laughter vibrated through the porch and into her feet, then slithered up to her chest, reminding her just what it was about Mitch Mathews that did it for her. What was likely going to be her undoing if she wasn't careful.

"God, what is that smell?" Mitch brushed a hand over his nose.

"I don't know." Simone leaned her hand against the glass, peeked in a side window. Newspapers littered an antique table. A lime-green crocheted, afghan lay over the side of a chair. A piece of pizza sat atop a paper plate on an end table. Dust littered the surface of most items in the living room. An unopened suitcase was pushed up against the far wall. "Doesn't look like anyone's home."

"I can smell why."

Foreboding washed over Simone. She jogged down the front steps. A flagstone path graced the side of the house.

"Where are you going?" Mitch asked, following.

She ducked under a low bush and pushed the gate open, giving them access to the backyard. "Reynolds was found in his pool."

"Whoa. Back up. I suddenly have a bad feeling about this."

Simone rounded the corner of the house before he could stop her. The stench was stronger in the backyard. A cat darted from behind a tree and disappeared around the side of the house. Her eyes widened when she saw the body, feet sticking out of rhododendron bushes near the back stoop.

She swallowed, hard. "So do I."

"Oh, hell." Mitch stepped in front of her, blocking her view.


Ryan's mother, Angela, tucked her auburn hair over her shoulder and laughed, flashing a wide smile. Candlelight from the dinner table flickered across her face. "So, Mitch is belaying at the top of the cliff, and Ryan slips."

Ryan watched Katie's brow shoot up across the table. Her apprehension at having to meet his parents had slowly diminished as the evening wore on. They were all seated around his dining room table, empty dishes in front of them, his mother telling embarrassing stories from his youth. In any other situation, he'd have put an end to it, but Katie looked thoroughly interested, and after her afternoon with Kari Adams, he figured she needed a few minutes of peace.

Even if it was at his expense.

Shifting Julia on his lap, Ryan shook his head. "Dumbo didn't close the system."

"What does that mean?" Katie asked with genuine curiosity.

Kathy Mathews rounded the table with a pot of coffee, refilling cups. "It means Mitch didn't tie a keeper knot in the figure-eight knot, and the end of the rope passed right through the belay device."

"You see," Angela went on, "Ryan had never climbed outdoors before. He'd only ever climbed indoors with Mitch, so when this happened—"

"Scared the crap right out of me," he said with all seriousness.

Everyone laughed but Katie.

"What did you do?" Her eyes locked on his, and he read the concern in those green depths. His heart bumped.

"There was a huge crack about shoulder level, so I jammed my arm in, elbow first, and dug the toes of my boots into the rock to brace myself. Found I could rest almost all my weight on that arm, though it hurt like hell. Then I shouted every profanity I'd ever learned up at Mitch."

"So that's where my boy learned those words," Kathy said, laughing.

"You could have been killed." Katie stared at him with wide eyes.

Whenever she looked at him with those soft, emotion-filled eyes, he wanted to wrap his arms around her and lose himself in her sweetness. Since both their parents—and their kids—were sitting around the table, he decided it probably wasn't the best time to do that. He'd have to save it for later, when they were alone. When he could drag her into his bedroom, lock the door, and show her just how much having her in his house meant to him.

"Yeah, tell that to Mitch," he said, trying to dampen the fantasy. "He about bust a gut when I finally got to the top. Thought it was the funniest thing ever."

Roger Mathews leaned an elbow on the table and sipped his coffee. "If you listen to Mitch tell it, the cliff wasn't all that high. Ryan would only have broken a leg, maybe two in the fall."

"Thanks a lot," Ryan shot at him.

Laughter resonated around the table. The phone rang, and Julia scrambled off Ryan's lap to answer it.

"I think," Ryan's father, Michael, said, running a hand down Reed's little back as he slept against his chest, "that was the last time you went rock climbing with Mitch."

"What do you mean, 'with Mitch'?" Ryan crossed his arms over his chest. "It was the last time I went period."

Angela leaned over and kissed her son's cheek. "I prefer both your feet on the ground anyway, sweetie."

"Dad?" Julia walked back into the dining room with the cordless phone. "It's Uncle Mitch."

"Speak of the devil," Ryan muttered, tossing his napkin on the table and rising.

Conversation continued behind him. "Hey," Ryan said into the phone. "Where are you?"

"Simone and I are in Vancouver."

Ryan clenched his jaw, looked over at Katie, then turned back toward the kitchen. He rounded the corner toward his office and shut the door. "I thought I told her not to go up there."

"Ryan, she barely listens to anything I tell her. What makes you think she'll listen to you?"

As he sank into the chair behind his desk, he heard Simone's voice in the background and Mitch's sharp intake of breath. "Tell her to quit hitting on you so you can explain why you're there."

They exchanged muffled words, and Mitch's voice came back stronger. "We found Walter Alexander. Medical examiner thinks he's been dead about three days."

"Son of a bitch." This was all Ryan needed to hear. He glanced up sharply when the office doors opened.

Katie stepped in, closing the double doors at her back. "Put him on speaker phone."

Shit. He didn't want her hearing this right now. She was just starting to lose that haunted look. When he only let out a breath, she walked toward him and reached for the phone.

Reluctantly, he pushed the button. "Mitch, I'm putting you on speaker. Katie's here."

"What's going on?" She leaned back against Ryan's desk.

"We found Walter Alexander," Mitch said again.

"And?"

"And he's dead."

Her eyes darkened. The color drained from her face.

Ryan squeezed her thigh. "Cops have any idea what happened?"

"No." Mitch said. "Looks like he was whacked over the head with something, but they haven't said what cause of death is yet. Autopsy won't be until tomorrow."

Katie dropped her head in her hands.

"Also looks like he'd only been in Vancouver a few days.

Suitcase was still packed, passport showed he went through customs not long ago." Mitch paused. "Ryan, he had a copy of a Seattle newspaper with a picture from your press conference on the front page."

"Shit," Ryan muttered.

"He also had some papers about a pharmaceutical company here in Canada. Gray-something or other. Simone's trying to con the detectives into sharing some of their info with her. The woman is a bloodhound."

Pinching the bridge of his nose, Ryan fought back the frustration. And the fear. "I want you guys out of Vancouver."

"We should be on a flight home tonight. Police have a few more questions for us, but I wanted to give you a heads up."

"Thanks," Ryan said. "Stay safe coming back."

"Will do. I'll call you when we know more."

The line clicked dead. Without waiting for a response, Ryan stood and drew Katie into his arms. Tension radiated from her body. Her face pressed into his chest, her hands against his biceps. His skin tingled under her touch, and he itched to take away all her worries.

He knew he couldn't.

Resting his chin on the top of her head, he closed his eyes. How could he explain any of this to her when he still didn't know what was really happening? When he didn't know yet who was behind it? If she knew what he suspected, he was afraid she'd bolt. And he couldn't let her do that. Not until he knew how she felt about him.

They were growing closer. She felt something for him. Something he hoped was love. He needed to tell her what he knew—soon—but he couldn't risk it yet. And he wanted to find some answers first.

"I don't want to know anymore."

Her muffled voice tore at him. "I'm not going to let anything happen to you."

She pushed out of his arms. "I never liked him. Walter was never nice to Reed. I didn't understand why. Now I know it's because he knew Reed wasn't his grandson. But even knowing he was somehow involved in all of this, I wouldn't want him dead." Her voice broke. "I wouldn't wish this on anyone."

"I know." He reached for her hand. "It's not your fault." In his heart, he hoped to God it wasn't his fault, either.

"I need to leave."

He tightened his grasp. "No way."

"I don't want anything to happen to you, or the kids because of me."

The muscles in his chest tightened. She had no idea what losing her would do to him. "You walk out on me now and I'll just track you down and bring you back."

Her eyes slid closed. "This is never going to work, Ryan."

"Don't pull that on me again, either."

"I don't know what to think or feel about you. When I'm with you, I feel like I've known you forever. Then reality sets in, and I realize how crazy this whole thing is. A few days ago, you couldn't even stand to be in the same room with me."

He grasped her other hand, lacing his fingers with hers, drawing her attention back to his face. "That's not true. I wanted to be close to you so much it hurt, and I didn't know how to get there."

When her eyes softened, he drew her nearer. "And you do know me. Your body does. Your heart does. It's just your head that's being stubborn. It always was," he added playfully. "That's nothing new."

Her body shivered under his touch. He trailed his lips across her temple. She had no idea what he'd do for her.

"This is happening way too fast for me. I don't know how to control it. I'm scared," she whispered.

Scared was good. It meant what she was feeling was real. That there was hope. He slid his arms around her waist, felt her breasts press against his chest, felt the soft sway of her hips against his own. "You've never been able to control it. Neither have I. What's happening between us started a long time ago. You can't stop it anymore than I can."

When her fingers tightened on his shoulders, he bent and brushed his lips over hers. Her soft moan made his stomach muscles clench, sent his heart soaring. He wasn't about to let her walk away until he knew she loved him even a fraction as much as he loved her.

And by then, he hoped she'd never want to leave. No matter what.


The first rays of dawn slanted through the open window. Sheer, pale blue curtains blew in the gentle breeze. Kate wiped her sleepy eyes and squinted toward the clock. Seeing the numbers, she sat straight up, blinked twice, and scrambled over Ryan for the robe she'd dropped on his side of the bed late last night.

Ryan rolled, trapping her under his muscular arm. "Don't go," he groaned.

She pried her way out from under his arm and thrust the red silk robe over her shoulder. "You said you'd wake me before morning."

A wicked smile twisted his mouth. "You looked too peaceful to wake." He eased up on his elbows. "Come back to bed."

"Not a chance, you idiot." She pulled the robe tight around her waist.

He sat up and tossed his legs over the side of the bed, then grabbed her by the hips before she could get away. Nuzzling her abdomen, he loosened the tie with his teeth.

"Cut that out. I need to get back to my room before anyone wakes up."

"Our parents aren't going to care."

She pushed out of his arms. Why on earth he'd ever suggested both of their parents stay with him was beyond her. She'd been a complete lust-driven fool to sneak into his room in the middle of the night with the house so full. "I don't need either of our parents thinking I'm easy."

Laughing, he followed and braced a hand on the door when she tried to open it. "You're not easy. You're my wife."

Her skin tingled, and she turned, trapped between his tantalizing male—very naked—body at her front and the hardwood at her back. Her muscles quivered as his lips brushed her ear. Electrifying sensations ran through her whole body.

There was no reasoning with him when he had that look in his eye. She swallowed hard, fighting back the arousal. "Okay, then, I don't need Julia knowing I was in here all night. She already doesn't like me. This won't make it better."

His arm came around her waist, and he pressed her back against the door. She felt his erection where he pushed against her. Felt her whole body tighten with anticipation in response. "She's just going to have to get used to it."

Her eyes slid shut when his mouth nibbled its way down her neck. Oh, man. If he kept that up, she'd never leave. All she wanted to do was let him drag her back to bed and repeat every wicked, amazing, X-rated thing they'd done to each other last night.

But she couldn't. Because there was too much at stake in the daylight with the house so full.

Taking one long, deep breath, she braced her hands against his chest and shoved. He stumbled back a step, and she yanked the door open before he could stop her. "Later, Harrison."

His sexy laughter followed her into the hall.

The door at the end of the hall opened.

Oh, crap. Kate looked right and left. Sweat broke out on her forehead. She was trapped with nowhere to go. She glanced back at Ryan's closed bedroom door.

# CHAPTER NINETEEN

Angela stepped out of the door at the end of the hall. A pink terry robe was belted around her waist. Fuzzy bunny slippers sat perched on her feet. A knowing smile curled her mouth. "Oh, good morning, honey. You look…refreshed."

Heat flushed Kate's cheeks. Crap. So much for hiding. She swallowed the lump in her throat. "Um, I was just—"

Angela motioned toward the stairs. "Come on. Let's get some coffee before the men wake up. We haven't had any girl time yet."

Shit. Shit. Shit. Like Kate wanted that.

With no other option, Kate followed Ryan's mother down the stairs, the whole time trying to think up a pithy excuse to get out of the morning's chitchat. Her brain was complete mush after a night of sex. For the life of her, she couldn't come up with anything clever.

She paused when she passed a mirror in the hall. Her mouth fell open at her reflection and she scrambled to fix her hair. Matted curls stuck out all over her head. Her mascara was smudged under her eyes, her lips swollen from Ryan's kisses, her cheeks entirely too rosy first thing in the morning.

"Don't worry," Angela said without turning. "You just look like a very well-loved woman. I wonder if Ryan has any bagels in that kitchen of his." She disappeared around the corner.

Kate closed her eyes. This was going from bad to worse faster than she could pray for an earthquake to hit and put her out of her misery.

Swallowing the rising bile, she eased into the kitchen. Angela was already making coffee.

"Look in the refrigerator for some cream cheese, would you, honey?"

Kate was going to kill Ryan; that's all there was to it. Biting back the curses she wanted to mutter, she made her way to the gigantic stainless steel refrigerator and fished out cream cheese. When the coffee was done, Angela poured two mugs, then brought them and a plate of bagels to the table.

Kate sank into the chair beside her. The caffeine was the only thing that settled her nerves.

"Ryan tells me you've been having some trouble with Julia," Angela said, sipping her drink.

Kate planned to have a chat with Ryan about the things he liked to tell. She shifted in her seat. "Some. This isn't easy on her."

"No, I don't imagine it is. She was very young when you left. It was hard on both of them."

Curiosity got the best of Kate, and she bit her lip, wrapping her foot around the leg of the chair. "Did Julia and I get along?"

"Oh, of course you did." Angela smiled. "You were very close. Julia isn't upset with you, honey. You have to understand that. She's just afraid of going through all that again."

"I would think most kids would be thrilled to have a parent back. But she's fighting me every step of the way."

Angela patted her hand. "Things were very hard for her. Ryan didn't handle your leaving well."

When Kate's brow wrinkled, Angela eased back in her chair. "He loved you very much, more than he probably should have. Losing you broke him. He walked around in a daze for at least two years. I don't honestly think he would have made it through without Julia."

Kate's eyes slid shut. If she weren't already falling for Ryan Harrison, that one statement would have pushed her right over the edge. Her chest tightened until she was sure she wouldn't be able to breathe.

"I think Julia's afraid of what will happen to him if you decide not to stay," Angela said softly.

Kate looked down at her coffee. Wisps of steam poured off the hot liquid. "I don't know what's going to happen there. I can't make any promises either way. Ryan and I…" She lifted a shoulder and dropped it in defeat. "We haven't made any decisions. But I'll always be around for Julia. That will never change."

Angela was silent for a minute, watching her speculatively. Finally, she reached for a bagel. "Ryan told you Michael's not his real father, right?"

"No, I didn't know that."

Angela brushed her hair away from her face. "It's not a surprise you two haven't gotten around to family stories yet. Michael and I met in college. We fell madly in love, had this wild affair. But he joined the military, and we broke up. I met Kevin Harrison, Ryan's real father, after Michael left. We got married, and a year later, Ryan was born."

Her voice softened as she looked down into her mug. "Kevin was a wonderful man. That's where Ryan gets his blond hair and blue eyes. And he adored Ryan." She sighed. "He died in a car accident when Ryan was two."

"Oh. I'm sorry."

Angela waved a hand. "It was awful when it happened. But then, a few months later, Michael came home. And it was as if we were still in college. Like no time had gone by at all. Wild chemistry, an unexplainable connection." She smiled Kate's way. "I'm sure you know what I mean."

Heat flushed Kate's cheeks again.

"Anyway," Angela went on, "Kevin had only been gone a few months, and here I was, madly in love with another man again. I didn't know what to do about it. I mean, back then especially, a widow was supposed to grieve for a respectable amount of time before moving on. Not me. No, ma'am. I jumped right into bed with the first man that came along."

Kate couldn't stifle the laugh that bubbled out. She covered her mouth with her hand, realizing how insensitive she was being.

Angela chuckled and set her mug down. "Exactly. Insane, right?"

When Kate glanced over, Angela clasped her hand. "Not really. Not when you think about it. God gave Kevin to me so we could make Ryan. He was a gift, one that I cherish forever. And when it was time for him to go, God gave me Michael. He knew exactly what Ryan and I needed. It doesn't mean I didn't love Kevin any less, just in a different way. Sometimes we spend way too much time questioning the gifts we're given instead of being thankful for them."

Kate closed her eyes. "This is a completely different situation."

"Maybe," Angela said. "Maybe not. Fate's a finicky thing to mess with. Somehow you made your way back here to Ryan and Julia. There's a reason for that."

Angela's words were still hanging in the air when Michael eased through the kitchen door wearing sweats and a Seahawks T-shirt. "What are you two doing up so early?" he asked as he headed toward the coffeepot.

Angela lifted her mug. "Kate was thirsty after a night of wild sex with our son."

Heat shot up Kate's face.

"Mom, you're embarrassing her." Ryan stepped into the room behind his father and flashed a quirky grin.

Holy hell. It couldn't get any worse. Kate rubbed the scar along the side of her head. On shaky legs, she rose. "I need to go take a shower before my parents get up."

"Don't rush on their account," Angela said after her. "Your parents' room is right next to Ryan's. We heard you all the way down the hall. I'm sure they did too."

Kate's eyes widened. She shot Ryan a look. With cheeks she knew were the color of strawberries, she made her way to the stairs as fast as she could.

Ryan caught up with her on the bottom step. He'd already showered; his hair was still damp, his body smelling clean and fresh. "Hold on a second."

"You did that on purpose." She tried to wiggle out of his arms, but he held her too tightly. "You knew your mother would be awake when I got up this morning."

"Guilty. Maybe I'm tired of hiding this."

"That was sneaky. And I don't like it."

"I agree. But you don't have much of an excuse anymore. I'm going to have a chat with Julia later today."

She stopped fighting. "Don't do that."

"Why not?"

Standing one step up, she was just about the same height as him. His sapphire eyes drilled into hers as Angela's words ran back through her mind. "I don't want her to get hurt again."

Those deep blue pools softened, tugging on Kate's heart. "Then don't give her any reason to get hurt. Move in with us."

Kate's eyes widened. That wasn't the response she'd expected. "What? Are you crazy?"

A smile curled his mouth before he kissed her. She only stared at him. When he pulled back, those eyes were sparkling. "Yes. I am. Crazy in love with you. Julia needs time with you. Reed needs time with me. We all need a chance to get to know each other again. Driving back and forth between your place and mine won't do that."

"You're nuts. I can't just move in with you. Ryan, my God, it's only been a week."

"A week is like a lifetime to me. I want you in my house. I'll even put up with you in the guest room for the time being if that's what you want."

The air clogged in her lungs. "Is that what you want?"

"Hell, no. I want you in my bed. Every night. But I won't push you."

Unexpected relief bubbled through her, insane thoughts that maybe he was right. "You've been pushing me from the start."

When she leaned into him, she felt the smile that curled his mouth against her shoulder. "I guess maybe I have. Please tell me you'll at least think about it."

Her eyes slid closed, and she wrapped her arms around his shoulders. How could she fight him on this when deep down she knew it was what she wanted? "Okay, I'll think about it."

His arms tightened around her. "Thank you, Lord."

Held firm in his embrace, she almost believed they could make this work. She eased back enough to look in his eyes. "I'd like to spend some one-on-one time with Julia today. I was thinking of taking her shopping."

"I don't want you out there alone right now."

"Ryan, a few hours of shopping downtown won't kill us. We'll be in a crowd. I promise not to take her anywhere dangerous."

She saw the hesitation in his eyes, so she pushed back. "You can't keep me locked up here like a prisoner, you know."

Indecision ran over him. Finally, he said, "Okay. I need to go into the office for a while. I can get John from security to go with you."

She shot him a look. "No way. I don't need some security detail hovering over us when I'm trying to connect with Julia. That'll make things worse."

"Katie—"

"But I know how you worry," she said quickly, seeing the persistence in his eyes. "So how about a compromise? I'll call you to check in. Just to ease your mind."

He frowned. "Every hour."

She rolled her eyes. "God, you're worse than a mother hen. Okay, every hour."

The look in his eyes said he didn't like the idea, but he wasn't going to argue. "Julia has softball practice this afternoon."

"I can drop her off, then come back and get you."

He nodded reluctantly. "I guess that could work."

"Do you want a list of where we're going too?" she asked,

smiling. When his scowl deepened, she leaned in and kissed him. "Will you please let me go shower now before my parents get up?"

He let go of her, but she knew he was still watching her as she headed up the stairs.

"Need any help?" he called.

When she glanced back, the sly smirk tugging at his mouth almost did her in. Right or wrong, she had a sinking suspicion she was going to end up giving him exactly what he wanted.


"How about this one?" Kate held up a pink sweater.

"Pink? Are you serious?" With a huff Julia turned back to the rack she'd been studying. She pulled out a frayed, neon-green, fitted T-shirt that looked like it had been through the ringer. "I like this." With a challenging smile, she held it out to Kate.

Across the front were the words, *Pinch Me. I'm Hot and Sexy.*

Metal clanged against metal when Kate grasped it and hooked it back on the rack. "I don't think so."

"Why not?"

Kate wasn't about to fall for it. She'd already seen Julia's claws today. "Because you're nine. And they won't let you wear that at school. And your father would kill me if I bought that for you."

"A lot you know. I go to a private school. We wear uniforms."

Kate stood in the middle of the junior section, staring after Julia. No truer words had been uttered that day. *A lot you know.* That was the problem here. She didn't know a lot when it came to Julia. Didn't know anything, as a matter of fact.

Feeling like a failure, she followed Julia out of the store. They climbed into Ryan's Jag, and the motor hummed to life. After texting Ryan for the hundredth time to give him a status update, Kate pulled into midafternoon traffic. She and Julia had spent the whole morning shopping and hadn't agreed on a single thing. If it were possible, this little excursion had done more to damage their relationship than help it.

Kate rubbed her aching head.

"Where are we going?" Julia asked.

Kate changed lanes on the freeway. "I need to run out to my house and pick up a few things."

Julia rolled her eyes and leaned back against the seat. "You could have dropped me off at home first."

Kate bit back her temper. She wasn't going to fall into Julia's woe-is-me trap. She pulled off the freeway.

"Why aren't you staying at your own house, anyway?" Julia asked.

"Didn't your dad talk to you this morning?"

Julia crossed her arms and looked out the window. "Yeah, he did. It still doesn't answer my question, though. I know why he wants you at the house, but why are you going along with him? You know you don't want to be there."

Kate's fingers gripped the wheel as she made a turn. "I do want to be there, Julia. Your dad and I both think spending time together as a family will help all of us."

"One big happy family? It won't last. Not with you." She turned so Kate couldn't see her face.

Kate breathed deep, her temper almost to a breaking point. "What's it going to take for you, Julia? I've been bending over backward trying to get to know you, but you keep butting heads with me. What do I need to do to prove I'm not leaving again? That I want a chance to make it up to you?"

"You want a chance?" Julia's blazing eyes shot to her. "I'll tell you what you can do. Stop seeing my dad."

"What?" The car swerved around a corner. Roaring waves crashed against rock off to the right. Cliffs covered in brush rose to the left.

"You heard me. Stop seeing my dad. You don't love him. You know you don't. The longer you let this go on, the worse it's going to be when you decide to leave again. You don't have any idea what he was like before. I don't want to go through that again!" Her gaze shot to the churning Pacific below.

Kate's chest ached with a fierceness she didn't expect. She wanted so badly to reach out to Julia, to comfort some of that raging anger, but she didn't know how. Hearing the words from Julia's lips reinforced all of Kate's fears.

What would happen to Julia if this relationship didn't work out? She couldn't put Julia through that a second time. And what about Reed? He was falling for Ryan in a big way. If she moved in with Ryan like he wanted and then eventually left, it would kill Reed's little spirit.

*You don't love him. You know you don't.*

That was the ultimate question, wasn't it? She was wildly attracted to Ryan, felt deeply connected to him, but was that love?

What she felt for Ryan was stronger than anything she'd ever felt before. She knew that, could admit it. Her heart told her it was love, but her mind was left questioning her judgment. She'd been so wrong about Jake. She didn't want to make another horrible mistake. Acting on an impulse would only make things worse. She had to be sure.

The car whipped around the next corner, faster than Kate realized. She eased her foot to the brake.

Nothing happened.

Confusion gripping her, she pressed down again. When the car still didn't slow, she pumped the brake. Instead of slowing, they seemed to pick up speed down the hill.

Fear prickled Kate's skin. She tried to keep her voice calm. "Julia, climb into the backseat. Put your seat belt on and—"

"Why?"

"Listen to me! The brakes aren't working. Get in the back now! Snap your seat belt and hold on. Do it!"

Julia's eyes grew wide. Without another word, she climbed into the back.

Kate's mind tumbled as she recalled the road. Ahead were some curves followed by a downgrade, which would inevitably speed them up, and another curve followed by a steady incline with a curve at the top. If she could keep the car under control until they got to the slope, they had a chance.

She tried the parking brake, but nothing happened. Her heart raced, and she glanced at the dash. A quarter of a tank of gas—it wouldn't run out in time. She swallowed the fear. "Julia. My purse is in the backseat. Find my cell phone. Call nine-one-one."

Julia fumbled with Kate's purse. "Can't you just turn the car off?"

"No. The steering will lock up if I do. I'm going to try to downshift. Hold on, it's going to give us a jolt."

She held the wheel with one hand and shifted the automatic transmission into third gear. Sweat trickled down her back, but the shift was smooth, slowing them only slightly. She was already into a curve, trying as hard as she could to keep the car on the road. She downshifted again when the road straightened. The car bucked slightly.

They slowed down a little, enough to make the next two turns, then hit the downgrade. Kate tightened her grip on the steering wheel.

Julia's muffled voice drifted to the front of the car as she spoke to the nine-one-one operator in a panicked tone.

They weren't going to die like this. Kate drew in courage. She wouldn't let them.

The car picked up speed, whipped around the next curve. A muffled sob tore from Julia as her body slid against the side of the car. Kate downshifted one more time into first, sending them rocketing forward.

Her hands were wet with sweat when she made the next turn, and the car whipped across the road, tires skidding over gravel. Julia screamed. Kate's muscles tensed, and she managed to straighten out the car. It slowed considerably. Optimism settled over Kate for the first time since realizing the brakes were out.

Then her eyes caught the last turn coming up.

Oh, shit. They weren't going to make it. She glanced down to check their speed. They were still going too fast. She'd miscalculated the number of turns. They should be on the rise by now, but they weren't.

The road veered off sharply to the left. Ahead and to the right, the cliff dropped thirty feet to a small bay. If she tried to make the turn, they'd roll. She knew it. They'd roll down the embankment and most likely die.

She had only a split second to make a decision.

# CHAPTER TWENTY

"Julia, hold on."

Kate gunned the engine. The car sailed off the cliff toward the water. Julia screamed again in the backseat, and for one terrifying moment, it was as if they were flying.

The car hit the water; the airbag deployed. Kate's head smashed forward and back, hit something hard. The car bobbed for a few minutes before it took on water and the weight of the engine started to pull them down.

Cold water seeping in at her feet brought Kate around. Her head pounded. Every muscle in her body ached. With frantic fingers she unbuckled her seatbelt, swore frantically when she couldn't get out of it.

They weren't dead. They weren't dead, yet.

"Julia!" Kate tried to shake the fuzziness from her mind. She climbed into the backseat where Julia's head lay against the window, her eyes closed. "No, no, no."

Julia's head moved to the side, and she slowly opened her eyes. "What…what happened?"

"Oh, thank God," Kate exclaimed. "Come on, we have to get out of here."

Kate pushed against the back door, tried the windows. They wouldn't budge. Shifting back to the front seat as water continued to spill into the vehicle, she found the windows there were stuck as well.

"They won't open. They won't open!" Julia shrieked.

Using her foot, Kate tried to bust the front windshield at the corner, but it wouldn't move.

Darkness tried to draw her down. Kate shook her head, blinked and forced herself to stay awake. She was having trouble thinking and seeing clearly. Everything in front of her was blurry. "Okay, just relax, Julia. Listen to me." She grasped Julia's shoulders as the ice-cold water reached their bellies. "Listen. We have to wait for the water to fill the car. Once it does, it'll equal out the pressure.

We can't open the doors right now because there's too much pressure pushing on them. Once the car fills, the doors will open."

"No, they won't!" Julia hollered, cradling her arm against her stomach. "We're going to drown!"

"Listen to me. They will. Trust me. Don't panic, baby."

"I'm scared," Julia whispered, grasping Kate's hand.

"I know. It's okay. We're not going to die in here, you hear me?" Julia nodded as the car continued to fill. "We're going to make it. Just think good thoughts, okay? Think about Daddy and Reed and what you want to do tomorrow." Kate's vision blurred again, and she shook her head to clear it.

She had to stay awake. She had to stay coherent.

When the water level reached their necks, Julia's fingers tightened.

"Just a little more, baby," Kate murmured and lifted her chin. She took one last deep breath, gestured for Julia to do the same, then tried the door again. When it didn't budge, her heart dropped.

Icy tentacles of fear wrapped around Kate's throat.

*Don't panic. Try again.*

This time Kate put her back into it. With one good thrust of her body, the driver-side door opened. She grasped Julia's hand and pulled her out of the sinking vehicle. Light flickered at the surface above. Kate kicked as hard as she could.

They broke the surface together, gasped for air. Kate treaded water, gripped Julia's shoulders, and checked her face for signs of shock. "You're okay," she told her. "We're okay. Kick your legs, Julia."

Julia spit water and tried to breathe deep.

"Can you swim?" Kate asked.

With a shaky nod, Julia tried to kick for land. Kate wrapped an arm around her when she realized Julia was having trouble. Gentle waves lapped at the shore of the bay. Crashing water pounded rocks on the other side of the spit. Kate's energy waned as she dragged Julia out of the water.

Sirens blared in the distance. Kate dropped to her knees next to Julia and sucked in air. Water dripped around her, sending shivers down her spine, but all she could focus on was her daughter.

Julia lay on her back, her eyes closed, her chest fighting for air as she cradled her arm against herself. Kate grabbed her hand. "Stay with me. Hold on, baby."

Relief bubbled through Kate when voices echoed from the road above. *Help. They'd made it.*

Julia's hand slipped out of hers.

Kate glanced down sharply only to realize Julia wasn't moving anymore.


Thrusting bills at the cab driver, Ryan sprinted from the yellow taxi. The automatic emergency room doors opened, and he dashed into the reception area. A woman holding a sick baby stood in line at the front desk, rocking back and forth. A man with a blood-tinged bandage draped over his hand waited behind her.

Ryan pushed his way to the front of the line.

"Sir, you're just going to have to wait your turn." The receptionist sent him a wicked glare.

Fear clenched its icy hand around his heart. "My wife and daughter were in a car accident."

The receptionist's face softened. "Last name?"

"Harrison." He shook his head. "And Alexander."

Time ticked by second after miserably long second while she checked her computer. The baby behind him screamed. Ryan raked a frustrated hand through his hair and was ready to climb over the counter to check the screen himself when the receptionist finally said, "Room five. Go through the double doors—"

He turned and waited for her to buzz him though. Pungent institutional cleaners cut through the hallway air. A crash cart was pushed up against a wall. Medical staff chatted around the nurse's station.

Terror clawed through him as he checked doors, frantically searching for room five. When he finally found it, the muscles in his chest tightened, and he whipped around, heading for the nurse's station.

A blonde intern leaning against the counter looked up. "Can I help you, sir?"

"Room five's empty." Panic made his voice crack.

The blonde looked over at a redhead in blue hospital scrubs seated behind the counter. "Didn't they take her up to surgery?"

Surgery? No, no, no. Ryan caught his breath.

The redhead checked a chart. "I think so. Car accident, right?"

"Where?"

"Um, let me see." She flipped papers on a chart.

Good God, couldn't they see he was dying here?

"Wait," the redhead said. "That was the woman in six. Five's in X-ray."

Sweet Jesus, did they take classes on how to torture family members? "Where's that?"

The blonde pointed down the hall. "Take the first left, go all the way to the end and turn right. You can't miss it."

He was already jogging down the hall before she finished talking.

The air choked in his throat when he rounded the last corner. Katie was seated on a chair in the hall, bent over at the waist, her head in her hands.

"Oh, my God, baby." He dragged her out of the chair and pulled her tight against him. His heart thumped out of control when her hands slid around his waist.

Grasping her face, he pulled back enough to look down. Her eyes were red and bloodshot, her cheeks streaked with tears. A square bandage covered a wound above her left eyebrow.

He swallowed, his eyes locking on the bandage. "Are you...?"

"I'm okay," she said, gripping his elbows. "It's just a scratch. I hit my head. I'm okay."

Her voice was weak, but her eyes were steady. On a relieved sigh, he wrapped his arms around her and pulled her close again. "Thank you, God."

She wasn't hurt. But she was alone. Reality settled in. Followed by a gut wrenching shot of fear.

"Where's Julia?"

Tears filled her eyes. "They're X-raying her. Oh, Ryan, I told her to get in the backseat. I thought she'd be safer there."

He took a calming breath. X-rays were no big deal. CT scans, MRI's...those were the things to worry about. "You did the right thing. Tell me what happened."

"The brakes weren't working. I didn't notice until we were on the coast highway. I wanted to get a few things from the house. I...I didn't think anything would happen."

"It's okay. I'm just thankful you're both okay."

He pulled her tight again, drew in her sweet scent. When the police had called about the accident, his heart had all but stopped. Losing them was not an option.

"Ryan, your car," she said against his shoulder.

"You think I'm worried about my goddamn car? That's the last thing on my mind."

"Oh, good," she breathed against him. "Because I think the interior's shot."

She was cracking jokes. Jesus, he'd nearly had a heart attack at the thought of losing her again, and she was cracking jokes.

He held on tight, rocked her back and forth. Tried like hell to steady his racing pulse. "Locking you in the house is looking more and more appealing."

"You don't think this was an accident?" she asked quietly.

He didn't want her worried any more than she already was. Swallowing the fear, he eased back and brushed a wet curl from her face. "I think it's just a bad car. I never should have let Hannah talk me into getting it."

The door behind them opened, and they both turned as a nurse wheeled Julia out.

Ryan let go of Katie and stepped up to the side of the bed. Her face was bruised, her right arm wrapped in towels, and exhaustion tugged on her little body. "Daddy."

"Hi, baby." He ran a hand over her curly head, fighting back the panic at seeing her so broken.

Her eyes closed. "I have a headache."

"I bet you do." He glanced up at the doctor and held his breath.

"Broken arm," she said, lifting the X-ray. "Rib's bruised but not broken, and she took a good knock on the head. But I think she's going to be fine."

"Thank you," he whispered. Relief poured through him. With a hand that was still shaking, he stroked Julia's hair. "You think this is gonna get you out of dish duty?"

A grin twisted her lips, but her eyes stayed closed. "I have to get a cast. I don't think they let you get it wet."

"No way," the doctor said behind her. "You're on the injured list, miss."

Ryan reached for Julia's good hand, brought it to his mouth, and kissed her fingers. "Scared me, baby."

"Scared me too," she whispered. Her lashes fluttered open. "Mom drives a mean car."

The muscles in his chest squeezed tight when he looked into the depths of her green eyes, so much like her mother's. Hope sprang to life at the term of endearment. "She does?"

Julia nodded. "Where is she?"

"I'm right here," Katie said behind Ryan.

He moved to the side, making room. With her hand still

clutching Ryan's, Julia reached for Katie, locking the three of them together.

Warmth encircled Ryan's fingers. He watched emotions flow over Katie as she looked down at their daughter, hands clasping each other. This was what he wanted. Just this for the rest of his life. His family.

That tightness gripped his chest with the ferocity of a lion. He needed to tell Katie what he suspected about her disappearance. If she found out before he had a chance to tell her himself, he wasn't sure what she'd say or do.

His eyes slid shut, and he tightened his hold on both of them. A few more days. If he didn't hear from his private investigator by then, he'd tell her regardless.

No matter what, though, he had to keep them safe. For reasons he'd never understand, he'd been given a second chance. He wasn't about to blow it now.

Kate flipped a page, made a mark with her pen, and rested her chin on her hand. Lifting her knees from where she was stretched out on the floor, she propped her elbow on her leg and kept reading.

Julia shifted on the couch behind her. "What are you looking at?"

"An article for work." Kate pushed her glasses back up her nose.

"What's it called?"

Julia's curiosity brought Kate's head up. The girl's bruises had faded to yellow, but she was still obviously sore from the accident. At the moment, she was lying on the couch, reading a book. The fact she even wanted to be in the same room with Kate brought a smile to Kate's lips.

"'Microseismic Investigation of Rock Fracture and its Application in Rock and Petroleum Engineering.'" Kate raised her brows, a smirk tugging at her mouth. No way that would interest the girl.

"Petroleum's like oil, right?"

"Yep."

"Uncle Mitch would probably like that article."

Kate smiled. "Yeah, he probably would."

Julia levered herself off the couch.

"You need something?" Kate sat up to help her.

"No. I want to show you something."

With a sigh, Kate set the papers on the coffee table. She slipped off her glasses and waited. Julia had opted to stay home with her today instead of going shopping with the grandmas, instead of going to a baseball game with Reed and the grandpas. Ryan was at the office for a few hours. It was just the two of them.

And that little fact made Kate shift nervously on the floor. She was probably foolish in getting her hopes up that she and Julia had finally found common ground. But she wanted to think that more than anything.

Julia stepped back into the room and handed Kate a magazine.

"What's this?"

"Page seventeen. 'Tertiary Western Cascade Magnetic Arc.'" With slow movements, Julia climbed up on the couch again and laid her hot-pink cast across her middle. When Kate lifted her brows, she shrugged. "The Cascade magnetic arc is the major structural element in the Juan de Fuca-North American plate boundary."

"How do you know that?" Confusion ran through Kate, followed by amazement Julia would even know how to pronounce those words.

"I read it."

"You did?"

"Yeah. My mom wrote it."

Kate swallowed as she looked down at the journal in her hand. On page seventeen, the by-line read, *Anne Harrison, PhD.*

"Daddy said you drilled that definition into his brain when you were writing it."

"Did he?" Tears stung Kate's eyes. Had she really written the article? "I wish I remembered."

Julia was silent behind her. And then she said, "I remember a lot of things."

"You do?"

"Yeah. Like how you used to take me to your office at the college and let me play on your computer. Or how you used to drag Daddy hiking with you in the mountains. He never liked that."

Laughing, Kate glanced back down at the journal. Julia had saved it, all this time. She'd memorized the words, even though she probably didn't understand what they meant. And today, she'd shared it. Emotions stirred in Kate. "Your dad's kind of a city boy."

A smile split Julia's angelic face. "That's just what Uncle Mitch says too." Then her smile faded. "Maybe someday we could go hiking like we used to."

Hope welled inside Kate's soul. More than anything, she wanted to bridge the gap between them, but she didn't want to do anything to make Julia pull back. This was a first step. A big step. So instead of reaching for her daughter and drawing her close like she wanted to do, she squeezed Julia's ankle. "I'd like that, very much."

The doorbell rang, and Julia looked up.

Kate pushed up from the floor. "You stay put, queen of the couch. I'll get it."

Two men dressed in suits stood on the other side of the door when Kate pulled it open. "Can I help you?" she asked.

The taller of the two pulled ID from his breast pocket. "Ma'am. I'm Detective Peterson. This is Detective Carson. SFPD. Are you Mrs. Harrison?"

Kate pushed the door open wider. Tingling fingers of dread tiptoed up her spine. "Actually, the name's Alexander. What's this about?"

His companion's eyes narrowed. "I recognize you from the newspaper."

"That's right," Detective Peterson said, recognition flickering over his face. "The press conference. You're the woman without a past."

Kate doubted they were here to chat about a picture in the paper. "What can I do for you?"

Detective Peterson flashed a smile. "We have a few questions about your accident the other day."

The accident. Of course. Silly of her to be on edge so quickly. Stepping back, she gestured inside. "Won't you come in?"

Shoes clicked behind her on the hardwood floor as the men followed Kate into the living room. Julia sat up from her spot on the couch. "Detectives, this is my daughter, Julia. Julia, these men have a few questions about the accident."

Detective Peterson stepped closer to the couch. "Cool cast. They didn't have nifty colors like that when I was a kid. You got lots of signatures on it?"

Julia shrugged. "Not yet."

"Bet you'll have it filled up before long." He studied her battered face. "Looks like you got a little banged up. How are you feeling?"

"Okay."

Detective Carson flipped open a notebook. "Ms. Alexander, can you tell us where you went on Thursday?"

"I was here in the morning. Ryan, Julia, and I drove into the city. We parked in Ryan's building garage. He went to work, and Julia and I walked downtown."

"How long were you away from the vehicle?" he asked, jotting notes.

"I'm not sure. A few hours, maybe."

"Did Mr. Harrison drive the vehicle after you left it in the garage?"

"I don't believe so, no."

He continued making notes. "Did Mr. Harrison know you were driving his car?"

"Yes. He knew I was going to take Julia to her softball practice when we were done, then come back and get him."

"So he knew you'd be alone in the car?"

Her eyes narrowed. "Yes. What's this about, Detective?"

Peterson stepped up next to Carson and smiled. "Just following up on some conflicting information. Are you living here, Ms. Alexander?"

Kate's adrenaline jumped. "Not exactly. You obviously read about me in the paper. We're taking some time getting to know each other again."

"Of course you are," Peterson said. "How would you classify your relationship with Mr. Harrison?"

"I don't know that I would." Nervous tension ran through Kate at the vague questions. "What does this have to do with my accident?"

"Are you aware Mr. Harrison's insurance company is grumbling about his repaying the claim he collected after you supposedly died?" Carson asked.

Kate's stomach clenched. "No. He didn't mention it."

"Probably didn't want to worry you." Peterson flashed that smile again. For some reason, it did nothing to calm Kate's nerves.

"Do you know how much that claim was for, Ms. Alexander?" Carson asked. When she shook her head, he raised his brow. "A million dollars."

Kate's eyes widened before she checked the emotion.

"That's a lot of money. Even for a man like Ryan Harrison. Especially five years ago."

Bile rose in Kate's throat. Knowing exactly where this was going, she turned toward Julia. "Honey, go upstairs."

Julia rose from the couch. "Mom—"

Kate ushered her toward the stairs. "It's okay. I'll be up in a minute." She waited until Julia rounded the corner, then set her jaw and turned back to the detectives. "If you're trying to imply Ryan had anything to do with my accident—"

"The brake line was punctured," Carson said.

"What?"

"Three holes. Too evenly spaced to be the result of a rock. We pulled the vehicle from the water this morning. You lucked out. If you'd gone in anywhere else along that highway, you'd have dropped right into the ocean, drown before help got there."

Kate eased down to the arm of the sofa. Someone had tampered with the car. Someone had intentionally tried to hurt her.

And Julia in the process.

"Would have taken a little while for the brake fluid to drip out, which is probably why the brakes didn't go out right away," Peterson added. "Whoever punctured the line knew that."

"Ms. Alexander," Carson said, "Did you drive Mr. Harrison's car Tuesday morning?"

Kate's brain was a mass of confusing thoughts. "No."

"Did Mr. Harrison?"

"Um." Why was she having trouble thinking clearly? Tuesday… She'd spent Monday night here. In the guest bedroom. The next day, they'd gone out to see Janet Kelly. She'd had her CT scan. They'd gone back to her house in Moss Beach and made love. She swallowed. "Yes. He went in to his office for an hour that morning, I think."

"Was he alone?"

"I think so. I don't know."

The detectives exchanged glances.

"Do you know this woman?" Carson asked, handing her a photo.

Kate studied the picture and shook her head. "No. Should I?"

"Her name's Janet Kelly. Her body was found yesterday."

Kate glanced up sharply.

"A black Jaguar matching the one we pulled from the bay was spotted in front of her house around the estimated time of death Monday morning, roughly nine a.m."

No. That wasn't right. They'd gotten a late start. They hadn't reached Janet Kelly's houseboat until after noon. She swallowed hard, unsure what to tell them, not wanting to give too much away. "You must be mistaken."

Carson handed her another photo. "How about this man? Do you recognize him?"

Kate's eyes grew wide when she looked at the photograph of Jake. Steel-gray eyes gazed back at her. Fear tickled the back of her throat. "Yes. Why?"

"Jacob McKellen was a silent partner in Grayson Pharmaceuticals, a Canadian company Harrison's conglomerate recently acquired," Carson said coldly. "We pulled his body from the bay last week."

# CHAPTER TWENTY-ONE

Kate leaned against the counter in Simone's kitchen and massaged her scar. Time ticked by silently on the clock above the stove. The only sound was the pounding in Kate's brain.

She stiffened when Simone swept into the room. "Well?"

Simone set the cordless phone on the table. "Ryan and his lawyer are at the station. So far, they're cooperating."

Kate braced both hands on the counter. Her heart felt like it was being ripped to shreds. Everything she'd believed up to this point was turning out to be a lie.

"Richard Burton's one of the best attorneys in the state, Kate. Their questioning won't last long. He won't let it."

"Oh, God," Kate muttered, unable to fight back the panic. "Ryan knew Jake didn't die in that plane crash."

Simone leaned back against the table and crossed her arms. "That's yet to be proven. What can be proved is that Ryan's secretary saw Jake in Ryan's office the day before that crash here in San Francisco. And that Ryan appears to be the last person to have seen him alive."

Kate's eyes slid closed. "Why?" she whispered. "Why wouldn't he tell me the truth?"

"I don't know. But there's more." When Kate glanced up, Simone shifted. "Jacob McKellen, a.k.a. Jacob Alexander, and Walter Alexander were both silent partners in Grayson Pharmaceuticals, a Canadian company with a specialized drug portfolio. AmCorp recently acquired Grayson for a good chunk of change, alleviating some of their cash-flow problems. With AmCorp's clout, they were about to push Amatroxin through for FDA approval, based on a series of clinical studies supposedly conducted in Canada."

"Amatroxin is Tabofren under a different name, isn't it?" Kate asked, already knowing the answer.

"There's no proof as of yet, but that would be my guess. The detective in Canada I chatted with mentioned paperwork taken from Walter Alexander's home referencing both drugs."

"Ryan knew about the possible link between the two." Kate drew in a breath to keep the tears of anger back. "He stood in Kari Adams's living room and pretended like he didn't know a thing about Amatroxin."

"Jake disappeared just after the merger went through. Ryan's secretary said she heard Ryan and Jake arguing that day in his office, although she can't say what the debate was about."

Kate dropped her head. "They think Ryan killed Jake. For what? Money?"

"Money's a huge motivator for some people," Simone said softly. "Ryan stood to make a killing if Amatroxin was approved. Jake developed it, he had a hand in testing it, but with him out of the way, the wealth floats to the top."

"You don't honestly believe that," Kate said, bile rising in her stomach.

"No, Kate. I don't. But that's the way the police are going to paint it."

"And Janet Kelly? They think he killed her to cover up the research study?"

"They'll be able to link Janet Kelly to Jake through the nursing home. They'll try to prove Ryan covered up evidence. If word got out illegal trials had taken place in the States, Amatroxin would never be approved."

Kate's eyes slid closed. "And the car?"

Simone sighed. "They'll try to say he tampered with the brakes, knowing you'd be in it alone. With you out of the way, he double-benefits. He doesn't have to pay back the life insurance claim, and there's no one to ask questions about Tabofren. You're the key to all of this, Kate."

A few hours ago, her future had looked bright and promising. Now, she wasn't sure how she'd get through the next hour without losing her slight grasp on reality. She wrapped her arms around herself. "I think I'm going to be sick."

Simone skirted the counter. Bracing both hands on Kate's arms, she said, "Listen to me. The police can't charge Ryan with anything at this point because their evidence is all circumstantial. You and I both know Ryan is not capable of any of that. I'm only pointing out what the DA's going to say if things escalate. Not what's reality."

Kate's eyes locked on Simone's. Her head and heart were caught in a fierce battle. The man she'd fallen in love with couldn't possibly be capable of murder, of conspiracy, of cover up. If he were, then it meant he'd known about her disappearance all along. And she couldn't believe that. Not after the things he'd shared with her, the emotions he'd pulled out of her in such a short amount of time.

But always in the back of her head was that nagging voice saying she didn't know the *real* Ryan Harrison. The steely businessman who'd built a pharmaceutical empire hadn't done so by being sweet and loving. There were qualities about Ryan Harrison, CEO, she knew he kept hidden from her. Were they finally emerging?

No matter how she looked at it, the lies that had ruled her life for five long years were once again consuming her.

Kate shook her head. "I don't know what I believe anymore, Simone. I just know I can't trust him. I don't know if I'll ever be able to trust what he tells me again."


Ryan ducked into Mitch's Land Rover. A handful of reporters closed in on them, trying to get a statement. Cameras were thrust against the windows, microphones held out for any sort of comment.

Dropping his head, Ryan rubbed his temples while Mitch pulled away from the police station. He tugged his cell from his pocket and dialed Hannah's number.

"Ryan, I'm glad you called. The press is hounding me."

"No comment, Hannah. Get a memo drafted for the employees. No one talks to the press. And I mean no one. Fax it to me at home before you send it out."

"The press is staked out on your front lawn, Ryan," Mitch cut in.

"Shit. Fax it to Mitch's house, Hannah. I'll be there for a while."

"Okay," she said. "Are you finished downtown?"

"For now." Disgust pooled in his gut at the accusations the detectives had thrown out. "I need you to get me the surveillance tapes from the building garage. Someone used my car last week without my knowledge."

"I can do that."

"And Burton may call with information. If he does, reroute it to me."

"Will do. Ryan?" she asked hesitantly. "Are you okay?"

"I'm fine." He shrugged off her concern. "Find Ron Grayson for me as well. I need him on this."

"I'll find him. Don't worry, Ryan."

*Don't worry. Yeah, right.* Like that was possible at this point. He closed the phone. Resting his elbow on the windowsill, he massaged his throbbing head. "Where's Katie?" he asked without glancing at Mitch.

"Simone's house." He hesitated. "Ryan, she knows about McKellen."

Closing his eyes, he drew in a steadying breath. He could only imagine what was going through that stubborn mind of hers. He should have told her sooner. He shouldn't have waited.

"What about the kids?" he asked.

"Mom and Dad took them to my place so they wouldn't have to deal with reporters."

He nodded. "I need to talk to Katie first."

"I figured. She's pissed."

"Yeah, tell me something I don't already know."

"Ryan—"

"Not yet, Mitch. I'll explain it all after I see Katie."

When they pulled up in front of Simone's house, Ryan eased out of the car and jogged up the front steps. Pushing the door open, he saw Simone on the phone. She waved him in. "I'll have to call you back." She hung up and glanced from Ryan to Mitch behind him. "I just got off with Hannah Hughes. She's found Ron Grayson."

"I'll call him later." Ryan glanced around the empty room. "Where's Katie?"

"Out back." When he stepped past Simone, she placed a hand on his arm, stopping him. "Ryan, I did the best I could."

He squeezed her hand. "I know."

Katie was standing on the edge of the deck, facing away when he eased the door open. One arm was wrapped around her middle; with her other hand, she rubbed that scar on the side of her head, the one she'd gotten when this had all started. Sunlight washed over her, bathing her in shimmering light. His arms ached to hold her; his fingers itched to slide into that mass of chestnut curls and massage away the tension and worry seeping from her body.

He hoped what he wanted and what she needed were the same. Swallowing the fear, he stepped up behind her. "Katie."

Her green eyes flashed when she whipped around. "You lied to me."

Fear spread to panic. She'd already made up her mind. He reached for her before she could step back.

"No, don't," she growled through clenched teeth, trying to pull away.

"Hold on. Let me explain."

She swatted at him, pushed hard against his shoulders. "No. No!"

Heartache ripped through her words, tearing at his soul, but he didn't let go. Couldn't. He pulled her tight against him.

His name was a strangled whisper from her lips. A sob tore through her. Shaky fingers grasped his face and pulled his mouth to hers. Her kiss tasted of urgency, of hunger, of desperation.

Thought slipped out of his mind as he kissed her back. This was all he needed. Just her, for the rest of his life. He could face any challenge as long as she was with him. As long as she believed in him—in them—they could get through anything.

"No," she mumbled against his mouth. Her hands rushed down to his chest, pushing against him. Tears slipped from her eyes as her mouth broke free. "No! Don't. Don't touch me!"

An icy rush of air washed over him when she pushed out of his arms. "Babe—"

She held out a hand to keep him away. "Don't call me that. You don't get to call me that."

He was losing her. Panic spread to bone-melting fear as a heavy weight pressed down on his chest. "Just wait. And listen."

"You knew Jake didn't die in that plane crash. And you didn't tell me. You knew!" She swiped at the tears. "How could you do that?"

He swallowed, hard. "I didn't know for sure. I suspected. And I knew if I'd told you, you'd have gone looking for him."

"So you lied to me? Why?"

He raked a hand through his hair, tamping down the resentment at the mention of Jacob McKellen. "Because you're *my* wife, not his. I needed you with me. I needed to know how you felt about me before I told you what I knew. It was wrong, and it was selfish, but I wanted more time." When her mouth dropped open, desperation tugged at him. "Don't you get it? I wasn't about to let you get anywhere near him after I knew what he'd done."

"So you let me believe a lie. You didn't trust me enough to be honest with me."

"No." It was coming out wrong. She wasn't getting it. "That's not it. I didn't want you to get hurt."

"And this is so much better," she mocked. Her eyes darkened. "You were working with him."

"No." On this, she had to believe him. "I swear, I wasn't."

"Don't lie to me! I know he was in your office. I know he was a partner in Grayson Pharmaceuticals. You acquired his company. You were planning on pushing Amatroxin through the FDA. My God, was this all about the money?"

The muscles in his chest tightened. Just the thought she would believe any of that sent the pain of a thousand daggers right through his heart. "I didn't know Amatroxin was linked to Tabofren when I went ahead with the merger. I had my suspicions."

"So you jumped on it?" A pathetic laugh rippled through her. "You were willing to do anything to get it?"

"No. I was willing to do anything to keep it off the market. I had an idea what McKellen was planning. Grayson was in trouble. They'd dumped all their money into that drug. I stepped in to make sure Amatroxin didn't go before the FDA. I put a stop to the process after we acquired the company. If anything, I lost money in that deal."

"You expect me to believe that?"

"It's the truth. That's why McKellen showed up at my office. He was pissed that I'd terminated the project a second time."

Disbelief swirled in her green eyes.

"Did you kill him?" she asked in a chilly tone.

"No." When she glanced away, he set his jaw. "But I would have. If I'd known what he did to you, I'd have ripped his heart out with my bare hands."

When she glanced back, he hoped she saw the truth in his eyes. "I would do *anything* for you."

"Anything," she whispered. "Including trying to cover up this whole mess by getting rid of Janet Kelly."

"No." He reached for her, but she stepped back. As his hand dropped to his side, frustration spurred his temper. "Do you honestly think I could do that?"

"Someone saw your car that morning. At her house. Before we even got there to try to talk to her. What am I supposed to believe, Ryan? You left me that morning. You said you were going to your office, but you didn't."

"And you believe I would go murder some woman?" Disbelief raged through him.

"I don't know what to believe anymore. Everything I thought I knew is a lie!"

That vise tightened around his heart. She didn't believe in him, not like he needed her to. She was pulling away, putting up those barriers he'd worn down over the last week.

"I didn't kill anyone, Katie," he said on a sigh. "I parked in the building garage that morning and walked three blocks to a private investigator's office downtown. Someone must have used my car while I was there."

"That's convenient, don't you think?"

"It's the truth."

"Why were you going to see a P.I.?"

"Because I wanted to find McKellen. I wanted to know if he was the one behind all this. I needed to make sure he wasn't planning on hurting you again."

She dropped to a bench on the deck. Curls tumbled across her face when her head fell into her hands.

He rested his hands on his hips and clenched his jaw as he watched her. He wanted to reach for her, but she'd made it clear she didn't want him touching her. "Are you going to ask me if I tampered with the brakes too?"

"I know you didn't," she whispered.

Finally. Sensibility. He ached to hold her, to reassure her. He stepped forward. "Katie—"

"Who killed him?"

"I don't know."

Damp lashes lifted so she could look at him. "Don't know, or won't tell me?"

"I don't know."

"You don't have any idea?"

"No."

She pressed the heels of her hands against her eyes. "I don't know what to believe anymore."

Kneeling in front of her, he placed trembling hands on her thighs. "Believe in me. Believe in us. I love you. I wouldn't do anything to hurt you."

"Don't you get it, Ryan?" she whispered. "You did hurt me. In the worst possible way." Tortured emotions brewed in the depths of her emerald green eyes. "You made me fall in love with you.

Then you took away the very trust that love was built on. How am I ever supposed to believe anything you say?"

The air clogged in his throat. She loved him. Her revelation was exactly what he'd wanted to hear since the day she walked back into his life, but never in a thousand years did he expect her to say it wasn't enough.

She pushed his hands aside and rose.

Fear and heartache clawed at his soul. He was going to lose her if he didn't do something to make this right. Rising, he fought back the tears stinging his eyes. "Katie, please."

She wiped at her cheeks. "I can't. I don't even know you."

"You do know me. You know everything that matters." When she turned for the door, his voice hitched. "Please. I can't lose you a second time."

She paused with one hand on the door. "Don't you understand, Ryan? You already did."


"Mitch, this is ridiculous."

Kate dropped blankets and a pillow on the couch. Calming waves tickled the shore in the moonlight outside her beach house, but the familiar sounds did nothing to settle the desolation in her heart. What she wanted was to be alone, to wallow in her misery. What she had was an overprotective brother who wasn't giving her an ounce of space.

"Don't even think about arguing with me on this one." Laying a sheet over the couch, Mitch shot her a frown. "You're not staying by yourself right now."

Frustration curled through her. "I'm not a child. I can take care of myself."

"Would you just stop arguing? You always were a pest when you set your mind to something." He tossed the pillow at the end of the couch, fluffed a blanket over the cushions.

"Did Ryan send you over here?"

"He suggested it. And I'd have listened if I hadn't already made plans to be here."

She let out a frustrated groan. "I need to be alone right now."

"No, you don't." He flopped onto the couch, toed off his shoes, leaned back against the armrest, and propped his feet on the cushions. "You need to be doing something to take your mind off Ryan. Making dinner for me would probably do it."

Her eyes slid closed, and she tried to muster up the exasperation he deserved. But instead, a pathetic laugh bubbled through her. She pushed his feet out of the way and dropped onto the couch.

Mitch sat up with a grin, tossed his arm over her shoulder, and chuckled. "See, isn't that better?"

As she dropped her head in her hands, the laughter turned to tears. Her chest tightened, the implication of what she'd done sweeping over her. Sobs wracked her body, and as hard as she tried, she couldn't stop the dam from breaking. She wrapped her arms around her head in embarrassment, some tiny part of her vaguely aware she wasn't alone.

"Oh, crap." Mitch's arms circled around her, pulling her tight against his chest. "It's okay. Let it out."

Her tears soaked into his blue T-shirt. She sniffled and tried to turn her head.

Mitch glanced down and waved a hand. "Go ahead. Use it as a tissue. It's just a Cubs shirt. They suck this year."

Gripping the soft cotton, she couldn't help but chuckle through the tears. She fought for control, dragged air into her lungs, only to have the dam break all over again.

Mitch ran a hand down her hair. "You're going to be okay. Cry it out."

How could she hurt so bad after only a few weeks? A month ago, she hadn't even known Ryan Harrison. Today, her world was tumbling down around her because she couldn't have him.

And what hurt most was knowing that even with everything she'd been through, knowing all the lies, all the deceit, she still wanted him. She wanted his arms around her. Wanted his body lying next to her. Wanted that family she'd never expected, never let herself hope for. In a few short weeks, he'd changed everything for her. And she didn't know if she'd ever be able to set it right again.

Somehow, she steadied herself. Pushed back from Mitch and drew in large gulps of air.

He brushed a tear from the corner of her eye. "You never were much for emotional outbursts."

Sniffling, she ran a hand across her face. "I'm still not. I told you I wanted to be alone."

"What can I do?" he asked softly.

"Nothing. There's nothing anyone can do."

"Kate, Ryan's not a bad guy."

"I know that. I don't want you caught in the middle, Mitch. I know you love him."

"I love you too."

Tears welled inside again, and she covered her eyes with her hand. "I know," she managed in a weak voice.

"Isn't there any way you two can work this out? It's obvious how much you love him."

"I do. Too much. But sometimes love just isn't enough."

His frown tore at her.

She swiped at her face again, desperate to change the subject. "Speaking of relationships…" She sniffled. "Simone tried to fire me today. Said she couldn't in good faith be my lawyer anymore because she's sleeping with you."

A cheeky smile spread across his face. "What did you tell her?"

"I told her she couldn't fire me because I was the client. And when she argued I told her if she brought it up again, I'd convince you to break up with her."

His smile widened. "And what did she say?"

"She backtracked rather quickly. I think she's got the hots for you, Mitch."

His smile turned to a full-blown grin as he leaned back against the couch and threaded his fingers behind his head. "Well, I'll be damned."

Seeing how happy he was made Kate remember how unhappy she was. Tears threatened again. She'd cried more in the last few weeks than she had in a year. She was sick of being such a girl. She rose, wiped her face again. "I need to go lie down."

He pushed off the couch. "Are you going to be okay?"

That was a ludicrous question at the moment. Her heart had just been ripped to shreds, and she still didn't understand what had really happened to her. But knowing that wasn't the answer Mitch wanted to hear, she mustered up a pathetic smile. "I'll survive. I've learned how to cope along the way."


Wind pelted the small house. A sliver of moonlight peeked through the sheer curtains in Kate's living room, shining right in Mitch's eyes. Tossing an arm over his face to block out the light, he muttered curses. Whatever happened to real curtains?

*Slap. Slap. Slap.*

Good God, what was that? He flopped onto his side and

yanked the pillow over his head to block out the relentless sound and obnoxious light. How the hell did Kate ever fall asleep in this place?

*Slap. Slap. Slap.*

No way he was sleeping with that incessant noise. On a frustrated groan, he tossed back the covers and moved toward the kitchen. Waves crashed against the sand outside. Placing a hand up to the window, he peeked into the backyard.

*Slap. Slap. Slap.*

The screen flapped furiously in the wind. Pulling the back door open, he eased down the back steps in his bare feet, shivering in the cool night air. Sand gritted between his toes. A gust of wind whipped his hair in his face, reminding him he needed another haircut already. Damn thing grew like a weed.

The screen hung carelessly on rusted hinges. He ran his fingers along the doorjamb searching for a hook or latch of some kind. No way Kate just let it flop around all day and night. Unable to find anything, he made a mental note to fix it for her tomorrow. If nothing else, he could give her a peaceful night's sleep.

A twig cracked behind him. His fingers paused on the wood. He turned. A shadow darted to the side. Pain exploded in the side of his head before he could follow the movement.

"Motherfucker." He gripped his head and made it up one step before everything went black.

# CHAPTER TWENTY-TWO

Light from the refrigerator spilled over Ryan into the dark kitchen. He stood with the door open, peering into the massive cavern. He wasn't hungry, and a beer wasn't going to quench the ache in the pit of his stomach. But lying in that bed upstairs remembering Katie next to him wasn't doing much to help him relax either.

He glanced toward the phone. He should call her. But he didn't know if she'd listen or just hang up on him. Rubbing a hand over the pain in his chest, he let out a long breath and closed his eyes. He'd give her a day. Then he'd try again. She wasn't getting rid of him that easy.

His cell phone rang, and he jumped. Slamming the refrigerator door, he reached for it on the counter. Hope pulsed through him. Hope that she'd finally come to her senses.

"Katie?"

"Ryan, it's Simone."

"Oh, hey." Disappointment flowed.

"Ryan, Mitch isn't answering his phone."

The hair on the back of his neck stood up at the panic he heard in her words. "What?"

"He's not answering his cell. He told me he'd have it on him at all times. Kate's not answering her home phone or cell, either."

Oh, shit. He didn't even think, just headed for the hall where he'd left his shoes. "I hired security to sit outside her house. They haven't called. It could just be the storm."

"Right," Simone said, but he knew she believed that as much as he did. "My PI finally emailed his report. My server was down today so I just got it. Ryan, Walter Alexander had two daughters. One of them died of cancer five years ago. Paula McKellen."

Ryan stopped with one hand on the front door, the keys to his rental car in his hand as realization dawned. "That's how he was linked to the McKellen name. He married into it."

"Yes. Walter Alexander is—or was—Karl McKellen, president of McKellen Publishing. His daughter Paula married a Jacob

Alexander eight years ago. She died after Tabofren was pulled by the FDA. I think she was in the clinical studies that were stopped."

"Shit, that's why he was so pissed." And that's why Ryan hadn't recognized Jake Alexander's name or put it together with the man he'd met and dealt with in his office. Because the son of a bitch had been using both names, staying under the radar as he ran his illegal drug study. And his father-in-law—Karl McKellen—had partnered up with him and Grayson Pharmaceuticals to get it pushed through the FDA.

"Yeah," Simone said as rain pelted his face while he ran for the car. He climbed in, started the engine. "But there's another daughter."

He pushed damp hair out of his eyes and backed out of the driveway at rapid speed. "Where?"

"Here in San Francisco. Ryan, she works for you."

"What? There's no McKellen in my company. No Alexander either."

"Ryan, his other daughter is Hannah Hughes."

"No. Are you sure?"

"Yes."

Oh, shit. Hannah, who'd been to Vancouver several times in the last month. Hannah, who'd headed the merger with Grayson. Hannah, who'd purchased that car for him and could have easily used it the day Janet Kelly had died when he'd left it parked in the building garage. And Hannah, who knew every detail of Katie's return because he'd been stupid enough to share it with her.

Urgency coursed through him. He gunned the engine. "Simone, Hannah knows Katie's out at the beach house tonight."

"I'm in the car on the freeway. I already called the police."

"I might beat you there. Don't go inside without me or the cops. Do you hear me?"

The line went dead. "Simone?"

Shit. He couldn't be sure if she'd heard him or not. He dialed the security detail he'd hired to sit outside Katie's house.

No answer.

*Shit!*

Foot heavy on the accelerator, he tossed the phone on the front seat and gripped the steering wheel.

\* \* \*

Warm water slid over Kate's skin. Bubbles surrounded her. Unable to sleep, she'd drawn a bath, hoping the warmth would ease the chill deep in her bones. So far, it wasn't working.

Her toe turned the faucet on and off in rhythmic succession while she stared at a spot on the edge of the tub. The occasional drip into the basin was the only sound in the room. Ryan's face flashed in her mind, and she closed her eyes, wanting the water to wash away her heartache.

After an hour on the phone with Tom Adams making plans for the next few weeks, she was drained. Disappearing probably wasn't the smartest plan at the moment, but it was the best she could come up with. Her parents would understand. Somehow she'd find a way to make Julia understand. And it wasn't forever, just until things died down. She just didn't want to know the truth anymore. Staying here while the press was swarming because of the story was only going to prolong her agony.

Running a hand over her hair, she let out a long breath and willed back the tears. Another waterfall wasn't going to help matters.

The lights went out.

She sat up, sending water lapping over the side of the tub. Drew in a breath and listened.

The wind whistled outside. The screen door tapping down below echoed up to her ears.

*You're jumpy, Kate. Get a grip. Mitch is downstairs. Nothing's going to happen. The storm probably knocked out power all over the street.*

She eased out of the tub and grabbed her white, terry bathrobe. After belting it around her waist, she headed for the stairs. Shadows danced across the hall, and she tripped over Reed's black Power Ranger. Pain shot through her toe. Biting her lip to keep from screaming, she hopped down the hall and tried to rub away the twinge. Couldn't one damn thing go right for her?

The stairs creaked under her feet. A dull ache settled around her toe. She sucked in a breath as she rounded the newel post, not wanting to wake Mitch in the living room.

Cool air blasted across her face when she stepped into the kitchen. The back door was wide open, the screen slapping against the doorjamb.

What the hell? She took a step toward the door and stopped.

She'd locked that door before going upstairs. Common sense trickled in. Her stomach muscles tightened. The air clogged in her lungs.

*Go get Mitch.*

She backed out of the kitchen. Bumped into a table in the hall. A lamp crashed to the floor.

Her adrenaline surged.

Good God. She was acting like a frightened teenager in a horror movie. Mitch was probably behind her laughing.

Pressing a hand to her belly, she turned and looked through the doorway toward the couch in the living room.

Empty.

She glanced back into the kitchen. "Mitch?"

No answer.

Sweat trickled down her spine. Her skin chilled.

*Think, Kate. Don't be a wimpy girl.* She spotted the cordless phone on the coffee table. Scrambling for the receiver, she turned it on with shaky fingers. The line was dead.

A gust of wind sent the screen slapping again. Kate jumped and whipped toward the kitchen.

Her purse was on the far counter with her cell phone and keys. She needed to get it. Taking a calming breath, she stepped through shadow and light.

Her foot slipped in a puddle on the hardwood floor. Grasping a kitchen chair for support, she was able to catch herself before she fell. She squinted through the darkness toward a trail of liquid from the back door that ran around the table.

Okay. That wasn't good. Something wasn't right. It was time to just go. She reached for her purse from the counter.

Something hard slammed into from behind. The contents of her purse went flying. Kate hit a barstool, bounced off the edge of the counter and tumbled to the floor.

Her arm took the brunt of the fall. Pain rocketed through her shoulder. When she tore open her eyes, Hannah Hughes was kneeling over her, holding a gun in her hand. "Welcome to the party, Kate."

Kate saw Mitch on the floor behind the table. His body was limp, his eyes closed. Blood oozed from his head.

Her stomach churned. Oh, God. That wasn't water she'd slipped in.

"No, look at me, Kate," Hannah said. "Do you have any idea what kind of mess you've made for me?"

What the hell was she talking about? Kate's brows drew

together. She opened her mouth to speak, but nothing came out.

"Don't play coy with me. I'm not falling for the whole 'I don't remember anything' routine like Ryan and Jake. You've been nothing but a pain in my ass since this whole thing started."

This whole thing. Jake. *No.*

"You," Kate managed on a ragged breath. "It was you? But you work with Ryan. I don't understand."

"Not very bright, are you?" A twisted smile graced Hannah's mouth. "Must have been all the drugs. Tabofren would have saved Paula. Ryan knew that."

Kate's brows drew together. Grasping her aching arm, she tried to sit up. "Who is Paula?"

"My sister. Ryan was so excited about Tabofren, he fast-tracked it into clinical trials. It worked. But he got cold feet when the FDA caught wind of the side effects and pulled the plug, stopped production. Paula died. That drug would have saved her life."

Kate swallowed. "You don't know that for sure."

"Oh, no? I think we do. Do you have any idea what it's like to lose someone you love, Kate? Or should I call you Annie? Which do you prefer?" Hannah's menacing laugh made Kate's nerves jump. "I forget who I'm talking to here. Of course you know what it's like to lose someone! Or better yet, Ryan sure does. We made sure of that."

"You—you did this on purpose? Why didn't you just kill me?"

"Hindsight is twenty-twenty. I was outvoted. Dad and Jake both thought you might be useful down the line. A kidnapping was better. Then that plane you were supposed to be on went down, and everyone thought you were dead anyway. It made sense to let Ryan suffer. And we were lucky that I had a friend working for the airline who made sure your name was listed on the manifest. People will do anything for money."

"You…you kept me alive on purpose?"

She shrugged. "Jake needed human tissue samples for his research if he was ever going to get the drug approved through a different company. We didn't really care if you had cancer or not. We were mostly interested in the side effects. Lo and behold, there you were."

With shaking fingers, Kate reached up and rubbed her scar. "But how did I—"

"That was the best part." She laughed. "You didn't go easily. Your struggling caused a car accident. Jake never lied to you about that. You did hit your head. And it did put you in a coma. That's what gave him the idea to use you in the study."

"Jake—"

Hannah's mouth curled in disgust. "Jake was stupid. Who knew he had a conscience? When he found out you were pregnant, he refused to do the tests on you. Did you know Paula was pregnant when she found out about the cancer? They had to choose—her life or the baby's. Then she died anyway. When Jake found out about your pregnancy, he figured it was payback. So we waited."

"Walter Alexander's your father," Kate said.

"Not so stupid after all." Hannah smiled. "He also goes by Karl McKellen. The head of McKellen Publishing. Your boss."

Sickness brewed in Kate's stomach. "What happened to Jake?"

Her eyes turned icy. "Cold feet."

"You killed him."

"I didn't mind that he wanted to use you to extract the ultimate revenge. To fuck Ryan Harrison's wife on a regular basis, to take his family and everything that had once been his? That was brilliant. But once Ryan killed Tabofren a second time, just after the Grayson merger, Jake lost his backbone. He was too worried about getting caught, about Ryan finding out about you and your boy. He wanted us to back off when we were so close to finally getting what we wanted. I couldn't let him ruin everything. I gave up my life to make sure that drug went through."

"Oh, my God." Bile rose in Kate's throat.

"Go ahead, be sick. Won't matter to me. You won't be around much longer to matter anyway." A smug smile graced Hannah's lips.

"You...you had the manifest changed so it looked like Jake died on that plane, just like me, didn't you?"

"Parallels. That was artistic, you have to admit. And everything would have been fine except for you. You just had to start digging into things that were better left dead and buried. And Jake, that dumbass. So stupid for leaving that picture in your fucking house. I should have killed him years ago."

Kate swallowed. No one was coming for her. Mitch wasn't moving. She didn't know if he was dead or alive at this point. "You killed the research patients."

Hannah didn't answer.

"And Janet Kelly. You took Ryan's car that morning. Was she threatening to turn you in?"

"Do you really think I'm going to answer your questions?"

Kate caught movement behind Hannah. "Did you kill your father too?"

"That was an accident." A hint of pain crossed Hannah's features. "We got into an argument. His sacrifice is nothing, though, compared to the number of people who have died because drugs that should be used to save lives are denied from the people who really need them. What's the purpose if they can't be useful?"

Mitch levered himself up at Hannah's back. Blood trickled down his forehead. He blinked twice and swayed.

Panic coursed through Kate. She needed to keep Hannah focused. "The FDA makes regulations to keep patients safe—"

Anger flashed in Hannah's eyes. "Don't lecture me about safety. If patients had access, my mother would still be alive. My sister would still be here today. If a few people have to die for the good of many, so be it."

Mitch rammed into Hannah from behind, knocking her back against the counter. The gun rocketed across the floor. On a moan, he fell into a chair and crumpled to the ground. Kate scrambled to her feet and reached for a candleholder on the kitchen table. When Hannah tried to push herself up, she swung.

The candleholder hit Hannah across the face. Kate skirted out of Hannah's grasp. She slipped in a puddle of blood. Hannah wrenched herself off the floor and launched herself at Kate. They struggled and rolled across the kitchen. Hannah pinned her to the floor.

Kate's arms ached, her muscles throbbed, but she wasn't going to die like this. Hannah reached for the gun. Kate kicked and clawed, managed to clamp her hand over Hannah's on the handle of the gun.

*No. No. No.* Not like this. She had too much to live for. Kate fought with every bit of energy she had. Reed. Julia. Ryan. She couldn't lose them.

When the gun went off, Hannah's eyes widened. Her body froze, and she looked down at Kate in shock.

The barrel of the gun was pointed at Hannah's chest. Her body slumped. She fell off Kate. The gun landed on the hardwood floor with a clank.

Kate scrambled to her knees, frantically checked Hannah's pulse. Nothing.

"Come on, Come on," she muttered, pushing down on

Hannah's chest. Blood pulsed from the wound, pooled on the ground around her.

Kate stumbled back, fell on her butt. Hand shaking, she looked around. And spotted Mitch lying motionless across the room.

Ryan's car screeched to a halt in Katie's driveway. He caught sight of the security detail's car parked across the street when he pulled in. A body was slumped over the steering wheel, and something red was splattered across the windows. His pulse jacked up as he killed the ignition.

Simone's car pulled in just after his.

"Stay here," he yelled through the rain as she opened her car door.

A gunshot echoed through the wind.

He tore across the front yard and thrust the front door open with his shoulder. "Katie!"

Simone was on his heels as he raced down the dark hall. His eyes locked on Katie on the floor of the kitchen. Blood covered her bathrobe.

His heart lurched into his throat. He dropped to his knees, frantically searching for a wound. "Where are you hurt?"

"It's not me," she choked out. "It's not my blood."

"Are you sure? There's so much."

"No. I'm fine. Oh, God, Ryan. Mitch."

Ryan tore his gaze away from her long enough to see Mitch lying on the floor, out cold. Blood trickled down his head. Simone was at his side, trying to coax him awake.

"Shit." Ryan pushed to his feet, darted around the island in the kitchen and tore open drawers. His stomach rolled when he stepped over Hannah's body. Blood oozed from the chest wound. Her lifeless eyes stared toward the ceiling.

He fumbled for towels in the cabinet drawers. Grabbing an armful, he raced back to Katie and Simone. "Press these against the bleeding."

"Mitch? Can you hear me?" Katie leaned over her brother while Ryan dialed nine-one-one on his cell and spoke to an operator.

"Mitch?" Simone said in a panicked voice. "Stay with us. Dammit, I'll get you that red leather outfit you want if you'll just open your eyes."

Ryan tried to talk coherently to the nine-one-one operator. Outside, sirens roared, but all he could focus on was the towels in Katie's hand, soaked in Mitch's blood.

Two minutes before, he'd prayed Katie wouldn't be hurt. Now he only wanted that for Mitch.

# CHAPTER TWENTY-THREE

Kate pushed the hospital room door open and smiled at the conversation she'd walked in on.

"Would you quit fussing at me?" Mitch swatted at Simone's hand as she tried to fix the blankets around him. "I'm not four."

"I swear, you are the worst patient ever. I don't know how these nurses put up with you." She shot him an annoyed look.

Kate eased into the room. Afternoon sunlight slanted through the window. "Grumpy?"

"A royal pain in my ass," Simone grumbled.

"You're a real peach, too, sweetheart," Mitch muttered.

Laughing, Kate stepped up to the bed and squeezed his toes under the blankets. "A knock on the head will do that to a person. Trust me, I know."

After two days, Mitch's energy was slowly returning. His head was still bandaged, and he'd lost some curls when they'd shaved one side of his scalp for the fifteen stitches he'd needed, but he was gradually inching back to his old sarcastic self.

"I need caffeine." Simone dropped her arms and headed for the door.

"Why don't you go pick up that red leather number while you're out," Mitch called. When she looked back with a shocked expression, he said, "Yeah, I heard you, gorgeous. And I sure as hell am not forgetting that promise."

Simone huffed and left the room. When she was gone, Kate smiled at her brother. "Congratulations, by the way."

"On what?" He reached for her hand and scooted over so she could sit on the side of his bed.

"On finding your penguin. Julia told me about the book she read."

He rolled his eyes. "I'm not marrying her, for shit's sake. We're just dating. At the moment, that's all I can get her to agree to."

"I know." Kate brushed a curl back from his face. "You should be nicer to her, though. She was really worried. You looked like death warmed over in my kitchen. I think she had flashbacks of Steve."

"Shit." His eyes slid closed. "I hadn't thought of that."

"I'm sure not. You are a guy, after all."

"And all men are insensitive, is that it?"

"Well…"

"Let's not go there, smartass." His face sobered. "How are you?"

Kate drew in a long breath. Aside from the press hounding her since the story broke, and the agony still coursing through her every time she thought of Ryan, she was surviving. Barely.

"I'm fine." She mustered up a smile she knew didn't reach her eyes. "I'll be glad when things quiet down. Mitch, I—"

"If you even think about thanking me, I'll kick you out of here."

A real smile curled her lips. "I wouldn't dream of it."

"Good." He frowned. "'Cause my image is shot. I got my ass kicked by a girl. Again."

"A psycho girl. There's a difference. And you weren't the only one."

His eyes softened. "How's the other guy?"

The other guy was the security detail Ryan had posted outside her house. The one Kate hadn't even known about. The one Hannah had shot in the chest before going after Mitch. "He's going to live. Paramedics got to him in time."

"Thank God," Mitch muttered. He squeezed her hand. "Did you talk to Ryan?"

Tears stung the backs of her eyes, and she swallowed to keep the flood from breaking again. "No."

"Kate—"

"Mitch, don't start. You have other things to think of now."

The door opened, and she and Mitch both glanced over as Ryan stuck his head into the room. A smile split his face, sending butterflies straight through Kate's belly. "Hey. Is Nurse Nitpick gone?"

"You just missed her," Mitch said.

"Good." Ryan tugged a bag from behind his back as he walked into the room. "She'd boot my ass out of here for this, guaranteed." He pulled a bottle of microbrew from the bag and handed it to Mitch.

"Oh, baby." Mitch reached for the bottle. "If I were gay, I'd marry you."

"Hate to break it to you, buddy, but you aren't my type."

Kate's heart bumped when Ryan looked her way. His blond hair was slightly mussed, his worn jeans hanging loosely off his hips. The white T-shirt he wore accentuated his tan.

She wanted those strong arms around her like they'd been before any of this had happened. For the first time, she wished she couldn't remember the misery of her life.

Simone pushed the door open. She stopped mid-step with a steaming paper cup in her hand. "What the hell is that?"

Ryan mouthed *Oh, shit* at Mitch before turning.

"Medicine," Mitch said, taking a long swallow.

Simone crossed to the bed, set her coffee on the tray at her side. "That's not allowed when you're on painkillers."

She reached for the bottle. Mitch held it out of her reach. She leaned over him to try to grasp it. Pressing it into Ryan's hands, Mitch wrapped his arms around her and pulled her on top of him.

"What are you doing? Let go of me. You're going to hurt yourself."

He tightened his grip. "Aw, sweetheart, you're the only one who cares about me."

She struggled. "I mean it."

"Me too." His voice softened. "I love you, Simone."

Her eyes took on that dreamy look. "Oh, Mitch."

Kate pushed off the bed, smiling for the first time in days. At least something good had come from this gigantic nightmare. "I think that's my cue to go. I'll come back later, Mitch."

"They're sending me home," he mumbled against Simone's lips.

"My home," Simone said between his kisses.

"Aw, sweetheart," he said in a sappy voice, "that's the best offer I've ever had."

Ryan set the bottle on the tray table and ran a hand through his hair. "I guess I'll go too."

"No more beer, Ryan," Simone ordered against Mitch's mouth.

"Okay. Yeah. I'll, uh, remember that. See ya, guys."

Kate stepped out into the hall. Her nerves vibrated when Ryan followed. It was the first time they'd been alone since that afternoon on Simone's deck.

The door snapped closed behind him. "Do you have to go?"

Her heart clenched when she looked up into those sapphire eyes. It would be so easy just to sink into his arms, to forget everything that had happened. But she knew it wouldn't help.

"Yeah. I have a thousand things to do today."

"The kids are with my parents. What do you have to do that's so important?"

She heard the need in his voice. And damn if it didn't make her want him more. "Pack. Ryan, I'm leaving."

"What? Where are you going?"

"Washington. It's just for a couple of weeks," she added when she saw the panic in his eyes. "Mt. St. Helens is grumbling to life. The journal wants to do an article on it. I talked to Tom about working on an assignment. I…I need some time away right now."

He was silent so long, she wasn't sure he'd heard her. Then he said, "When are you leaving?"

"Tomorrow night. I talked to my parents about staying on until I get back. They'd love the time with Reed. I didn't know if you'd—"

"He's my son. I want him with me."

Of course he did. That was stupid of her. No matter what had happened between the two of them, he'd fallen for Reed in a big way. "I know. It's just that you work. And I didn't want to inconvenience you."

"Katie." His voice softened. "You're never an inconvenience."

Oh, man. If he kept looking at her with those emotion-filled eyes, she'd never get out of here. She swallowed hard. "Are you okay with them keeping him during the day while you're at work?"

"Of course. You don't need to ask that."

A dull ache filled her chest. This was going to be impossible. Sharing the kids would kill her. Having to see him on weekends when they exchanged, knowing if she weren't so damn stubborn she could have exactly what she wanted.

But she still hurt. She hurt from his lies. From the fact he hadn't trusted her enough to be honest. She was so tired of the lies and secrets that had ruled her life for way too long. Deep inside, she was afraid she'd always wonder if he were telling her the truth.

"Okay." Silence stretched between them. When she couldn't stand it anymore, she said, "I, ah, need to go finish packing. I'll tell Julia when I see her this afternoon." She turned for the elevator.

His hand on her arm stopped her. Heat spread along her skin, ignited a fire inside her. "Wait. We need to talk about us."

Emotions she didn't want to deal with poured through her. She tried to steady her quaking voice. "I know, Ryan. But I can't right now. I need some time to figure everything out. Things between us happened so fast. I'm not sure what I need."

"How long do you think it's going to take you to think things through?"

"I don't know. I…I don't expect you to wait for me."

"Ah, babe. I'd wait for you forever."

Her eyes slid shut to block the tears. He knew exactly what to say to make her heart tip right over the edge. "I have to go, Ryan."

She eased out of his grasp and stepped into the elevator. He was still watching her when she turned, hands shoved deep into his pockets, heartache stamped across his handsome face.

As the doors closed, she had a pretty strong hunch that face was going to haunt her forever.


Glancing down at her boarding pass, Kate made her way through the crowded terminal. She checked her watch. She had almost an hour until her flight up to Portland. She didn't want to sit at the gate that long. With a sigh, she headed toward the coffee cart at the end of the corridor and grabbed a latté.

Sinking into a chair, she sipped her coffee and told herself she'd done the right thing. If she was lucky, a few weeks away would clear her head, give her something else to focus on besides the craziness that had become her life.

And maybe when she came back, she'd have a clue what she was going to do about Ryan.

She listened to the muffled conversations around her. An attractive couple strolled up to the coffee cart, arm in arm. The man smiled, brushed the woman's blond hair away from her neck, and kissed her ear. The woman leaned into his chest and grinned. The glint of bright gold on their fingers signaled they were newlyweds.

A young girl with dark hair, roughly Julia's age, ran up to them. A warm smile spread across the man's face as he wrapped an arm around the girl and his wife paid for their drinks.

Kate's eyes slid closed. She could have that. If she really wanted it, she could have that and so much more.

*I'd wait for you forever.*

Tears stung her eyes. She loved Ryan. That wasn't the issue. At this point, she didn't even question what she felt for him. She couldn't fight it any more than he could. But was it enough? Would she be able to forget the rest of it? The lies? The hurt? Would she ever be able to trust him again?

The couple from the coffee cart settled around a table next to her.

"How long are you going to be gone?" the young girl asked, slurping her drink through a straw.

The man's deep voice made Kate glance sideways. "Long enough for your mom to realize she can't live without me." He lifted the woman's hand and kissed her fingers.

The blonde ran her hand across his rugged face. "That, I already know."

He smiled. "Took you long enough to figure it out. You made me wait forever."

A redhead walked up and sat in the empty chair at their table. Kate had seen her with the young girl before she'd run to her parents. "Good thing you're both so forgiving. You let all that other crap get in the way much too long. Who said what to whom and when. I swear, words cause more trouble than they're worth sometimes."

*All that other crap.* Kate swallowed. Was that what she was doing? Letting circumstances rule her life? Letting what Ryan had or hadn't told her interfere with what she felt in her soul? If she let her heart make her decision for her, she wouldn't be sitting here wondering what the hell to do next.

He loved her. Anything he'd kept from her, he'd done to keep her safe. She knew that. Even if she didn't like it, she knew everything he'd done was only for her.

The muscles in her chest tightened. Suddenly, forever seemed much too long. All this time, she'd been searching for a past she thought would save her, when she should have been trusting her gut. It was the love buried deep inside that had the power to show her what was real. Nothing else mattered. Not really.

She clamored to her feet. Her latté spilled across the table.

The blonde at the next table leaned across the chairs between them and tossed a pile of napkins over the spilled coffee. "Here, let me help you."

"Thanks." Kate mopped up the mess. "I wasn't thinking."

"It happens." When Kate looked up, concern flowed through the woman's pale blue eyes. "Hey, are you okay?"

"No. Yes." She reached for her bag, not sure if she was going to laugh or cry. "I have to go. You have a beautiful family."

The blonde smiled. "Thanks."

"No, thank you."

"For what?"

"For reminding me what really matters."


Ryan tugged on the collar of his tux as he sat at a table in the packed ballroom. Men and women in formal attire swayed across the floor. The band cranked out notes to an ancient jazz number while light glittered from the massive chandeliers above.

He didn't want to be here. The last thing he needed tonight was to be surrounded by a bunch of people he had no use for. What he wanted was to be home with the kids, maybe drowning his sorrows in a bottle of whiskey after they went to bed.

He couldn't even remember what this damn charity event was for. The homeless? Public schools? Models in need of plastic surgery? He didn't care. If he hadn't already committed to it, he'd have come up with an excuse to get out of it. And he hated that he'd taken his new PR director's advice that showing his face tonight would be a good thing for his company.

The last thing he cared about right now was his company. He shouldn't have listened.

"They're really making a killing tonight."

"Hmm?" The woman's voice to his left dragged him from his thoughts. She had to be about eighty years old, with snow-white hair, a silver, beaded, long-sleeved dress, and the biggest rock on her finger he'd ever seen. He vaguely remembered she was related to some bigwig in state government. How the hell he'd gotten stuck at this table was beyond him.

He should have brought a date. Then, at least, he wouldn't have to listen to the old woman's monotonous voice. Problem was, he couldn't even think about dating anyone now. Didn't think he ever would. There was only one woman he wanted, and she was on a plane, halfway to Portland by now.

"The Inner City Youth Authority, of course," the old woman said. "I can't believe how many people are here supporting them. It's wonderful, don't you think?"

Inner City Youth Authority. Right. That was it.

"Yeah." He feigned interest in the conversation. "Raking in the dough." Barely listening, he calculated how much longer he had to stay before he could sneak out.

"Terrible news about that nasty business you were in," the old woman next to him went on. "I heard your wife left."

His gaze snapped to her. "What?"

She waved a hand. "Oh, honey. No one can keep secrets in this town. My daughter just went through a divorce. She's about your age. I should give you her number."

Bingo. That did it. Ryan pushed out of his chair and mustered up a polite smile. "Would you excuse me?"

He weaved his way through the crowded dance floor. Was afraid he just might implode if he didn't get out soon. Freedom teased him from the corner of the room. He was stopped a handful of times by business acquaintances. Each one grated on his already frayed nerves.

Excusing himself from the last conversation, he stepped toward the door, only to be stopped by a familiar voice.

"Mon cher, it's so good to see you."

*Oh, shit. Monique.*

He stared into her perfect face surrounded by that thick mane of red hair and couldn't for the life of him remember what the hell he'd seen in her. "I had no idea you'd be here."

"My agent roped me into it since I was in the city. Good publicity."

That made sense. She obviously wasn't here because she cared about inner city youth.

"You look good, mon cher." She stepped closer. "So sorry to hear about your recent drama."

"Yeah, I bet you were."

She smiled seductively, batted her long lashes. "You never told me about your wife."

"Well, we never got around to discussing anything serious, did we?"

She eased closer, slid her arm through his, leaned in a breath from his ear. "Why don't you and I go somewhere quiet, and you can tell me all the sordid details. I'm a good listener."

Being alone with her was the last thing he wanted. He pulled her hand from his arm. "Don't you have a date?"

Stupid question. Of course she did.

She waved a hand. "Oh, he's around somewhere. A complete bore, though. I'd much rather catch up with you, mon cher. You owe me anyway."

*Not gonna happen.*

"You know, as tempting as that is, I think I have to pass." His eyes darted toward the door, judging the distance to freedom. And the air clogged in his lungs when Katie stepped into the room.

She was dressed in jeans, a snug, orange T-shirt, clunky loafers, and a leather jacket that hung off one shoulder. Her curly mass of chestnut hair was wild around her face, and her cheeks were flushed, as if she'd just run ten blocks. And standing there, surrounded by women in ten-thousand-dollar gowns wearing every jewel imaginable, she was the most beautiful thing he'd ever seen.

She was also supposed to be on a plane. Surprise morphed to worry. He headed her way, barely hearing Monique as she called out to him. When Katie spotted him, she pushed through the crowd, making a beeline straight for him.

"What's wrong?" he asked when he reached her. "What happened?"

"Nothing," she said. "Everything. I mean…"

She was flustered. She was never flustered. That worry ramped up a notch. "Katie—"

Her gaze dropped to his left hand, and she sighed, reaching for him, sliding her fingers along his, touching his wedding band. "You're still wearing this."

"I always wear it."

"You're an idiot, Ryan Harrison. You were going to sit here and wait for me to make up my mind, weren't you?"

"I told you I would."

"I don't deserve you."

Hope welled inside. "Are you saying you want me?"

She tightened her fingers around his. "I've been fighting who I am and what I want because I can't remember my life. Tonight, sitting in that airport, I realized that you and the kids *are* my life. I've let too much other garbage get in the way. I don't want to do that anymore."

She wanted them. His heart swelled even as his eyes slid closed. "You'd better be sure, because I can't go through losing you again. Twice in one lifetime is too much. If you want me, it's got to be forever."

"Ryan, look at me." Her soft fingers against his jaw brought his eyes open. "I'm still upset that you lied to me. But I understand why you did it. I know it was because you love me, and you were trying to keep me safe. But in addition to your love, I need your trust. I need to know that when things get bad, you're always going to be there for me. That I can count on you."

"I will be. You can."

"And I need to know that deep down, no matter what, you believe I'll be there for you. Marriage is a partnership. It doesn't work without trust."

She was talking about marriage. His heart felt like it grew three sizes in his chest. "Katie—"

She stepped close. So close he could feel the heat from her body, smell the lilac of her skin, see the tears glinting in her eyes. "I'll tell you what I want. I want you to kiss me like you did at my house, to make love to me like you did at yours. I want to wake up with you every morning and go to bed with you every night. I want our kids and our life together. I want it all, but mostly, I just want you."

He couldn't breathe. She wanted him. Really wanted him. Even after he'd screwed things up so badly between them.

Her thumb brushed his bottom lip, sent sparks of heat straight to his soul. "I love you, Ryan Harrison. I always have. I was just too stubborn to realize that's the only thing that really matters."

He cradled her face in his hands and swiped away a tear that had fallen from her lashes. "Why did it take you so damn long to figure that out?"

She smiled as he kissed her, as her arms wound around him, as she pulled him so tight, what was left of that ice he'd built up inside finally melted away. "I have brain damage, remember? It takes me a little longer to figure things out."

"Oh, is that what it is?" Relief and joy mixed through him to meld with the music drifting in the ballroom, already lightening his spirits. "And here I thought you just loved to see me suffer."

"Only in the bedroom. And only when that suffering leads to pleasure for us both. Speaking of which…" She smiled against his shoulder. "I could go for a little of that pleasure, right now, in fact. If you don't mind leaving this party early, that is."

His whole body tightened at the erotic implications of her words. He couldn't wait to get her home, strip her naked, and lay her out on his bed. On their bed.

He eased back, and his humor faded as he looked down at the woman he'd loved and lost and would never be stupid enough to let go again. Somewhere close he was aware of a camera bulb flashing but for the first time, he didn't care. "I'm sorry. I'm so damn sorry for not being honest with you. For not trusting what was happening between us. I was so afraid of losing you again that

I did exactly what I was trying to stop. I pushed you right out of my arms. It won't happen again. I promise. No more secrets."

"No more secrets," she agreed. "Unless it's Christmas. Or my birthday. Or our anniversary. Come to think of it, today…" her eyes glinted with mischief "…this would be a good anniversary to remember in the future. The day we finally found our way back to each other."

She was cracking jokes. His heart felt like it sprouted wings. Like it just might fly right out of his chest. His Annie—his Katie—was the only person in the world who knew exactly what he needed.

"I love you," he whispered. "So damn much. So much more than I ever did before. Please don't ever leave me."

Her face softened. And love—a love he'd never expected to have again—shone in the depths of her green eyes under the sparkling chandelier lights. "Never again, Ryan. Never ever again."

Read on for a sneak peek at

# STOLEN *Fury*

Book 1 in the Stolen Series

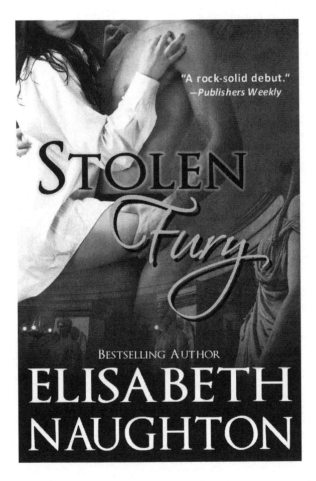

"A rock-solid debut."
—*Publishers Weekly*

STOLEN *Fury*

BESTSELLING AUTHOR
ELISABETH
NAUGHTON

*To unearth a centuries-old secret, an archaeologist must team up with the rakish thief who's stolen both an ancient relic and her heart...*

Elisabeth Naughton

# CHAPTER ONE

The floor was still at least twenty feet below her.

Surrounded by utter blackness, Lisa Maxwell tipped her head so the cone light from her helmet could slide over the interior of the cave. Then wondered what the heck she'd gotten herself into.

"You okay down there?"

The man's voice echoing from above drew her back to reality, and she shook off strange feelings of self-doubt as she continued her descent into darkness. Her hand slid down the rope as she let out slack inch by inch. When her boots hit the slippery rocks at the bottom, she unhooked the rope from her harness and stepped back. "Off belay," she called.

"Belay off," the voice yelled back.

She rested her hands on her hips and drew a breath of damp air. Mildew and the rich scent of earth filled her nostrils.

The ray from her carbide lantern bounced off thin, pointed stalactites hanging from the ceiling, orange and red sediments swirling through the fragile structures. Scattered throughout the room, large columns covered in white residue flowed from floor to ceiling, and everywhere, dripping water echoed through the vast dark space.

A shiver raced down her spine, so she pulled up the zipper on her coveralls. It might be nine million degrees outside in the Jamaican sun, but underneath all this limestone rock, it was downright cold.

Metal scraped against rock above, and she glanced up while her brawny guide descended the rope and dropped to the floor next to her. He unhooked his harness, letting the rope hang from the small hole in the ceiling they'd just come through.

"This room is bigger than the maps indicate." His thick Jamaican accent hung in the air.

As she turned to get a better look, her light swept over the darkness, landing on a translucent structure suspended from the ceiling. Though she'd have liked to spend time examining that drapery, there were more pressing issues at hand. She gestured to the left. "You start over there, Simeon. I'll look to the right. Be sure to note any tunnels or passageways."

"Ay, mon."

He disappeared into the darkness, his light bouncing off structures he passed, his feet shuffling along the rock floor. Lisa began her own in-depth search while he worked. As she moved, she checked her watch periodically, calculating how long they'd been below the surface, as was her habit whenever she was caving.

Simeon wasn't one for talking, and today she was thankful for the quiet. She skirted a small rimstone pool filled with murky water, picked her way around columns, careful not to touch any in the process. A gypsum flower jutted out of the wall, the presence of the curling, rosette-shaped calcium-sulfite structure indicating this cave was more stable than she'd thought. The knowledge calmed her.

"Anything?" she asked after they'd been searching nearly fifteen minutes.

"A couple small tunnels. None big enough for a man."

Damn. She wasn't going to get discouraged yet. They'd only been in this cavern a few hours. There were lots of rooms left to check.

She resumed her search. When she reached the far side of the room, she glanced up and a stream of light from her helmet spilled over the cave. The undulating drapery now hung above her, the banded structure blocking her view of the opposite wall.

She needed a wider perspective. Without looking behind her, she took a step back. A loud crack resounded through the quiet, followed by the rush of flowing water. Lisa lost her balance, and her arms flew out to the side to steady herself, but it was already too late. She managed one shrill scream before the floor dropped out from under her.

"Dr. Maxwell!"

Brisk air whooshed around her as she plummeted with the falling rock into a tunnel below. She hit the ground with a thud. Her light went out when her helmet cracked against the rocks. Pain ricocheted through her torso just as a surge of icy water washed over her body, pulling her through the darkness.

Instinct took over before she could panic. She kicked frantic legs, gasped for air and lashed out with her hands to grab on to something to slow her descent. Her fingers slipped on the slick rocks as she made useless attempts to stop herself.

The rush of water yanked her over sharp rocks and cave formations. Jagged points stabbed into her back, sliced up her hands and arms. She fought the fear, tried to keep her wits as her body was bruised and beaten. If she could just get one good grip, grab on to one solid rock...

Then the tunnel took a steep drop. A blast of cold air hissed over her, and a terror-filled scream tore from her chest as she fell feet first into the blackness below.

Her boots hit a pool of frigid water. She plunged beneath the surface, wrenched down by the sheer force of gravity. The muscles in her chest constricted while her lungs burned at the lack of oxygen. Kicking as hard as she could, she tried to swim up, but her senses were so disoriented in the darkness, she had no idea if she was heading in the right direction.

Just when she was sure she was going to drown, she broke the surface, gasped and pulled damp air into her blazing lungs. Heart thundering, she tried to slow her breathing. Long minutes passed before she opened her eyes and peered into the darkness.

She couldn't see a thing. The new room she'd tumbled into was pitch-black, the only sound the fall of water somewhere to her left.

Maybe caving in Jamaica hadn't been the brightest idea after all.

With unsteady hands, she flipped on her helmet light, praying the whole time that it wasn't damaged. Her fingers passed over dents in the metal cap, and her breath caught at the realization that without the safety gear, she'd probably be dead now.

As that lovely thought settled in, her light flickered on, and she heaved out a long sigh of relief. Not dead. Not yet anyway. She looked up and took survey of the new room.

The ceiling was at least thirty feet above, the pool surrounding her wide and vast, reflecting stalactites hanging down from above. Large columns and stalagmites jutted out of the cold liquid. A waterfall spilled from a hole in the wall at least twenty feet up and to her left.

She swallowed hard. Had she landed on one of those stalagmites, she'd have knocked herself out, drowned before Simeon figured out where she'd gone.

*Don't think about that now.*

Shaking the fog from her head, she swam toward the edge of the pool and hauled herself out of the water, then sucked in a breath and shivered in the cool air.

In the fourteen years she'd been an archaeologist, she'd encountered her fair share of tight scrapes in the field—a mudslide in a trench in Asia when a wall of sediment had caved in after a torrential downpour, a rockslide in Peru that had seriously tested her resolve and almost taken her life, and an underwater accident that had made her wonder why she'd taken up scuba diving in the first place. But in each instance, she'd gotten back up and kept going, because that's what she did. She was a woman proving herself in a male-dominated profession, and she was doing it pretty damn well.

And after all that, there was no way she was letting one measly cave in Jamaica do her in. Especially not on her vacation.

She stood on sore, achy legs, tried not to think about the throbbing cuts on her arms and back or the fact hypothermia would set in if she didn't get out soon. What mattered most was figuring out how the heck she was going to get back up to the top of that waterfall. If she was lucky, Simeon was somewhere up there looking for her.

If, that is, she was paying him enough to stick around and haul her ass out of this dark pit.

"Dr. Maxwell!"

Simeon's muffled voice echoed from somewhere above. Lisa was sure she'd never been as happy to hear another voice in all her life.

"Down here!"

"Thank God." His deep voice bounced off rock and limestone. Lisa glanced toward the waterfall just as Simeon's tense face came into view. He propped dark arms against the wall of the tunnel, kept his feet shoulder-width apart to keep from slipping. "You alright?"

"Yeah, I'm fine. It's a big drop. Be careful."

"I be right down. Sit tight."

He secured the rope, braced his feet on the wall of the cave and slowly lowered himself into the room. When he was five feet above the water, he kicked his legs to get a good swing in the harness and propelled himself to the ledge of the pool. He dropped onto the flat rocks, unhooked the harness and looped the rope around a nearby stalagmite.

Lisa resisted the urge to lecture him about not touching the structures. Playing teacher wasn't going to save her life. Instead she shifted unsteady legs forward and wove around stalagmites as she made her way to join him.

"You hurt?" he asked.

More than she was willing to admit, but there was no way she'd let that stop her. "No. I'm fine. Just knocked the wind out of me, that's all."

He didn't look convinced. "I think we done for the day. You freeze in here if we don't get you out."

Disappointment flowed through her. He was right, but she hadn't found what she'd come for. "Since we're already here, let's do a quick sweep of this room first, then we'll go."

"I don't think that a good idea."

"Why not?"

He nodded toward his left and shone his light between a massive column and a broken stalagmite. "Last guy not fare well."

Lisa's gaze followed, and her adrenaline spiked first with fear, then with intrigue, as her light illuminated the human remains Simeon had already spotted.

Carefully, she stepped across the slippery rocks and knelt by the remains. The skeleton was leaning against a massive rock formation, pieces of tattered fabric stuck to its bones. Leather boots still covered the feet, and a large knapsack was near the right hand.

"He's been here a while." She fought the excitement, tried to think rationally. This was probably nothing more than an unlucky caver. But something in her gut said it might be more.

Simeon crouched next to her on the rocks, a wary look in his eye. "Bad spirits in this cave." He glanced around. "Not good to disturb the dead."

Barely hearing him, she lifted the front pouch of the sack and extracted a worn wallet. She opened the leather folder. "Donald Ramsey. Born in 1946. ID reissued in 1982."

Simeon glanced at the license in her hand. "He been down here close to twenty years."

"That'd be my guess." She looked up and around again. "If he was caving alone and tumbled in here like I did, he never could have gotten out."

And that was the reason a sane person never went caving alone.

Lisa pawed through the front pouch some more and pulled out a worn map and a few sheets of yellow paper. "Looks like the guy was a treasure hunter." She showed Simeon the frayed map. "There's even an $X$ on that one."

A smile twisted Simeon's dark face. "$X$ marks the spot."

"Yeah, right," she said with a slight grin. "Only in Hollywood."

But her smile faded as she took a closer look at the aged papers. They detailed the location of a sunken Spanish galleon off the coast of Jamaica.

Her heart thumped against her ribs.

Fingers shaking, she opened the top pouch of the pack and peered inside. And her pulse beat frantically as she drew out a rectangular piece of marble roughly nine inches tall by twelve inches wide. When she turned it, the relief on the opposite side came into view, and she drew in a sharp breath.

The marble depicted a woman dressed in a Greek toga. Her arms were crossed over her chest and her gaze was fixed down toward her feet. Bare toes peeked out from beneath the robe, her bent knee indicating her weight was perched on one foot. Small wings jutted out of her back, and through her hair, snakes encircled her head like a wreath.

"Holy Mother o' God," Simeon mumbled, looking toward the relief.

The cold of the cave slipped to the back of Lisa's mind. "Trust me, this isn't the Virgin Mary."

She turned the relief in her hands, ran her fingers along the smooth back. The number one was carved into the bottom right side.

"It looks like there are cutouts on the side," Simeon said. "Like it fits together with another piece."

Perspiration tickled Lisa's skin in the damp air, and she swallowed. Six trips to the Jamaican caves over the past fifteen years, and she'd never found a single trace of the Greek goddess now in front of her. And today she'd simply stumbled across it when the floor had caved beneath her.

"Two other pieces," she said quietly. "It's one of three."

"Three? Where are the other two?"

*Definitely not here.*

Ignoring the question, Lisa shrugged out of her pack, extracted a thick piece of black fabric and wrapped it carefully around the relief. She slid the marble inside, latched the flap and stood as she slung the knapsack onto her shoulder. "It's time to go."

Wide-eyed, Simeon rose. He didn't question her, simply let her step past him and move toward the rope. She was paying him enough to keep quiet about their little excursion and not ask questions, and he knew that.

With the pack secured to her back, she strapped on the harness and started her ascent to the top of the waterfall. Simeon controlled the rope from the bottom. At the top, she waited while he scaled the wall of water, the pack heavy on her back. Heavier than one small marble relief should feel.

She pushed aside the thought as they silently made their way back through the cascade of water, careful to keep their feet wide to avoid slipping. Twice Lisa lost her balance, and the strong Jamaican stopped her from sliding back down the tunnel.

Okay, so he'd more than earned his pay. She'd have to give him a nice tip and a good recommendation.

When they reached the spot where the floor had given out beneath her, Simeon's hand covered her arm. Lisa flashed him an annoyed look, but paused when he held a finger to his lips. "Shh." He lifted his hand and flipped off his lantern. Hearing movement above, Lisa did the same.

Voices echoed from the vast room—thick Jamaican Creole she couldn't understand, followed by a softer voice speaking English. She strained to listen, could barely hear the tones, but couldn't make out any of the words.

With a firm hand, Simeon pressed her back against the wall of the tunnel. "No sound," he whispered.

Two voices. Maybe three. Male. Angry.

Crap, they'd found the Jeep parked outside in the brush. She thought they'd hidden it well enough to avoid a run-in.

Simeon tugged her back down the wet tunnel. For once, she didn't argue and try to take control.

He pushed her into a small tunnel to her right. She dropped to her hands and knees. The pack hit the roof of the cave, and she paused, wiggling out of the straps. Rolling to her side, she shoved the pack in front of her and slithered through the tunnel. Without light, she had absolutely no clue if the tunnel was getting bigger or smaller, or even where the heck they were headed.

Simeon's breathing at her back was all she could hear. That and the pounding of her heart echoing through her head.

The tunnel took a sharp right turn, and Lisa curved her body to mold to the space. The walls closed in tighter. The oxygen level dropped as the tube grew smaller. Her helmet hit the ceiling, both shoulders brushed the walls, and she stopped, fearing she was at the end of the line.

"Keep going," Simeon whispered from behind.

"I can't. It's too tight."

"This tunnel goes through. I checked the map before we came down."

He *had* to be kidding. No way she was purposely turning into a sardine without seeing the map or tunnel for herself.

"I'm going to turn on my lantern."

"No!" he whispered sharply. "They still back there. Go."

Holy crap. She didn't want to spend the next ten years in a Jamaican clink, or worse, wind up dead. She'd been warned—in no uncertain terms—not to trespass on private property again. And obviously, she hadn't listened. But then, she didn't exactly take kindly to unsolicited advice.

Drawing in a deep breath, she peered into the blackness ahead, contemplating her choices. This was the stupidest thing she'd ever done.

Before she could change her mind, she kicked over onto her side, dropped her head against the floor of the tunnel and wriggled deeper into the tube. The walls pressed in on her, front and back. She couldn't lift her head more than an inch off the ground. With the pack in front of her, she tried to slither through the shrinking space.

The tunnel took a sharp turn to the left. She folded her torso around the corner. This was it. She was going to get stuck in here and die, with the first of the Furies in her grasp.

No way. She wasn't giving up.

Blowing out all the oxygen in her lungs, she kicked her legs and gave one last thrust into the tunnel. Her chest burned, every muscle ached, and just when she thought she was a goner, the cave widened.

Warm, sweet air filled her lungs. The steadily rising ceiling allowed her enough room to lift her head. Just ahead, the soft flicker of light shone through the darkness.

She suppressed the glee rolling through her and kept moving forward, slithering until the tunnel widened enough so she could push herself up to her hands and knees, then finally stand when the ceiling took a sharp rise.

Hands braced on her thighs, she bent over at the waist and drew in large gulps of musty air. She could hear Simeon still struggling in the cave. If she'd been stuck, he had to be in serious trouble. The man was at least twice her size.

She crouched in the darkness, calling out to him softly.

"Almost there," he croaked. Metal scraped against rock, and then she heard him scrambling across the tunnel floor toward her.

Lisa grappled in the darkness and reached out, wrapping her fingers around his thick arms. Mud covered every part of their bodies. She helped him to his feet. His muffled coughing filled the space.

"How the hell did you get through there?" she asked in a whisper. "I barely made it myself."

White teeth flashed in the darkness as he straightened. "I pray to Olorun to make me small as a snake to slither through the cave. He answer my prayer."

Lisa frowned and let his answer roll right off her. She wasn't going to get into a religious debate with him, and there was no way she was touching that one.

She slung the knapsack over her shoulder, turned and headed for the crack of light ahead. "Come on. Let's get out of here while we can."

"Your goddess pull you through that tunnel?"

Was he serious? She suppressed a laugh. Sheer female determination had saved her ass, as always. "No."

"She will," he said behind her. "You let her, and she'll pull you to the light."

Lisa glanced over her shoulder. In the dim light she could just make out his serious expression. "Thanks." She shifted forward and kept walking, feeling the need to put as much distance between her and this cave as possible. "But I think I've got all the light I need."

"You think that, but you don't. You in the dark, Dr. Maxwell. Pitch dark. But things change. You see."

Her guide had lost some serious oxygen in that tunnel, but he was right about one thing—something had definitely changed. She finally had what she'd been seeking for nearly fifteen years. With a little luck she'd be on her way to the second of the three Furies real soon. And she knew just where to start looking.

# About the Author

A former junior high science teacher, *USA TODAY* Bestselling Elisabeth Naughton traded in her red pen and test tube set for a laptop and research books. She now writes sexy romantic adventure and paranormal novels full time from her home in western Oregon where she lives with her husband and three children. Her work has been nominated for numerous awards including the prestigious RITA® awards by Romance Writers of America, the Australian Romance Reader Awards, The Golden Leaf and the Golden Heart. When not writing, Elisabeth can be found running, hanging out at the ballpark or dreaming up new and exciting adventures.

Visit her on the web at www.ElisabethNaughton.com.